Angel FALL

Angel FALL

COLEMAN LUCK

A NOVEL

ZONDERVAN®

ZONDERVAN.com/
AUTHORTRACKER
follow your favorite authors

ZONDERVAN

Angel Fall

This title is also available as a Zondervan ebook.
Visit www.zondervan.com/ebooks.

This title is also available in a Zondervan audio edition.
Visit www.zondervan.fm.

Requests for information should be addressed to:

Zondervan, *Grand Rapids, Michigan 49530*

Library of Congress Cataloging-in-Publication Data

Luck, Coleman.
Angel fall : a novel : Coleman Luck.
p. cm.
ISBN 978-0-310-28398-0
1. Children of divorced parents—Fiction. 2. Survival after airplane accidents, shipwrecks, etc.—Fiction. I. Title.
PS3612.U256A8 2009
813'.6—dc22 2009005148

Interior design by Christine Orejuela-Winkelman

Printed in the United States of America

09 10 11 12 13 14 15 • 25 24 23 22 21 20 19 18 17 16 15 14 13 12 11 10 9 8 7 6 5 4 3 2 1

To my children, Cole, Chad, and Cherissa,
who believed in this story from the beginning
and waited so long. This book is dedicated with love to you.

ACKNOWLEDGMENTS

When a book is written over a period of twenty-five years there are many people to thank who gave encouragement along the way. Sadly, the memory dims. If I have forgotten a name please forgive me.

My deepest gratitude ...

To the memory of my father, Dr. G. Coleman Luck, who passed away long before this book began, but who laid the foundation for it by reading great stories to me when I was a child.

To the memory of Jim McAdams, Hollywood Executive Producer of the old school, trusted colleague, and dear friend, who, though he was dying of cancer, read the manuscript and offered wonderful encouragement as he had done with all of my writing for over twenty years.

To Heidi Schneider who came with her family to visit and from that moment began reminding me that I had left three young people in a dangerous world and needed to bring them home. Then, with her sister Hannah and brother Roy, organized a little reading group. Together they read the manuscript in the most agonizing way possible, two chapters at a time with big gaps in between. The other members of that group were Nicholas Ganssle, Elizabeth Ganssle, and Erica Weston.

To Rick and Soozie Schneider and Jim and Karen Covell for their support and encouragement not only for this book, but in many ways over many years.

To Amanda Culp Luck, my daughter-in-law, who critiqued the manuscript with the calibrated eye of an attorney and graciously allowed me to use her name.

To Tori Ellsworth, my granddaughter, who read and also let me use her name.

To Slade Wheeler, my son-in-law, for his visual artistry and constant encouragement.

To individuals who took the time to read the unwieldy stack of paper that I handed to them and offer their thoughts and help: Sarah Beach, Mary Reeves Bell, Martha Cotton, Christopher Covell, Paul Karrat, Dan Korem, Amy Luck, Melissa Pollack, Erin Wheeler, Denise Wilkerson, Margo Zych, and the writers' group of Northridge.

Special thanks to Andy Meisenheimer, my editor at Zondervan, who labored long and patiently and did so much to help this story become what it is.

Most of all, my gratitude goes to Carel, for over forty-two years my wife, lover, and closest friend, who believed in me and my writing since I was seventeen years old. Carel, without you this book would not exist.

Angel
FALL

1

WIND SUNDAY

It was the stillness.

That's what they remembered most about the beginning. A stillness that hung like ancient mold in the trees. But who could forget anything about Wind Sunday? The sharp acrylic memories painted themselves on their hearts and refused to dry. And ever after, touching the canvas brought tears.

On Wind Sunday there were secrets to be learned. And the first one was this—that waking periods of light and sleeping periods of darkness have names just like the people who live through them. Who gave them the names, no one can tell. But one thing is certain—when a day has two names, it speaks with a voice that demands to be heard.

And when it's over, it leaves echoes.

Do you know what I'm talking about?

You do if you've lived through one.

Divorce Wednesday.

For the children it was three years ago. A day that crackled with screams and tears and hatred. Since Divorce Wednesday, Alex, Amanda, and Tori had lived with their mother. Ellen Lancaster was not a bad mother. She was just a very brokenhearted and lonely one. Her children, who really weren't children anymore, didn't understand the look in her eyes. The look was there because a voice in her head kept whispering that she was a failure.

Just look at them.

If you had been a better wife and mother they wouldn't be this way.

There was not a day when the whispers didn't plague her. They were lies and the voice was not her own, but she didn't know that. And the more it whispered, the more desperate she had become.

Something had to change. For their sakes. She loved them more than life, and she was losing them. So something had changed, driven by the unexpected. After much agony and many tears shed alone in her room, the decision had been made. For them. All for them, though they didn't understand that.

But on that Sunday the Wind blew all her plans into a darkness beyond the stars.

Warnings about weather come from scientists. Highly respected men and woman check their satellites and computers, then tell the pretty TV weather models what to say. But on Wind Sunday the whole system fell apart. It crumbled because not a single scientist believed that such a wind could be possible. It was outside their frame of reference. Naturally they had logical reasons for their disbelief. A wind larger than a planet would have to come from outside the planet. And *outside* meant space. But there isn't any air in space. And this was a wind made of air. Without air you can't have wind. So, by definition, it was impossible. That's what the scientists said, and, of course, they were correct. Which created a certain amount of cognitive dissonance since they were both correct and wrong. With all their equipment and equations, they had forgotten something that people long ago had known very well. They had forgotten that the wind of this world, the wind that we can measure with instruments and feel in our hair, is only a shadow of something far greater. But such collective memories, which are beyond scientific observation, had been blotted from their brains.

On that morning Alex Lancaster had gotten up early. But he was pretending it was like any other Sunday morning when he never got up early. At sixteen he had perfected the art of sleeping until noon, but the truth was, last night he hadn't slept much at all. His room looked strange and cold with the posters gone. Only a few days ago the walls had been alive with superheroes, sports stars, and rock stars, silent images loud enough to blow your eardrums out. Now they were neatly rolled and packed into sixteen cardboard mailing tubes. Half the night he had stared at an infinity of plaster.

Haven't you stood in an empty room where the only residue of your existence was nail holes in the walls?

Sunday morning and not a frigging thing to do.

His computer was sealed in a box, and the rest of his electronic junk had been stuffed into a bulging backpack. The last thing he wanted was to dump that mess on the floor. So what was left? TV? Boring. The newspaper? How retro. Did they still get a newspaper? He thought maybe they did because his mother didn't like computers.

Alex peered out the window. There it was, lying on the front lawn soaking up the dew. He hoped it hadn't landed in dog poop. On this street jerks walked their stupid dogs and never cleaned up after themselves.

So go get the thing.

With great stealth Alex began the journey through the house. It was a trick getting past the other bedrooms without waking everybody. The problem wasn't Amanda or his mother. They could snore through a nuclear holocaust. It was Tori. He had considered renting her out as a guard dog. She heard every creak of the floor. And when she woke up, everybody woke up.

Curling his toes so his flip-flops wouldn't flop, he sneaked down the hall and through the living room. At the front door he moved even more cautiously, opening it with excruciating slowness to keep the hinges from squeaking.

The moment he stepped onto the porch, Alex knew that something was wrong. He stared up and down the street. The neighborhood looked like it was going to puke. The edges of everything had softened and the colors seemed to be muddling into a yellow blur. Or maybe it was his eyes. He rubbed them but nothing changed.

After retrieving the newspaper, he went back to his room. But for some reason his favorite chair wasn't comfortable anymore, not even when he propped his feet up on the boxes. And the newspaper—what a bunch of crap. How could people kill trees to print this stuff? Somehow, as he stared at the pages, a blur came into his eyes.

Soon the remaining Lancasters were up and about. Amanda and Tori wandered down to the living room, but neither seemed interested in their favorite Sunday morning pastime: arguing over the TV. Strangest of all, this morning neither girl tried to irritate Alex. Which proved that everything was screwed.

Breakfast. Scrambled eggs, bacon, sausage, pancakes, doughnuts, and hot chocolate. Enough carbs to stoke a football team. Comfort food that brought no comfort. Alex glanced at his watch. An hour before the cab would arrive. He wished the time would go faster. He was sticking a doughnut into his face when the stillness outside was broken. From somewhere within the blur came a high whistling call just beyond the range of human hearing. Around the world scientific instruments measured it, but only the dogs understood what it meant. Untold millions of them began howling their lungs out.

Soon, like all prophets, they would be beaten to silence.

While the dogs howled, experts in large cities debated about what was happening. Most of their debates disintegrated into raging arguments. Finally political sensibilities prevailed and an explanation was negotiated. The explanation was purely speculative, which is another way of saying bogus, but that didn't matter. What mattered was coming up with a consoling statement for TV viewers. In times of crisis TV viewers won't sit still for bogus speculation unless it's easy to understand and delivered as though it were ironclad truth. On both counts they were obliged. Not to worry; the odd stillness and the visual distortions were the result of capricious sunspots — unimportant disturbances with little effect beyond the messing up of cell phones and satellite signals. Rest assured they will pass.

Now, precisely how sunspots could generate high frequency whistling was not explained because the whistling was never mentioned. Why bother telling people about things they can't hear? For the cameras, all questions were answered quickly and authoritatively by an axe-faced spokeswoman from the National Weather Service who displayed a series of incomprehensible but sleekly designed charts, plastered with unintelligible nonsense. Since the spokeswoman looked exactly like a scientific spokeswoman should, when she was finished everyone was satisfied. There was even an ounce of truth in what she had told them. Yes, there were sunspots, but they weren't minor. They were the largest in recorded history. And she didn't talk about the most disturbing facts, because her minders had forbidden it. The trifling problem of the visual distortions had nothing to do with sunspots. They appeared to represent a fundamental shift in the equations of reality. And the whistling was getting louder.

Apart from that, everything was fine.

2

MALLEUS

It had taken Alex, Amanda, and Tori months to pack for their trip, but finally everything they owned had been distilled into a collection of suitcases and shipping crates. Their rooms stood empty. It had been an agonizing process. Now it was done, and the only thing left to do was leave.

The family gathered in the living room, if "gathering" was what you could call it. Ellen and Tori were at one end of the couch, Amanda at the other, while Alex slouched by the door. And no one was talking.

Amanda stared down at her shoes. They were new and black and boxy. She had bought them yesterday at the mall. Alex had told her they were ugly, which made her like them even more. Most important, they weren't what a child would wear. Because she wasn't a child. Thirteen going on thirty, that's what the psychologist had said, and he was right.

Amanda glanced at her sister, but a glance was all she could bear. They were completely different, but that didn't keep them from understanding each other. Their understanding came from many nights of crying—sometimes together, but mostly alone.

It was hard for strangers to believe that Amanda and Tori were related. Tori, with her light skin, blonde hair, and blue eyes, was beautiful. While Amanda had given up the dream of being beautiful. Mirrors do not lie. She looked like their father. Brown hair without a wave or luster in it, a chin too large to be considered delicate. Dark, sensitive eyes often kept averted. Not that she was ugly. She just wasn't anything at all. At least, that's the way she viewed herself.

Of course, her mother had told her that with a little effort she could be very pretty. Which made her want to throw up. She hated lies. Amanda had accepted her looks and knew her place within the family. Tori was the doll-like child, her mother's favorite, while she was the smart one, the lover of books who used to get straight A's. Used to. Tori was all bubbles and laughter and light, while Amanda was the one who could stare at nothing for hours, drifting in a place where no one else could come. Her therapist had tried to reach that place and had failed. The twilight room of her heart was locked tight.

At the other end of the couch Tori laid her head on her mother's shoulder—in one way, the youngest Lancaster was very much like her sister. Both were proficient at dancing the family minuet. At nine Tori was an expert at the game that kept them all alive. Each child had an unconscious role to play. Hers was to remain a happy Barbie doll. She hated Barbies, but that didn't matter. To perform her role, Tori carefully pretended to love her mother's collection. The game had started out fun, but she had grown tired of it. Not that being tired meant it could end. The game must never end. It had to go on because it made her mother happy. And when her mother was happy, everything was fine.

The closing moments in the living room were very painful. Ellen moved down the couch so that she and Tori could be close to Amanda. Which made Amanda hug her corner even more tightly. And then the whispering began.

Alex tried not to hear what his mother was saying, but he couldn't help it. And the words made him furious. They were the same words he had heard from his earliest childhood, meaningless promises about the wonderful days ahead and how very much she loved them all. Soon Tori was crying. He swore under his breath. He couldn't stand it when his sisters cried. When they did it late at night, he would slap on his headphones and crank up the volume. He was about to search for the headphones in his backpack, when salvation arrived in the form of a honking wheeze.

Alex got up and opened the front door. Squatting in their driveway was a decrepit rust-red limousine that looked like an escapee from a demolition derby. From bumper to bumper it was battered and bashed as though someone had taken a sledgehammer to it—except for the windows which were shiny and clean and tinted metallic blue.

The wheeze came again from under the hood. Definitely an attempt at a horn. Smirking, Alex turned to his mother. "I think the cab's here. If the pile of junk on the driveway is what you called for us." Grabbing their suitcases, he lumbered outside.

The others followed. On the porch they entered the stillness. Everything was so quiet and the air was thick with a smothering blur. For a moment none of them moved. Then slowly, with a tortured scream of metal, the limousine door creaked open and out stepped the driver. In front of them stood a gangling old man in a ragged chauffeur's uniform.

"You folks ready to travel?"

He was even more decrepit than his car. A shock of white hair stuck out from under a threadbare cap. Plastered beneath his nose was a straggling mustache that made him look like a malnourished walrus. Alex's smirk widened into a deathly grin. Excellent. Their driver was a homeless bum. Just the sort of derelict to take them to the airport. He loved it because he knew it would drive his mother insane.

"Are you … from Central Cab?" Ellen's voice quavered as she stared first at the man and then at his vehicle.

"Sure am, lady. Jerry's all full up. Told me to come and get you. He's got calls runnin' out the nose. A lot of cars aren't startin' today. 'Course, I don't have no trouble with ol' Malleus here."

"Malleus?" Alex snickered.

"Now, I know we aren't what you was expectin' …" The man pulled out a set of keys and walked to the trunk. "But this here ol' boat knows his way to the airport better'n anybody. That's where this crew's headin', aren't it?" With a metallic shriek, the trunk opened.

Ellen gulped. "Uhh, yes, but … I was thinking … maybe I should drive them myself."

"Not the day to drive, ma'am. Take my word for it. I know we aren't pretty, but we're safe."

"So those dents must have come from hitting air pockets," Alex said.

"Half of 'em came from air pockets and the other half just flat-out old age. Sorta like metal wrinkles. That's what happens when your odometer tops a million."

Alex glanced at his mother expecting to see her fall apart. But to his shock, she was *smiling*. So was Tori. Even Amanda's eyes had a twinkle in them.

"Yeah, ol' Malleus an' me got some miles on us, but these young people are gonna be safe, ma'am. You kin bet your stars on it. How about it? You want to ride in my ol' junker?"

"Yeah!" Tori's tears were gone.

Alex couldn't believe what he was hearing. She was gonna let them do it—ride with a bum in a car that would fall apart if it ever reached twenty miles an hour. Instantly his rage returned. There you go, just another example of how little she cared about them. Clear proof of how much she wanted them out of her life. Well, *fine*. The sooner they were gone the better.

But in his rage he hadn't noticed something. While he had been staring at the dents in the car, his mother had been looking into the old man's eyes, and as she looked, all her fears had vanished. Somehow, beyond words, she knew that her children would be safe with him, safer than anywhere else in the world.

But then Ellen looked at her son and her fear returned. "You ... you do think it's all right, don't you? I mean ... if you'd rather, I could take you myself."

"Hey, forget it. We'll be fine." Utterly disgusted, Alex picked up their luggage and stalked to the trunk. He saw the tears she fought back and didn't care.

But then the old man approached and spoke gently to Ellen. "Don't you worry none about your boy, ma'am. You done the best you could, and that's all that matters. Now, you listen to what I'm sayin'. When all's said and done, he's gonna be fine." Such strange words from a cabby. But when he said them, they brought great comfort. Then the lines in his face crinkled into a smile. "Hey, will you look up at that sky? We got a touch o' weather comin'. Now you take my advice. Go inside an' shut your windows an' doors. Then get a little rest. Nothin' like sleepin' with rain on a roof to wash the sorrows away." The man picked up the remaining luggage and loaded it in the trunk. "All right, now ... you lovely ladies climb in the back an' this young gent can ride shotgun next to me. How's that for a plan?"

The last moment was the most painful of all as Ellen kissed and hugged each of her children, hugged them as though she might never see them again. When Alex's turn came he stiffened, but she kissed him anyway. His coldness only deepened when she whispered, "I love you."

Their eyes didn't meet because he wouldn't let them.

The girls climbed into the rear of the limousine, while Alex slid into the front. Then the engine started, and with a creak of loose gears, the old tub rattled out onto the street. Amanda and Tori waved out the back window until their home vanished behind them. Alex stared rigidly ahead. For him, his home had vanished a long time ago.

When they were gone, Ellen Lancaster walked back into her house. As she entered her living room, she broke down in tears. So empty. Just like her soul. The pain was almost overwhelming. And not just in her heart, in her body. It had been growing for months. The terrible secret that she had not told them, because if she had they never would have left. And leaving was for the best. Struggling to her bedroom, Ellen fell onto her bed. Tomorrow the treatments would begin. Paid for by the man she had loved since she was seventeen. The man who had left her. Was it going to rain? She wished it would rain a river that would drown her soul.

3

TIME SPIRIT

Forty-five minutes to O'Hare, the worst airport in the Western world. Alex slouched on the tattered seat, wishing their walrus of a chauffeur would close the glass partition so he could be completely separated from the passenger compartment. One glance had told him that his sisters were enjoying themselves, enthroned like princesses on the way to a junkyard ball. Tori had discovered an old TV set bolted into the ceiling and was watching cartoons. Amanda had found a paperback novel, just her kind of trash.

Alex examined his surroundings. If anything, the limousine was worse inside than out. He guessed that four thousand years ago the upholstery had been red. What was left was barely visible between long strips of duct tape that kept the whole mess from sliding onto the floor. But that was better than the dashboard, which was a shattered mass that looked as though someone had taken an axe to it. Unquestionably his mother had consigned them to a garbage truck. Alex knew that only a total dork would arrive at the airport in such a wreck.

There was one small consolation, however. As bad as the limousine was, it was better than riding with their mother. Of course, she had talked for days about driving them herself, but he had been firm in his refusal. Like always, getting his way in things that didn't count. True, Ellen had been hurt (he was trying to think of her as "Ellen" now), but that was good. She deserved to be hurt. While the scales of justice were hardly balanced, retribution had to begin somewhere. He hoped that she was miserable.

In spite of his best efforts he fought a growing lump in his throat, hating himself for allowing the slightest trickle of emotion. Shifting his mind into neutral, he tried to lose all feeling in the trance of the highway. It was odd how smooth the old junk heap ran. Not the slightest bump or rattle. Laying his head back, through half-closed eyes, he watched the liquid blur of trees and buildings.

Blue town.

The town of the tinted window.

A metallic river of speeding shapes that meant nothing.

The trance was almost complete when the driver's grating voice jarred his eyes open. "Come on, Malleus. Get up there, boy. Don't let that wind stop you." Suddenly it was blowing much harder. The old loon was having a difficult time steering the limousine up the ramp onto the tollway. "Ever see such crazy weather? 'Nough wind to carry off the whole dern city. What airline you kids want?"

"American." Alex intentionally mumbled the word.

"How's that?"

"I said *American*."

"That's what I thought you said. Goin' a long way, are you?"

Alex groaned. What a stupid question, and if he answered it, it would lead to a hundred more. Only one way to deal with this. Long ago he had discovered that a few well-timed grunts kept old people blathering with no need for him to talk. Staring at the road, he grunted out a half-word that sounded vaguely affirmative. As expected, the driver started to babble.

"Don't ever fly in planes myself. Too dangerous. Was drivin' right by when that DC10 crashed in '78 ... or was it '79? Anyway, I said then what I say now. If the good Lord wanted us to fly in planes, He wouldn't have give us perfectly good cabs. Never fly in a plane when you kin take a cab. It's a good rule, son, 'specially on a day when the time spirit's movin'."

Alex was all ready with another grunt, but the man's last words strangled it in mid-articulation. He stared at the lined face. "What did you say?"

Dim, whimsical eyes peered back at him. "I said, don't never fly when you kin take a cab."

"No. After that. Something about a spirit."

"Oh, the time spirit. I said he's movin'. Look up at that drippy, blurry sky. That's what he does, makes things seem like they're slowin' down, when they're speedin' up. 'Course usually he's a little quieter about it. Bet you never heard o' the time spirit, did you, boy?"

Suddenly everything was clear to Alex. They were being driven to the airport by a certifiable lunatic. Of course, there was no way this idiot could be from the cab company. His mother would have discovered that with a single phone call. Picking them up had been a scam. Alex even knew how it had been pulled off; all it took was listening to a two-way radio. When the pickup order went out from the dispatcher, you raced over and beat the cab to the door. Very likely the real driver had arrived a few minutes after they were gone. Alex wondered if Ellen was worried. Maybe she was trying desperately to find out who had stolen her children. Maybe soon there would be an Amber Alert.

The thought amused him.

"Yeah, nobody talks about the time spirit these days. Can't blame 'em none. He's nobody to mess with."

It occurred to Alex that since he was stuck with a lunatic, he might as well enjoy it. A sarcastic smile twisted the corner of his mouth. "Bet you've seen a lot of spirits."

"More than my share."

"Hey, you'd better look behind you, 'cause there's one on your tail right now."

"Really?" The old fool stared in his rearview mirror. "What you talkin' about, boy? There ain't nothin' back there."

"Oh, he's there all right. It's the junkyard spirit, and I think he wants your car."

As soon as he had said the words, he wished that he hadn't. There was a long pause, then the old man smiled and turned to look at him. And with that look, everything changed. From being dim and whimsical, his eyes took on a clarity and power that Alex had never seen on any human face.

For an awful moment he couldn't speak. He couldn't even breathe.

"You like music, don't you, son? Why don't we just stop talkin' an' listen to the radio." He punched a button, and rock music blasted from the dashboard speaker.

After that, the man never said another word until they reached their destination. Alex rode slumped down, staring sullenly out the window, trying to make the blur resettle over his brain. Finally they turned off the Tri-state and headed down the ramp toward the Kennedy. Moments later they arrived.

Outside the terminal their bags were removed from the trunk. Then the old man got a cart and loaded them on it. Amanda and Tori went inside while Alex paid the driver. For some reason, the tip was more generous than he had planned, but still he couldn't look into the old man's eyes. Cramming his wallet back in his pocket, he was about to push the cart through the automatic doors when he felt a tap on the shoulder.

"Got a mind to tell you somethin'."

Alex turned.

"Listen to me, boy. When you don't know where to go, follow."

"What?"

"I said, *when you don't know where to go ... follow.* Now, you an' your sisters have a good trip to England. And don't forget what I told you about cabs." With that, he got into his car and drove off. It wasn't until later that Alex realized he hadn't mentioned anything about England.

4

THE CLOTH OF TWILIGHT

Amanda stared around the terminal and mumbled, "This is creepy." The huge room was jammed, and the noise should have been deafening, but instead, there was total silence. Nobody was talking at all. Not even the kids. And on every face there was a slight bewilderment as though the blur outside had entered their brains. She turned to her sister. "Come on, let's find a restroom."

As they walked away, Alex stared at the crowd. Amanda was right. Everybody looked half asleep, or maybe half dead. Pushing the luggage cart to the center of the room, he scanned the huge board that listed departures. Every slot flashed with a single message.

FLIGHT DELAYED—SEE REPRESENTATIVE

So that was it; the airport was jammed because no planes were taking off. But that made the silence even weirder.

Everybody should be yelling.

Travelers always yell when the slightest thing goes wrong. But at the ticket desk a fat little man in a red jacket actually whispered in answer to his questions as though he were giving out secret information: "Flight 466 to London, with a stop in Boston, has been delayed until three o'clock. Watch the board for more information." It was like a recorded message. He never even looked up from his computer screen.

When the girls returned, they processed their tickets and began the endless journey through security, then passport control, then baggage, then more security, and more security after that. At the gate everything sludged down into a blurry bore. Amanda read her book, Tori played a video game, and Alex sat with earbuds stuck in his head, not really listening, just staring out the window.

Three o'clock came and went, and nobody appeared at the desk.

At six o'clock he checked his cell phone. No signal.

He checked again at six-thirty and seven. Finally a few bars appeared, but no messages. His mother hadn't even tried to call. Big surprise—for all she cared, they could be dead and buried on a farm in Wisconsin. He told himself it didn't matter.

Hour after hour the delay was extended. By the time the call came to board, it was ten o'clock and Tori was whining. She had been asleep since eight-thirty. Amanda wasn't much better. She had been asleep too and remained uselessly groggy, which left Alex with the task of getting all of them and their backpacks onto the plane.

To make matters worse, even after they were buckled into their seats, the wait wasn't over. There was still another forty-five minutes of sitting at the gate. The girls went back to sleep, but Alex couldn't close his eyes.

At last there was movement. Slowly the big jet eased away from the terminal, crawled across the tarmac, and got in line for takeoff. Thirty minutes later they roared up into the moaning darkness.

Alex realized something odd. The airport had been crowded, but their plane was half empty, plenty of room for everyone to stretch out with pillows and blankets. Which he and his sisters did as soon as the fasten seatbelt sign had been turned off. Lying in the gloom, half-formed thoughts flickered through his mind.

England. Flying away to live with a father he hadn't seen in over a year. A father with a new "family." He and his trophy wife even had a son. How much would this new "family" want three leftovers from Chicago? About as much as Alex wanted to live with *them*. As far as he was concerned, they were streaking away at six hundred miles an hour toward nothing, and nothing was what his life had become. In the last moments before sleep, it was easy to pretend that their jet would never land. With his heart at the controls, Alex kept on flying.

Away from Chicago ...

Away from London ...

Away from houses where they didn't belong ...

Into the silent coldness beyond the stars.

It seemed that no time had passed before a flight attendant was shaking him.

"Is this ... London?" His eyelids felt like they had been stuck shut with superglue.

"No, we're about to land in Boston. Please sit up and fasten your seat belt. And maybe you could help your sisters with theirs."

It took a great deal of effort, but finally the girls were buckled into position, though still fast asleep. With a screeching bump, the jet landed. Then it taxied to the gate and stopped. The big door slid open and a few haggard passengers straggled out.

That's when the weirdness began.

Suddenly, onto the plane rushed a man and a woman in heavy overcoats and gloves. The woman was carrying a baby. They seemed nervous; every move had a kind of jerky twitch about it. The woman held the baby in a funny way, stuck out in front of her as though he had peed on himself and she didn't want to touch him.

Overcoats and gloves in August? Alex thought. Maybe Boston was cold at night, but it couldn't be *that* cold.

Their seats were one row up and across the aisle. Without taking off their coats and gloves, they sat down. Alex stared at the baby. He was a little boy about one year old, with a chubby face and reddish hair. As the baby wriggled into a new position, maybe it was only the light, but for a moment his eyes flashed with a dark, silvery glow, almost like those of an animal caught in the headlights of a car.

Alex blinked.

When he looked again, the baby was staring straight at him. It wasn't a trick of the light. His pupils were shining silver. It was unlike anything Alex had ever seen, and the intensity of the shining was growing every second. But then the little boy smiled. Instantly all the anger and exhaustion that had made Alex so miserable in the past few hours were gone, replaced with a mysterious warmth.

The feeling remained until the woman turned the child away.

Then all the ugliness rushed back.

The longer Alex stared at the woman, the more convinced he became that she looked exactly like the pictures he had seen of his father's new wife, Cynthia. She had jet-black hair that hung straight and silky, and her chiseled features made her look like a mannequin. It took only a little imagination for Alex to believe that the touch of bronze on her cheeks wasn't makeup, but places where the fake head was showing through. Just the kind of female his father would think was *hot*. And her traveling companion was a male copy. The coat couldn't hide it. The guy was ripped. Clearly a workout freak loaded with enough steroids to play professional baseball. Whoever they were, Alex knew that they couldn't be the baby's parents. No way. Not the slightest chance. People like that hated kids. And just look at how she was still holding him—like he was poison. So if they weren't the parents, who were they? His mind raced. Kidnappers. That was it. Why else would they act so weird? Important thought: If they were kidnappers and he turned them in, there might be a reward. Not only would he get rich, he'd be on cable news. Heroes always got on cable news.

Suddenly the man twisted in his seat and stared straight at him; the look was so menacing that it drained the fantasy right out of his head. *Stupid fool.* That's what the look said, and Alex withered. With a sneer the man turned away, and it was as though he had awakened from a trance. He stared at them. Suddenly, try as he might, he couldn't find anything unusual at all. Kidnappers? They were just two people with a baby on the seat between them reading magazines—*Sports Illustrated* and *Cosmopolitan*.

No joke. He really was going nuts.

Alex was seriously contemplating his loss of sanity when a grinding rumble almost made him jump out of his seat. He noticed that the flight attendant had swung the huge door shut in preparation for departure. That was it. He rubbed his eyes. First, weird babies and kidnappers, and now he was jumpy enough to explode out of his skin. He had to get some sleep or he would go stark raving wacko. Forcing himself to relax, he closed his eyes.

Then he jumped again and swore.

Someone outside the closed door had begun pounding on it as though with a sledgehammer. The whole plane shook. The startled attendant rushed over and looked through the porthole. Instantly the pounding stopped. After unlatching the door, she pulled it open.

No one was prepared for the person who walked onto the plane. Handing her boarding pass to the flight attendant was a blind woman led by a seeing-eye dog. But there, all touch with the world Alex had known came to an end, for she was almost seven feet tall, and the head of the dog came to her chest. Both were old, so old that Alex couldn't imagine any living thing more ancient, yet in neither was there the slightest weakness or quavering. Mist drifted in the woman's clothes and the animal's fur, as though they had just walked through an ocean fog. Yet the darkness outside was clear and windy.

And the attendant … what was wrong with her? She acted as though everything was totally normal—as though every day of the week seven-foot-tall people got on planes after pounding on them with sledgehammers.

Turning toward the aisle, the old woman stared vacantly in Alex's direction. A glistening film covered her eyes, but if anything, it added to her majestic presence. On her face was the shadow of a great beauty, creased with a thousand lines and careworn by age. Her iron-gray hair was pulled back into a long braid that hung almost to the floor and around her shoulders was draped a tattered shawl coarsely woven like a fisherman's net. In her hand she held a worn leather bag.

Reaching down, she touched the animal standing motionless beside her. For some reason the fur on the dog's neck was bristling. But Alex didn't really notice because he was transfixed by the creature's eyes. They were blue, haunting, and somehow didn't fit the rest of his body. Nothing so young should have been in anything so old. He was old, grizzled beyond description, a misshapen mongrel; and he was covered with scars … terrible scars … as though he had spent his entire life locked in vicious battles. Something about the way he stood spoke of endless pursuit, deadly peril, and bloody victory. Here was an animal both brave and dangerous beyond imagining, and he was gazing steadily at the man and the woman in the overcoats—staring at them as though, at any moment, he might leap across the seats and tear them to pieces. Alex had never seen a dog stare like that—with absolute, unwavering intensity. Then his lips drew back in what could have been nothing less than a canine grin of pleasure.

His teeth were like knives.

The response of the people across the aisle was not hard to understand. They were frozen with terror for a moment, but then the moment passed. The flight attendant led the new arrivals to a seat several rows up, where, with aching slowness, the old woman sat down. The dog stretched out on the floor next to her and promptly closed his eyes. The old woman rummaged in her bag, mumbling in exasperation, until finally she drew out a small book attached to a golden chain. Carefully placing the chain around her neck, she opened to a page marked with a purple ribbon and began to read.

Alex leaned forward. For a brief moment the woman held the book high enough for him to see its pages. As he had expected, there was no printing on it. He had seen books for the blind. But as he continued to watch, he realized that something was wrong. To read Braille you had to move your fingers across the paper touching dots, but the woman never moved her fingers. She held the empty book as though she were reading just like anyone else. Alex was completely mystified. But before he could think any more about it, he was pushed back into his seat by the thrust of the engines.

As soon as the plane was in the air, the old woman closed the book and folded her arms. Alex tried to keep watching, but his eyes just wouldn't stay open. Before he knew it, he had plunged into a deep sleep.

A jarring bump, and then another, and Alex lurched into total awareness.

The flying was getting rough. Sliding over to a window, he looked out. It was dark—and that was strange. He checked his watch. They had been heading east for a long time. The sun should be rising. But it wasn't.

As the minutes passed, the bumping grew worse. Then the seatbelt sign came on, and the flight attendants began waking everyone. Alex got Amanda and Tori buckled into the seats next to him. The girls were afraid, especially Tori who had awakened with no memory of where she was. For their sakes he tried to appear calm. But this kind of bumping wasn't normal. As he stared out the window, he couldn't help imagining that there was something thick and heavy in the air. They must be flying into a storm, but there were no clouds. Far below, moonlight sparkled on a furious ocean.

Soon the bumping grew to bashing. There was a crash as though a giant fist had struck the underbelly of the plane, and instantly it dropped from the sky, only to climb again moments later like a speck in a hurricane. Amanda and Tori screamed. Alex's ears popped. His head swam as all of the air was sucked from the compartment. Oxygen masks tumbled down. They struggled to put them on.

Just as the plane leveled off, lightning appeared. Through the window Alex could see it falling like torrents of glowing rain. And with it was thunder.

The jet plummeted as though off a cliff.

Amanda and Tori clutched wildly at each other. Everybody was screaming. The terror was indescribable—except in one person. The old woman didn't seem to notice that anything was wrong. She was still reading from her book, mumbling and staring at it with rigid concentration. And the dog? Well, that was the most amazing thing of all. He had climbed into the seat next to her and was wearing an oxygen mask. Not only did he look ridiculous, it barely covered his nose, but it appeared that he was enjoying every moment of it—huffing and puffing into the mask with total delight.

Then came a roar that made every other crash seem like a whisper. The jet groaned and lurched, and the lights went out.

The captain's tense voice crackled over the loudspeaker. "I'm sorry to tell you this ... but we've experienced total engine failure. I have no choice but to land in the ocean. Please remain calm. We have rafts and your seat cushions are made for flotation. Prepare for impact. And God be with us all."

Horrified, Alex pressed his face to the window. The jet was only a few hundred feet above the water. Waves like mountains raged and vanished beneath them. Jagged streaks of lightning crashed into the foam with a thousand blue-green explosions. No one could land in that and survive. They were going to die. Strangely, with the loss of hope, his terror vanished. Pulling the shade, he turned to Amanda and Tori. More than anything he wanted to say something, but he didn't know what, so all he could do was stare at them helplessly.

From the windows of the aircraft no one saw what was happening high above. Over a screaming wind from deep within the universe, a brilliant star was beginning to shine ... as an ancient voice sung from the pages of an empty book ... hanging from a chain of gold ... above the cloth of twilight.

5

WORLDFALL

Slowly Tori Lancaster opened her eyes.

Something warm was against her cheek. It was a blanket. To her surprise she discovered that she was lying on a little mountain of blankets in the center of a huge raft. And the raft was floating on water. It was a dream, she told herself.

Amanda was in the raft too, lying half-hidden, snoring away, under a blanket of her own. Tori was about to close her eyes and doze off again when a wonderful smell made her turn and glance in a new direction. Instantly she was wide awake.

Someone else was in the raft and this person wasn't asleep at all. Near the pile of blankets sat a battered airplane chair, and seated in it was a very tall old woman, smiling. Tori had never seen anyone so odd. Everything about her was strange: her hair, her eyes, and especially her clothes. A faint mist drifted around them.

In her hand she held a steaming cup and on her lap sat a plate of freshly baked cookies. That's where the delicious smell was coming from. And if all that wasn't freaky enough, next to her chair sprawled a dog the size of a small couch with a baby asleep between his paws.

"Good evening." The woman's voice was deep and creaky but not unpleasant. She took a loud sip from the cup and snorted deliciously as the steam circled her nose. "Cookies. Cookies here. Want a cookie? They're fresh. Baked one half minute ago."

Tori was so surprised that she couldn't say a word. All she could do was reach across the blankets and grab her sister. The only response she got was an unintelligible grunt that sounded like, "Go 'way, jerk."

But Tori wouldn't go away. She just kept poking.

"I said, *go away.*"

If there was one thing Amanda hated, it was being awakened on a Saturday morning by Tori. And it happened every Saturday morning. Every single time she wanted to sleep in, Tori bugged her to death until she had to wake up. Well, she was *sick* of it. Rolling over, she was about to give her a whack when her eyes opened and she saw where her sister was pointing.

An old woman ... a dog ... and a baby ... in a raft in the middle of the ocean.

Suddenly she began to remember. And what she remembered was absolutely terrifying. The last moments before the crash. The screams. The plane hitting the water. Everything breaking apart. Then darkness. Jumping up, she stared at Tori. The look made Tori remember too. They stared around.

"Alex ..."

He wasn't in the raft.

"Oh no ..." Tori's lower lip began to tremble.

"Now, now, now, now, now, I know everything's upset. A little jerky. Twisted upside down. But it's going to be fine." The old woman spoke quickly but with great gentleness. "The gangly one. The one with lots of hair. That's who you're looking for, isn't it?"

"He's our brother. Do you know where he is?" Amanda could hardly get the words out. It felt like someone had punched her in the stomach.

"Well, I can tell you this. Not a thing was lost in the flying. Certainly not your brother. Never something like that. A chair maybe. A pillow. A hundred indigestible meals. But not a brother. He's alive and well. Not comfortable, not quite that. His landing wasn't as padded as ours. Bumpy, but all right. You've got my word, and I always tell the truth."

"You mean he's on another raft?" Amanda felt a glimmer of hope.

"Yes. Specifically, another raft. Seriously, that indeed."

"But ... how do you know that?" She stared at the old woman's eyes. It was obvious that she was blind. "I mean ... I mean ... you couldn't have ... seen him."

"A minor detail. You'd be surprised how much a blind person knows. And that's a fact. Now, Grandfather is taking care of your brother, and he couldn't be in safer hands anywhere in the universe. No indeed. Not ever."

"But ... we don't have a grandfather." Tori's voice sounded small and scared. "We were traveling by ourselves."

"*By yourselves?* What's that? What did you say?" A strange catch came into the woman's voice. "Surely, positively, you can be certain of one thing. You've never lived a minute, not a second, not a day or two, never ever ... *by yourselves.*" Turning away, she dabbed at her eyes and cleared her throat. "Now, I know you're frightened, who wouldn't be? Who indeed? But this is not a time for sadness and tears. We've got enough water all around us. No need for it to drip out of our faces. Your brother is going about his business, and we must be about ours. Which, at present, is eating cookies. So nibble one of these before I give them to our very large friend over here, who could eat the whole platter in a single gulp." At this, the old dog perked up his ears.

There was a moment of uncertainty. Tori wanted to cry over Alex and couldn't understand why he wasn't there. Yet being with this peculiar woman seemed to make everything all right. A tear trickled down her cheek. But then she reached out and took a cookie. One bite made her feel much better. It was the most delicious cookie that she had ever eaten. And it was *hot* ... as though right out of the oven.

"Now, you—you, my dear. A cookie for you."

The plate was extended to Amanda, who shook her head.

"No, thanks. I'm not hungry."

In fact, Amanda wanted to throw up. None of this could be real. Dogs and babies and weird old women in rafts? Not a chance. So if it wasn't real, that meant it was a nightmare. Or worse, she was dead. That made a lot of sense. No one could have lived through that crash. The truth must be that she had died, and because of her evil life, God had stuck her in a raft with a wacko blind woman, a baby, a dog, and Tori to wake her up every single morning forever. Amanda felt the contents of her stomach move closer to her throat. But then she looked up to find the woman's mysterious eyes gazing at her. And there was something coming from deep within them that looked like a glowing mist. When it touched her skin, it warmed the fear away. Suddenly she felt loved. Loved almost more than she could bear. It hurt, like tasting something wonderful when you've been starving. The first touch on your tongue brings aching pain.

"Is your dog a guide dog?" Amanda was glad that Tori had asked the question. It made the woman stop looking at her.

"Oh, he guides all right. Yes, he does indeed." She chuckled. "But he has his own way of doing it, and he doesn't stop for traffic lights."

"I think I remember when you got on the plane." Tori crossed her legs and leaned against the side of the raft. "I was mostly asleep, but it was in Boston, wasn't it?"

The old woman nodded, "Yes, Boston, Boston. Massachusetts, somewhere. Foggy place."

"We're from Chicago. Did you have to wait long at the airport? We had to wait forever. I got tired and slept almost the whole flight. I usually don't sleep on planes. But this time I did. We were going to London. Where were you going?"

Suddenly Amanda wanted Tori to shut up. "Everybody was going to London, Tori. That's where the plane was going." She gave her sister a withering look.

"I wasn't."

Both girls stared at her. For a moment Amanda thought she was joking. But she didn't laugh.

"What do you mean? Were you on the wrong plane?" It seemed impossible that anyone could make such a mistake. Surely the airline people would stop them, especially a blind person.

"No mistake. It was the right plane. But London, the bigger foggy place, wasn't where I was going. Planes go up, but they never go down where you want them to. Unless you make special extremely unusual arrangements. And that's always expensive."

Amanda realized that every time the old woman spoke it grew harder to understand what she meant.

"Our dad lives in England. We were on our way to visit him." Amanda didn't know why she said it. It wasn't even true. They were on their way to *live* with him.

"I know. Indeed, yes, everything, all about it." There was a sadness in the creaky voice that made Amanda glance up at her.

"Yes, I know the Lancasters, each and all of them. Five. Then four. Before that six. Eight. Seven. Back and back and back, and so forth, etcetera, etcetera, many, many years."

"What?"

"Families, families. Lancaster families. The number of people in them. And you. I've seen both of you, all three of you, many times. Times over times. A lot of times."

The mist around the woman's eyes became glistening drops. "Your name is Amanda … Manda-Manda of the many questions. Amanda who hides on top of the garage to cry."

Amanda sucked in her breath. The look on the woman's face was disturbing. The sightless eyes focused with full attention. Not at all the way adults usually "listened" to teenagers. And yet it was so odd and loving. If the love hadn't been there, she would have been terrified. Nobody knew about the roof. Not a single soul. The high place under the tree. It was her secret. Yet, somehow, a complete stranger knew all about it.

Then the mysterious face turned toward her sister. "And you. You are Tori … Tori-Tori who buries dolls under bushes. The lilac purple kind. Tori who dreams and dreams, so many dreams. And in the dreams she cries for her father. The doll's name? My brain doesn't remember. Tell me, tell me."

"I … I've forgotten." Tori hadn't forgotten at all.

"In a bag you buried it. The girl who loves to bury things. But love can bring them back again. See? See here?"

From under her shawl she removed a dirt-covered plastic bag and handed it to Tori. Inside was the doll that she had buried so long ago. A princess doll with golden hair and a flowing gown. The one her father had given her when he went away.

"Something Wendy. Wendy-Wendy. *Golden Wendy.* That's it. That's the name."

At that moment Amanda understood a great deal about her sister that she hadn't known before. On the outside Tori had seemed strangely unhurt by their father's leaving. For a few weeks she had cried at night, and Amanda had gone in to comfort her. But after that she seemed okay. Once in awhile she had whimpered in her sleep, but not often. Everybody has bad dreams.

All bubbles and light ... that was Tori. Always trying to make their mother happy.

Except for a few times, when she destroyed things. Smashed them. Ripped them up. Always her own things. Never anybody else's. Things that had been precious to her like the Golden Wendy. She'd said she had lost it. Buried under the lilac bush. How had the old woman known?

Neither girl could speak.

"Wondering, wondering ... the young ones are wondering. Don't wonder how. Hows and whys and whens and wheres—who cares? Oh yes, I know Amanda and Tori and Alex-Alex their brother. I know them very well."

Rummaging in her shawl once more, the mysterious lady pulled out a handkerchief and dabbed her eyes. "Now look here, just look at this. You've got me crying. And there's nothing to cry about, not anymore, not yet anyway. This is one of the grandest days in history and we're not going to waste it with puddles of tears. Just look out there."

The girls turned and looked at the ocean.

"Grandfather's bubbling right along. He's doing his job. Every bit of it. And you don't see him crying. So let's just stop this silliness right now." She blew her nose loudly and continued staring at the water as though if she looked at the girls more tears would come.

Amanda and Tori had a thousand questions. But they didn't ask a single one. A great peace settled over them. Nothing made the least bit of sense, but it didn't seem to matter. All they knew was that they were with a perfect stranger who understood them better than anyone ever had in all their lives. For a long time the raft drifted through gently rippling water.

Suddenly Tori crawled to the edge and started to reach over the side. "Is it okay if I get a drink?" Cupping her hands, she was about to dip in. Instantly the lined face jerked to attention. "No!" The command was so loud and sharp that both girls jumped.

"Don't even think such a thing. Not once. Not ever. It'll make you sick. What's worse, it'll make *him* sick. He's got a very delicate constitution. Doesn't like being in people's mouths. Can't say I blame him. Gives him gas and we don't want that. There's nothing worse than riding on his belly when he starts to burp."

"Who?" Amanda stared at her as though she were crazy.

"Grandfather. The Old Man of the Ocean. Who else?"

"The old man of the ocean?"

"He's down there, you know. Deep down, close to the surface, everywhere. All eyes. Never stops watching. But what *is* the matter with me? Of course, you're both thirsty. What have I been thinking about? Come right over here. Come, come, come, right now."

As the girls watched, the old woman mumbled something to herself, then reached into her leather bag with both hands. To their surprise, out came a small blue tea kettle covered with strange symbols. Hanging on the side were two metal cups like the one she had been using. As Amanda and Tori stared, the pot began to puff and rattle and steam shot from its spout.

"All finished. Didn't take long. Quick as a wink."

To the girls' amazement, when the kettle was tipped into the cups, out came ice-cold lemonade. "That should do the trick. Lemon-lemon. From the stand you had last summer. Very good. Just like yours. Exactly the same recipe, I think."

One sip and they knew that it was the best lemonade they had ever tasted. Only after they were satisfied did the woman pour from the kettle into her own cup, which promptly filled with steaming tea from the very same spout. Then she tucked everything neatly back into the bag.

"How do you do that—get hot and cold stuff out of the same pot?" Tori was enthralled.

"Ask it, talk to it, that's how. Doesn't your teapot take orders?"

"I don't think so."

"Well, are you friends?"

"With a teapot?"

"Of course. But it does take time to build their trust. They're very shy, you know. Shy and never into politics. And they do have feelings—not at all like microwaves. But teapots are a little hard of hearing. It's because of the *steam*. That's the truth, I never lie."

The words were spoken so gravely that Tori roared with laughter. Amanda couldn't help smiling too. At that moment they heard a gurgle. The baby's eyes were open and he was smiling at them.

Tori bent down. "Oh, look, he's awake. He's so cute. Can I pick him up?"

The woman nodded.

To her surprise she discovered that he was light as a feather. "He doesn't weigh anything. Poor little guy. I wonder what happened to your parents."

"His what, his what?"

"His parents. I think I saw them on the plane."

"Those were not his parents." The words were so cold that the mist around her eyes turned into glittering crystals. *"Never ... ever speak such things again."*

Instantly Tori felt like burying herself under the blankets. But then the frightening look vanished and the old woman sighed, "Forgive me. Do forgive me. I'm tired and that turns my brain to rocks. How were you supposed to know? Indeed, you couldn't even. It's just taken so long. But at least he's with us now." A great weariness seemed to come over her as she sensed the girls' lingering fear. "Half to death, I've scared you. Now your heads are filled with questions that you're afraid to ask." She paused and looked out over the water. "My dear young women. Both of you ... all two of you ... you haven't known me long, but trust me, please, in spite of how I sound. Outsides change, but insides—never. You must get to know me inside, because we will be together for a while."

Amanda stared off at the endless horizon and shivered. Okay, maybe there was just a chance that she wasn't dead and all of this was real. "Don't you think they'll be out looking for us? I mean, after the plane crash and everything." She couldn't keep her voice from trembling.

"Looking for us? Oh, they're looking for us, looking everywhere. But we're well hidden. Hidden where their eyes can never see."

"What do you mean?"

There was another pause, and then the woman turned toward her. "Amanda. Manda-Manda, what if I should tell you strange things? New things. Things a girl from Earth has never heard. The truth. Questions answered. And it might as well be now. The large plane, the one from Boston. It didn't crash by itself. I told it to. Just me. Alone."

"What?"

"Crash. Unpleasant word. Let's say unscheduled landing in the ocean. Something else. A small but important detail. Don't be disturbed, but it isn't one of your oceans. It's one of mine on a slightly different world."

"You mean ... we're not on Earth?" Tori's eyes were wide. "We're on ... another planet?"

"Another planet. Yes. Exactly, precisely other. Look up."

Both girls stared at the sky. Above them a pale sun was setting, and above it there were stars. A sun and stars together. Tori gulped and her lower lip began to tremble.

"Now, don't be afraid. You're safe, so very safe with me. Did I not tear the twilight to come to you? And did I not call the Wind? It blew and blew and carried us away. Too old to do it now—not as young as then—aging with my world, and so it ought to be."

"Who are you?" Amanda was staring at her with hard eyes.

"Who?" The woman spoke softly and smiled. "Not just who, but *what*. What and what and what. The Watcher of two girls from the mornings they were born. Who? Many names. Names on names. But only one that matters. On Boreth, I am *Bellwind*." As she spoke her name, the mist around her sparkled like a thousand tiny diamonds, and from far away there was a whispering echo as though something unseen had heard and answered. Suddenly the dog began barking joyously, and they all turned to look.

In the distance fog was rising from the ocean, growing in billows like heavy smoke from a giant furnace beneath the sea. And it was moving toward them. As it drew nearer, a vague shape began to form. What they saw was an island made of mist. Cloudy cliffs and dim forests drifted in the haze. Before they knew it, the fog was all around them and they found themselves entering a river of shadows.

Bellwind rose and beckoned. The girls joined her at the front of the raft. Tori stared down at the baby in her arms. As they drifted in the stillness, he was changing. His skin took on a gentle pearl-like hue, and in his hair there were flecks of gold. He was even more beautiful than before, but now there was something wild about him, as though a flower from another world had begun to bloom. He sat, pulling at her sweater, gurgling just as any baby would. Yet, in him, there was mystery and strangeness.

Tori looked up. Bellwind was smiling at her. But the ancient face was not the same. It was her eyes. The silver coverings that had made her appear blind had vanished. Tori was staring into the loveliest eyes that she had ever seen, filled with pale blue mist. And as she stared, from deep within the shadow island, a haunting voice began to sing.

6

GRANDFATHER

Heartbeats.

Clanging.

Sounds without meaning.

Slivers of light and pain.

Alex's eyelids flickered open ... then shut.

More than anything, he didn't want to wake up. But the very act of willing himself to remain asleep was so annoying that it only awakened him further. And the more awake he grew, the more he knew that everything was wrong. To start with, his whole body ached, even his hair. And his mouth — it tasted like he'd been sucking garbage all night.

More aggravating awareness.

He was lying on something cold and clammy, and it was *moving* ... rolling back and forth ... in the most stomach-churning way. And every time it rolled, it made a nasty sound.

Roll-slosh ... Roll-squish ... Roll-slosh.

He forced himself to crack open one eye. It was a very brief experiment. The lids were stuck with mucus and the light made his head swim. Which didn't do one thing for his queasy stomach. His aggravation grew to anger.

What was going on here?

He opened his eyes and stared up into a dark blue sky. He hated camping, so he couldn't think of one good reason why he should be sleeping outdoors. Then he began to realize that the sky wasn't right. A pale sun was setting and above it there were stars. Sunlight and stars do not go together.

He groaned and turned his head, and the sky vanished. Two feet from his nose bulged an inflated rubber wall. With a great effort he lurched into a sitting position, which made his stomach want to leave his body. He was alone in a huge life raft. He rubbed his eyes. His head was splitting. How in the world had he gotten here?

Then, the terrible memory.

Shrieking wind and noise ...

A roaring explosion.

Their plane had broken apart.

Alex forgot the weirdness of the sky and the ache of his body. Amanda and Tori ... where were they? Desperately he scanned the horizon. And then he knew the truth. The plane had crashed and he was the only survivor. His sisters, the last people who mattered to him in all the world, were gone. In the agony of his imagination he saw them struggling, screaming, slipping away in the wreckage. And he saw himself in the raft, unconscious, floating off to live while they drowned. Alex shrieked and kept on shrieking until his voice was a rasping croak. Then he sobbed until there were no tears left and all that remained was a black stillness in his heart.

Alone.

Left alone.

First by his parents and now his sisters. If there was a God, He was hideously evil. Far better to die than to go on like this. And so Alex sat, staring at nothing, willing himself into a trance of the dead. In this state he might have remained for many hours but for one unpleasant reality: thirst. His mouth was so dry that his tongue felt like sandpaper. Try as hard as he could, not a drop of saliva would come. He remembered stories about people who had died of thirst in the middle of the ocean—about how your mind could play tricks on you, making you see weird mirages, like rows of ice-cold drinking fountains, squirting water. No ghost drinking fountains yet, but they couldn't be far off.

An hour passed and his desperation grew. He tried to think of other things—anything to take his mind off the agony. But it always came back to one thing. He wondered how long it would take to die. How much would he have to suffer? And after he was dead, how long would he float before someone found him? He felt for his wallet. Gone. They wouldn't even know who he was. Just a pile of rotting bones. They'd probably use his skull in some dental school for students to practice drilling. And that would be his reward for brushing every day. But the thought of brushing made him remember sloshing water in his mouth. He swore that never again would he waste a delicious mouthful of tooth-water spit. And the more he thought about tooth-water spit, the more it forced him into a desperate decision.

Why should he die of thirst when he was sitting in the middle of an ocean? People said you weren't supposed to drink ocean water, but if you were going to die anyway, what did it matter? Besides, salt's not so bad. Crawling to the edge of the raft, he dangled his fingers in the cool darkness.

How deliciously wet it was.

How good it would feel on his cinder-block tongue.

Suddenly he couldn't stop himself. Cupping his hands, he bent over the side and drank. And with the first swallow, he cried out in shock.

It wasn't salty.

The water was as sweet as a mountain spring.

His mind reeled. Oceans were always salty.

But that was as far as he got before thirst took control.

Alex stuck his face in the water and began to drink. And the more he drank, the more wonderful it tasted. He cursed himself for suffering needlessly. Gulping as fast as he could, he sucked it down until his stomach was so full it wouldn't hold another swallow—until he felt like a bloated whale. Gasping for air, he was about to pull himself back into the raft, when he opened his eyes and looked down into the depths below.

The ocean was even darker than the sky and nothing should have been visible. But something *was* visible. Many fathoms down, a mass of glowing light was moving. At first, it looked like a school of luminous fish, shifting back and forth. Then the glow changed to *fire.*

As Alex stared, the floor of the ocean cracked open. Huge fissures appeared, spewing out red-hot lava. To his amazement, a shape was beginning to form. It looked like a massive head, with a face of unearthly coldness. Eyeholes, ringed with flame, stared up at him. A mouth of jagged teeth the size of mountains hung open as though in a watery scream. He tried to tell himself it wasn't real. But then the mouth twisted wider, and out of it came a rumbling groan that exploded in a gigantic bubble. With a yell, he lurched back into the raft as stinking gas burst all around him.

It was then that the illness struck. A terrible spasm wrenched his stomach, and he began to heave. He kept on heaving as the raft twisted and plunged through steaming mountains of ocean that crashed around him. He puked until every drop of water that he had drunk had been expelled. Then almost instantly the sickness passed, and the ocean settled back into a glassy calm.

For a long time Alex lay with his cheek pressed against the clammy rubber, wanting to be dead. But the only way to accomplish that would be to drown himself. And the thought of jumping into the ocean—straight down to the "thing" at the bottom—was even more horrible than staying alive. He let out a miserable sob. So the decision was made, he would drift until his skull was ready for the dental school.

For some reason the thought of turning into a soggy skeleton brought back the unpleasant memory of his grandfather's funeral. What had the minister talked about, "The great ocean of eternity"? Could that be where he was, floating in a raft on an ocean that went on forever? But that would mean that he was already dead. He told himself that it just couldn't be true. But where was the proof? His stomach gave a slight residual lurch. Was vomiting proof? Was it even possible to vomit after you had kicked off? He doubted it. Unless, of course, an eternal cycle of thirst, drinking, and puking was punishment for an evil life.

An ugly idea.

He decided the proof of his current status must come from outside his body. But where?

The sky? Earlier there had been a sun ... and now there were stars. At the funeral all the minister had talked about was water. The "ocean" of eternity. A sun and stars must mean that you were on a real world. And that would mean that you were alive. Suddenly Alex wanted to see the stars, in fact, was desperate to see them. Struggling to roll over, he looked up ... and almost stopped breathing.

Instead of the stars, he saw *the Mountain*.

In all the time he had been drifting, he had been so miserable that he had never imagined actually going somewhere. But he had been going somewhere. As he sat up, what he saw made him forget everything else. Looming above him in the starlight was the silhouette of a mountain so gigantic that it took up half the sky, and behind it rose the knife-edge of an eerie rust-red moon.

Something told him that what he was seeing now would make every other mountain in the universe look like an insignificant pile of rocks. Alone it stood in its forbidding vastness, like a Mighty King towering over the world. And in the moonlight, around the summit, hung a faint red mist like a crown of blood.

As Alex stared transfixed, inside him grew feelings that he had never known before. Smallness. Insignificance. Overwhelming awe. And from those feelings came a strange desire; no, a hunger. He had never worshiped anything in his life. But without knowing it, at that moment, *worship* was what he wanted to do. He hungered to fall down before the mountain above, to prostrate himself in the shadow of its vastness and never rise again. Instead, all he could do was tremble, knowing that such a mountain had never existed on the world in which he was born. Sinking back, he let the vision sweep over him. Even his thirst seemed unimportant now. All that mattered was drifting ... and seeing ... and feeling.

But then, in a single instant, everything was gone—the Mountain, the moon, even the stars, and he was engulfed in total darkness.

7

BELLWIND'S HOUSE

Red moonlight turned the mist crimson as the raft carrying Amanda and Tori drifted up the river of shadows. Around them was a forest of such ghostly splendor that it seemed to live on the edge of dreaming. The current took them past hazy banks dappled with soft ferns, beneath the smoky hair of dangling willows, and through clusters of blossoms that drifted like little clouds. In the ancient trees they could see the gnarled and gentle faces of old men and women nodding, whispering . . . then fading as they passed. And always the strange, lovely voice sang on. As the island drew them deeper, more voices joined it, some deep and rumbling, others clear and high. Through it all, Bellwind knelt at the front of the raft with her arms outstretched and her face shining. "The trees. My very trees. Do you hear them? I have missed their voices for so long." As the girls looked up at her, for the first time they saw how beautiful old age could be, how strong and filled with joy.

Night settled more deeply and the trees grew luminous. As they drifted beneath a rock draped with vines, a rain of mist fell on Amanda, making her skin glow. She looked at Tori who was still holding the baby. A circle of shimmering moss had settled in her hair like a starry crown. For a moment she wasn't a girl anymore. She was a lovely creature of the forest who Amanda feared might dissolve away.

Bellwind looked down at them and knew what was happening. The island had taken them in its arms. The peace that entered Amanda and Tori that night would remain with them always. During all the terrifying things that were to come, they would never forget the singing trees and the misty river that had whispered love into their hearts.

The girls were almost asleep when the raft floated around a bend and entered a lagoon bathed with moonlight. On the bank stood a strange house, and from the roof rose a tower so high that its top was lost in the clouds. Bellwind gazed at it. "Home ... my home. Finally, finally, I am back home." As they drifted nearer, the girls saw that the house was covered with gables—little boxy projections with windows and miniature roofs that stuck out in the oddest ways. Not a single one was like another. There were tiny balconies and lattices and frosted glass windows with candles burning inside. It reminded Amanda of an old Victorian cottage.

The raft came to rest against a little pier, and Bellwind wiped her eyes. "Forever and goodness, what a journey. But getting—arriving—home is always the best part. Which goes to show that I wouldn't make a good travel agent, because I'd only sell one-way tickets back to where you came from."

Stepping onto the pier, she walked up a little path toward the cottage. Then she stopped and looked back. The girls weren't following. "Well, come-come along. Don't be shy. Do you want to spend all night out here when there are good beds inside? Now, that would be immeasurably strange for girls from the outlying limits of the universe, the very suburbs of Chicago. And bring the baby with you. I'd ask our friend the dog to join us, but I'm sure he has other obligations." As though in answer, the dog jumped from the raft and splashed off into the woods.

Amanda and Tori stared at each other ... and at the pier. The pier was the problem. It seemed entirely too misty to hold anything up. It was true that Bellwind had stepped on it, but she could do a lot of things that no one else could. Solemnly Tori turned to her sister. "You first, you're fatter. If it doesn't break with your weight, it'll be okay for me and the baby."

"Oh, really?"

"I didn't say *fat.* I said *fat-ter.*"

Bellwind cleared her throat. Giving Tori a dirty look, Amanda began crawling up onto the foggy wood. First an arm. Then a leg. Finally her whole body. To her relief, it was solid. "It's okay. Come on."

Holding the baby against her shoulder, Tori climbed out, and then the girls followed Bellwind toward the house. Stepping onto the porch, the old woman smiled, walked forward, and promptly vanished. There wasn't any door; where one should have been there was a solid wall of blue bricks. Amanda ran her fingers over them. Definitely real and hard. "So, what are we supposed to do now?"

"Come in. That is precisely, exactly what you're supposed to do." It was Bellwind's voice, but she was nowhere to be seen.

"Uhhh ... we can't seem to find a door." Amanda had hardly spoken the words when the old woman's head appeared above them, sticking straight through the wall like a mounted hunting trophy. "You don't need doors to get into my house. Doors-barriers-barricades are to keep things out. And there's nothing to keep out here. Not on this island. It belongs to me. Just walk through any place wherever you choose. Naturally, the porch is recommended. For instance, and thinking about the possibility, if you walked in under that gable over there, you'd knock over my bookshelf. Immeasurably not to be recommended." Bellwind's head looked so peculiar that the girls laughed.

Amanda tapped on the wall. "You mean ... just pretend like the bricks aren't here?"

"Who said anything about pretending? Was such a word ever, mostly never, mentioned? Pretending, imagining, and such and such, take thinking. And some things you just have to *do*. That, precisely, and consequently, is the trouble these days and why walking through bricks is a lost and dying art. But such will not be the case with you. Come into my house this very instant." With that, her head vanished and the girls were left staring at the place where it had hung.

Tori gulped. "You first."

"No way. You're *skinnier.* You could slide between the bricks like a little worm."

They heard Bellwind clear her throat again. With a grimace Tori reached toward the wall. When she touched it, both were amazed to see her arm vanish to the elbow. Then she felt someone take hold of her hand and before she knew it, both she and the baby had been pulled inside. Amanda watched her disappear and then heard her yell, "Hey, you've gotta see this."

Closing her eyes, Amanda walked forward. When she opened them again, she found herself in a most unusual room. The inside of Bellwind's house was much larger than it appeared outside. The room the girls had entered was long and narrow and at the center stood a spiral staircase with a huge banister that wound upward into the shadows. But what was so wonderful was the furniture. It looked as though it had come from garage sales and swap meets all over the universe. Not that it was dirty or trashy. Everything was very clean and in perfect order. But it was a stacked and jumbled kind of order. And no matter where they looked, they saw odd things.

Against one wall stood a huge coatrack made of plumbing pipes bent and twisted like the limbs of a tree. Hanging from them were rusting pieces of junk automobiles that had been reshaped into medieval armor. There was a breastplate with old radio knobs and a helmet with a turn signal on the visor. Beside the coatrack sat a moth-eaten love seat with blinking Christmas tree lights stitched into the upholstery. Relaxing on it were a Victorian dress flowing with ripples and ruffles, and a stiff Victorian suit with a watch fob hanging from the pocket. They were frozen in place as though the bodies that had worn them had simply disappeared. Near the love seat hung a gigantic wind chime made from ten thousand pieces of gaudy costume jewelry. Next to that huddled a pile of crates that looked like a musical instrument. It had a keyboard with little hammers that tapped on three hundred soft-drink bottles filled with different amounts of orange soda.

But the strangest decorations were above the fireplace. There, side by side, hung seven antique picture frames. All were huge and deeply carved with overlays of gold. And all were *empty.* In each frame there was nothing but dark blue glass. Amanda would have asked about them if she hadn't been more interested in Bellwind herself. The old woman was ensconced in an overstuffed chair upholstered in living moss. She had taken off her shawl and was wearing a long dress covered with real flowers. On a little table in front of her sat a tray laden with peanut-butter sandwiches and hot cocoa. Two smaller chairs were waiting for her guests.

"Come, sit down entirely and immediately, and gather yourselves to eat. I don't suppose young women from Earth like hot cocoa."

The young women from Earth assured her that they did. The food was delicious, and as they ate, Amanda and Tori began to relax and ask questions. "Where'd you get all this cool junk?" Tori licked peanut butter off her fingers.

"Oh, I'm a collector. Garages sales, swap meets, flea markets, there isn't one in the universe that escapes my attention. But I've gotten choosy—picky-picky—as the years have passed. Space is limited. Not much room left for treasures. So sad."

"Why don't you throw some of it away? Then you'd have plenty of room."

Aghast, Bellwind stared at Amanda. "Throw it away? Get rid of it? My sweet but most insensitive young friend, how, in a hundred worlds, could I throw away such infinitely priceless feelings?"

"Feelings?"

"Do you think I bought all this junk because I like the look of it? Feelings. Feelings. Those are what matter. Every single piece in my house is stuffed, stacked, jammed with them. Why, right here in this room, in this very place beyond all others, is the most complete set of feelings ever assembled. A thing isn't anything until someone has glued a feeling on it. And if the glue is strong enough, they stick like bugs in amber. What kind of feeling do you like, excitement? Just stand next to my gym shoe collection." (Not far away a hundred old gym shoes hung nailed to the wall.) "And musicy thrills? What can compare with the healthy slurp of thirsty people? Wait until you hear my soda bottles. Oh, do not be mistaken. No, indeed, young ladies. True feelings are hard to find. And there are plenty of fake ones on every world. But you can tell the frauds in a minute. They're the ones that hang around old TV sets. Fake feelings cranked out to make you think they're real so they can sell you more fake things. And who would waste a dime on any of those?"

The old woman took them on a tour of her living room. They found that what she had said was true. Each piece had a different feeling attached to it. Their favorite was the old love seat, the way it whispered words like "sweet dumpling cakes" and "I'll kiss your ruby lips forever." When Amanda asked about the frames, however, the only answer she got was vague and sad. Something about old friends who had gone away. And beneath the frames was the only place where they weren't allowed to stand.

But Bellwind was so merry that it didn't seem to matter.

The evening ended with buttery toast and misty marmalade that tingled on their tongues. Then the girls snuggled up in soft chairs while Bellwind played her "bottle-odeon." That's what she called the boxes with the keyboard and the bottles of orange soda. It made a gentle, haunting sound, not at all what they had expected. And while they listened, they couldn't imagine ever being thirsty again.

Whether it was the music, the overstuffed chairs, or their overstuffed stomachs, soon both girls began to feel very drowsy. Amanda saw Tori nod off, and it wasn't long before her eyelids grew extremely heavy. The harder she tried to keep them open, the heavier they grew. Bellwind was singing something silly about the plants that covered the island and a costume party they had each year. Amanda wanted to listen, but the words became more and more indistinct until everything melted into a dream.

In the dream, strong arms gently lifted her and carried her up a staircase. And for a moment she was a little girl again with her daddy carrying her off to bed just as he had done so long ago. Amanda didn't wake up until much later. Not until everything that was about to happen had happened.

And when she awoke, the whole world had changed.

8

NIGHT WALK

When the Mountain disappeared, Alex was so shocked that he almost jumped out of the raft. The truth was that he had been so engrossed in looking upward that he hadn't watched where the strong current was taking him. Silently the raft had drifted toward a shore of black cliffs that were hardly visible until he was upon them. In those cliffs was a rift with a jagged formation across it. The sky had vanished because he had entered the rift; over him now was a wide expanse almost like a stone archway, and when he emerged on the other side, only a few stars and a sliver of moon were visible.

Alex stared around. He was floating up a narrow gorge. Shafts of rust-red moonlight glinted on the water. On either side and to his front rose stone walls hundreds of feet high. He had come to land. But what land?

At first the walls of the canyon appeared to be natural formations, but it was hard to tell exactly what they were because they were covered with thick vines. The longer he stared, the more he thought he saw strange shapes spaced uniformly along the top, piles of rock almost like the battlements on a medieval castle. But in his overwrought imagination they could have been anything. A light wind had begun to blow, and its keening wail made him shiver.

The farther Alex drifted, the more the walls of the gorge became irregular, bending and twisting like the body of a huge snake ripped open in the moonlight. And with every bend the vines grew longer, spiraling out to brush the raft like tentacles. Constantly he jerked his head this way and that, straining to see every crevice and weaving form. The harder he looked, the more his imagination painted the gorge with horrors.

It wasn't natural.

He was sure of it now.

Ages and ages ago someone had carved it out of solid rock. And he knew something else. It grew out of an awful feeling that welled up until his skin crawled. From the moment he had drifted into this place something had been watching him.

Abruptly there was a soft bump that almost made him jump out of his skin. The raft scraped to a stop against an odd embankment. Beside him in the moonlight was a ruined wall with ancient steps carved into it. For a moment all he could do was huddle in terror with his mind racing; he tried to see where the stairs went, but they vanished around a stone outcropping. They must lead to the top, but the thought of climbing into the darkness was beyond imagining. Yet what else could he do? He couldn't keep floating forever. Pushing back out into the canal could mean landing somewhere even worse. And he had no oars. Alex might have sat shivering all night, if it hadn't been for his thirst.

Suddenly it was unbearable.

No choice.

He had to find water.

Reaching out, he grabbed some vines and dragged himself onto the embankment. But when he tried to stand, he almost fell back into the canal. After floating for so long, his legs were like rubber. It took a few minutes before his balance returned. Then slowly he began groping up the stairs. He had to be careful because they were covered with debris. When he passed the outcropping, he stopped. They led into a vine-covered hole.

How could he do this? How could he bring himself to go in there? But he had to. His thirst was terrible. His throat felt like he'd been swallowing hot coals.

Gritting his teeth, Alex pulled back the curtain of vines. Beyond was a pitch-black passage with more stairs leading up. Creeping in, he smelled a sickening mustiness. Half gagging, he began to climb.

Alex found that the staircase twisted back and forth and was clotted with rotting vegetation. Many times he tripped and fell. Many times he jumped back shivering, brushing sticky webs from his hair and clothes. But always his thirst drove him on. At one point, after a nasty tumble, he discovered a stick. This he used as a sort of brush, swishing it in front of him. The stick helped with the webs, but it didn't help with the small creatures that scurried past on the ground. Once, something larger brushed his leg, causing him to yell and almost fall backward. But he caught himself, sweating, trembling, and trying not to be ill.

At several places he came upon landings, like little oases. Each had a break in the wall that allowed in a glimmer of moonlight. Through them Alex was able to look out and mark his progress. Soon the dark gash of the canal was lost below. The cliffs were much higher than he had imagined; he began counting the stairs—one hundred, two hundred, three hundred, four hundred. Somewhere in the fives he lost track, and they just kept on.

It was at the end of the darkest and steepest passage, when Alex was sobbing from sheer exhaustion, at the very moment when he was ready to give up and die, that he broke through a mass of vines and found himself at the top. What he saw made him think that he was dreaming.

Spread out in the moonlight were the ruins of a vast and terrible city. Before him stretched the jagged hulks of ten thousand ancient buildings. Huge pyramids, domes, obelisks, towers, arches, all lay in rubble like the rotting bodies of stone giants. And blanketing all of it were vines. Like waves of long black hair they drifted in the wind that moaned through the desolation.

Cowering in the staircase, Alex couldn't comprehend what he was seeing. *This* was what he had climbed so far to reach? Better to die at the bottom of the ocean. He was about to turn and run back down to the canal when he heard the one sound that mattered more than anything else.

Splashing water.

Faint.

Far away.

But very clear.

Suddenly not even the terror of the dead city could overcome his thirst. Where was that sound coming from? Alex scanned the buildings. Directly in front of him stretched a broad avenue lined with massive columns. The splashes were coming from that direction, he was sure of it. He told himself that he would find the water, get a drink, then go back down to the raft and try to float out into the ocean. Just one drink, that was all.

Cautiously he stepped from his hiding place and began creeping down the avenue. But the farther he went, the more jittery he became. The buildings were hideous. Where the vines didn't cover the walls, he could make out huge grotesque slashes like letters in a strange language. And carved into the street were monstrous flat heads with wide eyes and gaping mouths as though trying to swallow the sky.

Alex did his best to think only of the water and how good it would taste. Instead, he thought more and more about the twisting shadows that loomed around him. On and on he went, but the splashing didn't seem to be getting any closer. Finally, ahead he saw it: a fountain. Like everything else, it was crumbled with age, but dusky moonlit sparkles still gushed from it.

He ran.

When he reached it, he fell down and let the cold liquid pour into his mouth. Unlike the ocean, it had a metallic taste, but he didn't care. And if it killed him, what did it matter? After drinking all he could hold, he let it splash over his head. He was drying his face on his shirt, when the same awful feeling returned.

He was being watched.

And this time it was close.

For an instant Alex was afraid to move, terrified of what he might see. And then the sound began. From everywhere came a mournful cry, as though the whole dead city had begun to weep with one unearthly voice. Starting in a low moan, it rose to a bloodcurdling scream . . . and then fell back, vanishing in a thousand echoes.

Alex thought he was going to be ill. Forcing himself to turn, he looked behind him. A hundred yards away, in the center of the street that crossed the avenue of the columns, stood a gigantic shadow, and it wasn't the shadow of a building.

In the moonlight loomed the silhouette of a bird with its huge wings outstretched. And it was staring straight at him with shimmering eyes. He froze; all he could do was wait for it to sweep down and crush him. But it didn't move. Squinting at it, he almost sobbed with relief. It wasn't a real bird at all. It was only a statue with moonlight shining through jagged holes in its head.

But it wasn't like any bird that he had ever seen. Instead of two wings, it had four, and its feathers looked like shards of broken glass. It had a yawning beak, lined with teeth, that hung open as though caught in an endless shriek, and above the beak were the *eyes*. Even after Alex understood that they weren't real, he couldn't rid himself of the sensation that they were watching him. So the bird was a statue, but that didn't explain the awful scream. The thought had barely come into his mind when it began again, wailing higher and higher. This time, as it faded, he heard something else: a dull clattering roar.

He knew that he had to hide and there was no time to run back to the stairs. Across the street was a building. Rushing over to it, he buried himself in the vines. Slowly the clatter grew. What was that sound? It was familiar. Then he recognized it; it was like *marching*. Thousands of feet marching, but not in unison. More like a shapeless mob. Soon the city shook with it.

The scream sounded a third time.

From where he hid Alex could see all the way back to where he had emerged from the staircase. He knew there was nothing beyond the wall but a sheer drop into the gorge. Yet from out of the vine-covered stone appeared a cloud of luminous shapes. At first they were indistinct, but as they drew nearer, he saw that it was a great mass of people—thousands of them, all swathed in black—marching toward him in utter silence. Their bodies were like mist, yet it was the sound of their feet that shook the city. He panicked. These must be the ones who had been watching. And now they were coming for him. He had to run, but he was too terrified to move. On and on the apparitions marched, down the street of the columns, until they were almost in front of him. Alex could hardly breathe.

But they passed right by.

They didn't even seem to know that he was there. When the first row reached the fountain, they turned and headed in a new direction. The street was jammed with shadow-forms. Men and women, old and young, so close he could almost touch them. Individual faces became visible in the moonlight, each was different, yet all were the same. They were like sleepwalkers, without the slightest trace of life in their eyes. And there was a dustiness about them, as though they had been wandering in a desert.

Finally Alex mustered enough courage to turn and see where they were going. They were headed straight toward the statue of the bird. When they reached it, they disappeared under its claws, almost as though they were melting into the stone. The moon was sinking when the last of them had vanished and the city was empty and silent once more.

Suddenly Alex felt desperately tired. He had to find some place to sleep. At his back was the building; maybe he could get inside. Groping through the vines, he began searching for an entrance. Gradually he worked his way down one wall. Then another and another. Nothing. Not even a window.

Finally he was at the place where he had started, and he discovered that wasn't a building at all; it was a solid block of stone. He wondered if the other ruins were the same, but there was nothing to do but step out into the street and take a look.

Creeping into the moonlight, he scanned the piles of rubble. Quickly he realized that what he had taken for buildings might not be buildings at all. Most were exactly like the one he had examined. Then, several blocks away, he saw a structure with a dome. Around the bottom were shadowy arches. Beneath them he thought he could make out entrances. To get there he would have to walk straight past the statue—down the same street the phantoms had traveled.

Alex told himself that there must be some other choice, but there were no other buildings like it anywhere.

From across the street came a new sound. A kind of scurrying and scraping. Definitely animal. Not a small animal either. He envisioned giant rats—the city might be crawling with them. Maybe they came out at night for food. And maybe they were looking for a nice pile of fresh, sweaty meat.

It was the dome or nothing.

Rushing out of his hiding place, Alex ran down the street. With every step the monstrous bird loomed larger. And with every step the animal sounds increased. Faster. Gasping for air. Finally he was beneath the statue's wings and could see the place where the ghosts had vanished. It was solid rock. But he only glanced at it. He was fifty feet beyond the sculpture when the animal sounds began coming from everywhere.

He stopped and froze.

A block ahead something was pushing through the vines. Out of the shadows crept dozens of huge black dogs. The animals had seen him. One gave a low growl that was answered by all the rest. He tried not to panic. Slowly he turned his head to see if they were behind him. His heart sank. The street on the other side of the bird was filled with them. He was surrounded. But then he noticed that at the base of the statue was a small open door. Maybe he could get to it.

More growls.

The dogs were coming toward him.

Very slowly Alex began to turn, hoping the gradual movement wouldn't be noticed. But it was like a trigger. Instantly the street was filled with enraged snarls ... and they were after him.

He ran for his life. When he reached the statue, the dogs were only a few feet behind. Rushing inside, he found an iron door that was still on its hinges. Though it was old and creaked horribly, he managed to slam it shut and throw his shoulder against it just as the first of the beasts arrived. In a mindless rage they threw themselves against the rusted metal. Alex knew he couldn't hold them off for long. Groping in the dark, his fingers found a latch.

Shoving it in, he tested it.

It held.

For the moment he was saved. Dripping with sweat, he staggered back—the snarling and crashing were horrible. How long could the door withstand such a beating? He scanned his hiding place; the statue was hollow all the way to the top. Moonlight flooded in through its carved-out eyes. There was just enough light to see that once, long ago, this must have been a storage chamber. Twenty feet up was a ledge, and a primitive ladder had been gouged out of the wall to reach it. Rushing to it, he began to climb.

A moment later Alex sprawled onto a platform of dusty stone and there he lay in an exhausted heap. Outside everything grew still. With an eerie abruptness, the howling stopped and the dogs ended their attack. He struggled to his hands and knees. Through a small crack he could see the street. It was filled with black dogs. Each sat in absolute silence, with its eyes fixed on the statue. What had made them grow quiet? It was almost as though they had heard a command.

Suddenly, the feeling came over him once more. He was being watched.

And the Watcher was somewhere above.

He looked up.

The moonlight had vanished. Suspended in the dark was a glowing blur. For a moment everything was still. Then, as he stared in horror, the blur began to descend. He heard again the scream that had brought the phantoms, coming from a face with huge luminous eyes, but this time there were words in it. Over and over it shrieked ...

"Unclean ...
Unclean ...
Raging colors
In rotting green ...
Lord of Shadows ...
Unclean ...
Unclean."

9

THE SEVENTH FRAME

There were no soft dreams for Tori.

In fact, there were no dreams at all.

When she awoke, she found herself wrapped in a warm blanket, alone on a bed in a small bedroom. Always before, waking up in strange places would frighten her. But now there was only confusion.

Where was she?

It seemed to be the middle of the night.

And there had been some kind of sound.

She sat up. Everything was quiet. Pale moonlight shone in through a gabled window. Of course, Bellwind's house. She smiled as she remembered. This must be one of the rooms in the tower. With a yawn she was about to lie back down when the sound came again.

Voices talking.

As the youngest of her family, she assumed she was missing out on something. It was always that way. She went to bed while everybody else stayed up having fun. Amanda was probably downstairs right now, stuffing her face with ice cream. It wasn't fair. And all because she couldn't stay awake. Sliding from the bed, she tiptoed across the room and cracked open the door. The voices became clearer. There were two of them, and if her sister was there, she wasn't doing any of the talking.

Cautiously Tori crept out of the bedroom. Beyond was a circular landing with a spiral staircase, and around the landing were more doors probably leading into other bedrooms. Dropping to her hands and knees, she crawled to a place where she could look down.

The voices were very clear now, but she still couldn't see anybody. The talkers were in the living room just out of sight. One voice belonged to Bellwind, but the other was new. And Amanda wasn't there. Tori was sure of it. The new voice was rough and gravelly as though it hurt to form words. With agonizing slowness it rumbled, *"You are ... you are ... to send them ... on the morning light ..."*

When Bellwind answered, there was fear in her voice. "But Seeker ... what, specifically and utterly, is to become of them? I, yes, I myself, have brought them here. They trust me. Are they to be endangered if there is no hope? The moment, the very moment they leave my island, they will be pursued."

"Ended ... Ended. No more answers will be ... no more answers can be ... given."

There was a long pause. When the old woman spoke again, it was with great weariness. "Forgive me. It has been so long, so very long and ever, since you have been among us. But you know my ancient heart. These Earth ones ... I love them. It is I, yes I, who have watched them grow and known their sorrows. Already they have carried a terrible burden. Can I not go with them? For such a joy I would give my life."

"The Law ... Watcher ... the Law ... remains. Upon the land ... no foot of yours must travel until Mountaincry. "

A great shadow fell at the bottom of the stairs, and Tori could almost see the strange speaker. But he didn't come quite close enough. She was sure they were talking about her and Amanda. And what was the word he had said? *Mountaincry?* It made her shiver.

"And what of the other one, the Alex one?" Bellwind seemed to be fighting back tears.

Tori leaned forward. Most of all she wanted to know about her brother. But all that came were more strange words.

"Walking in shadows ... until the end."

There was a long pause. Desperately she wanted Bellwind to ask more questions about Alex. Instead, the old woman moved into a part of the room that Tori could see. Standing in front of the fireplace, she looked up at the seven frames. "And what, what of these? You have walked the land, Seeker. Why and why have they not answered for such an immeasurably longness of time?"

"Lost in pain . . . lost in sorrow. Sing to them. Yes, sing."

"But I've sung and sung for years upon centuries. And no one ever answers."

The voice whispered so low that Tori could barely hear. *"Sing."*

Drawing a deep breath, Bellwind bowed her head and nodded. Then she circled the room three times making peculiar reaching motions with her fingers. On the fourth circle she began to sing in a dreaming kind of language. Bellwind's voice was beautiful. As she walked and sang, a thick vapor began to grow. Rising up out of the floor around her, it swirled and shimmered as though the song itself were taking form. Higher and higher it rose until the room was enveloped in silver radiance.

Six times.

Six circles.

And at the end of the last one the sparkling mist gathered around the frames. Something was happening. In all but one the midnight blue was fading. Only in the seventh frame did the darkness remain. Bellwind had stopped and was staring up at them. Behind each glass was a struggle of swirling fog. Then the third frame came into focus. It was a portrait of a bell tower, surrounded by rays of light. The tower was made of blue bricks and the bell was silver. From out of the frame came a deep, echoing peal. Bellwind didn't seem surprised. Her attention was on the others and the vagueness moving in them.

Suddenly a dim outline appeared in the first frame—a dark, forbidding shape with wings and glowing eyes. It was some kind of bird. From it came a distant, haunting scream that rose, and echoed, and died away. When the sound was gone, the picture faded. Nothing more happened and in a few moments all six were as dark as before. But the old woman was ecstatic. "Rindzac, my little brother, he was almost here. The first, the only-only in time upon centuries. For so long, all I have seen has been my own tower. Something is happening. A message. He was trying to give it."

The Rough Voice answered from the shadows, *"Allowed not . . . before. Shaken. Death and awakening."*

"Not-not *allowed*?" The joy left Bellwind's voice. "How, and tell me how, for I do not understand, could anything stop a Worwil from answering the call?"

There was no reply. The Great Shadow vanished from the floor. Bellwind called out, "Seeker, wait. Where-where are you going?"

Still no answer.

"When, please, when will you return?"

The Voice was filled with sadness. *"Perhaps again ... never. But in the garden ... now ... walk with me ... toward the shore."*

Tori heard them leave the house. Unable to control her curiosity, she crept down the stairs hoping to see the one who had sounded so strange. Something in his last words had made her want to cry. However, by the time she got to the window, no one was visible in the misty forest.

Disappointed, she turned back and headed upstairs. Maybe she could find Amanda and tell her what had happened. Walking through the moonlit room, she passed beneath the frames. Suddenly she was afraid of them. Shivering, her step quickened. She had almost reached the stairs when an icy breath touched her ... and a soft voice whispered her name.

She stopped.

Her eyes grew wide.

Something was in the room.

Something she could feel but couldn't see.

Rushing to the stairs, Tori began to climb. But on the third step she froze. An icy wind was blowing on her. Without wanting to, she turned and looked back.

The moonlit room was changing. Once more it was filled with sparkling mist, but this time it was oily green, and it was drifting from the seventh frame. The glass had transformed from midnight blue to jade and in the center was a swirling Shadow that began oozing down the wall. Softly the voice called her name again.

And she knew who it was.

Her mother!

Tori tried to answer, but the sound froze in her throat. Terrified, she watched as the Shadow crept across the floor. She tried to run but her legs wouldn't move. She tried to scream but no sound came out. Now it was on the stairs … around her shoes. It was swirling up her legs. And when it touched her, the fear vanished. Her mind became drowsy. The voice of her mother told her to sleep.

Sleep and don't be afraid.

Higher and higher the Shadow rose until it enveloped Tori's body. Then she was lifted. But all she knew was that her mother was calling … calling her home. And she wanted to go to her. She wanted to go home. And the way was through the frame. She would sail through the Shadow like a little star … back to her mother's arms.

Suspended in the cloud, Tori floated across the ceiling to the frame.

Closer and closer … until she could feel the coldness of the glass …

Then she was sliding through …

At that instant Bellwind rushed back into the room. With one look the old woman saw it all. From her came a scream of terror and a raging command. Lightning answered. Out of her mouth streaked fire that smashed into the seventh frame. Thunder shook the house as she leaped, trying to grab Tori.

Bellwind touched Tori's ankle, but that was all. Then, like a feather sucked into a hurricane, Tori was gone. Instantly the black vapor disappeared and the frame was nothing more than scorched wood and broken glass hanging empty above an oily stain.

The old woman collapsed, sobbing. Behind her there was movement in the shadows and the rumbling voice spoke again. *"The journey … it is now. Do not … any longer … delay."*

Bellwind turned to cry out. But the giant of the moonlight was gone.

10

TOWER CALL

Night.

And there was something wrinkling the air.

A kind of rustling disturbance just on the edge of hearing.

Amanda felt it as soon as she awoke. Without taking her head from the pillow, she looked around. She was in a room that flickered with dim light. A figure was standing at the foot of the bed holding a candle. It was Bellwind and her eyes were full of pain.

"Wake up, child."

"What's wrong?" Amanda sat up. The rustling was growing and it frightened her.

"This world and all that's in it. That's what's wrong."

"Something's happening outside."

"My people are preparing to defend their home. Now, hurry. No time to talk. Breakfast awaits." Placing the candle on the dresser, she left the room.

Amanda got out of bed. It wasn't cold but she was shivering. She found that she was still dressed except for her shoes; they had been removed and placed beside a chair. Pulling them on, she went to a window and looked out.

The island was undergoing a transformation. Below, in the moonlight, indistinct shapes were sweeping through the fog. Some looked like bushes and vines, others had the vague appearance of men and women—but not human—more like smoke drifting across the ground. Suddenly a shape passed in front of her and she screamed. It was a tree, and in the heart of its branches glistened a lovely phantom with wild eyes staring at her. As Amanda watched, the tree began to change; its branches moved as though blown by a strong wind. Masses of leaves dropped away, and out of every branch grew a blood-red thorn. When the transformation was complete, the phantom gave a terrible cry and flowed away with the rest.

Amanda rushed to the door. When she reached the bottom of the stairs, she found Bellwind waiting. The living room was ablaze with light. Candles of every shape and size burned everywhere. And dozens were gathered beneath a broken frame.

"What's going on?"

"Breakfast is going on. That precisely. And it is right now." On a table sat a plate heaped with bacon, eggs, and sweet rolls.

"I'm not hungry. What happened to that frame?"

"Eat, child, you must. Strength, the very strongest of it, will be needed for what is ahead."

"Where's Tori?"

There was an awful pause. "Amanda, Manda-Manda ..." The pain returned to Bellwind's eyes. "How can this be told? Your little sister is not here."

Amanda stared at her. "Where is she?"

"She has begun her journey."

"What are you talking about? She isn't supposed to go anywhere without me."

"Both ... you both ... were to travel together. But now, that ... immeasurably ... has changed."

"Where has she gone?"

The old woman looked toward the blackened frame.

Amanda followed her gaze. And slowly a creeping horror came over her. Within the frame she saw a vague shadow burned into the broken glass. It was the barest outline of a girl.

It was the outline of *Tori.*

Amanda started to scream, but the scream died. Something was behind the glass. A Darkness that she could sense but not see. *A Darkness that was alive.* She felt invisible fingers groping, probing in her mind, peeling away layers of memory like scabs from a rotting wound. Slicing open every ragged scar. Squeezing the pus from all her rancid sorrows. And in the horror of that moment she felt *eyes.* Felt them knowing, yearning, hungering to taste every brokenhearted agony.

And she *knew* those eyes.

Then it all turned to sobbing, shrieking rage. Picking up a burning candle, she smashed it on the broken fragments of the glass.

"No, no, my child." Bellwind grabbed her and took her in her arms. But Amanda fought her with all her strength, spitting, gnashing, screaming every vile word she knew, desperate to murder, to destroy. On and on the old woman held her until the rage turned into exhausted, half-human croaks.

Finally a black stillness settled, and Amanda hung like a dead thing in Bellwind's arms.

"My daughter, would you do something, please, now do something for me?" Rising, she lifted Amanda to her feet and handed her a candle. "Will you climb my tower? Yes, climb ... even all the way to the very top. At the top many questions will be answered. I will be waiting when you arrive. Will you do it? Will you climb?"

Amanda stared at her barely able to understand. "I ... I can't," was all she could get out.

"Yes, you can. And you must. Climb, my child." And then Bellwind vanished.

"Where are you?"

A voice echoed from high above, "Climb, daughter, now."

The rage returned. Amanda yelled, "No. You come back down here. Where is my sister? What have you done with her?"

Silence.

"Answer me."

But there was no answer. So then, now was her chance to destroy with no one to stop her. Snarling, Amanda turned toward the frame. But the instant she did so, she felt long invisible fingers wrap around her throat and drag her toward the frame. Strangling, gagging, she flailed to escape, desperately trying to reach the stairs. Flopping onto the first step, the fingers loosened. Pulling herself up, she struggled to climb, and slowly the fingers fell away.

Then Amanda ran—past the second floor, higher and higher, sobbing, gasping.

Soon the walls became a blurry spiral and only the cold dampness of the banister told her that everything was real. In her terrified rage, Amanda stumbled and fell many times, raking her flesh until the blood ran. Each time she screamed and swore. But then Bellwind's calm voice would whisper, *"Keep climbing. Don't give up."* Which made her even more furious.

Finally, from the gloom of the staircase, Amanda rushed out into crimson moonlight. She was in a large, open bell tower surrounded by an iron rail, and above her hung a gigantic bell. She was *alone.* She almost screamed again, but then she looked out into the darkness. What she saw drained her rage away.

The climb had brought her above the clouds that covered the island. In the distance, soaring into the sky, stood a jagged peak so vast and majestic that it seemed to rise beyond the stars. Like a King in splendor it stood, crowned in crimson brightness. Never had she seen such a Mountain. Walking to the rail, she gazed up at it. Then a soft voice whispered, "Amanda. Manda-Manda."

She turned but she was still alone. "Where are you?"

"Look up."

Amanda looked. Inside the bell shimmered a face of silvery loveliness surrounded with masses of softly drifting hair. It was Bellwind, but it wasn't.

"What happened to you?"

"I have become myself. Walking down below makes me old and tired. And my words stumble with my feet. Here, I am as I was at the beginning."

"But ... where's your body?"

"All around you. I am the bell and the tower. This is my place to see and remember. Isn't the Mountain beautiful?"

"It's so *huge.*"

"Yes, it is greater than all. And you have come because the Mountain has called you."

"What do you mean?"

"Amanda, listen to the song of a dying world."

> *Sing wind,*
> *Of ice hearts,*
> *Echoes of children who will never be,*

Lost ones crying soft in the darkness,
Their song,
Bloodsong,
Sing.

Sing wind,
Of Star Curse,
Of blood-gorged rivers that rush to the sea,
Why did you answer the call that he gave you?
His song,
Bloodsong,
Sing.

Sing wind,
Of Iron Tongue,
His lies like daggers pierced through me.
Oceans of teardrops, the wombs are dying.
Birth song,
Bloodsong,
Sing.

Sing wind,
Of childhood's end,
On burning altars and bleeding trees,
Crimson axes slash in the moonlight,
Blade chant,
Bloodsong,
Sing.

Amanda shivered. As she stared out toward the dark land beneath the Mountain, she heard strange, moaning cries. "What is that?"

"Desert and forest, swamp and rock, crawl with things that were never meant to be. That is Boreth now, once the land of the whispering garden. My island is a fading memory of all that was. What you hear are the ghosts of those who gave their souls away."

"Were they people?"

"Yes, creatures like you."

"What happened to them?"

"Death and choosing. Lying and listening. They lived in golden cities across this world. At their creation, seven powers were brought to guide them. The Worwil—the World Walkers—and you must learn their names. Thunderer. Weaver. Watcher. Caller. Singer. Painter. Healer. These are the Seven, and in the beginning they walked together. Their joy was in the Song of Songs. But then one turned and broke the chain forged when stars were born. It was he who went to war against the others. And he has almost conquered, for strength was held in oneness. The people followed him ... and they are gone. The memory of his shadow was what you saw in the frame."

"I saw something else. I saw Tori. Where is she? And where is my brother?"

"All that's happened is because of the baby."

"What do you mean?"

"He was born in blood in a time of horror and was taken to your world to hide him from their eyes. But they found him and stole him. And if they could, they would have killed him. I was the messenger sent to bring him back, but now my work is done. Every moment they grow more desperate. They will stop at nothing to keep him from reaching his home. Amanda, I brought him through the stars, but the most dangerous part of the journey lies ahead. He must be carried to the Mountain. That is why you and your sister were brought here ... and now you must go alone."

"What ...?" Amanda stared at her.

"He is very light and will not be a burden. Provisions are ready. There is no other way."

"But you didn't ask us whether we wanted to do this. You just kidnapped us."

"If I had asked would you have come?"

"No."

"Then what would have been the point of asking? Child, if the decision were mine, I would surround you with armies and march across the darkness with the strength of light. But it is ordained that he must be carried by a child unprotected. And for this purpose you were born."

"I can't do that by myself. You carry him and I'll go with you."

"The Worwil are bound by law. Unless I am called, I can never leave my

island to walk upon that shore. And since Boreth was formed, I have never disobeyed."

"So, you're one of those ... *things*."

"Indeed, yes, one of those things. I am the Watcher."

"Well, if you're a Watcher, maybe you watched where my brother and sister went."

"I will tell you what I can. Alex is alive, but his steps are hidden. He has entered Boreth in another place. The purpose I do not know. And Tori ..." There was a long pause, and Amanda felt warm drops falling on her. Bellwind was crying. *"Your little sister has been stolen from my house this very night. She has entered a place from which no one has ever returned."*

Amanda stared at her, then whispered, "Is she ... dead? Is my sister dead?"

Silence.

And in the silence Amanda knew. In the silence she saw the burned image in the glass and heard the echo of Tori's screams and heard them die. Suddenly, over her swept all the pain of her whole life in a single drowning wave. And it was more than she could bear. Something tore within her. If her little sister was dead, she didn't want to live anymore. She couldn't live all alone. If Tori was dead, she wanted to be dead too. If death would take her to her little sister, then let it come.

No, make it come.

With a scream Amanda rushed to the rail and looked down. All she had to do was drop into the soft darkness and the pain would end. Closing her eyes, she climbed over the iron. Now, all she had to do was let go.

And she did let go.

But at the edge of falling something caught her. Something pulled her back. Invisible arms wrapped around her. Not the arms of Bellwind. The arms of the one in her dreams. Strong yet infinitely caring, the way she had always wanted her father to be. At first she fought them, then finally sank into them, sobbing until the desire for death passed into a stillness not unlike death.

For a long time she lay on the floor and felt the arms fading. When she opened her eyes, she was alone. Struggling to her feet, she caught sight of the Mountain. How close it was. And out of it flowed soft waves of crimson light. In that light there was glory. Exaltation. The light was the source of all loveliness, and it wasn't far away—just at the top of the Mountain. If only she could touch it. Live within it. As her heart flew toward it, from the Mists came singing, lovely voices calling her name. Among them she thought she heard her little sister calling her to come.

Amanda leaned against the rail. But this time she was straining upward. Her sorrow remained, but with it there was a terrifying, mysterious joy. It wasn't pretend. All of it was *real.* The Mountain had called her to walk away from everything that she had ever known … to follow a path that led into shining. And with that call came the strength to carry the baby home. She still felt small and weak, if anything, smaller and weaker. But somehow what *she* felt no longer mattered. Her questions were still there. But for every one there was an answer. To learn them all meant walking, then climbing, even if it took forever. And forever wasn't far. Not when the Mountain knew your name.

Suddenly Bellwind's voice echoed from the bottom of the stairs, "Amanda, it's time. Walk down, yes, walk down, my child."

Turning away from the Brightness, Amanda Lancaster moved down through the blue shadows of the tower toward agony and glory, called to the singing mists around a Crimson Throne.

The great sickle moon cast a dull redness in the fog as a raft drifted away from Bellwind's island toward a mysterious shore. In one corner, beneath a blanket, huddled Amanda with the baby in her arms. The little boy was asleep cuddled in a sling against her breast. She could feel his gentle breathing. Nearby was a backpack filled with food.

Suddenly she was very lonely. Somehow everything was different down below. She looked back—past the trees and vines at the island's edge. Above them she could see the tower—the place where she had stood. Was it her imagination or did it actually change into the form of a beautiful woman—almost like an angel looking down? There came the peal of a silver bell and the ghostly image faded.

As the sound echoed over the water, it was answered from far away by a raging cry and a series of trembling wails. After that … stillness. Water lapped against the raft.

The journey had begun.

11

THE MUTT

An ant crawled out of a thick patch of brown hair ... across a dirty forehead ... and onto the bridge of a nose. Alex jerked straight up and brushed it off.

Daylight.

He stared around. Where was he? Two dusty shafts of sunlight glimmered high above, and a dizzying twenty feet beneath him lay a dirt floor. He was on a ledge. It took Alex a moment to collect all the pieces. Was he actually inside a statue? Could all of that have been real? He remembered the eyes and the shrieking voice.

Definitely a nightmare, he decided. He had gotten sick on the raft. He must have had a fever. That was the only logical explanation.

Rolling over on his stomach, he looked out through the crack in the wall.

Well, the city was real. A dismal sun had risen over the ancient, vine-choked wreck. It was an ugly place. He wondered if he had come ashore somewhere in South America. Maybe there were natives close by. Or even archaeologists. Somebody had to be digging in this mess. But then another thought. What if the natives were headhunters? What if they collected heads and shrunk them to the size of potatoes? Of all the possible ways to end your life, the least attractive had to be hanging in a hut with strings running through your lips. Definitely something to be avoided.

As he gazed down at the street, he saw the dogs, hundreds of them still sitting just as they had been the night before, looking up at the statue in eerie silence. They were so motionless they could almost be statues themselves. He stared harder . . . and rubbed his eyes.

They *were* statues.

And they were crumbled and worn as though they'd been sitting there for a thousand years. But how could they have seemed so real last night? He could still hear them raging and crashing against the door. He'd been totally nuts. Absolutely wacko.

But then he squinted through the crack. Down the street a block away something *was* moving. Another dog. And unquestionably this one was real. He watched as it trotted briskly in his direction with its tongue lolling out as though on a morning stroll. When it arrived beneath the statue, it stopped, sat down, cocked its head, and *barked*. It looked a little like the dog that had been on the plane, but how in the world could it have gotten here? As he stared in amazement, the old mutt jumped up and chased its tail, barking. Then it sat down and seemed to look straight at him. Alex laughed out loud. The dog pricked up its ears, tilted its head, and went around to the metal door and began scratching. Climbing down from the ledge, Alex lifted the latch and cracked the door open.

"What'd you do, lose the old lady and swim ashore? You must be a good swimmer. You look different."

He was sure it was the same dog, yet it was smaller than he remembered. *Much* smaller. Like normal size. He told himself that he had been half asleep and must not have seen it clearly on the plane. Everything else was the same—well, no dagger teeth, just regular ones—but all the rest, the scars and ragged fur.

"You are one old bag of fleas. And I guess you look friendly enough. So what happens if I let you in? You gonna bite me?"

As he opened the door, the dog trotted back out into the street, sat down, and stared at him.

"Here, dog. Come here, boy."

The only response was a slight tilt of the head.

"I said, *come here*."

What followed was an embarrassing series of attempts to get the animal to obey. These included hand gestures, verbal wheedling, insults, and whistles, all to no avail. If anything, the dog seemed to be enjoying the show. It continued staring at him and grinning, but without budging an inch. Finally Alex gave up.

"Stay out there, then. That's fine with me."

He was about to shut the door when it walked over and licked his hand. The move was so startling that for a moment he was speechless.

"So you aren't deaf after all."

He scratched its ears, then tried to pull it inside. This was no easy task, because it had no collar. And clearly, *inside* was not where it wanted to go. Finally it jerked away, grabbed his sleeve, and tried to drag him in the opposite direction.

"Hey, stop that."

But the dog was very insistent.

"You got spit all over my sleeve."

Trudging back into the middle of the street, it started barking.

"Be quiet. Shut up. You're gonna wake up the whole city."

As they stared at each other, Alex became aware of a rumbling in his stomach.

"Okay, you're right. I can't stay in here forever. I gotta find food. What have you been eating?"

The dog turned and trotted off.

"Hey, where you going?"

Pausing, it looked back, then continued on. Alex knew that he had to make a decision. If he was ever going to leave his hiding place, there was no better time than now. Maybe the mutt would protect him. Cautiously he stepped outside.

"All right, I'm coming."

The animal waited. Alex gulped. To follow it, he had to walk past the dog statues. They were huge, almost as tall as he was. And the memory of the night before was so creepy that he half expected them to come alive and tear him apart. Why would anybody put hundreds of dog statues in the middle of a street? It didn't make sense. Finally he was beyond them. But even then he kept looking back to make sure they hadn't moved.

The old dog led him to the fountain, and there they both took a long drink.

"Okay, here's the deal. Your job is to find me breakfast. And I don't want any rotten stuff. You got that? Just find me something."

Grinning, as though he knew exactly what Alex had said, the animal walked away. As Alex followed, he told himself that this might not be the wisest idea. The mutt wasn't going to lead him to a Taco Bell. But he *was* a seeing-eye dog. Maybe he was trained to take orders like "go find food." Blind people had to eat. And sometimes wasn't it possible that they could get stuck in weird places ... like *dead cities*?

Why sure, that made perfect sense.

The city was like a maze, and very soon Alex was hopelessly lost. His guide ambled up one street and down another, past hundreds of monstrous piles that looked like buildings but probably weren't. Often he thought he heard scurrying sounds, but nothing ever appeared. They were headed inland and the walking wasn't easy. The streets were clotted with rotting vines, and it was a struggle just to stay on his feet. And not one thing around him ever started looking *normal*. Creepiest of all, there were ugly carvings everywhere—twisted serpents with gargoyle faces, giant beetles with long tweezer-thin legs, and hundreds of roach-things with stingers in their tails. The roach-things seemed to have been an especially popular motif. They came in a variety of delightful sizes.

The whole place was beyond disgusting.

The farther he walked, the more he began to believe that it wasn't a city at all. What if it was a giant graveyard? He thought about the ghosts that had passed so close to him. What if they hadn't been a nightmare? What if they had been coming home to their graves?

The "city" was even larger than Alex had thought. But the old dog seemed to know exactly where he was going. He moved at the same brisk pace, never stopping, even when Alex had to crawl through slimy tunnels of green vine-gunk. Invariably he emerged, cursing every leaf that had smeared him. Eventually he started cursing the dog. But the animal didn't seem to care. It never looked back.

After an hour the "buildings" became smaller and the vines thinned out. Which made walking easier but didn't improve Alex's mood. The rumbling in his belly had become a cramp.

"Hey, you stupid mutt, I'm starving to death. They eat dogs in China, you know! I could go for a big Western bacon dog-burger right now."

No response.

Finally they entered an avenue lined with overgrown gardens. It was under a large tree with a limb that jutted out over the street that the animal stopped and looked up. Every branch was heavy with golden fruit. Suddenly Alex's hunger was overwhelming. Picking a piece, he examined it. It was soft and smelled like roses. He was just about to take a bite, when he stopped. *Strange fruit could kill you.* It wasn't so much dying of poison that bothered him, but the thought of going irretrievably nuts with a bad case of diarrhea on top of it. If seawater could do what it had done to his brain, the wrong kind of fruit might turn him into a howling, pooping maniac. In spite of his hunger, he was about to toss it away when the dog walked over to a piece that had fallen on the ground ... and bit into it.

Alex stared. "A dog that eats fruit. Did they train you to do that in seeing-eye school?"

He took another bite.

"Okay, I get it. I just hope you're not stupid enough to kill us both. I guess we're gonna find out."

As though forced to take awful medicine, Alex bit into the piece he was holding. Never had anything tasted so delicious. Fear vanished as the sweet juice dripped down his chin. The flavor was hard to describe—one mouthful was like cherries, the next like peaches; there was even a little pineapple in it. He ate and ate, making a pig of himself. When he couldn't hold another bite, he stuck half a dozen pieces in his shirt. Instantly the old dog trotted off again.

"Hey, wait. Where you going? I like this place. Let's stay here awhile."

He didn't stop. Irritated, but not knowing what else to do, Alex followed. A few minutes later they turned a corner and he found himself at the edge of the city. In front of him stood a massive arch with broken walls on either side. Beyond lay a road leading into a gloomy forest. Without slowing, the dog headed toward it.

Alex hesitated. He didn't like the look of it, but the alternative was spending another night in the city and finding out whether the ghosts were real. Not a difficult choice. Alex hurried toward the forest.

The road through the trees was ancient. It would have disappeared long ago if it hadn't been made of heavy paving stones. For centuries iron wheels had rolled over them creating deep ruts and ridges. After that must have passed centuries when no one used the road at all, because the stones were broken and heavy with slick moss. It was like trying to walk on clumps of greasy cotton. But if walking *on* the road was nasty, walking *beside* it was worse. The ground was blanketed with thorny weeds that could send you sprawling. Cursing under his breath, Alex chose to slip and slide in the ruts.

Hours passed . . . and the dog was tireless. On and on it loped through the gloom with Alex stumbling after it. The deeper they went into the forest, the more oppressive it became. An eerie, dead kind of feeling hung in the trees. Other than the dog, never did he see another animal or even hear the chirp of a bird.

Several times they stopped for water. Each time Alex ate a piece of fruit.

Then it was on again.

Daylight turned into twilight, and the forest transformed into a surreal world of giant, misty shadows until Alex could barely see. After a particularly bruising fall he yelled, "That's it, I'm finished." He was about to slump to the ground when the animal ran up, took hold of his pants, and started pulling.

"Hey, stop that. Get away from me."

But it didn't let go.

"Jerk dog." He kicked it as hard as he could. The blow landed on the animal's stomach and it groaned. As it let loose, a strange hurt came into its eyes. Instantly Alex was filled with guilt. "Okay, I didn't mean to do it that hard. But you gotta stop pulling on my clothes. I'm tired and I can't go any farther."

To his disgust, the mutt took hold of his pants and started pulling again.

"I don't believe this."

But it only did it for a moment; then it ran across the road and disappeared into a jumble of trees and bushes. Then it barked, clearly wanting Alex to follow. Aggravated, Alex crossed the road and pushed through the weeds. He hadn't gone more than twenty feet when he came to a large boulder. The dog disappeared behind it, and when he followed, he found the entrance to a shallow cave — the perfect place to spend the night. Grumpily he crawled in and discovered a soft bed of pine needles.

"Why didn't you tell me this was where you were going? It would have made things a lot easier." It was a dumb thing to say, but he was too tired to care. A moment after lying down, he was asleep.

Darkness came ... and with it a chill. The dog never closed his eyes. He lay at the entrance to the cave, watching and listening. And while he watched, Alex slept. The chill never touched him. It couldn't get past the crimson shadow at the entrance that loomed like a living wall.

12

TREE IN THE SKY

When the night mist burned off, Bellwind's island disappeared with it, which made Amanda feel even more lonely. She looked down at the little boy asleep in her arms; how strange and beautiful he was, so peaceful and content. She whispered to him, "Little baby, if you knew what was happening right now you'd freak. I'm gonna do the best I can, but I'm really scared. You know, it's funny, Bellwind didn't even tell me your name."

All that day they drifted. When the baby awoke, Amanda played with him and fed him a few pieces of fruit. That's all he wanted. Not once did he cry. Finally the sun set and the moon appeared.

Amanda was napping when she heard the sound of water on a beach. Turning her head, she stared. Several hundred yards away lay a narrow strip of sand and beyond that a jumble of low vegetation. Bellwind had said there would be a path, but she had warned against traveling at night. At night her enemies had great power. If they landed in darkness, the plan was to find shelter and wait until morning. Amanda hoped morning would come soon.

As the raft drew closer to the shore, she saw something odd: sticking out of the vegetation at the edge of the beach was a row of mysterious shadows. Leaning forward, she squinted. They were rectangular silhouettes, like sections of a broken wall. She was straining so hard to see, that it was a shock when the raft ran aground on the sandy bottom.

"Don't tell me this is as close as we're gonna get. *Come on, move!*" She tried rocking back and forth, but it wouldn't budge. Disgusted, she pulled the knapsack over her shoulders. Should she take off her shoes? If I cut my foot on a stone I'm screwed, she thought. Reluctantly she decided to leave them on.

After rolling her jeans as high as she could, Amanda picked up the baby and stepped into the ocean. The water was cold and came to her knees. Cautiously she waded up onto the beach; the area covered by low vegetation sloped gradually upward for several hundred yards until it met larger shadows that she took to be a forest. All around her was a feeling of strangeness and gloom.

She had to find someplace to hide.

Not far away were the moonlit shapes. Walking toward them, she discovered that they were individual blocks of stone crumbled by the wind and rain of centuries. Hundreds stood in long rows that stretched away into the darkness, but only their tops were visible above a heavy mat of vines. She examined one; there was carving on it, letters in a strange language, and above the letters, a face with ghostly eyes. The stone next to it was the same, except the "face" was smaller.

"I know what this is. This is a graveyard. I've gotta spend the rest of the night next to a bunch of graves." But she wasn't going to freak. If she freaked, she'd scare the baby. Bellwind had said the path would be close. Maybe she could find it and hide near it.

Amanda began walking up the beach. After a hundred yards there was still no break in the vegetation.

"Okay, so, where's the stupid path?" It was supposed to come right down to the water. There was enough moonlight; she should see it. But she didn't. The thought occurred to her that Bellwind had never been here. Not exactly the best person to give directions. And there was no place to hide except in the vines next to the graves. She shivered. Crawling in there would be totally creepy. As she tried to think of what to do, suddenly there was an odd sound.

It came again ... a whirling rush like wind in the treetops.

But there was no wind.

The third time it was much louder—and *closer.*

As she stared into the darkness, Amanda realized that the air above the graveyard had changed. It wasn't clear anymore. High up, a vague shadow had formed; at first she thought it was her imagination, but then she knew it wasn't. The shadow was growing, and as it grew, it blocked out the stars. A voice in her head yelled, *HIDE.*

Hugging the baby, she dropped to the ground and crawled into the vines. There she waited, trembling. For several minutes everything was quiet. Finally her curiosity got the better of her and she peeked out.

The shadow in the sky was transforming. From black it turned to gray and then to white. And as it became visible, it boiled and surged like a thunderhead. Then with a mighty rush it shot upward into a pillar thousands of feet tall. For a moment it hung motionless.

Then lights appeared.

From inside the pillar flashed gigantic beams of red and green, blue and purple. Up and down they swirled, leaving trails of glistening mist. As they moved faster and faster, out of them dropped thousands of smaller lights that raced and spun in every direction like a dance of fiery stars. Amanda stared at them. She had never seen anything so beautiful. As the lights grew brighter and swirled faster, her fear vanished and she felt a dreaming kind of ecstasy. Suddenly nothing mattered but seeing the lovely lights.

Laying the baby down, she walked out into the open. They were like streaming angels, and seeing them made her want to dance. Stretching out her arms, Amanda began to twirl.

If only she could fly.

If only she could dance with them.

Dance with the angels forever.

Filled with joy, she cried out, "You're so beautiful. I love you."

Instantly from the bottom of the pillar appeared a brilliant shaft of light that shot down into the middle of the graveyard. And in the light Amanda saw the path. "There it is. That's why you came, isn't it? To show me the way. Oh, thank you, thank you."

She had barely spoken the words when the beam shifted straight onto her. Bathed in the shimmering brightness, she looked up ... and her smile faded. The joy changed to confusion; and then to horror.

She couldn't move. Her arms and legs ... her whole body was frozen.

The pillar began to gnarl and glow, and then caught fire. Above her hung a blazing tree, and from it grew a thousand twisted limbs and branches that spread upward in a raging mass. Out of the bottom fell steaming roots that dangled to the ground. Amanda saw them slithering toward her. Still she couldn't move. In a moment she was surrounded. Only when there was no escape did the light release her. Collapsing to the ground, she gasped. All her strength was gone.

A burning tendril appeared on a gravestone above the baby. The little boy was lying on his back, cooing and clapping as though it were the most fascinating thing that he had ever seen.

Amanda screamed, "No!" It felt as though her body had turned to lead. With every ounce of will she dragged herself across the sand toward him. The roots were everywhere. As she crawled, one of them slithered over her ankle. The pain was so great that she almost passed out. When her vision cleared, she screamed again. The tendril was dangling toward the little boy.

"Get away!"

Lunging forward, she tried to hit at it. But it was like hitting mist. Everywhere she touched it, it burned her skin. The root was inches from the child. Then the most unexpected thing happened. The child reached out his hand ... and with one tiny finger ... *touched it.*

The tendril froze.

For a heartbeat nothing happened.

And then suddenly there was a rushing, sucking wind and a blood-red explosion. Sweeping out from the baby's touch roared crimson darkness. Higher and higher it streaked ... up the roots ... up the trunk ... and out to every limb and branch across the sky. Then with a shriek and a gigantic flash ... the tree disappeared.

Amanda stared. Gurgling happily, the little boy clapped his hands. Above them the sky was clear and the universe was filled with stars.

13

PATH THROUGH THE TREES

It was midmorning when Amanda finally awoke, and waking up wasn't easy. Her sleep had been filled with horrible dreams. Nightmares about Tori. Nightmares about Alex. And other nightmares that she had had so many times before. For a moment she lay shivering, trying to remember.

Where was she?

What had happened?

She was lying on her back in the sand. Towering above her was a gravestone covered with scorch marks. Sitting up, she turned to look for the baby. The movement made her gasp—every inch of her body ached. But the most awful pain was in her hand and ankle where the roots had touched her.

It was all the proof she needed that the worst nightmare had been real.

The little boy was awake, sitting quietly, looking at her with his strange eyes. She tried to smile at him. "Hi. Hope you slept better than I did. I'm not doin' so good this morning." She examined the burns. They were streaks of white surrounded with haloes of dusky red. The skin was hard and there was a sickly sweet odor about it. "You saved us last night. How'd you do that? What kind of a baby are you?"

The little boy only smiled and cooed. A bubble formed on his lips. As it grew larger, he stared down at it. When it popped, he jumped. His look was so comical that Amanda laughed in spite of her pain. "Well, that was a pretty normal baby thing. I guess we'd better eat before we start out. But I'm sure not hungry." When she opened the knapsack, though, she realized how weak she was. Every move took a tremendous effort. "I hope I feel better soon, or we're not gonna get very far."

Breakfast was light. Little cakes, a piece of fruit, and sips of water from a bottle. Neither ate very much. Finally she packed it all away and put the baby in his sling. Then, with the knapsack in place, she stood up. Instantly she was almost overcome with dizziness and had to grab a gravestone to keep from falling.

"Oh, God, what am I gonna do? I'm really sick." She started to cry. Suddenly, more than anything, she wanted to be home with her mother. Her mom would put her in bed and wipe her face with a cool damp cloth. Her mom always knew how to make her feel better. Funny how little she had appreciated that until now. But something inside whispered that she would never see her mother again. Amanda gritted her teeth. "Just shut up. Stop thinking that." With a tremendous effort she wiped her eyes and took a deep breath. The dizziness was fading. She forced herself to search for the path.

The vines that had choked the graveyard had been burned away. Now a thick layer of white ash covered everything. With the vegetation gone, the path was clear. But with the first step came a deathly exhaustion. After only a few feet she had to stop and lean against another stone.

How am I gonna do this? she thought. I'm never gonna make it. More tears welled in her eyes. Then she looked up. Far away loomed the great Mountain. "Oh, please ... if I'm supposed to come to you, you've gotta help me ... and you've gotta do it right now."

Nothing seemed to change. But in a few moments she found the strength to walk a little farther. And after that, a little farther still. Then she was on the path and there was nothing to do but keep going. At the edge of the graveyard she found gateposts covered with carvings. Walking between them, Amanda entered the forest ... and the Mountain vanished from view.

The path wound through a jungle of delicate ferns. Dense trees with long willowy branches drooped overhead. Amanda barely noticed any of the beauty around her. Very soon her face was covered with sweat, and her head became so heavy that all she could do was stare at the ground. Looking at the baby helped a little—as he hung in his sling against her breast, he seemed to be making a scientific examination of her hair. A curl was in his tiny fist and he kept trying to taste it. "No, that's yucky." But she couldn't say any more because forming the words was too exhausting.

As she struggled on, slowly her body seemed to grow heavier. Every few minutes she had to stop and rest. And the burns made her want to scream. Instead of screaming, she became very angry.

How could Bellwind have sent me out this way? She knew there were terrible things out here, things that could kill me. How many miles is it to the Mountain? Hundreds? Thousands? We're never gonna make it. Why does the baby have to go there anyway? I never got a single reason. We're gonna die in the forest, and it's my own fault.

Around and around the dark thoughts circled. And as the pain grew worse, out of the despair came the darkest thought of all. *Why keep walking? It's too hard. All I have to do is lie down in the soft leaves and close my eyes. Just lie down ... and die.* But Amanda refused to do it, though often she could barely see for the tears. What kept her going was the baby. When the tears fell, he would touch her face with his tiny hand and look into her eyes with such concern that it made her smile. "I'm sorry. I don't want to scare you. I don't know what's gonna happen to us. I just can't go much farther."

But her love for him had grown very deep and one step led to another.

The forest remained unchanged until the middle of the afternoon. Gradually the underbrush grew thicker, and the path began to twist through shallow ravines. They had just rounded a bend when in front of Amanda was a dead tree. Finding a dead tree in a forest shouldn't have been unusual, but even in her pain she realized that this tree was very odd. It was in the center of the path and nothing else was growing around it. Once it had been large, but long ago it must have been struck by a blast of lightning. A black scar ran down its trunk and all that was left was a single branch with a few twigs at the end that stuck out like broken fingers. But what was oddest about it was the wood. It was deathly white with streaks of crimson and from it came a sickly sweet odor, the same odor that was on her skin. She hurried past. But a few hundred yards farther, she came to another one standing by itself in a little clearing.

And after that there were more and more.

It was late in the afternoon when Amanda knew that her strength really was gone. Every time she took a breath she felt a stabbing pain in her side and her legs had begun to cramp and stiffen. She scanned the woods for a place to spend the night. Thankfully there were no more dead trees around. For some reason she had come to dread them. A few yards off the path she found a sheltered place in the ferns. Enough leaves had dropped to the ground to make a soft bed. Here she spread the blanket, and after gently laying the baby on it, she collapsed beside him. With her last ounce of strength she opened the food. The little boy ate a few bites of cake and drank a sip of water; Amanda drank some water, but that was all. She was burning up. Lying on her back, she fell into a trancelike sleep.

As the hours passed, the afternoon faded into darkness. Shafts of moonlight fell through the trees. She lay soaked in sweat, gasping for air. During the night she had two strange dreams, and they were so vivid they didn't seem like dreams at all. In the first one she awakened with a start. Her head was splitting and her eyes wouldn't focus. The baby was awake on the blanket beside her.

She had heard something.

In the distance ... a deep, pounding roar.

Was it thunder?

It couldn't be thunder, because it didn't stop. It just kept going.

Where had she heard a sound like that? She struggled to remember. Horses. It was like galloping horses. A lot of them. And they were coming closer. But she couldn't see them. All she could do was hear them *pounding* in her head ... pounding and pounding until the crashing was everywhere. When it was gone, the illness was much worse.

The second dream was even weirder. In it she was lying on the blanket unable to move. A terrible heaviness was on her chest, and she knew that she was dying. With a great effort she turned her head toward the baby. All she wanted was to see him one last time. He was sitting up, looking at her with starlit eyes.

Then she heard rustling, dragging sounds. Something heavy and lumbering was coming toward her. The sounds came very close ... and stopped. With dim eyes she stared upward. *She was surrounded by dead trees.* Their diseased bark seemed to glow in the moonlight. At first she was afraid. But then she looked at the baby, and without knowing how, she knew that he had called them.

As Amanda watched, the broken, twisted arms of the trees spread out above her and from their branches fell drops of cool liquid in a soft rain that bathed her burning skin. The largest tree was at her head, the one with the black scar on its trunk. Slowly its branch reached down to her lips, and the drops entered her mouth. She was too weak even to swallow, but as they ran down her throat she felt life enter her body. Shortly after that the fever must have broken because the dream faded and she slept.

When Amanda awoke the next morning, her pain was almost gone. The burns on her hand and leg were still there, but they didn't hurt at all. When she looked at the little boy, he was smiling at her. She smiled back. "Well, good morning. You look happy. Was I ever sick last night! And I had really weird dreams. But I'm feeling a lot better. Are you hungry? I sure am." They both ate a good breakfast. Not far away she found a bubbling stream with cool, clear water. After washing herself and the little boy, she filled their water bottle and rolled up the blanket.

Once more they set out on their journey.

The path continued through the forest, and this time the walk was almost pleasant. Amanda was amazed at how good she felt. Her body still ached a little, but the improvement was so great that she didn't even notice. She even sang nonsense songs to the baby. And he was happier too — the only shadow came when they approached one of the dead trees. She still didn't want to look at them. It was true that in the dream they had taken away her sickness, but that was just a nightmare caused by fever. She told herself that being afraid of dead trees was stupid, but it didn't help.

Finally Amanda became disgusted with herself. The next one she saw was close to the path, and it was very small. "All right, I'm tired of this," she said. "We're gonna put a stop to it right now." With a determined look she walked right up to it. "This is a dead tree. You've seen a lot of dead trees. So stop being a dork." She forced herself to touch one of the branches. The strange bark made her shiver; it felt almost like skin. And from it came the sickly sweet smell. Then a terrifying thing happened. As she examined the branch, she seemed to hear a small voice whisper in her mind, *Don't be afraid. Don't ever be afraid, no matter what.* With a cry she jumped back, and hugging the baby, she ran and didn't stop until she was far down the path. Exhausted, she dropped to the ground, gasping, "I hate this place." After that the journey was much less pleasant. Every time she saw a dead tree, she ran past it as fast as she could. And there were many of them.

As the afternoon became evening, Amanda started looking for a place to spend the night. This wasn't as easy as before, because the ground had become swampy. Everything beyond the path was mud and weeds. When it was almost dark, the thought occurred to her that it wouldn't hurt to spend one night in the open. Bellwind had warned her to hide after the sun went down, but the old woman couldn't expect them to sleep in the mud.

Suddenly she saw something deep in the forest; far away in the shadows stood a very large building. Who'd put a building in the middle of nowhere? she thought. Well, whatever it was, she didn't want to stop and visit. Just looking at it creeped her out. But as she continued walking, there was a rumble of thunder and raindrops began to fall.

"I can't believe this. *It's raining.* If we get wet now, we'll be wet all night." Reluctantly she looked back at the building. "I guess we'd better check it out." With a sigh she left the path and began squishing through the weeds. The building was farther away than she had thought, and by the time they got there, they were drenched.

The storm brought an early darkness, and lightning crackled across the sky. As Amanda approached the hulking structure, she shivered. It was a gigantic heap of rubble covered with dripping vines. With each lightning flash she saw more. It looked like a stadium. It was circular and the outside was lined with columns. Once it must have stood twenty stories tall, but now it was a broken ruin.

Sloshing through the mud, she looked for a place to get out of the rain. Another lightning flash. Not far away was a massive arch that looked like the main entrance. Cautiously she crept inside and found a broad tunnel that led off into darkness. The echo of dripping water was everywhere and the walls reeked of decay. Close to the entrance she discovered a little alcove that was dry. Dropping the knapsack, she wrapped herself and the baby in the blanket.

"Well, this is better than sleeping in the rain. Are you hungry?"

She groped into their supply of food. The little cakes were all gone, but the next layer down was brownies, and they were delicious. As she fed one to the baby, tears came to her eyes. They tasted exactly like the ones her mom used to make.

Instantly, in her memory, she was back home in her own warm kitchen. Amanda cried for a while; then she looked at the little boy. She could just make out his face in the lightning flashes. How mysterious he was; he never cried and he was always happy. And with one touch he had saved their lives. She told herself that even if she never got home again, as long as they were together, everything would be okay.

Then she fell asleep.

It was the middle of the night when Amanda woke up. The rain had stopped and everything was quiet. Why had she awakened? The baby was awake too. She could feel him moving. She listened. Had she heard something? From the darkness of the tunnel came a strange low sound, like air pushing in and out.

Slowly ... softly ... over and over.

Breathing!

It was exactly like breathing ... as though something huge were breathing in the darkness.

It was breathing!

Grabbing the baby, Amanda sat up. Suddenly she was trembling so hard that her teeth chattered. The sound continued for a moment. Then came a deep whisper: "*Who ... are you?*"

Utterly terrified, she huddled against the wall.

The whisper came again: "*Who ... are you?*"

Amanda thought she was going to be ill. She didn't know what to do. Should she run? She couldn't run. Whatever it was was right out there in the tunnel.

The voice spoke with great gentleness. "*You're a child ... and you're afraid. I can feel your heartbeat. Child, it is no accident that you have come here. Tell me your name. Who ... are you?*"

There was such calm in the words that Amanda stopped shaking. Gulping hard, she mumbled, "I'm ... I'm Amanda Lancaster. Who are *you*?"

"*A friend to those who travel to the Mountain.*"

"That's where we're going."

"Then, come, child . . . and talk to me."

"I'm talking to you right now."

"No, come to where I am."

"Where's that?"

"Follow the tunnel."

"But . . . it's dark and I don't have a flashlight." Her voice was trembling.

"There is nothing that will hurt you. Walk with your fingers against the wall."

"How do I know . . . *you* won't hurt us?"

"You don't know. But you must have faith."

"Have you ever heard of . . . Bellwind?"

The answer came with such loving emotion that Amanda was surprised. *"Heard of her? Oh, yes. Long ago, I knew her well. So very long ago. Is she, then . . . still living?"*

"We were just with her."

Now the great voice was trembling: *"Come to me, child. Walk to the end of the tunnel . . . and don't be afraid."*

Slowly Amanda got up. Hugging the baby, she stepped from the alcove. As she did so, she whispered, "I hope I'm not doing something really dumb." With one hand against the wall she began groping down the stone corridor. Everything was pitch black. "I don't see you. Where are you?"

"Keep walking. It isn't much farther."

Suddenly ahead she saw a patch of moonlight. As she moved toward it, it grew large. Finally Amanda emerged from the tunnel into the open.

And what she saw lying on the ground took her breath away.

14

CRYSTAL CORRIDOR

Gooeyness.

That was the first sensation.

When he awoke, Alex discovered that he had forgotten to take the remaining fruit out of his shirt and his stomach was covered with slime. His second discovery was equally unpleasant. He was alone. Crawling from the cave, he looked around. A few shafts of pale sunlight fell through the trees giving the forest the appearance of late autumn, and everything was deathly still.

The dog was gone.

For a few minutes he wandered around calling, but finally he had to accept it. The dog had deserted him. As he stared into the silent forest, Alex felt like a lost child. As aggravating as the animal had been, he was all he had. Suddenly he was furious with himself. What kind of stupid idiot follows a strange dog off into nowhere? Anybody that dumb deserves whatever happens to him.

But as he raged, there came a cold awareness. He'd better figure out what he was going to do or he would die out here. Okay, one step at a time, he told himself. Even though he wasn't hungry, the first thing to do was eat. Picking up a piece of the squashed fruit, he stared at it. It looked like a handful of brown rot, but he forced himself to take a bite. Not nearly as good as yesterday, but better than nothing. While Alex ate, he considered his options. This was easy because he didn't have any. He wasn't going back to the city, which meant that wherever the road led, that's where he was headed. He wondered how long it would take to find civilization. How many miles would he have to walk? Hundreds? Thousands? It couldn't be thousands.

When he was done eating, he found a little stream, and there he washed the fruit slime off his body. When he was finished, he remembered that he still had two pieces of squashed fruit left—probably his only food for the day. And the only way to carry them was in his shirt. So much for washing. With a grimace he tucked the slick lumps against his skin and headed toward the road.

It occurred to him that it might be good to have a weapon—the thought came mostly because he felt like beating something up. It didn't take long to find a thick branch that made a good solid club. He almost wished something would run out of the forest and attack him so he could beat on it. Swinging the club made him feel better; he actually started to hum as he walked but soon stopped because it sounded weird in the deadness.

As the morning passed, the forest changed. The trees around him became much taller, and by the middle of the day they were gigantic. Alex remembered one summer just before his parents divorced; his family had traveled to Yosemite National Park and he had walked among the sequoias. The monsters on either side of him now would make the redwoods of Yosemite look like sticks.

It was late in the afternoon when the road began to climb. Gradually the paving stones disappeared and all that was left was a weed-covered path. The trees were thinning out; patches of sunlight became visible. This cheered him, but now fatigue was setting in and he was very thirsty. He had just decided to stop and rest when he came to a fork. To his relief, beside it ran a little spring. After a drink he slumped against a tree and ate the last of his squashed provisions.

Okay, which direction should he take?

What he wanted was to find people, and for that, one way might be as good as another. Which was the same as saying no good at all. Alex stood up and brushed himself off—there was only one way to get foolproof guidance: use the system that had never failed him ... *eeny, meeny, miney, moe ...*

And so it was decided. It would be the right-hand path. The gods had spoken.

He began to walk, but he hadn't gone more than a hundred feet when he rounded a bend and discovered that this path led back down into the forest. Darkness would come much earlier there. He hated the thought of spending a night in the woods without any shelter. Okay, maybe the gods *hadn't* spoken. He was about to retrace his steps when he heard barking coming from up ahead; he knew that bark. Instantly Alex was both relieved and immensely irritated. So, the mutt had returned, and now it expected him to follow. *Come. I am the master, you are the slave. Run and stumble and fall while I drag you along.* It was disgusting. Well, no way—if the mutt wanted him to chase it down this path, then he would do the exact opposite. The bark came again. Somehow, it was different, urgent. But still Alex thought: screw that.

As he hurried back to the fork, he yelled, "Bark all you want. I'm not coming. You can follow me for a change." Instantly there was silence.

No question about it, the left-hand path was much more to his liking. Though it was steeper, the sunlight was brighter. Definitely the right choice. As he walked, he kept looking back to see if the dog was following, and apparently he wasn't. Alex felt a strange kind of hurt, but there was something else. The farther he walked up the left-hand path, the more an odd fear crept over him. He couldn't shake the feeling that he'd gone the *wrong way* ... that he should turn back immediately. Several times he stopped and was about to do it, but each time, a voice in his head whispered, *Don't be an idiot*; *there's nothing wrong with this road. You're just giving up. If you go back it'll prove you're pitiful*; *you can't go anywhere by yourself.*

Instead of turning back, Alex walked faster, swinging his club, telling himself that the sunlight was wonderful. Much better than the gloom of the forest. Going this direction, he felt good. In charge of his life. No more running and stumbling. No more being dragged around by a stupid animal.

Soon the trees gave way to a rocky landscape pocked with tall scraggly bushes that kept him from seeing much of anything. And the path was steeper. As he climbed, Alex tried to whistle. It was a pathetic attempt because he'd never really learned to whistle. It was hard to whistle with earbuds stuck in your head, which is the way he'd spent most of his life. So, the puffy squeak that came from his lips didn't exactly brighten his spirits.

It was almost evening when the road took a sharp turn, the bushes disappeared, and he was in the open. Alex stopped. He was much higher up than he had imagined. Ahead, the crumbling path wound off into the distance, snaking toward an eerie mountain of tremendous size. Although it was only a foothill compared to the Great Peak that he'd seen from the ocean, there was so much haze above it that no other mountain was visible. So this was where the road was taking him. He didn't like the look of it. Just beneath the summit stretched a sheer rock face that must have been thousands of feet tall, and while the rest of the mountain was gray, the cliffs near the peak were streaked with red as though giant claws had raked the stone and drawn blood.

Maybe he *had* gone the wrong way. Well, there was nothing he could do about it now. The only choice was to push on and hope for the best. There were still several hours of daylight. Maybe up there in the rocks he could find a cave.

It wasn't long before the path disintegrated into a narrow track that took him higher and higher. As the sun began to set, the air grew cold. Shivering, Alex zipped his jacket. He tried to console himself with the thought that the path must lead somewhere. Someone had built it for a reason. Though it was narrow and dangerous now, maybe long ago it had been wider. People had traveled on it and travelers needed shelter.

Yeah, right, he thought. A *thousand years* ago travelers had needed shelter, and it looked as though the "path" hadn't been used since then.

Darkness came, and with it a piercing wind. The moon hadn't risen yet, so he could barely make out where he was going. As he groped along, he stumbled on a rock and fell to his knees. Groaning and swearing, he decided his only choice was to stop and wait for the moon. While Alex crouched, he took the opportunity to curse everyone and everything that had brought him to this place ... his mother, his father, his father's bimbo, his father's baby, the storm, the plane, the ocean, the city, the road, and especially ... *the dog.*

Finally the moon appeared and he could see a little. What he saw made him tremble. Next to him a sheer drop vanished into yawning darkness. If he had fallen that direction he'd be a grease spot at the bottom of the mountain. Struggling to his feet, Alex began climbing again. He had to keep going until he found shelter. It was just too cold to sleep outside.

Another hour passed and he was so exhausted that he could barely walk. Not a single cave had appeared and the wind was blowing harder. He had to keep moving because if he didn't, he'd freeze.

The red sickle moon was at its zenith when he gave up. He was shivering so badly that it was hard to breathe and his legs just wouldn't go any farther. Huddling and hugging himself, he stared into the darkness. How high up was he? He had no idea. He'd been climbing for a long time straight into the wind. It tore through his clothes, but strangely he didn't feel it. All he wanted to do was sleep. He had read that freezing to death was like falling asleep — maybe this was hypothermia. Well, there was nothing he could do about it; there was nothing he wanted to do about it. Alex's head began to nod.

Suddenly he lurched awake. At first he thought he'd dreamed it. Then it came again.

A moan.

He tried to tell himself that it was the wind. But he knew it wasn't. Shaking, he prayed for silence. A moment later it came a third time, rising higher and higher into an awful wail. A dozen times the wrenching spasm echoed across the mountain.

In the stillness that followed Alex heard a woman screaming. Between the screams he heard: *"Help! Help me! Somebody help me."*

He thought he was going to be ill. He tried to plug his ears, but he could still hear it. How much he had wanted to find another person, but not this way. Horrible images flashed through his mind. She must have been walking on the road ahead of him. Probably somebody else from the crash. Maybe the thing that had been moaning had caught her and now it was tearing her to pieces. So what was he supposed to do? He couldn't fight a monster. If he tried to help, it would just mean two people dead instead of one. He had to run. He had to escape. But a mocking voice whispered, *Sure, run, you little coward. You wanted to be a hero, well, here's your chance.* Then it laughed at him. Alex groaned. As much as he wanted to run, he couldn't leave her. He would never be able to live with himself. Grabbing the stick, he jumped to his feet and rushed up the path. It looped in a hairpin turn around a jagged ridge.

When he reached the other side, he stopped in amazement. In front of him stretched a narrow gorge, and what was left of the path had crumbled into a narrow ledge, inches wide, that clung to one of the walls. There was nothing to hold on to. To warn of the danger, a burning torch had been placed at the entrance, but as terrifying as all of this was, there was something worse: the gorge was choked with transparent strands that glistened in the moonlight like masses of crimson hair. He sucked in his breath. He knew what that was; it was a spider web. Shimmering between the walls hung a web larger than he had ever imagined possible.

The woman screamed again. Her voice was coming from beyond the gorge. Squinting to see through the web, his mouth dropped open. Beyond the walls loomed the rock face that he had seen from down below. Jagged cliffs towered thousands of feet above him, but it was what stood at the bottom of those cliffs that almost made Alex stop breathing. Before him lay an insane nightmare carved in stone; hundreds of spires and flying buttresses sheered upward, reaching like broken fingers from walls that twisted and turned as though writhing in agony. He was at one end of a vast ancient building that was so huge, the other end was lost in darkness across the mountain.

A castle? Could that be what it was? He couldn't tell; the whole structure was covered with the same shimmering web that choked the gorge—billions of strands draped over every spire, pinnacle, and parapet, like the body of a dead giant wrapped in a delicate shroud. As he stared at the web, Alex knew that all the spiders in the world couldn't weave anything so gigantic.

Then he saw the spider's tunnel—twisting down from high above was a corridor of crystal laced through the web. It was huge.

Suddenly the voice shrieked again, *"Help ... Help me!"*

"Where are you? I can't see you." Alex peered through the shimmering strands.

"I'm over here."

Beyond the gorge a dim figure stepped from the shadows. It was a girl with long black hair, dressed in a flowing gown. Perhaps it was because he was looking through the web, but somehow she didn't appear quite real. Around her drifted an aura of moonlight.

"I see you. What's the matter?"

"I'm trapped. I can't get back inside and the spider's coming. Please, help me."

Alex shivered. He had always hated spiders, and the thought of the one that had made this web was too horrible to imagine.

"Where is it? I don't see it."

The girl didn't answer. She just started screaming again. Not knowing what else to do, Alex lifted his stick and struck the web. Not a single strand broke, but something else happened. The instant the stick made contact with the strands there was music... a thousand exquisite notes rippled through the air as though he had struck a giant harp.

The girl was even more terrified. *"Why did you do that? Now, you've called it!"*

Suddenly the whole mountain was filled with soft melodies, as though unseen fingers were sweeping across a million strings. The girl stood transfixed, staring upward.

"Tell me what to do," Alex yelled.

No answer.

Then he saw it.

Creeping down through the moonlit tunnel was a spider. In his wildest nightmares he had never imagined that such a monster could exist. Not only was it *huge*, it was completely transparent, as though made of glass. A hundred legs, so delicate that they seemed on the verge of breaking, touched the strands, and with each touch, the air was filled with trembling melodies, a thousand songs within songs woven with harmonies so complex that no harpist on any world could have played them. If only Alex could have closed his eyes, he would have heard music of such wistful loveliness that it would have washed away his terror. But he couldn't close his eyes. The terror wouldn't let him. As he stared up at the thing, his skin crawled. And somehow the music made it even more hideous.

The girl wailed, *"The music kills. Don't listen to it."*

With mysterious slowness the creature drifted through the web toward him. As it drew nearer, the crimson moonlight shone through its body, and Alex saw that there was something inside ... a soft, flickering glow. He cringed. Sweat poured down his face.

The girl screamed, "Get the torch. Burn it."

Dropping his stick, Alex grabbed the torch. But as he did so, from behind him came a deep, rumbling growl. He spun around.

The dog.

But he almost didn't recognize it. It was so much larger. Its teeth were bared—teeth like knives. And its eyes were burning. With a snarl it rushed at him, grabbed his jacket, and pulled him off his feet. He tried to get away; his jacket tore and he was loose. Struggling to get up, he heard the girl scream,

"Look out!" The spider was dangling at the end of the tunnel. Alex grabbed the torch and was jabbing it at the spider, when a roar shook the mountain. He swung around. The dog had gone mad. Its jaws dripped with foam.

It roared again and moved toward him.

Alex lunged.

It attacked.

Razor teeth pierced Alex's forearm and wouldn't let go. He screamed, desperately beating its head with the torch. Finally he jerked free, but the creature came at him again. With all his strength, Alex burned it and bashed it, slowly forcing it to the edge of the chasm. Then with one fiery, screaming lunge Alex pushed the beast into the void.

"Look out!"

He turned.

The spider was above him.

Delicate crystal legs were reaching ... groping the air. In a last desperate move Alex flung the torch at it. The instant the fire touched the web, the strands exploded. With a howling roar the blaze leaped through the gorge and raced across the mountain, consuming the web in an inferno. And as each strand burned and broke, it combined with millions of others in a hideous discord, as though all the strings on every harp in the universe were breaking. Most terrifying of all was what the flames did to the crystal spider; the creature didn't writhe, it didn't even move. It simply hung, trembling, as its legs melted. Then came the wonder.

Suddenly the glow inside the transparent body burned with a shimmering brightness. And in that brightness ... a *face* appeared. A woman's face of ethereal beauty filled with overwhelming sorrow. Alex looked into soft eyes that had never held the slightest hate. *And those eyes looked at him.* From out of her agony a sweet voice began to sing.

Burning, burning,
Forever turning,
Icy ashes fall away.
Melting, reeling,
The end of feeling,
Crimson strings will never play.

Soft hearts broken,
Death words spoken,
Childhood's blood from yesterday.
Webs of crystal that you gave me,
Words to weave and harps to sing,
Through the universe I served you . . .
Now, to your heart . . . my soul I bring . . .

As the creature's body melted and the web gave way, for one moment the lovely face hung above the chasm. Then with a wordless whisper it dropped into the gorge. But at the very instant of dying, the light, which was her soul, flashed upward, carried away like a spark on a mighty wind.

Alex saw . . . and she was gone.

Far away, in a room on an island of mist, an old woman stood trembling. Her eyes filled with tears. She was looking up at a picture frame that hung with six others; its glass flowed with crimson, and it echoed with the last notes of a harp.

"Farewell, Weaver," Bellwind whispered. "You were the most beautiful of us all. What a price you paid to hold him in. But now the Destroyer has come. Farewell, Faylin . . . my little sister . . . until the Mountain calls."

15

CATHEDRAL OF SORROWS

A freezing wind blew through the empty gorge, but Alex didn't feel it. He clung to the rock wall, shaking, gripping the stone so hard that his fingers turned white. The face, the web, the music, all were gone, leaving only a fading sweetness in the air. He couldn't understand what had just happened. The face of a beautiful woman inside a spider? It wasn't possible. It couldn't be real. But the memory of her overwhelmed him. It was the most beautiful, gentle face he had ever seen, and as she died she had looked at him — a single piercing gaze filled with *love.*

Love for the one who was killing her.

All of his life Alex had dreamed of being a hero. In his dream he had seen his face in the posters that hung on his bedroom walls. The blazing rock stars and sports stars. The superheroes. Nothing could touch them because they were like gods. And someday he would be a hero too. All he needed was a chance. As he had waited for it, he had dream-lived it. Dream-lived it through his anger and loneliness, dream-lived it through the nightmare of his parents' divorce, dream-lived it through all the tears and screaming rage. In his mind he was the hero who kept his family together, who protected his sisters, who carried the hurt of his parents' selfishness, who wasn't like his father — that *scum* who had run away.

But in a single look the dream had shattered. A hero? He had burned to death the most beautiful gentle creature he had ever seen. And a voice whispered that he had been warned. She had played the harp for him, filled the air with the music of Heaven. When he wouldn't listen, the dog had tried to stop him, but he had killed it too.

In the eyes of the woman he saw himself for what he really was. A hero to his family? He had despised them all. Amanda and Tori he had teased and mocked for no other reason than it brought him pleasure. And his mother—he had hated her for the weakness that made her wallow and sob. To the people who loved him most he had been like a murderer. The dream was gone, burned with the body of the crystal spider. But if he couldn't be a hero, who would he be at all? Better to stop living.

Alex inched out onto the ledge. As he gripped the rocks, he stared into the chasm.

So easy to let go ...

So easy to make the pain end forever.

But just as he was about to do it, he turned his head and saw her—the girl standing in the moonlight with her black hair swirling in the wind.

"You saved my life. You're *very* brave."

Brave? Is that what she'd said?

"It tried to kill me. Did you see its ugly face?"

Slowly his mind took hold of the words. *Yes, he had seen it and it was ugly. What had he been thinking?*

"I've watched it eat people—tear them to pieces and suck their blood. I was so scared. A lot of men have tried to kill it, but the music fooled them. It made them see things that weren't there. But it couldn't fool you. You were too smart."

The music. That was it. The music had tricked him. It was like a drug. There was no beautiful face. And the whispering in his mind—it was just a lying echo trying to make him kill himself.

"I don't know what I would have done if you hadn't saved me. You're such a hero."

Instantly Alex's world stopped crumbling, and all the shattered pieces fell back into place. She had said it. He really was a hero after all, and the truth was all that mattered. He was so relieved that he almost sobbed.

"What's the matter? Are you all right?" The girl moved a step closer to the gorge.

"I'm ... I'm fine." He hoped she didn't hear the quiver in his voice.

"It's freezing out here. Come on inside and get warm."

"Inside?"

"The cathedral. It's where I live."

"You *live in there*?"

"I know it looks a little strange, but it's okay." She sensed his hesitation. "You aren't afraid, are you?"

"No." The question aggravated him. Hadn't he just killed a monster?

"Do you need help getting across?"

"I think I can handle it."

The girl laughed. It wasn't a friendly sound. "Well, what are you waiting for? Come on."

Fighting his irritation, Alex began creeping across the ledge. Instantly he felt a stab of pain. *His arm—the dog had bitten it.* He'd been so caught up in the battle with the spider (yes, that's the way he was remembering it now) that he'd barely noticed the wound. His forearm was slashed to the bone. Not much bleeding ... which wasn't good. Slowly the stabbing pain gave way to a throb. He was losing strength in his left hand.

"The dog bit you. Is it bad?"

"It's pretty deep and it may have been rabid."

"There's help inside." She hurried toward the building.

Alex crept forward. Soon he almost forgot the ache in his arm because every inch took him closer to the most awful monstrosity that he had ever seen. When he reached the other side, all he could do was stare at it in shock. The thing that she had called a "cathedral" lay like a gash on the face of the mountain. The web had masked its true ugliness and squalor. Now all the chaos was visible in every writhing detail. Hundreds of broken towers jutted toward the sky. Grimy spires and pinnacles crowded in senseless profusion. Tortured walls coated with filth twisted and turned, mile after mile across a wide rock ledge.

Was it really a cathedral?

Just looking at it, Alex felt a crushing weight of misery and madness. Out of it seemed to rise a miasma of agony, as though all the groaning prayers and grinding penance of endless centuries had congealed into a haze of silent screams. Far away he could just make out the tallest pinnacle of all. It rose like a bloody needle above a gigantic vaulted chamber. In front of it, spilling down the face of the mountain were thousands of broken steps that ended in a moonlit gorge. Long ago, people must have climbed those steps. But why? Why would anyone want to come to such a place of terror? As his eyes traced the insane heap, suddenly he was overwhelmed with such despair that it felt as though his life were being sucked into a sewer. His gaze shifted to a wall a few feet away. It was covered with deep-carved eyes. The heaviest cluster was around a massive door banded with iron. In front of it, at the top of a crumbling staircase, waited the girl. And she was *smiling.*

"Come in and we'll take care of you." She reached for a handle.

"You said you were locked out."

With a soft laugh she opened the door ... and vanished inside.

So she was lying.

Slowly Alex walked to the steps and looked up. Though the eyes in the wall weren't real, they seemed to glare at him with revulsion as though he were a rodent that had crawled out of a hole. More than anything he didn't want to climb those stairs and go through that door. Something told him to run and never look back. But in his misery he knew that he couldn't do that either. If he ran, where would he go? Back out to freeze on the mountain? To die of an infected wound? He told himself that he was an idiot. Okay, she had lied about being locked out, but the spider really was going to kill her. And this old building where she lived, maybe the people who built it thought stomach-churning ugliness was pretty. And who was he to say they were wrong? There was no such thing as "wrong." Just different. He'd learned that in school.

Forget the building.

Think of the people.

Hadn't he come all this way to find other people? Well, he had found them. Inside was a beautiful girl who thought he was a hero. And he needed help. His arm was throbbing. So why was he standing out here in the cold?

But try as he might, Alex couldn't bring himself to walk up those steps. Each time he lifted a foot, a horrible pain shot through his arm. As he stood unable to move, he suddenly heard a sound that made him forget the terrors of the cathedral. From behind him came the same haunting moan that had echoed across the mountain. But now it was much closer. Slowly it rose into an agonized wail. Alex turned ... and stared.

Something was coming up out of the gorge ...

Above the chasm hung the shadow of a dog.

And it was growing.

The beast had come back from the dead to attack him, to tear him to pieces for what he had done. Around him echoed a cry of heartbroken sorrow. But all Alex heard was a roar.

He ran up the stairs ... pulled the door open ... and stumbled inside.

With a thundering crash the huge door slammed shut behind him.

Panting ... shaking ... he tried to catch his breath. Instantly he felt like a jackass. What was wrong with him? There was no ghost dog out there. The thing was dead, lying in a bloody heap at the bottom of the mountain. The shadow was only a mist in the moonlight. And the moan—just the whistling of the wind. He hoped the girl hadn't seen him.

As Alex cursed himself, he slowly became aware of his surroundings. He was standing in an oily darkness, the air damp and warm and filled with a cloying stench like the reek of a filthy toilet. A large chamber surrounded him, lit only by a shaft of moonlight. And it was hot. *Really* hot. Sweat began trickling down his face. Peeling off his jacket, he almost screamed—his arm felt like it was about to drop off. Where was the girl? He needed medicine and a bandage. Carefully he wrapped the jacket around the wound.

As the pain subsided, he heard dripping ... a slow, thick plop like gravy into a bowl. A few feet away stood an ancient fountain in the shape of a tree with branches like hands with long drooping fingers. They were covered with softness like furry gray-velvet skin. He realized that the softness was everywhere. Walking over, he touched it ... and drew back in disgust. It was mold. Like on old food in a refrigerator. And it was so thick that it must have been growing for a thousand years. The fountain was full of it. A pool of furry slime rippled with each drip. His stomach gave a queasy lurch. What a hideous place to live. He was turning to search for the girl, when he saw a broken reflection in the ooze.

He looked up.

In the ceiling hung a stained-glass window, a tapestry of red and purple moonlight, and embedded in it was a figure cut from jagged crystal, a man with black hair and a long robe. His ghostly face was so utterly cold and his squinting eyes so real that they made Alex shudder. Where had he seen that face?

The plane!

It looked exactly like the man who had been with the woman and the baby on the plane. And just like on the plane, the man was glaring at him with such hate that it felt like any second he would crash down from the glass.

Then the figure moved. The arm shifted an inch. He was sure of it.

And that was it! Even the freezing wind and the ghost dog would be better than this. Rushing to the door, he tried to pull it open, but it wouldn't budge. He pulled harder. Was it jammed? Suddenly fear prickled the back of his neck. *It wasn't jammed. It was locked.* At that moment the girl's soft voice called to him.

"What're you doing?"

He spun around. Across the chamber a flicker of candlelight came through an open doorway. But the girl wasn't there.

"Unlock this thing, I want out."

Soft laughter. "You can't go out that way. That door's only for coming *in.*"

"Open the frigging door right now."

Another soft laugh. The candlelight began to fade as though she were walking away.

"Hey, come back here. Where are you going?" As he ran across the room, he was so enraged that he never saw the change in the window above. The image of the man had vanished. All that remained was a silhouette in empty glass.

Rushing into the next room, Alex was ready to let loose with a string of profanity, but he never got the chance because the candlelight was gone. In a split second all his fury drained. She was playing a game with him. A stupid *game.* Why would she do that? She knew he was wounded and needed help. Now she was screwing with him.

Suddenly he hated her. She was just like everybody else. If she was trying to freak him out it wasn't going to work. So the dirty, ungrateful little witch wanted to play games. He'd show her. He'd find her wherever she was. And when he did . . .

Alex scanned the room. It was like the hall of an old castle. Red moonlight flooded through a hole in the ceiling. By the dim glow he could just make out the walls. They were covered with hundreds of paintings. It was some kind of gallery, and the paintings were portraits. Alex didn't know anything about art, but he didn't need to. Even in the moonlight he could tell that they were the work of a great master. Each was lifelike to the smallest detail. Especially the eyes.

And as he stared at them, a strange realization came over him. All the portraits were of children — every single one. And they seemed to look back at him with anguish and pleading. It was eerie, almost as though they were watching him, following his every move. Suddenly finding the girl didn't matter. He had to get out of this awful place. And if the only way out was through the locked door he would break it down.

Alex was about to run from the room when the dim candlelight flickered through another doorway at the end of the hall. With it came whispering and laughter. "You're so slow. What kind of a world do you come from? It must be full of turtles."

It was then that he knew the truth: he was caught like a rat. She had lured him here, and now she was playing with him. Terrified, he turned and tried to run back into the room with the fountain, but instead, he crashed into a wall of paintings. The door he had just come through wasn't there anymore.

Another trick.

Feverishly Alex shoved the paintings aside and groped in the mold. It had to be there, but he couldn't find it. Swearing, he pounded on the wall, and once more, the soft laugh whispered around him. He had to play the game. There was no other choice. The only way out of the gallery was to follow the candle. And the glimmer was fading.

As the shadows merged into darkness, a terrible thirst swept into him. And it wasn't a thirst for water. It was a thirst for light. Suddenly nothing mattered but light. To be without light was to shrivel and die. As the flicker disappeared, the thirst took control, and all he could do was run after it.

So Alex ran into the next room.

It was a library; three of the walls were lined with shelves, but there were no books. On the fourth loomed a gigantic stained-glass window, and in it was a woman with a face of power and dark beauty. It was the woman from the plane, but Alex barely saw her. The thirst for light was blinding him. The glimmer had moved on and he had to follow.

And so began a staggering, stumbling chase of horror. No matter how fast he ran, the candle was never closer than the room beyond. Chamber after chamber. Hall after hall. Through narrow passages. Up and down staircases. Around corners. Beneath echoing domes. And everywhere, rippling laughter with muffled, meaningless words. Everywhere thirst and terror. Running. Falling. Screaming with pain. Then on again. Sweat dripping. Clothes slick with mold. Loathing himself, choking with rage at his own weakness. Dragged as though chained to the fading glow.

And on every wall there were paintings of children, always children, only children, paintings crammed and jammed without an inch between.

16

THE PORTRAIT

As Alex ran, the air gradually grew hotter and thicker until he could hardly breathe. Blinded and choking, he was about to drop from exhaustion when the chase ended. Rushing around a corner, he crashed into a stone wall with such force that he fell backward and hit his head on the floor.

Slowly he sat up and groaned. His eyes wouldn't focus, and his arm burned with such agony that he wanted to tear it off. But what was this? All around him was falling a soft shower of light. And he heard singing. From somewhere came the deep rumble of a thousand male voices joined in a roaring chant.

Alex rubbed his eyes trying to make them work. Slowly they began to focus. The wall he had crashed into had a large hole in it. That's where the light was coming from. A mist of glistening drops lay on his skin like clusters of tiny pearls.

Liquid light. Light that you could drink.

Suddenly the desire to drink it was like a sickness. He licked it off his hand. So sweet! So delicious! Sticking out his tongue, he drew in his breath, trying to suck it from the air. Not enough. He had to have more. In spite of the pain, he pulled himself up. Then, like a dog on three legs, he scrabbled through the hole. As he passed to the other side, the chanting pounded into him with such ferocity that he sprawled on his face.

Struggling to his feet, Alex stood in awe. He was at the back of a cathedral so magnificent and soaring that he felt like an ant on the floor of Heaven. High above, the ceiling was lost in darkness. Below rose a forest of pillars taller than the tallest trees and littered among them were crumbled statues with golden wings, twisted bodies, and contorted faces. They looked like angels frozen in a writhing dance.

But it was the light that Alex cared about. The light and nothing else.

Fiery mist swirled and spiraled between the pillars, falling around him in clouds of glistening rain. And in the light flowed billows of silvery mold. The chamber was awash in an ocean of it. Clots and strands in exquisite patterns sailed through the air. Furry webs of filth floated to the walls and slicked the floor.

Gasping, he let the rain fall into his parched mouth.

Where was it coming from? He had to find it ... then run and leap and drink until he drowned. He craned his neck. He couldn't see between the pillars. Trembling, he crept out and cowered behind a statue. With one eye he peeked around it ... and the vision froze his heart.

The cathedral was infested with phantoms.

Thousands of them hung suspended from floor to ceiling, and each was draped in a shroud of softly swirling mold. Far away he could see splashes of brilliance, but he couldn't tell what was causing them. Whatever it was, the ghosts were staring at it as though in perpetual amazement. Finally Alex's thirst overcame his fear, and he began skulking around the edge of the vast room; from pillar to pillar, he crept and each one brought him closer to the phantoms. Finally he was able to catch a glimpse of their faces.

And he knew who they were.

They were the sleepwalkers who had marched through the dead city. When they disappeared into the statue, this is where they had come. Even though he was moving close to them, they didn't seem to know he was there. With dead eyes they just kept staring straight ahead. It took several more minutes for Alex to reach the last pillar, and with his face pressed against the slime, he inched around it.

Everything opened before him.

The congregation of ghosts was gathered around a golden staircase that led up to a wall a hundred feet high, and down it poured cascades of flaming light. In the light hung a gigantic painter's canvas. The great expanse of cloth was empty except for a thick coating of dark green oil that rippled down in heavy waves. When each wave reached the bottom, it flowed onto the golden stairs. The steps must have been very hot because when the paint touched them, there was a hiss, and the oil bubbled into the fiery light that billowed through the room.

Most horrifying of all, between the canvas and the stairs hung a grotesque shape. It was the sculpture of a golden hand with fingers the size of tree trunks. The monstrous thing was suspended, palm upward, as though a giant were reaching through a curtain of oil. And the sculpture was alive; the fingers were slowly moving. As the burning waterfall ran through them, they opened and closed, grasping the shimmering brightness.

Suddenly Alex felt ill.

The heat was overpowering, and the stench smelled like boiling vomit. Fiery streaks were pulsing through his arm, and something slimy was running through his fingers. Lifting his hand, he stared at it. Green pus was flowing from the gash. His stomach knotted. His mouth filled with saliva. Squatting behind the pillar, he retched. The taste made his thirst for light disappear. Suddenly all he wanted was the cold of outer darkness, a place where he could go and freeze and die alone.

It was time to die. He could feel it.

Desperately he looked for a way out of the cathedral. In the dimness of his suffering he remembered that at the back he had seen massive doors. But they had been chained shut. Maybe there was a little space underneath them—just enough for him to crawl out like a maggot, then rush to the cliff and throw himself off.

He was about to run for the back when a bolt of agony shot from the wound with such force that he gasped and staggered—and shrieked.

The chanting stopped and there was deathly silence.

As Alex sobbed, around him echoed a whisper as soft as the billowing mold,

Enter me . . .
I am the flesh of diamonds.
Feast on me . . .
Drink my light . . .
And die.

Then the cathedral thundered with singing that shook the mountain.

Slowly all the phantoms turned and thousands of dead eyes stared straight at Alex. The voice came again, but this time like a hurricane.

"Child of the Wind ... look at me."

Instantly an invisible force picked him up and threw him out from behind the pillar. Like a bag of dirt, he slammed to the floor. The phantoms parted, opening a corridor that led to the golden stairs. The invisible force dragged him to his feet. As Alex stood teetering on the brink of unconsciousness, out of the shadows a new host appeared. Among them were the man and the woman from the plane. They towered above him in glittering brightness as though their flesh were made of glass.

The voice cried out, "Child of the Wind ... come to me."

And Alex knew that he must obey. He was desperate to obey. The thirst for light had returned. All he wanted was to grovel and lick the glory—suck the burning oil that shimmered on the stairs.

As Alex Lancaster stumbled toward the golden staircase, suddenly his arm didn't hurt anymore. In a steaming cloud the brightness swirled around him. He opened his mouth. Softly it caressed his lips and tongue. So delicious! But still not enough. He wanted more! And more came. As he drank the mist, he felt a tingle in his stomach ... a strange warmth ... then waves of shivering ecstasy.

He understood now!

His mind was clear and soaring!

The cathedral was Heaven; he was surrounded by angels, and the mist was the Blood of God!

As Alex stumbled down the corridor between the phantoms, he saw her. The girl with the long black hair. She was standing at the top of the stairs near the frame, and she was smiling. How beautiful she was. Such soft lips. The body of a goddess. All his blazing pleasure at her beauty distilled into an ecstasy of perfect hate. Until that moment he had never understood the splendor of unpolluted loathing, loathing untainted by the slightest love. As he traced her form with his eyes, he longed to let the loathing crush her. He longed to punish her for what she had done to him—to torture her for what everyone had ever done to him.

But then she vanished from his consciousness like a wisp of smoke, because above him loomed the waterfall of light and flowing oil. As he gazed at it, everything else was forgotten. In the journey through the cathedral, he had been reborn. And from within the oil came an answering joy. It bled in streaks of yellow, swirls of crimson, slashes of gold. It flowed in colors that he had never seen, as though a palette had been drawn from the veins of heaven. Above him on the canvas were a thousand rainbows, circles of fiery brilliance flowing down from the stars. And in them appeared a face. When he saw it, he dropped to his knees, knowing that his existence was over. Nothing could look into eyes of such glory and live.

God and Beast!

Hunger and yearning!

The Crashing Chaos behind the thrones and altars on uncounted worlds.

To look into those Eyes was to have every question answered. In one moment Alex understood the horror of his filthy, reeking insignificance. Crouching beneath the Eyes, he felt them piercing through his body . . . searching for the breath that made him live. And having found it, the Hungering God bent close and groaned. The whisper came again: "Pray to me for I can taste your soul. Pray to me that, as I drink it, I will leave a drop of you alive."

And Alex prayed, shaking, screaming, retching out meaningless words.

Then the whisper rose into a wail. "Live until the gift of dying. Live until death is all that remains. Worship me for I am Lammortan, Painter of Heaven. Worship me, drink my light, and never rise again."

Down roared an avalanche of splendor. Alex's face blazed and from his throat came a screaming song. The voice was not his, and his lips formed words in a language that he could not understand, a language of stuttering madness, of ranting, spewing, babble, of jabbering hate in ten thousand tongues, a language of agony, but never had he felt such raging joy. As he shrieked, the ghosts of the cathedral answered.

Praise to that which has fallen.
Praise to the Lord of Night.
Sing the Song of the Lost Ones.
Glory to the God who burns away light.

Alex's body convulsed in hideous spasms. Crashing to the floor, he writhed and jittered, and his mind floated free. All his life he had been searching for this moment ... to worship ... to offer up his soul ... to burn himself in shrieking glory. One last time he screamed, and the veil of his spirit was ripped to shreds. Slowly the writhing stopped. The sacrifice was finished. Lust for lust. Hate for hate. Rage for rage. Every ounce of him had been conquered. And in the conquering was his exaltation. In the rape of his soul he had met his God.

The Voice spoke again: "Crawl beneath my hand."

Slithering, quivering across the floor, Alex clawed up the steps. Where he touched the oil, his skin blistered, but there was no pain. Streams of pus oozed from his wounded arm, but he felt nothing. Finally he was beneath the gigantic hand.

"My enemies have damaged you. Lift your arm."

Alex obeyed. At the place where the dog had bitten him, his flesh lay open to the bone and was slathered with green pus.

"Look up."

Alex tried to look up but his vision swam. The giant fingers seemed to be on fire. Flashes of liquid gold dripped between them onto the wound, filling the rip in his flesh, turning the pus to steam. Then the gold wove around his arm in a seamless band. As he stared at it, his vision cleared. The wound was no longer visible. Once more he heard whispering. But now it came from within his head.

Stand up. Walk down the stairs.

Slowly Alex obeyed. When he reached the bottom, he paused. Looking back at the canvas, he received the greatest thrill of his life. Painted on it in the colors of heaven was a majestic portrait, a picture of himself the way he had always wanted to be. A conqueror; a hero; a god! And the face was perfect in every detail but one—the eyes were not his. Alex didn't care. His dream had come true, that was all that mattered. And he *felt* like a god. All the phantoms in the cathedral and all the crystal creatures lay prone before Him, singing, worshiping the glory of His Presence.

Suddenly there was a rumble ... and the singing died.

In the blink of an eye the multitude vanished.

To his amazement Alex found that he was alone. The gigantic chamber was empty. Dazed, he turned back toward the canvas. His portrait was gone.

All that remained were flowing waves of oil. Instantly his fear returned. What had happened?

A figure rushed from the shadows. It was the girl.

"Where'd everybody go?"

"Daylight is coming. We've got to hurry."

"What do you mean?" Alex stared into her eyes. For some reason she couldn't look at him.

"Quick, follow me!" She turned and ran.

"Hey, not this again. Come back here." To his amazement she obeyed. Not only did she return, she dropped to her knees. It was so shocking that for a moment he didn't know what to do. "Well ... okay ... good." Bending down, he glared at her. She was afraid of him. He could feel it. And her fear made her beauty even more delicious. "What's your name?"

"Melesh. Please, we don't have much time ..."

"All right, but no screwing around. No running ahead and losing me. You got that?"

"Yes."

Quickly she led him away. This time the journey through the cathedral was much different. Though the girl hurried, she never left him. Once Alex ordered her to stop just to make sure he was in control. Turning back, she knelt at his feet. It made him feel so good that he laughed. "Hey, I like this."

"If you like it, I'll do it always. I'm your slave. But please, we've got to go to our rooms."

His slave? Into his mind came thoughts so cruel they were unspeakable.

Jumping up, she hurried on, through a part of the building that was without the strangling heat and mold and portraits of children; no haunting eyes full of sadness to watch him. They didn't go much farther. After climbing a staircase and rushing down a hall, the girl ran to a wooden door. Throwing it open, she pulled him inside. Alex found himself in a room with high windows. It was very stark with only one piece of furniture, a large four-poster bed.

"It's time for sleep."

"And what if I don't want to sleep?" He moved close to her.

"I can't stay. But I'll come back. I promise." She was trembling. He liked that.

"Well, you can't leave until I get some answers." But before he could say another word, a tiny beam of sunlight flashed through the glass and fell close to her. She screamed, "I have to get back to my window or I'll die." To his amazement, she rushed into the shadows ... and disappeared.

"Hey!"

At the place where she had vanished hung long curtains with a drawstring. Thinking she'd gone behind them, Alex pulled them back ... and *froze.* Under the curtains hung a life-size portrait without a trace of mold. It was of a little girl, and the image was so real that the tears on her cheeks looked as though they were actually falling.

The portrait was of Tori. And the paint was still wet.

As Alex stared at it in horror, a beam of sunlight struck the gold on his arm and he felt a terrible weakness. Then came the sound of cracking and ripping, and he was no longer in his body. It was as though his flesh had grown flat and hard and his blood had congealed into veins of lead.

And Alex Lancaster slept—seeing nothing through eyes of crystal—a figure of power and dark beauty in a window of stained glass.

17

SANDALBAN

From darkness . . . to crimson moonlight.

When Amanda emerged from the black tunnel, she found herself at the entrance to a huge stadium. Above her rose a hundred tiers of crumbled seats covered with thick moss that blanketed every stone. Masses of vines hung like clumps of matted hair above gaping arches. Once, long ago, screaming crowds must have gathered here. Now all that was left was rotting emptiness. But it wasn't the stadium that had taken Amanda's breath away; it was what she saw in front of her.

In the middle of an arena loomed a gigantic form, a horse ten thousand times larger than any horse that she had ever seen. The stupendous creature lay on its back, a haunting image of rage and misery, as though it had been thrown down and quick-frozen in the peak of a thrashing battle. Its legs rose high in the moonlight. Its huge head was wrenched up and its teeth were bared as though shrieking against an invisible foe. Every muscle, every line screamed power. But it was power under brutal control. The horse was chained to the floor, weighed down with gigantic iron links pulled taught and embedded in the stone.

Slowly Amanda began to realize that it was a statue . . . the greatest sculpture of a horse that she had ever seen. But as she looked at it, she was filled with inexplicable sorrow. It was so wild and beautiful. Why had it been thrown down and chained? And why had someone destroyed its eyes? For where eyes should have been there were only gouged-out holes.

"Don't be afraid. Walk out into the arena."

Amanda looked around. "Where are you? I don't see you."

"You see me very well. Come quickly, Bellwind's friend. I have been waiting for this moment through a million sorrows. The little one . . . I can feel his presence . . . bring him to me."

"Are you . . . the statue?"

"I am."

Still Amanda hesitated. "Well, if you're the statue and you're talking, why can't I see your mouth move?"

"Why would I tell you that I'm the statue if I'm not?"

"I don't know. Maybe you're like a ventriloquist and you're trying to fool me just to get me out there."

"If I were a ventriloquist wouldn't I make the mouth move so that I could fool you?" There was a hint of irritation in the voice.

"Okay, good point. But how do you know Bellwind?"

"I am Sandalban, Worwil of the Winds, Thunderer of the Storm. If you've come from my sister she will have told you my name."

"Thunderer. But how can you be one of them? You're a big, carved rock and they're like . . . angels."

"Child, I see that among your many gifts is the gift of aggravation. You think that rocks are dead? I tell you they are not. No, not on any world. They feel and cry out. But their voices are too deep to be heard by deaf little creatures like you. For endless eons the rocks of my world have been weeping, for over them have washed rivers of innocent blood."

"Why are you chained down?"

"Long ago there was a great war. Across this world people slaughtered people until almost all were dead. But the most terrible battles were fought by the Spirit Lords. I led a mighty host, but we were overcome. There is only one who was strong enough to capture me. He brought me here so that his creatures could take pleasure in my pain. They came by the thousands to watch me tortured."

"That's horrible. Where are they now? It doesn't look like anybody's been here in a long time."

"The war went on for many centuries. The Worwil were overcome until only two remained, and they were weakened. But at the moment when the Enemy was about to be victorious, the prophecies were fulfilled and the child you carry was born. With him came strength. The Enemy was bound and his fortress shrouded

with the Music of Heaven. But he was not destroyed. His spirit has remained powerful in the hosts of his crystal lords. They tried to kill the child. His mother was murdered. But he was hidden from their eyes. And so Boreth has dangled on the brink of death waiting for ancient words to be fulfilled. Now that he has returned, the end is near. Quickly, let him touch me. But stay away from the chains. They're linked through the ground to the heart of Evil."

"Why do you want him to touch you?"

"Because within him is the Spirit of Joy, and I have waited so long for a single drop of it."

Cautiously Amanda began walking out into the arena. She came to the first chain—it was easy to step around because each link was larger than her body. She was almost to the horse's head when there was a distant rumble.

"Too late, they're coming." The great voice no longer whispered. "Find shelter! Hide! But not in the tunnel!"

Holding the baby tight, Amanda ran back to the edge of the arena and began scrambling up over the stones. The sound grew louder. Gasping for breath, she hid in the vines above an arch. From there she peeked out at the stadium. The rumble turned to thunder. That sound—she had heard it before. It was the sound in her dream—the sound of galloping horses. Looking up, she stared in horror.

From the moonlit sky a long, dark cloud was descending. It swirled downward until it vanished behind the far wall. Then with a crashing roar they appeared. Flying straight out of the stone came a thousand jet-black horses, and on each sat a ghostly rider. As the stampede raged forward, they streaked and blurred as though their bodies were made of painted smoke. When their hooves touched the ground, they dashed madly around the statue, and the ruins echoed with the pounding roar. But gradually the insane race slowed until every horse and rider stood in silence facing the great chained form. And somehow, the silence was more awful than the noise. Then, as though at a mysterious signal, they turned and looked toward the sky.

A terrible voice echoed in the gloom, "Live until the gift of dying. Live ... until death is all that remains."

When Amanda heard it, the words made her feel terrible things, like joy at the suffering of others and hate for the happiness of a single soul. She wanted to scream. To keep from it, she bit her tongue until it bled.

As the voice echoed into silence, down from the sky swirled a huge stallion that shimmered in the moonlight. On it rode a shadowy image of smoke and fire. The horse landed by the statue's head. Then slowly the Fiery Shadow raised the vague form of a hand and spoke.

"Sandalban ... my brother ... the spider's web is broken. Our sister is dead. This is the night that was foretold in the prophet's singing. Soon I will have a body of human flesh in which to ride; I will be transformed into the glory that I was when the stars were new. Beg for your life and I will give it. Pray to me and we will ride together as we did so long ago. No one will stand against us. We will conquer the Crimson Throne."

From the horse came a majestic whisper. *"Mourn, I mourn for you, oh, Lammortan. I mourn for the rainbows that sang at your awakening. I mourn for the glory of your birth at the gateposts of the dawn. I mourn for the flashing colors of your splendor. But most of all I mourn for the blood that you drank ... and the lives that are gone."*

The Fiery Shadow leaned close to the statue's head. "Sandalban ... the little beast and the thing she carries ... they have been here. I can smell their trailing stench. Give them to me and your dying will have no pain."

Quietly came the answer, *"The creature ... Lammortan ... the creature must do and obey. The Song will be sung again, and my voice will join with it."*

Instantly the Shadow let out a scream of rage and drove its burning hand deep into the socket of the gouged-out eye. A cry of unspeakable agony echoed through the ruins, and a river of dark blood gushed from the empty hole. The horde saw it and went insane with joy. But they had only begun their celebration, when there was a thunderous roar. The mob leaped back as great cracks appeared in the statue. The agonizing cry of Sandalban faded into a gasp as his body split open and granite flesh fell away, revealing bones. Then they too crumbled and broke until the arena was littered with dust and jagged pieces. Finally, all that remained of the great horse was his head lying on the stadium floor.

With a shout of victory the dark riders gathered behind their leader and began a triumphal march. To Amanda's horror she realized that they were heading straight toward the tunnel beneath her hiding place. Huddling down, she tried to flatten herself against the stone. As the stallion and the Burning Shadow passed below, the air was filled with a stench so horrible that she gagged. In a few moments the last of the horde had clattered out of the building. Then, with a thunder of hoofbeats, she heard them rise into the air. A moment more, and they were gone.

When Amanda could breathe again, she started sobbing. Once more came the whisper of Sandalban, but this time it was very weak. *"Bellwind's friend ... come quickly. Bring the child. Let him ... touch my head."*

Trying to control her sobs, Amanda climbed down and made her way through the bloody dust and broken bones.

"Little girl ... dry your tears and turn toward the Mountain. Think of nothing else ... than completing your task."

"But he's looking for me. He wants to *kill me*."

"The One Who Lives Above ... He is greater than all. Your life ... is in His hands."

"But I'll never make it to the Mountain. They're gonna catch me."

"While you carry this little one ... you are hidden in his light. Your enemies live and see only in darkness. But they sense his presence ... and are filled with fear. Remember this. Help may come ... in shapes that are unexpected. This much I can tell you, your path ... is filled with pain. But at its end ... lives joy forever. Trust ... and walk on ... as quickly and as far ... as you can. Now, let him touch me ... for my life is slipping."

Amanda lifted the baby. The little boy reached out both his tiny hands. As soon as he laid them against the broken stone, a wonderful thing happened. The pieces of the sculpture began to glow. Suddenly, out of the destroyed remains there rose the form of a gigantic, shining stallion. Not a stone horse, but a creature with the breath and fire of the stars. As though awakening from a long sleep, he stood and shook himself. Then, raising his head, he gave a joyful cry.

"Father of the Mountain ... I come!"

Washed in waves of brilliance, the spirit of the mighty Worwil leaped into the air. Higher and higher he flew until he became a streak of lightning. And when the lightning vanished, thunder roared—the whole stadium began to shake. Huge fissures appeared in the walls. The ground began rising and falling with such violence that all Amanda could do was drop down and try to shield the little boy. Then, with one rolling crash, the building fell away.

In a moment all that was left of Sandalban's prison were great mounds of moonlit stone.

Amanda awoke.

She didn't feel good. Not good at all. Where was she? Beneath her was a slab of dusty granite. With a jolt of terror she sat upright.

Where was the baby?

Struggling to her knees, she looked around . . . and saw him. He was playing in the dust under the statue's head. Though she was stiff and her body ached, she rushed over and scooped him up . . . then gave him a big hug.

"You gotta stop crawling away like this. You're gonna scare me to death."

He smiled and dropped a tiny fistful of dirt on her clothes. Brushing it off, Amanda stared at the shattered ruin. Nothing was left of the stadium but giant piles of rock. After the earthquake she had been afraid to move and had remained on the ground, trying to protect the little boy until they both had fallen asleep.

"Look at this place. We are in trouble. The tunnel's gone. I don't even know where it was. And our backpack is buried under a million tons of rock. I'm starving and I'll bet you're hungry too. I guess we should try to find the path."

After placing him in his sling, she began picking her way between the mounds of rubble. Several times she slipped and almost fell. Finally she managed to climb out into the forest. A small stream was nearby, and at the edge stood a scraggly apple tree. Water and half-rotten apples became their breakfast. When they were finished, Amanda climbed onto a stump and tried to figure out where they were, but nothing looked even slightly familiar. And trying to see the Mountain through the trees was useless—they were too thick and tall.

"I guess we'll just have to walk around the building until we get to where we came in. I hope we can find it." But by the time she had stumbled three quarters of the way around the giant heap, her legs ached and her arm hurt so much that she wanted to cry. The disease was back and it was a lot worse.

After a short distance they found the entrance to a trail. "Maybe this'll take us to the path. I sure hope so 'cause I'm starting to feel really bad." But it was only a narrow animal track that wound through dense underbrush. As she pushed through, Amanda did her best to protect the baby from sharp branches, which meant that she couldn't protect herself. Soon she was covered with scratches and scrapes. A few more minutes, and the trail sloped downward into a shallow ravine. By then it was clear that it wasn't leading back to the path, but she was too tired to retrace her steps. All she could do was continue on, hoping for a view of the Mountain. But the view never came.

The ravine broadened into a narrow valley bordered by jagged cliffs. The bushes receded, which made walking easier, but now she felt such pain in her joints that every step was agony. The patches of dead skin were getting bigger, and there were new ones on her chest and stomach. At one point she fell and scraped her knee. The skin broke but there was no blood. Instead, from the wound came a sticky pale-red ooze, and the pain was almost unbearable. Though she cried, she kept going.

In the middle of the afternoon a cold fog began to rise. The night was going to be miserable. Shivering, Amanda hugged the baby. "At-at least ... you're warm. If only ... I could ... catch my breath. I ... just ... can't ... seem to get ... any air."

Suddenly she smelled smoke. "S-something's burning. With my luck ... it'll be ... a ... forest fire." The smell grew stronger, and in it was a foulness like charred meat.

The trail led into a mass of tall bushes. As she pushed through, to her surprise she came upon a rusty iron gate. "Look at this. Maybe somebody lives here." When she tried to open it, it fell to pieces. Beyond lay a path through gnarled trees. Another hundred feet and she came out into a clearing. Squatting in the middle of it was the ugliest house that she had ever seen. Black moss hung from the eaves and all the windows were broken. Once it had been large, but sometime in the distant past lightning had struck and most of it had burned. Now it was a shanty of rotten wood. Through the windows Amanda could see a fireplace. Flames and smoke were billowing into a crumbled chimney.

"Somebody *does* live here. Maybe they'll help us." Trying to stop shivering, she called out, "HELLOOO ..."

No answer.

Carefully she climbed creaky stairs onto a creakier porch.

"Is . . . anybody home?" She knocked on the door.

Still no answer.

Almost overcome with exhaustion, Amanda tried the knob. The metal felt greasy, but it turned and the door swung open. Stepping inside, she looked around.

"Is . . . anybody here? Anybody . . . at all?"

Before her lay a room of unutterable filthiness. There was no furniture except for a rat-chewed couch facing the fireplace and a broken table lying in a heap near the door. Thick cobwebs hung from the ceiling and the walls were caked with grime. The chimney must have been partially blocked because wisps of foul smoke drifted everywhere. She coughed. The smell was nauseating. At any other time in her life Amanda would have run from such a squalid hovel. But the fire was hot and her body ached so much that the only thing she could think about was getting warm. She walked over to the couch. It was crusted with soot, but she just couldn't stand up any longer. Holding the little boy so he wouldn't touch the filth, she half fell onto the cushions.

"Okay . . . we'll just stay here for a minute. Then we'll leave." But as soon as she sat down, she was asleep.

A crash!

Amanda's eyes flew open.

It was dark. The only light was coming from the fireplace. She was still on the couch in the filthy room. Suddenly from behind her came a screeching, grating voice, "Well, well, well, so what have we got here?"

18

ABOUT TREES

At the sound of the voice, Amanda jumped up and turned. The quick movement was so painful that she almost fainted. Standing in the doorway was a little man of immense ugliness: black sparkling eyes and a scruffy beard that sprouted in long tufts from his grime-smeared face. The rest of his head was bald. Tattered rags thick with dirt hung from his scrawny limbs. The crash had come because he had dropped a load of firewood. Amanda was so terrified that she couldn't move.

Slowly the little man stalked toward her. "Well, well, well, well ... an intruder in my house."

"Look, I'm sorry. I didn't mean to ..."

"Sorry? You saw the signs. They're everywhere. Keep Out! Private Property! No Trespassing! Intruders Will Be Executed!"

"I didn't see any of them."

"Then you're either blind or stupid. And where did you get that baby? Did you kidnap him? You're a kidnapper, aren't you?"

"I'm not. He belongs to ... a friend. I'm ... taking him home."

The little man glared at her. Then a shrewd look came into his unblinking eyes. "Are you ... ill?"

"Yes. I'm ... really sick. We need ... help."

"*Is that right?* Well, how fortunate you are. First, because I'm a kindhearted man, and even though you're an intruder I see that you haven't stolen any of my possessions, So I shall overlook your felonious entry. Second, I happen to be a physician. My name is Doctor Pilfius Bordre Wanderspoon, and I don't mind saying that I am a medical prodigy of the first order, a learned professor of the physical sciences, a master of the arcane virtues that pertain to the mysteries of primary, secondary, and even tertiary pubescent senescence. In a word, I am an intellectual colossus. But I'm sure you understood the nature of the master who lived here from a single glance at my magnificent library, in which resides the sum of all wisdom." His hand swept toward the empty walls. But then he leaned close with a menacing look. "You didn't touch any of my books, did you?"

Amanda was confused and frightened. "No … but … I don't see any books."

Instantly his eyes crackled with rage. "No books? Really? You don't see any books at all? None there … or there … or there?" He dashed from one side of the room to the other pointing at empty space. Miserably she shook her head.

"Well, what exactly do you see?"

"Just … a room … with nothing in it. Except a couch … and a broken table."

The rage vanished and was replaced with dripping sympathy. "My poor child, it's as bad as that, is it? The disease has progressed that far? Well, describe my home. How does it appear to you?"

"It's … old … and … a little … dirty."

"Dear infected creature, my home is spotless, and you are surrounded with rapacious luxury. The walls are hung with masses of silver brocade, and the floors writhe with the endless intricacies of the finest golden filigree. The stairs are a torrent of marble, and my chandeliers drip with precious stones. You can see none of that?"

"No."

He shook his head. "Then I have all the information I need to make a complete diagnosis. Many times I have encountered this horrible disease. Oh, yes, thousands of times. In its advanced stages there is a total dislocation from reality. The sufferer believes the exact opposite of that which is actually true. Black becomes white, cleanliness becomes filth, good becomes evil. What am I wearing?"

"Kind of … like … rags?"

"I am dressed in a spotless white smock and trousers befitting a world-renowned practitioner of the medical arts. Here, give me the child and let me examine the skin on your stomach."

Stepping closer, he reached out grimy hands. The little boy was staring at him intently. For a split second Wanderspoon's eyes locked onto his. Instantly the man jumped back as though he had come face-to-face with a cobra. Sweat beaded on his bald head. "On second thought, you hold the brat. I can examine you just fine the way you are." He began circling the girl. "Pitiful, pathetic, vile, horrid. Are you aware that you are dying?"

Amanda gulped, fighting back tears.

"And when you are dead, do you want to know what you're going to look like?"

Rushing over to the firewood, he picked up a log, then ran back and stuck it in front of her. She thought she was going to faint. It was cut from one of the white trees. Beneath the bark she could see the shadow of a face. A girl's face. And there was no life in it.

"Go ahead, take a good look. Very soon that will be you. And as you die, you'll be in excruciating, mind-wrenching, gut-ripping agony."

He threw the log into the fire.

"But I am such a merciful man. Whenever I find someone like you in the forest, as an act of kindness, I cut them into pieces and burn them up. Perhaps I should do that right now and put you out of your misery."

Amanda's legs collapsed. Landing on the couch, she stared at the burning log.

"Ah, has my penchant for honesty overcome you? Has the plenitude of my propinquitous rationality given you pause? Forgive me, my dear child. As a physician, I know well the value of a positive outlook in the direst of circumstances. How else can one travel through this horrendous morass that we call living, which concludes in an endless nonsentient void? So, no matter how hopeless and utterly vile your situation, never give up! Push on! Keep a stiff upper lip! Hope for the best! Think good thoughts! Pray for that miracle that will never come! However, while you're praying, I would suggest that you consider a medical reality. Wherever you're going, forget it. You'll never get there. Look at your stinking arm. Look, look, look."

Amanda stared at her arm. From her hand to her shoulder it was covered with thick white bark.

"Now, if you don't mind, as you continue to maintain an uplifting, positive attitude, I'd appreciate it if you'd walk into the yard and turn into a tree out there. Then, when I chop you down my spotless floor won't get covered with human sawdust."

She began to cry. What he had told her was true. She was dying. The journey was over. Her arms and legs were so stiff that she could barely move them.

Wanderspoon bent close, being careful not to touch the baby, who continued to stare at him. "My poor young friend, who could have sent you alone into this awful wilderness? Well, whoever it was they knew that you would die here. A kind of human sacrifice, I suppose that's what you are. Someone gave you this infant to take somewhere. Well, they didn't do it themselves, did they? Child abuse, that's what it is. Double child abuse. And I cannot abide child abuse. If you're going to kill a child, do it quickly, do it mercifully. Be humane about it. Don't let it suffer. Don't send it on useless journeys. Whoever did this is an evil coward."

As she listened to the droning voice, Amanda was overwhelmed with the blackest despair that she had ever known. Like foul smoke, it choked her mind, making it impossible to think. All she could do was cry as she stared into the leering face. But then the sly look returned to Wanderspoon's eyes.

"However, there may be one glimmer of true hope, a single pustule the size of a rat dropping. But hope is hope and it must never be discounted. If we hurry, there might be someone who can keep you from suffering inordinately as you disintegrate into a foul-smelling, deciduous stalk of wood. Have you ever heard of the Worwil?"

Amanda was so startled that she stopped crying. "Yes. One of them sent me on this trip."

"Aha." The little man's eyes glittered. "Well, that explains everything. Most of them have gone bad, you know. Utterly rotten and evil. But there may be one who can still be trusted. Her name is Melania. She's called The Healer. Have you heard of her?"

"I have." Suddenly Amanda felt hope. Sandalban had told her that help would come in strange shapes, and no stranger shape could there be than this repulsive little man. "The Healer ... could she ... make me well?"

"Oh, that's far too much to ask. Your case has advanced beyond extremity.

I don't know what she can do. Probably nothing. In fact, I'm not even sure she's still alive. I've had no contact with her in at least five centuries. But because I'm a noble and compassionate man, perhaps I'll help you try to find her."

"Would you? Oh, please ..." She started crying again.

"Stop that! Crying only makes it worse. The disease loves to be watered with tears."

With a great act of will, Amanda forced herself to stop.

"We'd better get going. Considering your advanced decrepitude, there's no time to lose. Come along. My wagon's outside."

The simple act of rising from the couch made her groan and stagger.

"Now, don't do that! Don't fall over on me! If you fall over, I'll leave you right where you are until you're dry enough to chop into firewood."

"I'm ... okay. I'm not ... gonna fall." But when she tried to walk, it was impossible to bend her legs. As she held the baby, she realized that her arms were frozen in a cradled position. Wanderspoon gave her no assistance at all. Instead, as she struggled, he berated her.

"Come on, you can do better than that. Keep moving, lazy girl. We've got to get out of here. Pretty soon you'll be completely stiff, and what am I supposed to do then? Do you think I want a dead tree cluttering my immaculate house? There's not even enough wood in you to make a decent pile of kindling."

Inch by inch Amanda crept out onto the porch. Nearby stood a broken-down wagon pulled by a ragged donkey. The back of it was filled with chopped logs from white trees. Rushing over, Wanderspoon began throwing them to the ground. When he was finished, he motioned to her.

"All right, get over here and lie down. The road we're going to take is dangerous. Not good to travel after dark. I'm risking my life for you. Bad things are loose in the world. For two nights I've heard them. They haven't been this way in a thousand years. Then two nights in a row. Now, I wonder what they want."

He gave Amanda a crafty look. But she didn't notice. It took all her strength and sweating concentration to creep across the yard and lower herself onto the wagon. Then she lay, holding the baby and panting for air. As Wanderspoon jumped onto the driver's seat and the cart creaked away, tears streamed down her cheeks. She whispered words so low that only she could hear them, *"I've failed. I'm gonna die. We're never gonna get help in time to save me. But please, please, God ... if You're really there ... save this little boy."*

She couldn't see her hands, but she knew that her fingers could no longer move. In fact, they were hardly fingers at all. They looked more like twigs growing from the branches of a small white tree. Too tired to think anymore, Amanda closed her eyes. But if she had kept them open, she would have seen an amazing sight. High up in the sky directly above her, so high that it was barely visible in the darkness, soared a great white eagle. From where it flew, the cart looked like a speck in the moonlight.

Suddenly the bird swooped down. In great spirals it fell until it was right above her. There it hovered on silent wings. If she had opened her eyes, she would have seen it bend its head, and with its beak cut into its own breast. A single drop of blood formed on the white feathers.

Amanda never felt the drop when it landed on her skin. But the baby saw it. With silvery eyes he watched as it disappeared into her body.

The pain eased and she slept.

For a few moments the eagle continued hovering. Then, without a sound, it flew away toward the Mountain and the Crimson Mists.

19

VISIONS

Someone screamed.

Alex's body slammed against the floor and his eyes jerked open. For a moment he lay without moving, trying to figure out where he was. All around him glimmered dim-red moonlight. His head ached and he was drenched with sweat. Against his cheek he felt a moldy carpet, and a foot from his nose stood the leg of some kind of furniture. He struggled to look up at it.

A bed. Had he fallen out of it?

And who had screamed?

With a great effort he pulled himself up to his knees. But his head swam and he almost fell over. So hot! Why didn't somebody turn down the heat? It's sweltering in here! His clothes were plastered to his body. Suddenly he couldn't bear the feel of his shirt on his skin. He ripped it off. Why couldn't he wake up? Where in the world was he? It smelled like a garbage dump. And why was the air so thick?

Then terror began to churn in his guts. He knew where he was—he was in the room where the nightmare girl had brought him. He looked up. Towering above his head was a gigantic window, and in it he saw the outlined image of a figure that looked amazingly like himself. And somehow he remembered being up there, flattened, cracked, and broken into a thousand pieces held together by black veins of lead. Blind and deaf, yet feeling the sun getting hotter and hotter as it shone through his transparent body, wanting to shriek, but unable to make a sound. Had he had fallen out of the window? That was insane. None of this could be real.

His arm hurt. *That* was real. It ached all the way to the bone. Looking down, he saw the golden band that had been poured over the wound where the hell-dog had bitten him. He tried to pull it off, but it was embedded in his skin. Growling like an animal, he tore at it, but all he accomplished was to give himself several deep scratches with his filthy nails and a worse headache. Finally he gave up.

So tired. Exhausted. And the exhaustion made him confused. If only he could really sleep, maybe his mind would clear and he would know what to do. Alex dragged himself up on the bed and flopped down. Instantly billows of mold rose around him.

He jumped up in disgust. What he had taken for a spread was actually a layer of soft gray spores so thick it looked like a quilt of rat fur. He looked down at himself. His sweaty skin was covered with it. When he tried to wipe it off, it smeared into gray slime.

"Oh, yuuuuck!"

But the revulsion cleared his head. Why was he spending one more second in here? He had to get out or he would choke to death. Where was the way out? In the corner he saw the door. But as he rushed toward it, he heard the sound again.

A scream. Coming from far away. Like a terrified child.

It made him remember something. A painting on the wall. Tori! A painting of his little sister! Had he dreamed it? There were the curtains with the drawstring. But they were closed. He had pulled them open, he was sure of it. Rushing over he jerked them apart.

Nothing! Just a frame with an empty glass. Why would somebody hang something like that? As he stared at it, he felt cold radiating toward him. He touched the glass. It was like ice. No, it was colder than ice. It was freezing terror. He staggered back. He was going crazy. He had to get out right now. Rushing to the door, he was just reaching for the knob when it swung open hard, jamming his knuckles. He yelled!

And there she stood, just as beautiful as the night before. The girl he had chased through the cathedral. Instantly his fear turned into rage. "I want out of here right now!"

All she did was stare at him.

"Did you hear what I said?"

Grabbing her arm, he dragged her into the hall.

"Please . . . you're hurting me."

He let go. "I can't breathe. I've got to get some air."

"It's cooler in my room." She placed her hand on his bare chest and looked into his eyes. The touch was like an electric shock. Her fingers were so soft. As he stared at her, his mind grew foggy again.

"You could rest on my bed." She moved closer.

He struggled to think. Why had he wanted to leave? He couldn't quite remember anymore. All he knew was that the most beautiful girl he had ever seen was inviting him to her bedroom.

"What was your name? I . . . forgot."

"Melesh." Her body was against his. "But you can call me anything you want. Just don't . . . hurt me again."

"Why would I do that?"

"Because you're angry after what I did to you last night."

"I am?"

"Yes, very angry. Don't you remember?"

Suddenly everything snapped into razor sharpness. Every detail of his agony slammed into him as though he were living it all again. Heat! Blood! Mold! Darkness! Terror! Her soft, laughing voice! What was wrong with him? How could he have forgotten? This was the filthy little witch who had tricked him, humiliated him, dragged him through the sewer like a dog on a chain, and all of that after he had *saved . . . her . . . life*. The most beautiful girl he had ever seen? He wanted to *gag*.

And she thought he was *angry*?

He almost laughed out loud. How about shrieking rage? Hurt her? He wanted to kill her. Hideous images flashed through his mind, but he kept his face icy calm.

"I am angry. Very angry."

"I know." She ran her fingers gently on his neck. "Do you remember what I told you last night when I brought you to your room?"

"Tell me again."

Dropping her eyes, she whispered, "I said I was your slave."

He stared at her coldly. "Does that mean I can tell you to do anything and you have to do it?"

She nodded.

"Anything?"

She looked straight at him. "Why don't you find out?"

The soft words scorched through his brain, boiling down into the depths of his belly. How he detested her eyes. Yet how he wanted her — desired her — with a vicious hunger. Find out? That's exactly what he would do. But not all at once. He would let the acid of his loathing pour over her drop by drop until he had paid her back a thousand times for all she had done to him. Slowly he reached out and ran his fingers through her long black hair. From it came a musky odor that drove him wild.

"If you're my slave, kiss my feet."

Instantly she knelt and obeyed.

"Now my hand."

She bathed it with kisses. Her tongue on his skin turned his blood to fire.

"Your room ... let's go." He struggled to get the words out.

Rising quickly, she led him down the hall. A short distance away they came to a black door. Opening it, she slipped inside. He followed. He expected a bedroom like the one he had left, but instead he was in a chamber large enough to hold a thousand people, the air was filled with what appeared to be slowly drifting mists of blood. At least that's what he thought they were until he realized they were only masses of spider webs, thick with mold, shimmering in the red moonlight.

Why was the moon so bright in here?

Looking up, his mouth dropped open. Above him hung a window of staggering size, a single panel of leaded glass that covered the entire ceiling. Suspended in it, executed with breathtaking artistry, was the gigantic form of a girl in crystal. Her arms and legs were outstretched, her gown and hair streaked behind her as though she were falling from a terrible height. Her horrified eyes stared downward, frozen in the last moment before a death-crash. Through the glass of her open mouth fell a silent shriek of crimson light that illuminated the only object in the chamber. Across the room stood a black dais with seven stairs leading up to it. On the top squatted an enclosure shrouded in rotting curtains.

Alex was stunned, all his rage drained away beneath the crushing weirdness. "This is your … *bedroom*?"

The girl nodded.

"Where's your bed?" He was struggling hard to get control of himself, to carry through with his intentions when what he wanted to do was run.

"Over there. Up those steps. What's the matter?"

"Nothing."

"Yes, there is. You're afraid. Don't be afraid." She moved toward him.

"I am not afraid." She thought he was a coward. Gritting his teeth, he rushed across the room to the dais. But when he looked back, she hadn't followed.

"Well, what are you waiting for?"

She smiled. As she walked toward him, her face was lost in darkness. And as she walked, she began singing in a low, soft voice. Alex couldn't make out the words, but the sound sent chills through him. *"Don't do that; I don't like it."*

Silence.

When she was several feet away, she stopped and stared at him. "Well?"

"Well, what?"

"Here I am. What are you going to do?"

"Anything I want."

"Really?" The girl chuckled. Alex blanched. She was laughing at him again. Grabbing her shoulders, he pulled her body against his. The feel of her took his breath away. His knees almost buckled.

"Remember, don't hurt me."

More derision. Her voice reeked with it. *Filthy mocking witch!* Pulling her head back, he mashed his lips against hers. The response was amazing. She wrapped her arms around his neck and kissed him with a terrible fury. For a long moment they remained locked together. Then suddenly Alex *screamed* and shoved her away. Staggering across the room, he began choking, his stomach wrenched in dry heaves. As though she didn't notice, the girl began climbing the stairs toward the bedchamber. And the eerie song began again. But this time the words were clear.

Lips that whisper of mourning,
Eyes that die at the dawn,

Mouth with the honey of sorrow,
Come to my bed, my love.
Death is the pleasure of knowing,
The promise of passion beyond,
A grave is the altar of worship,
Come to my bed, my love.
Come to the place where they laid me,
My beauty asleep in the dust,
Die in the moonlight with me.
Come to my death, my love.

Slowly Alex's choking and heaving subsided. He turned and stared up at her as though she were a living plague. *"Your mouth ... what's wrong with you?"*

In answer, the girl pulled back the curtain. "Come and see."

Inside the enclosure stood a large bed and something was lying on it. As she looked down at him, there were tears in her eyes. What he wanted to do was run, but he couldn't. There was no choice. He had to see what she wanted to show him.

"What is that up there?"

She didn't answer. As though drawn by an invisible force, Alex climbed the stairs. When he reached the top, he froze. On the bed lay a nightmare, splayed out on the filthy sheets, a body so old it was mummified. The skin was wrinkled and cracked as though it had been there for a thousand years. Much of it had turned to dust revealing bones. But most awful of all, still attached to the skull was a shroud of long black hair.

"I was so beautiful. Look what they did to me," the girl whispered. "Soon, only my hair will remain." Dropping the curtain, she turned toward him. Her eyes held a terrible longing. "Help me, please. It won't be as bad next time. I promise. In a little while you won't taste anything at all."

She tried to touch his chest, but Alex jerked away. As he did so, he stumbled backward down the stairs and sprawled on the floor. The girl began descending toward him.

"Give me back my life and I'll give you pleasure such as you have never known. A goddess will be your slave."

Terrified, he jumped up and rushed to the door. Lurching through it, he ran ... down one hall after another ... trying every door he found. All were locked. But as he ran, he felt himself growing weaker and it became harder to breathe.

And then the fever hit him.

Sweat poured from his body, and he shook as though in a freezing wind. A purple darkness shrouded the edges of his vision, making the hallway look like a tunnel into death. His run slowed to a walk, but still he pushed on, desperate to escape. Then his legs began to go numb. A few more steps and he couldn't feel them at all. With a groan he crashed to the floor and writhed. His skin was burning. If only he could have a sip of water to wet his smoldering tongue.

Instantly cool hands lifted his head and delicious water dribbled into his mouth. He looked up, but his eyes wouldn't focus. A vague shadow was giving him a drink from a glistening pitcher. Then he heard the soft voice of Melesh.

"Little boy from far away, it won't do any good to run. Don't you understand? You belong to us now."

The water stopped, and he felt her lips press against his. Once more he tasted the sickly sweet rot of death. But he was too weak to pull away or even to gag. All he could do was cry.

Alex drifted in and out of consciousness. What followed seemed like endless nights of burning fever, thrashing in a moldy bed interspersed with endless days hanging blind and flattened in the scorching sun. At dusk he would crash to the bed and roll off on the floor. There he would lie too weak to move until the girl came and dragged him up to begin a new night of horror. Through it all she sat beside him, chanting in a low, soft voice with red moonlight in her eyes. And as she chanted, Alex would dream.

First came nightmares. Gashes and wounds of memory. Home. Sisters. Mother. Father. Screaming. Divorce. These were mingled with jittering cuts and freeze-frames of all the horrors he had seen, one image after another retching across his brain like a movie slash-edited by an axe murderer. On and on it went, for what seemed like a thousand lifetimes. But somewhere in the endless dreaming, the images changed. The chanting became a lilt. Gone was the movie from hell. As the girl whisper-sang, his eyes seemed to open; he lifted out of his body and soared high in the air.

Light! Wind! He was free!

If this was death, he didn't care. All he knew was that his body didn't hurt anymore and he was gone from the sweat-reeking bed in the Cathedral of Horror. He sailed through misty clouds. Alex had never believed in heaven, but what he was experiencing now made him change his mind. He wondered if he would meet some angels. He looked over his shoulder—no wings, which was confusing. He thought everybody in heaven had wings. Then he looked down and almost cried.

Below him was a breathtaking garden-world laced with rivers of liquid light. Dazzling waterfalls poured into shimmering streams that rushed through forests with trees so tall they were crowned with clouds. In them lived thousands of iridescent birds that soared into the air, then swooped and swirled like rushing rainbows. Laughing with joy, he tried to fly with them.

But then came more chanting and the vision changed.

He found himself above broad plains where millions of animals raced madly in gigantic herds for nothing more than the joy of running. Each species was a different tint and hue, some gaudy, others soft and gentle. They rushed toward each other, but instead of crashing, they converged and flowed, blending into chaotic torrents of rippling hide that surged, then parted, and raced on again. Alex had never seen anything so wonderful. He realized that he was flying above a masterpiece, the work of an Artist greater than any other in the universe who had turned a planet into a canvas and painted it with joy.

And then he saw cities built on mountains.

He had never seen beautiful cities before. In his world there was always darkness in them, slums next to skyscrapers, for every mansion a thousand hovels. But these shone like star-clusters draped across the mountain cliffs. Their buildings were of burnished stone, and in the sunlight, they glistened with soft fire. And the people of the cities—how beautiful they were. They walked the quiet streets without rushing desperation, without exhausted fear. They laughed and talked as though they had nothing better to do in all the world. Alex tried to fly down to join them. But when he got close, the vision disappeared.

Then, as though from far away, he heard the girl chanting.

Instantly he was back in the Cathedral. But no longer was it a place of horror. Gone were the darkness and the mold. The halls were filled with sunlight and laughing children. He followed as they raced from room to room and out the open doors to pick fruit in the gardens, then back to dance in the chapels and splash in the reflecting pools.

Finally the chanting drew him into the Great Sanctuary. Ten thousand voices were singing with such joy that he couldn't hold back the tears. The massive doors were thrown open, and an endless river of people was flowing up from the valley. Families brought their children for blessing. The aged raised their hands in praise. Every inch of the gigantic room was filled with rejoicing. And all were reaching toward the amazing loveliness at the front. The painting towered above them, and out of it rushed the colors of heaven in a waterfall that sprayed glowing mist into the farthest corners of the room. The touch of the tiniest drop brought ecstasy. Walking among the people were the Beings that Alex had seen in the windows, but how differently they looked now; they were majestic, like gods, yet their eyes were soft with love. They reached out to everyone around them touching and blessing wherever they went.

Then he saw the girl.

She was seated in a corner, and hundreds of children were bringing her flowers. A baby was asleep in her arms. If he had thought that she was lovely before, her appearance now stunned him. Gone was the pallor of the Cathedral. Her face glowed with joy. Her hair seemed to glisten with starlight. And as she looked at him, he felt ravishing love. But then her face began to change. Slowly it transformed into the face in the moonlight and her chant was of sorrow and fear.

Once more he was flying above the garden-world. But now gigantic columns of smoke rose in the distance, spreading out like black rivers in the sky. The beautiful cities were burning, crushed into piles of red-hot stone. The streets were filled with death and horror. The mountains shook with thunder that seemed to come from beneath the ground. Across the plains loomed monsters, a spider with legs that uprooted trees, a bird that shrieked and made cities fall, a horse with wings of lightning that struck fire wherever he flew. And above them hovered a terrifying shadow that seemed to cover half the world. What it was, Alex couldn't make out. But as it moved across the land, destruction spread beneath it. Burning stones dropped from the sky. The world that was a heaven was transformed into hell.

And then he found himself in the Cathedral. But now the doors were closed and the children gone. All that was left of them were painted pictures. He stared out a window and saw the spider weaving a shroud; as it pulled great strands from its body, the voices of the Cathedral sang anguish and doom.

After that came the most frightening vision of all.

Alex heard a hideous roar and something huge and covered with green flames streaked through the air down the hallway. From its wings and glowing body came a searing wind that charred his lungs and burned his flesh to scarlet. And from its mouth came a Song. With terrible, unknown words, it sang the desolation. When it was gone, fiery ashes settled. As they cooled, they turned into the mold that swirled in every crevice of the great building. When it touched the majestic "gods" of the Cathedral, they began to die. Their skin shriveled and cracked, and they dropped to the floor. He saw the lovely girl struggle up the steps to her bed, then fall face down and breathe her last.

After that he awoke.

It was night. The only light came from the red moon shining through the window. Standing at the foot of his bed was Melesh.

20

ANGEL TOMB

"How long have I been sick?" As Alex lay in the bed, he felt weak, but his mind was clear.

The girl replied, "Long enough."

"What does that mean?"

She didn't answer.

"I almost died. I saw horrible things."

"The Master gave you the dreams so you would know who we are and how we got this way."

"All of that really happened?"

She nodded.

Suddenly he was famished. "I'm starving. Is there any food?"

"Can you walk?"

"I . . . think so."

He struggled to sit up, then to stand. Though his legs were wobbly, he managed to follow her out into the hall. Turning a corner, she led him down a narrow passage. As they walked, he stared at her. "In the dreams everything was beautiful—and then it was all destroyed. I saw monsters."

"The Worwil."

"The what?"

"The Worwil. The World Walkers."

"Where did they come from?"

"They're the brothers and sisters of our Master."

"He's one of *them*?"

"The greatest of them all. He was their king."

"What happened?"

"Jealousy and hate. They became jealous of his beauty and the worship the people gave him."

"That's why they wrecked everything?"

"They wanted all of us to die. They trapped us here and tried to kill us. But in his power our Master found a way to keep us alive. When our flesh stopped breathing, he painted our spirits into glass and gave us forms to serve him."

"So your body ... isn't real? It felt real." The words came out before he could stop them and he was embarrassed.

"It's just a shadow of what I was. We await the dawn when our flesh will live again. The ancient prophecies foretell that a warrior will come from another world, and if he is victorious our living death will end."

"And you think that's me?"

"You killed a World Walker. No one else could have done it."

"But how the heck am I supposed to save you? I don't know how to do that."

"You'll be told, but it needs to happen quickly. You're one of us now. If your flesh dies before you free us, you'll be here forever and all hope will be gone."

"So, how long have I got before my body disintegrates?"

"You're young and strong. Probably a week."

"A week?" Alex was appalled. He grew enraged again. "You did this to me. The disease came from your mouth."

"No, the kiss only joined our spirits so I could enter your mind. You started dying when you breathed our air."

"That's your fault too. You could have stopped me from coming in here but you didn't."

"There was no other way. The prophecy said you had to be one of us."

"Why should I believe you? Maybe everything I saw was a lie."

"Believe what you want, but you were shown the truth. Don't you understand *anything*? Lies are evil. Evil is ugly. So if something is beautiful, it can't be a lie, it *has* to be true."

Alex was silent. What she said made sense, but a nagging doubt remained.

Then for a moment he saw her the way she had been in the vision, a goddess with starlight in her hair and love in her eyes. A voice in his mind told him to stop being an idiot. Hadn't he felt wonderful in the world they had shown him? Hadn't it been so much like Heaven that he wanted to stay there forever? What more proof did he need? Before he could think about it anymore, a delicious odor wafted through the hall and all of his attention focused on his belly.

"*Food!* Oh, that smell, it's fantastic. I'm so hungry."

Turning a corner, they arrived at a set of ornate doors encrusted with filth. The girl pulled them open, revealing a majestic, moonlit dining room. Heavy chandeliers swathed with spider webs hung above a long gilt table. Around it sat a dozen chairs rotten with mildew. Though the room was grimy, Alex didn't care. The smell of the food was so wonderful it made him weak. It was coming from a collection of platters arrayed on a large sideboard. Rushing over to them, he stopped and stared in surprise. Though steam rose from them, the platters were empty.

"Hey, what is this, some kind of trick?"

"What do you mean?"

"Where's the food?"

"Right in front of you."

"There's no food here."

"Are you sure?"

"Of course I'm sure. Do you think I'm blind? All there is is steam."

"Look closer."

He bent down. To his amazement, in the dim light, he saw that the platters were covered with exquisite *portraits* of food. A painted ham. A painted turkey with dressing. Painted prime rib with horseradish sauce.

"They're just *pictures*. What am I supposed to do, lick 'em?"

"You *are* blind. But I have something that'll help." Opening a door in the sideboard, she pulled out a carafe filled with dark liquid. Then she poured some into a goblet and handed it to him.

"What's this?"

"Sweet wine."

"I hate wine."

"If you want to eat, you'd better drink it."

Alex brought it up to his nose. It smelled like chocolate. He took a sip. "It's chocolate and cherry." As he drank it down, a hot tingle filled his throat.

"Give me some more."

"Eat first."

Turning to the platters, he was shocked to see that now they were slopping over with food.

"What happened?"

"Just eat."

He didn't need another invitation. Grabbing a plate, he began heaping it with prime rib, country ham, turkey and dressing, and a giant mound of mashed potatoes ladled with thick gravy. On top of that he stacked hot rolls with large pads of butter. As an afterthought, around the edges he tucked in a helping of cranberry sauce. Then he sat down and began stuffing his mouth. With the first bite, the pleasure was so intense that he groaned. Bending close, he almost buried his face in the heaping plate, scooping in the food as fast as he could chew. Soon his cheeks were bulging like a giant squirrel.

When the plate was empty, he filled it again. This time he found platters of fried chicken, corn-on-the-cob, cheeseburgers, and four different kinds of pizza. When that plate had been sucked down, he filled the next with buttery lobster, cheese soufflé, and baked potatoes with sour cream and bacon. Again and again he went back. Soon there were platters of cakes, pies, and warm chocolate chip cookies along with bowls of ice cream and stacks of candy bars. But gradually Alex began to realize that there was something odd about this meal. Even after emptying a dozen platters, he wasn't getting full, not even a little bit.

Finally Melesh said, "That's enough. It's time to go."

"But I'm still hungry."

"This food isn't meant for that."

"What do you mean?"

"It's just meant to taste good."

He stared at her. "What are you talking about? I chewed it and swallowed it. Did it vanish before it got to my stomach?"

"Our Master is such a great artist that he can paint from the hunger in your mind. Being full isn't important. All that matters is the taste and how delicious it is."

"But that's *crazy.*" Alex looked at the platters. He had eaten enough for twenty people, but his stomach was still growling. "What good is the taste if you're starving to death? I want real food, even if it's just a hunk of bread."

"We have nothing like that here. All we can give you is the pleasure of a memory."

"So this was all *fake*?"

"It was a gift." Her eyes flashed with anger. "You're so selfish. You never think about anybody but yourself. Did you see *me* eat anything?"

"No."

"Why do you think that is?"

"You don't get hungry anymore."

"You're wrong." Tears were in her eyes. "I die with hunger every minute."

"So why didn't you eat?"

"Because I can't taste anything. All I can do is smell it. Do you know what I went through just watching you eat?"

"I'm sorry."

"Forget it." She wiped the tears away. Once more she poured a glass of the wine and handed it to him. "Drink this. It'll help the hurt in your stomach for awhile."

"What is this stuff?" He stared at the goblet.

"Don't ask, just drink."

He downed it. For some reason it didn't taste as good as before, but it did dull the ache.

"We've got to hurry. The Master wants to see you."

A chill passed through him. "About what?"

"Come on." She headed toward the door.

"Hey, wait, what does he want?"

"Just come."

Alex gulped. Suddenly he wasn't thinking about hunger anymore. Getting up, he followed her out into the hall. As he left the dining room, he looked back. On the sideboard sat the serving platters, cold and empty.

Melesh walked fast. Still weak, Alex struggled to keep up.

"Look, what if I'm not who you think I am? I mean, what if I'm not this big warrior from outer space?"

"You're the One, we know it."

"Yeah, well, the problem is *I* don't know it. And what if … I can't do … whatever it is … he wants?"

In a cold voice she replied, "Here is what will happen if you fail. One evening you'll wake up to agony worse than you've ever known. You'll grovel and shriek in your bed until it feels like you're tearing yourself to pieces. Then you'll leave your flesh never to return. After that you'll find out what hunger really is. You'll remember everything you've ever wanted and want it more. Every desire will be like a burning wound. You'll thirst with a fire that no water can quench, lust with a passion that no touch can fulfill, fear with a terror that no love can soften. Every beautiful thing you've ever known will become a desperate longing, and you'll scream, trying to forget, because remembering will be such agony, but your mind will make you live it all again, every touch, every taste, every thought, every smell from your whole life, over and over. You'll rage, and the rage will only make you remember and hunger more. You'll weep tears enough to drown a world, but not enough to drown your memories. You'll spend forever longing for the things that were … and might have been."

"Is that the way … you are now?" Alex was stunned.

"Every second."

"It sounds like … hell."

"Don't say that word." She screamed at him, trembling with rage.

"Okay. All right."

Quickly she got control of herself. "Just remember, you must not fail." A moment later they reached the door to his bedroom and stopped.

"What are we doing here?"

"I told you, the Master wants to see you."

"He's in *there*?"

"He's everywhere."

She opened the door and held it for him. But when he was inside, she didn't follow. The door slammed shut.

"Hey!"

He tried to open it again but it was locked.

"Hey, what's going on?"

Suddenly strands of coldness touched his back and a shudder passed through his body.

Slowly he turned.

The *frame.*

Something was happening inside it.

It had changed from gray to black.

What Alex saw was a universe without stars, a living night. And as he watched, it began oozing like a cloud, out of the frame and down the wall. He tried to cry out, to run, but he couldn't move. In horror he stared as the darkness crawled across the floor toward him, and he heard a soft singing voice, calling his name, whispering for him to come. The mist touched his shoes and moved up his legs. He felt himself rise into the air and begin drifting toward the glass. Though no sound came from his mouth, his mind shrieked with terror. Gradually his body turned until he was floating face down, and inch by inch he moved with excruciating slowness. With every inch the coldness grew. Finally, when the glass was only a foot away, it became unbearable. He closed his eyes. Then he felt the top of his head touch the freezing surface. It was so cold it felt like fire burning through his hair. But the glass didn't hold him back. He began passing through it, entering whatever was beyond. He felt knife-edges of frost scrape down his head and shoulders until they reached his elbows.

Then he stopped.

His body hung with his torso half inside the frame and the rest of him suspended in the room. Opening his eyes, he *screamed*! He was hanging over the edge of a sheer cliff above an abyss that seemed to go down forever. The wall beneath him was of crystal and within it raged tongues of dark fire. They leaped toward him like living shadows, stopped only by the transparent barrier. Alex knew that if his whole body slid through the glass, he would fall and never stop. He was desperate to pull back inside, but he couldn't move.

Deep in the abyss a form was rising toward him. Though he couldn't make out what it was, he knew it was vast and covered with rippling light. Sweat poured down his face. More than anything he had to get away. Whatever was down there, he couldn't bear to see it. He fought to break the glass. Better to be cut to pieces than to look at the thing rising out of the dark. But his efforts did no good.

Nearer.

His mind began to freeze and he stopped struggling. He was like a tiny animal chained in a trap, waiting to die in the jaws of a tiger. He tried to close his eyes, but his eyelids wouldn't work.

Closer.

As the thing floated upward, Alex saw that the light was coming from ripples of flame, streaking back and forth, fading and congealing, across what appeared to be a smooth mountain of ice. He struggled to understand, but it was incomprehensible. Then slowly the form beneath the fire began to take shape. He was looking down onto the top of a gigantic head that was rising toward him. Behind the head, attached to the shoulders, were two huge appendages. Gradually he saw that they were *wings*, tightly closed, as though unable to move.

Yard by yard the monster came nearer. In a few moments its wings rose past him and then towered above. The top of its head was very close now and as he looked down at it, to his amazement he found that he could see straight into the skull. Its bones and skin were of glass and inside surged rivers of blood in ten million colors.

Slowly the forehead of the giant ascended in front of him. Alex was like an ant staring at a mountain. And then its eyes came level with his.

He had never seen such eyes. In them were grandeur and purpose, rage and disdain, arrogance and hate. Yet how lovely they were, the colors of Heaven streaked with the shadings of hell. Alex knew that he could look into those eyes forever, for this was his god, Lammortan, Painter of the Universe.

And the eyes were crying.

From them flowed tears of blood.

As he stared, transfixed, a voice whispered, "Child of the Wind ... *look ...*"

He had no choice but to obey. His eyes were made to stare downward. The body of the giant seemed to go on forever and through its crystal flesh, he could see organs surging with blood the color of rainbows. But the creature couldn't move. It was bound hand and foot with mighty chains of crimson, and horrifying wounds covered its flesh. From them flowed blood in steaming rivers that fell away into the abyss.

Then the voice whispered again. *"Now, I will teach you all that you must know."*

21

MR. HYDROGEN

From the moment she entered the darkness, the experience hadn't been horrible at all. For something to be horrible, you had to "feel," and all "feeling" had ended. There had been a flash of coldness when her body reached the glass, but after that Tori had found herself in a swirling, dreamy place, drifting on a soft wind through a universe without stars. The voice—her mother's voice—had vanished. As she drifted, her memories seemed to jumble together and fade into gray fuzziness. It occurred to her that in a little while even her name might fuzz away and she would go on forever not even knowing who she was. The thought was vaguely disturbing, so she decided to make herself remember who she was. Over and over she repeated, "I'm Tori. That's my name. T-o-r-i. *Tori* ..." But after a few minutes she couldn't remember why remembering it was so important. Then she couldn't remember what it was that she was trying to remember, so she stopped. The fog in her mind whispered that the only important thing was to sleep. The idea was so nice that she closed her eyes.

But then she opened them again.

A very unusual sensation was prickling inside her. At first it was mildly irritating and she tried to ignore it. Then it got worse. Slowly it began to feel as though she were seeping out of herself, as if the thing that made her who she was had begun to congeal in a mist just outside her skin. It didn't hurt, but a weirdness about it kept her awake. The strangest moment of all came when she heard a popping sound and could see her body as though she had split in two. After the "pop" her mind became clear. She remembered everything.

So there she was.

Tori staring at Tori.

Twins tumbling through the universe facing each other.

And the Tori in front of her wasn't looking so good. Her clothes were rumpled as if she had slept in them all night and her hair was a terrible mess. If only she had a brush. Then she started laughing. What was she going to do, float through the universe brushing her own hair? Suddenly she understood the silliness of it all. How worried she had always been about looking perfect, wearing just the right clothes, saying just the right things, because if she didn't, no one would like her. But all of that was about the "outside Tori," and it was the girl inside that really mattered, because when you came unstuck from yourself, whatever was living under your skin would go on forever.

As Tori watched, her "twin" began drifting away. She waved to her, but the twin didn't wave back, which wasn't very friendly considering all the time they had spent together. After a few moments she was gone.

Alone in the universe once more.

But at least her brain wasn't fuzzy and she didn't want to sleep. However, she did hope something would happen, because floating this way could get *really* boring. It was then that everything got even crazier. Drifting in *nothing* as she was, out of the corner of her eye she saw *something* pull up beside her. Where it came from she couldn't tell, but rolling along in the emptiness was an ancient Cadillac limousine, faded-red with blue-tinted windows. Hunkered behind the wheel was the same funny driver who had taken them to the airport. The old man smiled and waved in the friendliest manner. His window was down so it was easy for them to talk.

"Well, howdy do there. How're you today?"

"Oh, I'm fine." Tori didn't even try to make sense of it. She was just glad to have some company.

"Just out for a little swim I see. Nice day for it too, even if the water *is* a little murky."

Swimming. What an interesting idea. She began to paddle with her arms and legs.

"Tell you what. Don't normally pick up hitchhikers, but in your case I'm gonna bend my rules. Think you might need a ride? How 'bout that?"

"Okay." She smiled happily.

"Good. Now, just kinda wiggle your arms like you're doin', an' swim over to the other side of ol' Jezebel and climb in the window."

Tori found that by turning her body and "swimming" it was possible to make her way over the roof of the Cadillac. Then, upside down, she pulled herself into the front seat. The old man laughed as she settled onto the cracked leather.

"Well, that's better now, ain't it?"

"This is *so* freaky."

"In a manner o' speakin' I 'spose you could say so. 'Course, it depends on what you call freaky. Ain't nothin' freakier to me than bein' on the Dan Ryan Expressway headin' into Chicago durin' rush hour. *Whewee.* Some o' the stuff I seen. Now that's what *I* call freaky. This here's just horseplay compared to that. Anyway, you better buckle your seatbelt. We gotta make a quick turn up ahead, and it might get a little bumpy."

It was more than a little bumpy. Suddenly Tori heard a shrieking sound as though the entire car was being torn to pieces. It was exactly like a movie she had seen of a spacecraft reentering Earth's atmosphere. The metal of the hood began to glow fiery red, then the limousine started flipping end over end. Finally there was a terrifying explosion. Tori looked out the window and saw that they were no longer in empty space. The Cadillac was driving along as smoothly as you please through a universe with a billion stars. Spread out in front of her were lovely wisps of galaxies and multicolored clouds of nebula. And the hood was cooling down.

"Totally freaky."

"And derned hard on the paint job too. I keep them cheapo paint places in business. Don't take too many reentry numbers to sandblast your door panels right down to the bone."

"Is this a space ship?" The hood was almost back to normal, but it did seem to be a shade or two lighter.

"You kiddin'? Wouldn't drive one o' them claptraps for the world. Terrible gas mileage. Cadillacs is cheaper and just about as strong too. Tried one o' them compact jobs once. You shoulda seen it after reentry. Nothin' left but a seat cover an' a steerin' wheel. Nope. Nothin's as good as ol' Jezebel."

"But we're in space. If this isn't a space ship, how do we breathe?"

"Hmmm, now that's a very interestin' question." The old man scratched his head. "Have to get back to you on that one."

"Are we in the Milky Way?"

"No, ma'am. Hold on a sec." He fumbled with a pile of maps stuck under the seat until he found the one he wanted.

"Milky Way. Let's see, that's B-20-601238549. There it is. That's in Universe Belda. This here's Zelda. Whole lot prettier, don't you think?"

"If you say so."

Wherever they were, it *was* beautiful. The Cadillac was leaving the edge of a blue-green cloud of star mist and driving into an empty region toward the tail of a slow-moving comet. For a little while Tori was silent. When she spoke again it was in a small voice.

"What happened to me back there? I was in a house, then I floated into a picture frame ..." Her voice trailed off. Strange thoughts and memories were pushing their way into her mind. Suddenly she turned toward the old man as though seeing him for the first time.

"Who are you? Cars don't drive in space."

He looked at her with a twinkle in his eye. "An' I don't normally neither myself, honey. I just make deliveries once in awhile off the beaten path you might say. An' you're right. We ain't been properly introduced. You can call me Mr. Hydrogen."

"Mister *what*?"

"Hydrogen. Got a nice ring to it, don't it? Saw it just the other day an' I thought, you know, that'd make a great name for me ... Hydrogen. It was on a bottle in a drug store. 'Hydrogen peroxide.' Course I only took the first part. Never did like them fancy pantsy hypheneutered kinda names."

"But it's not your *real* name."

"It'll do." He looked at her. "You couldn't pronounce my real name anyway."

Suddenly Tori's attention was drawn to the front. The car was rapidly approaching a strange object hanging in space, a gray rock the size of a mountain. She had seen something like it once in a video at school. "I know what that is. It's an asteroid."

"Home sweet home."

"You *live* there?"

"I know it's a humble place. Never make it into one o' your highfalutin' House an' Vegetable magazines, but it's cozy enough for me."

As the Cadillac flew nearer, Tori saw that carved into one side of the boulder was the face of a gigantic clock. It had hundreds of hands of different sizes and was marked off into millions of hours instead of just twelve.

"Why is there a clock on it?"

"To tell what time it really is instead of what people want it to be."

Every moment the clock was getting bigger. The Cadillac flew on until only a little piece of it was visible because it was so close. In fact, it began to look as if they were going to crash into it.

"Don't you think you'd better stop?"

"Just give a minute here. We'll be fine." The old man picked up a rusted metal box from the floor and pushed a button. Nothing happened. "Drat!" He pushed it again. Still nothing. "Drat, drat, drat!"

They were getting dangerously close. Rummaging under the seat, he found an ancient oilcan. After dousing the rusty metal with generous squirts, he banged the box on the steering wheel.

"We're gonna crash!" Tori closed her eyes.

Once more he jammed the button. At the last possible moment a section of rock slid open and they flew inside.

"Sorry 'bout that. Been tryin' to get a new garage door opener. But last time I checked, they were out of 'em at the Home and Doohickey Depot."

The limousine had pulled to a stop inside a massive cavern at least a mile long and hundreds of feet high. Far above were the intricate workings of the huge clock. But beneath it the cavern appeared to be a storage chamber. Every inch of space on the walls was covered with little clocks, millions and millions of them in every imaginable size, shape, and color. Hundreds of steel ladders led up to a maze of crisscrossing catwalks where there were more clocks. It was like a vast warehouse in space for the greatest clockmaker in the universe. The old man opened the door and got out. Tori was right behind him. She stared in wonder. The whole room was filled with ticking, clicking, and bonging.

"Why are there so many clocks? All of them in the world must be here."

"Oh, there's more'n that. Lots, lots more."

"But why?"

"Well, these aren't your regular clocks." He began leading her through the cavern. "They keep a special kinda time."

Tori noticed that the nearest clocks weren't keeping time at all. They weren't even running. And they looked very old. The ticking clocks were still ahead.

"How come these are stopped?"

"'Cause the people stopped."

"What do you mean?"

"There's a clock in here for every person who ever lived or ever will. And as long as their body keeps chuggin', it keeps tickin'." They entered a section of ticking clocks, but even as they walked, Tori heard gentle chimes and saw that many were coming to a stop.

"You mean, when they don't tick anymore, the person is dead?"

"That's what some people call it."

"Can't you wind them up again?"

"Nope. Spring's only good for one lifetime."

For a while they walked along in silence with Tori looking at the clocks. Suddenly, ahead, she saw a different section. In it, none of the clocks were operating, but they looked brand new.

"What are those?"

"Those are for little ones that aren't born yet."

But even as he spoke, thousands of them began ticking merrily.

"Hear that? I like this part best of all. Nothin' like the sound of a new clock when it's just gettin' started."

Tori stopped and looked back down the cavern. Being in this place filled her with awe. It was as though she could see life moving in a wave that had started long ago and was just now reaching to where she stood, a wave of time in a cavern of clocks. She turned and looked ahead. Far in the distance there was an end to the cavern where there were no clocks at all.

"What's that up there, that empty place?"

"Oh, that's where there isn't any time anymore."

"No time?"

Just then a little blue grandmother clock nearby started to chime gently. Then it was silent.

"That one just stopped. It's so pretty."

The old man stood looking at it with her. "Ol' Grandma Watson. Been tickin' away almost a hundred years. Wonderful lady. Did nice things for lotsa people. But her spring finally just wore out."

"Can't you fix it and make it run a little longer?"

"Nope. I'm not the clockmaker. I just tidy up the place."

"Could I see mine?" Mr. Hydrogen nodded and led her to an out-of-the-way corner. There, sitting on a tiny shelf, was a pink and yellow clock covered with blue flowers.

"Oh, I love it. But ... it's stopped."

"Only for awhile. You see? It's got a lot o' time left on it. Lots an' lots of time."

"Does it mean I'm ... half dead or something? Are you sure it will go again?"

"For you, there's special instructions. Happens once in a great while."

"You can make people stop living ... and then live again?" Tori felt a twinge of fear. The old man saw it and took her hand.

"Not all by myself, honey. I'm just the caretaker. An' you know that big clock outside? That one's for me. Even the time spirit don't go on forever."

"That's who you are?"

"Yep. An speakin' of time, there isn't much left for our little visit. We pulled a snaffle on 'em an' we gotta stay on our toes."

"What's a snaffle?"

"A trick. Ol' Paint Buckets thinks he's got you like all the rest. But we fooled him."

"Fooled who?"

"The nasty one who pulled you into that frame. Have we got a *surpriiise* to stick in his canvas!"

Tori shivered. Suddenly she was remembering the singing darkness that had taken her away.

"He thinks he's so high an' mighty. Thinks he kin steal time, an' I been lettin' him do it. But things are changin', you just wait. Now, come out to my observatory. We gotta parlay."

Walking fast, the old man led Tori through a doorway tucked in the shelves, and they stepped into a glass bubble. The view was breathtaking. It was like standing in the middle of the stars, floating in sparkles and darkness. But then something far away caught her eye.

"What's that way out there?"

"Now, I gotta show you somethin', and it isn't very nice. So buckle your seatbelt."

The thing grew larger. It was some kind of monstrous building floating like a ghost in space. Smoky tentacles reached out from it in every direction.

"Sometimes when your body gets sick, there's one place that's causin' the whole trouble, an' you gotta fix that one spot so everything else can get well. You understand what I mean?"

"No."

"You ever had a bad pimple?"

"My sister did. It got infected."

"That's just exactly what I'm talkin' about. Now that right there's like a big nasty pimple right on the nose of the universe. An' it's been gettin' pussier for thousands of years."

"My mom had to pop the one on my sister. She screamed."

"An' this one's gotta get popped too. Remember in your sister's pimple there was a puky little knot right at the core?"

"I didn't look at it."

"Well, there was. An' there's a puky little knot at the core of this one. Except it's a person. Remember what pulled you into that picture frame?"

"Old Paint Buckets?"

"Exactly right. He's the core o' the pimple."

"Why do you call him Paint Buckets?"

"'Cause he thinks he's a great artist when he's nothin' but a copycat. If he stuck to paintin' ugly little pictures it'd be bad enough, but he kills people. He went bad a long time ago, an' that's all I can say about it. But somebody's gotta stop him before he makes the whole universe turn into rot. Now listen to me, 'cause we don't have much time. I'm a good friend of that old lady Bellwind. We ain't spoken for years on end, and she don't know nothin' about what I'm doin', but we're fightin' on the same side, if you know what I mean. Now your brother got himself in all kinds of trouble ..."

"You know about Alex?"

"'Course I do."

"Where is he? I want to see him."

"Well, he's in a bit of a pickle."

"I could help."

"Only way you can help is by listenin' hard and doin' exactly what you hear. The thing that's got hold of your brother ain't nothin' to mess with. I call him Paint Buckets, but his real name's Lammortan, and he lives in that big pimple out there. That's where your brother is, an' that's where you gotta go if you want to help him. You willin'?"

Tori gulped. "Yes."

"You're a spunky little kid. Remember the snaffle we pulled? Well, this is what we done. He thinks he's got you right where he wants you, an' he's half right. But we tricked him. He got the half that don't count. He thinks you're stone dead and in his power, but the Painter's a fool. Comes from sniffin' too much enamel in closed-up places. Now, in a few seconds I'm gonna send you back to join your sleepin' half an' you'll be where he lives."

"What am I supposed to do when I get there?"

"Don't need to know that right now, 'cause there's gonna be somebody to help you every step of the way."

"Will you come with me?"

"Nope, no place to park the limousine. But I'll keep up with what's goin' on, you can bet on that."

"Well, who's gonna be there?"

"Don't you worry none, honey. You'll meet a new friend. Just do whatever he says. Now you're gonna fall asleep for a while, an' when you wake up it'll be in a scary place, but don't be afraid. This new friend'll be right there with you. You got that?"

"Okay."

"An' whatever happens, remember this. Help always comes in the strangest packages. Oh, yeah, I got somethin' for you. A little gift."

He reached into his pocket and pulled out a silver chain. Dangling on the end was a tiny stone filled with starlight.

"Oh, it's so pretty."

He fastened it around her neck. "Now, tuck this away and don't let nobody see it. There's somethin' buried under the light. At the right time you'll know what it is."

Tori stared at the pendant and was about to ask another question, but Mr. Hydrogen only shook his head and put his finger to his lips. Suddenly there was a powerful blast of wind. The glass bubble seemed to dissolve, and once more she was flying away into darkness. The last thing she remembered was her friend standing in the observatory, waving and blowing kisses. This time, flying was like falling asleep.

22

MIRICK

First there was humming, a tiny buzzing noise. Though it was soft, it penetrated through the darkness of Tori's mind, and slowly she began to awaken.

What *was* that sound? It was annoying, and it was very close to her ear.

Then it started calling her name. "Torriiiizzz ... Toriiiiizzz ... zzzz ... Toriiiiizzz ... zzzz ... Toriiiizzz ..." The sound left her ear, and a little breeze fluttered over her cheek. Then something settled on her nose making it tickle. Her eyes popped open. The first thing she saw was a tiny light. The humming sound seemed to be coming out of it.

"*Yick*, a bug." She brushed it away.

The light fluttered above her face, and a small voice angrily said, "Don't do that. Keep your gigantic hands to yourself." The voice was coming from a moth. But it wasn't a normal moth. Its body was glowing. "I can assure you that I find humans just as unpleasant as you find me. However, did I say, 'Yick, a girl'? I did not. I restrained myself, and I suggest that you do the same. Yelling 'Yick, a bug' does not establish a friendly working relationship."

"A *talking* bug—and you're *funny looking*." In front of the wings was a miniature face, and it was quite comical.

"Please! Have you no self-control?"

"Are you real?"

"Look, if something is right in front of your nose you'd better assume it's real until it proves otherwise."

"My sister has a bug collection."

"Now that was uncalled for. What if I told you that my brother has a people collection—all stuck on gigantic pins—how would it make you feel?"

"I'm sorry. It's just hard to get used to a talking bug—*yick*. Where I come from, people don't talk to bugs, they squash 'em."

"I am well aware of the brutal proclivities of your race." The moth had put a little more distance between himself and Tori. "We have a lot to do and not much time to do it in. Squashing me will slow things down considerably. So restrain your natural instincts."

"Are you the one Mr. Hydrogen told me about?"

"I don't know any Mr. Hydrogen, but I do know that I'm assigned to you for better or for worse. Probably the latter. My name is Mirick. Do you get scared easily?"

"Of bugs?"

"Of *anything*."

"Pretty much. And when I get really freaked I start screaming."

"Well, if you don't mind, try not to do any screaming right now. Stuff some hair in your mouth—you have enough of it. The place we're in is rather unpleasant, but it looks a lot worse than it is. Now take a deep breath, then sit up slowly. And whatever you do, don't scream. Is that clear?"

"I'll try not to. Is it full of bugs?"

"I am the *only bug* present."

"Good. Okay."

Tori sat up and almost did scream. She was in a huge cavern that stretched away in every direction as far as she could see, and it glimmered with eerie light. The light came from thousands of blue candles that burned on slender candlesticks spread throughout the chamber. By their flames she could see row after row of small stone tables, and on each lay the body of a child. There were thousands of them, from little babies to Tori's age, and all were covered with layers of dust as though they had been there for a very long time.

"Are they all ... dead?"

"The maker of this place thinks so."

"What happened to them?"

Before Mirick could answer there was the distant creak of a door.

"All right, they're coming. Quick, lie down and pretend to be dead."

"Who's coming?"

"*Just do it.* I'm going to hide in your hair."

Frightened, Tori lay back down and the moth crawled in next to her ear.

"Yick, bugs in my hair."

"*Please be quiet.* Now, nothing can hurt you as long as you don't move. So go to sleep or something."

A moment later coldness filled the air, and there was the sound of many footsteps. Trying to see, Tori narrowed her eyelids into slits which made everything blurry. Moving toward her were dozens of strange shapes, half people, half colored shadows, and each was carrying a small crystal bottle. A tense whisper filled her ear.

"Stop twitching or you'll give us away."

Suddenly, directly above her head, appeared the cruelest face that she had ever seen. It was a regal-looking woman. Then came more faces until she was surrounded. Some were men and some were women, but all were filled with a breathless kind of hunger like wild animals gathered around a kill. They watched as the regal woman placed her bottle on Tori's chest just above her heart. Then, bending down, she covered the opening with her lips and began to suck.

It was the most awful thing that Tori had ever experienced. It felt like her soul was being pulled up into a knotted little clot. Desperately she tried to control her terror, but the harder the woman sucked the worse it became. The other faces watched with ravenous anticipation.

Just when Tori was about to scream, a strange warmth radiated through her body. It started close to her throat, where the pendant the old man had given her hung. When it filled her chest, the awful clotted feeling vanished. Suddenly, instead of wanting to scream, she felt like shrieking with laughter. The whole situation was so totally stupid. A funny-looking woman was sucking on an empty bottle. And it looked like she might suck Tori's shirt right into it, and the whole thing would clog in her mouth in a great big wad. The image was so hilarious that Tori didn't think she could stand it.

Finally, with a cry of frustration, the woman jerked the bottle away. "What's wrong with this filthy little beast? She's like an empty husk. Don't the offspring of her world have souls?"

A shadow-faced man edged her aside. "You're not sucking hard enough.

Some of the older ones need vigorous concentration." Placing his bottle on Tori's chest, he started sucking like a vacuum cleaner. She could almost hear the motor in his mouth, which made her want to laugh even more. Finally, with a roar of rage, he gave up.

"Let me try, let me try." Next came another woman, but her suction was pitiful. A fourth made a half-hearted attempt that wasn't even worth talking about.

"The Master must have taken every drop," the man growled.

"But he always leaves us the crumbs." Whined another voice. "He always does that. This is worse than not eating at all."

The regal-faced woman screamed, "Shut up! If only he would let us consume each other, I would devour every one of you so I wouldn't have to listen to your pathetic moans."

At that moment a deep male voice yelled, *"The dawn is coming."*

The faces vanished. Tori heard footsteps rush back across the cavern. The heavy cold that had been around her disappeared. A moment later a door opened, then slammed shut. Mirick fluttered out of her hair.

"Not badly done, not badly at all." Landing on the edge of the candlestick, he stared at her. "I have to say I'm surprised. I thought you were going to scream, and then we'd have been in a very nasty mess."

"I almost did." She sat up. "I was afraid they were gonna suck my shirt off."

"What an odd creature you are. It wasn't your shirt they wanted, it was your soul. They've lost their own, and it's the only thing that will appease their hunger. They were particularly aggressive because they haven't had a meal in quite a few centuries. Come along, we have work to do." The moth fluttered off in the opposite direction from the one the strange people had taken. Tori climbed down and followed, but as she hurried along, she couldn't help staring at all the children lying in neat rows around her.

"Did they suck the souls from all these kids?"

"They tried."

"It's so horrible. How did they get so many of them here? Did they steal them from their parents?"

"That's the worst part. The parents brought them and gave them away."

"How could they do that? Didn't they know what was going to happen to them?"

"They knew enough."

"It makes me want to cry."

"Many tears have been shed in this place."

Finally they reached the far side of the cavern, and Mirick settled to the floor next to a crevice in the wall.

"This is the way out. You've got to squeeze through this opening."

"Are you *serious*?" Tori knelt down and tried to look into it, but it was pitch black. "I can't get through there."

"Yes, you can. And you must."

"I *can't*. I'm *too big*."

"While you were asleep, I took careful measurements. It'll be a tight fit, but you can do it."

"What'd you measure with, a moth ruler?"

"It doesn't matter."

"Where does it go?"

"Before this building was constructed, a beautiful castle stood here that belonged to the first king of Boreth. A monster called the Painter thought he destroyed it, but there are hidden parts that still exist. This leads to an ancient staircase."

"But what if I get stuck?"

"You won't. After a few feet it opens out into a corridor with enough space for even a giant like you. Now, let's go." With that, he disappeared into the wall.

"Why can't we go through the door those people-things used?"

Mirick's voice echoed from inside. "Because it leads to where most of them are sleeping, and we've got to stay hidden as long as we can. Now, do you want to help your brother or not?"

"Are we going to find Alex?" Suddenly Tori was excited.

"That's what all of this is about."

"All right, I guess I'll try." Lying flat on her stomach and pushing with her feet, she was able to slide her head and shoulders into the crevice, but it was very tight. By the light from the moth's body, she could see a few feet ahead.

"It's too small. I can't get through." She wailed.

"Yes, you can. Keep pushing."

Inch by inch, grunting and struggling, Tori forced herself into the narrow gap. Finally her whole body was inside, but she could barely move. *"I'm stuck."*

Mirick burned brighter and his voice deepened. "Tori Lancaster, the power to be and to do has been given to you, but you must try harder than you have tried to do anything in your life. *And you must do it right now!*"

She began pushing and pulling with all her might.

An inch.

Six inches.

Tears came, but she kept on going.

A foot.

Then the crevice grew wider.

She could raise her head a little.

After that her shoulders.

Suddenly the top half of her was out, but the bottom half was stuck.

"You're almost through. *Pull!*" The moth fluttered in front of her nose. With one last great effort she flopped onto a stone floor. There she lay exhausted, sobbing.

"Excellent, if I do say so myself." Mirick was glowing normally again. "Of course, I have to take a bit of credit for some wonderfully precise measurements, but getting your giant body through that hole did require a bit of courage."

Instantly Tori was so aggravated that she stopped crying. "I do *not* have a giant body. I may look big to a creepy, little bug, but I'm *not* a fat person."

"Semantics. Clearly you don't know how to take a compliment. However, I shall overlook your lack of social graces. Now, we have a few minutes for you to rest and eat."

"Eat? Is there food in here?" Slowly she sat up and looked around. She was in a small square chamber carved from solid rock. By the tiny light from Mirick's body, she could just make out the bottom of a staircase. The moth fluttered to a small pile that lay on the floor. It was a mound of nuts and dried berries. Crawling over, Tori picked up a handful.

"Is this all there is?"

"Don't tell me you don't like nuts and berries."

"I don't like crunchy things."

"Crunchy things?"

"Stuff that crunches when you chew it — except cheese snacks. They're crunchy, but that's okay. Mostly I like food that comes wrapped in paper. You know, hamburgers, chicken strips, that sort of thing."

"We have no cheese snacks, hamburgers, or chicken strips, whatever they are. It sounds like the food of monsters. Do you know how long it took to bring all this down here so you could fill your stomach? It had to be done one nut and one berry at a time. And they came from far away. This is a month of hard work. Now, are you hungry or not? I can assure you there will be no food 'wrapped in paper' for a very long time. Chicken strips. Ugh."

"I *am* hungry."

"Then eat. We don't have time to sit around talking about your repugnant gastronomic practices."

Reluctantly she put a berry in her mouth and chewed. "Well, they're not too bad."

"I'm so glad they meet with your tepid approval."

She took some more. "I'll bet flying them in was hard work for a bug."

"Oh, I didn't bring them here."

"Who did?"

"Two very dependable and hard-working rats."

"Oh, yick, rat food!" Tori spit out what she had been chewing and tried to scrape the residue off her tongue.

"Don't tell me you're prejudiced against rats too. I suppose your sister has a rodent collection."

"They're awful. They're dirty. They're full of disease."

"I beg your pardon. My friends would be deeply insulted at such slanderous allegations. Whatever rats are like in your world, in this one they are quite clean."

"They are?"

"Immaculate. They cleanse themselves thoroughly twice a day with their tongues."

"OH, YICK!"

"Well, what did you want them to do, take mineral baths? You are a very exasperating creature. Now stop thinking about how the food *got* here, and be grateful for the fact that it *is* here."

"I can't. I just can't eat it."

"Fine, then let's go. But when you're starving you're going to wish that you hadn't been so picky."

Tori stared at the pile. She was *very* hungry. "You're making me do a lot of nasty things." She whimpered, "If I die from eating rat stuff it'll be all your fault."

"I shall take full responsibility."

With a look as though she were eating poison, Tori picked up several berries and put them in her mouth. Instantly into her mind came the image of little rat fingers wrapped around them and she started to gag.

"Oh, please." The moth stared at her disgustedly. "They are delicious."

In spite of herself, Tori knew that he was right. She took some more. And then a few nuts.

"I'm thirsty."

"Come over here." The moth flew to a corner and hovered above a little pool of water. Tori crawled over and stared at it.

"How'd this get here? Did the rats carry it in their cheeks?"

"*It came from the ground.* Do you see those drips running down the wall?"

She squinted. "I think so."

"Well?"

"Okay, I guess it's all right, but it is on the floor. I suppose you don't have any cups."

"No, we have no cups, goblets, or golden chalices."

"That means I have to drink like a dog." Bending down, she drank. It tasted wonderful. Finally she sat up and wiped her mouth.

"Now put some 'rat food' in your pockets. You're going to need it. We've got to get going. We've wasted too much time here." The moth fluttered toward the stairs. When her pockets were crammed, Tori followed. The steps were old and worn, and if it hadn't been for the light from the insect it would have been easy to fall.

For a few moments Tori climbed in silence. Then she asked, "Why did the mothers and fathers give away their kids? Did they stop loving them?"

"They loved themselves more."

"There was a baby girl on one of those tables. She looked so sweet. If I had a baby like that I'd never let anyone hurt her, even if I had to die. Why were we brought to this awful world where they give away their children? We weren't bothering anybody. We were just flying in a plane to be with our father."

"You were with Bellwind. Didn't she tell you anything?"

"Not much."

Mirick sighed. "Well, there are things that you should know, and it's time for you to hear them. Your family on Earth is not what you think it is."

"What do you mean?"

"A thousand years ago you had a grandfather. But he was not born on your planet; he was born on this one."

"How did he get to Earth?"

"That isn't important. Who he *was* is all that matters. He was the last of our great kings. During the time of the Great Dying he took something to Earth to hide it. While he was there, he married and had a son. Down through all the generations your family has been watched and feared. Invisible enemies have tried to destroy you. But through it all your ancestors were protected. When the time was right, Bellwind came and brought you home."

"What do you mean *home*? This isn't my home."

"But it is. You are a child of two worlds, and I will tell you the story of this one. It should be sung, but the sadness is too great for me to make it rhyme. Once this world was called Boreth the beautiful, Garden of the Seven Stars, because seven Great Spirits of Light were chosen to live here. There is a word for them in your language. I believe it is angels."

"I've seen pictures of angels."

"None looked like the images in your mind. If you saw one right now it would appear very strange. They were called the Worwil. Their job was to watch over everything. But one was more powerful than the rest. He could splash the sky with sunsets and streak rainbows in the clouds."

"You mean Old Paint Buckets?"

The moth fluttered backward so he could stare at her. "Who told you that name?"

"Mr. Hydrogen."

"And where did you meet this individual?"

"In outer space. He gave me a ride in his Cadillac."

"You confound me, child. Many strange things are happening right now, and I don't pretend to know them all. But if you ever come face-to-face with Lammortan, I suggest that you refrain from calling him 'Old Paint Buckets.' He is not known for a scintillating sense of humor."

"Okay. But I hope I never see him. Mr. Hydrogen told me he's like a pimple on the nose of the universe and he needs to get popped."

"What a fascinatingly crude but accurate analogy."

"You said he was like an angel. I thought angels were supposed to be good."

"Oh, he started out good. For countless years he brought beauty to everything he touched."

"Then what made him turn into a pimple?"

"All over Boreth people loved what he did and told him so. The more he heard how wonderful he was, the more he wanted to hear it. Finally he lied and said that he was the one who had created everything. He told the people that if they didn't bow down to him he would stop the rain from falling and keep the sun from rising in the sky."

"Could he really do that?"

"No, but he was in charge of painting the clouds. So he just started painting them darker with a very dry brush."

"So everyone did what he wanted?"

"Not at first. The kings, your ancestors, joined with the other Worwil and fought against him. There were many battles. The war continued for centuries, and Boreth was almost destroyed. But slowly the Painter began to win. People saw what was happening and became afraid. They were tired of war so they believed his lies. Lammortan built a great cathedral where they could worship him. So they brought their gifts and became his slaves. But they had forgotten the most important thing of all. There is one who is above the Worwil, and he is so much greater that they are like tiny candles compared to his Burning Fire. On this world he is called the One Who Lives in the Mists, for his home is on a Mountain that reaches to the crown of the sky. He is so high above that the people had stopped believing in his existence. But he is the true Artist who paints all things."

"So what happened?"

"When Lammortan had almost won, a terrible plague struck the world. The people began dying. The Painter told them that there was only one way for them to be healed. They must give him their children. A life for a life. He promised if they obeyed not only would their sickness go away, he would make them live forever."

"And they believed that?"

"Most did, but not all. Some cried out to the One Who Lives in the Mists. Lammortan hated them above all others. To those who would not sacrifice their children he gave a hideous disease that hardened their flesh and killed them with agonizing slowness."

"But the rest brought their children."

"They did. When it was too late, they found out that he had lied. The sacrifices didn't save them. They died, but their spirits live on, forced to go back each night to the place where they gave their children away and remember the terrible thing they did. Then they must stand and worship the murderer."

"Those people-things back in the cave? Were they some of the parents?"

"No. And they aren't people."

"What are they?"

"Spirit creatures who followed Lammortan into darkness. He keeps them alive to serve him."

At that moment they turned a corner and came to a blank wall.

"The stairs don't go anywhere."

"Yes, they do." The moth fluttered to a small crack in the stone. "Stick your left hand in and pull it out quickly."

"Why? What's inside?"

"It will open a door."

"I don't see any door."

"Just do it."

"Are there bugs in there?"

"There are no bugs."

"Some other yucky thing?"

The moth began beating his tiny head on the stone.

"What are you doing?"

"Expressing extreme frustration."

"Don't do that. You'll hurt yourself."

"Will you please stick your hand in the hole so we can get out of here?"

"All right, but you don't have to get upset. You're not used to kids, are you?" Cautiously she inserted her hand in the crack. To her surprise, it felt like her fingers were sliding into a stone glove that fitted perfectly. Quickly she pulled it out.

"Okay, where's the door?"

There was a scraping sound, and a section of the wall slid away revealing a hole just large enough for her to crawl through.

"All right, let's go." The moth landed on her shoulder. "And from here on out you've got to whisper because we don't want to wake the sleepers."

"Who are they?"

"You'll see in a minute."

Kneeling, Tori crawled through. On the other side hung a heavy curtain. She pushed it back and a cloud of mold billowed around her making her sneeze.

"Shhh."

"What do you want? I can't stop a sneeze."

The stone panel slid shut. She stood up and looked around. Shafts of dusty sunlight revealed what appeared to be a gloomy chapel. Grime-encrusted tapestries sagged from the walls, and masses of cobwebs draped from the ceiling. Twenty rows of broken pews faced toward a low platform at the front. On it squatted a grotesque chair with stumpy legs and a high, round back that was deeply carved with twisted gargoyle faces. Clawlike armrests extended outward making it look like a throne. On the chair sprawled a pile of bones and dirt.

And at the top rested a blackened skull.

23

THE MAGNIFICENCE OF WANDERSPOON

To her surprise, when Amanda awoke she discovered that she felt a little better. The skin on her arm was rough and hard, but it didn't appear like tree bark anymore, and while it was still difficult to move, the stiffness in her joints had diminished. She sat up. The baby was playing quietly with the edge of her shirt, gently grabbing and releasing it while he stared in fascination at his own fingers. It was early morning, and Wanderspoon's wagon was creaking down a dirt track that ran through a desolate gorge. Sheer walls rose on either side, and not a bush or a tree could be seen anywhere.

Amanda forced herself to turn and look toward the front of the wagon. The effort was painful, but at least she could do it. The greasy little man was hunched over asleep. His loud snores were perfectly timed to create a kind of antiphonal response to the periodic squeak that came from the rear axle. It was hilarious, but the humor was lost on her. She was very thirsty, and a water jug was hanging on the seatback. Struggling hard, she managed to crawl over to it. But the instant her fingers touched the strap, Wanderspoon jerked awake.

"What? What–what? *Stop thief! Put that down!*"

He stared at her as though she had been trying to steal gold from his pocket.

"I'm really thirsty and I need a drink."

"Oh, you do, do you? Did you ever think about asking?"

"You were asleep."

"That's right, I was asleep, so you decided to take advantage of me."

"Look, I just want some water. And I need some for the baby."

The little man squinted at her. "What's happened to you? Why are you moving around? Last night you could barely get into the wagon. You should be stiff as a steel plate."

"I don't know, but it doesn't hurt quite as much today. Now, could I *please* have a *drink*?"

Reluctantly he handed her the bottle. "One sip. Not a drop more. There's no use wasting water on someone's who's as good as dead."

"Thanks, I appreciate your concern." Pulling out the stopper, Amanda put the bottle to her lips, but before she could take more than a swallow, he jerked it away. "That's all, that's enough you greedy girl!"

"The baby needs some."

"Oh, fine, use it all up. Have no consideration for your generous benefactor who might have special needs of his own."

Glaring at him, Amanda took back the jug. But when the water touched the baby's tongue, he made a terrible face and spit it out.

"Look at that—the ungrateful little brat!"

"Well, your water tastes like swamp scum."

"Well, neither of you have to drink it then, do you?" Jerking the bottle away from her, he put it between his feet.

"How much farther do we have to go?"

"Oh, very far. I'm sure you'll be dead long before we get there."

"But you said this person, Melania, might be able to help me."

"If we get there in time, which I highly doubt. Even if we do, 'help' is a relative term. Deep inside disordered brains such as yours, there exists a whole series of synaptic connectors autoprogrammed to trigger a set of pitiful responses to a grid of simplistic beliefs. Precisely focused, bolstering verbal/visual stimuli may create psychophysical responses that could mitigate the progression of your psychosomatic dysfunction."

"I have no idea what you just said."

"Of course you don't. Let me try to put it into semi-simian terms. Because your species is marked by stupidity and delusional tendencies, you will believe any horse defecation that's handed to you. Therefore the presentation of a countering delusion may nullify the intensity of your current debilitation, which I have diagnosed as a severe case of dysmorphophobia, an excessive preoccupation with a minor defect in your appearance. Ergo because your arms are turning into branches you have convinced yourself that you are becoming a tree."

"But you said I had a disease that was turning me into one."

"I said you *believed* you had a disease that was making you into one. I was simply condescending to your ignorance."

"Well, do I have a disease or not?"

"Do you believe you do?"

"I feel miserable, I'm stiff, my skin looks like bark, and my fingers are changing into branches ..."

"There you have it. Perception is all that matters. First we must discover why you feel the need to *perceive* yourself as a tree. When that is accomplished, we will begin the arduous task of constructing a more positive self-image. Of course, small steps must come before larger ones. From a tree, we'll try to convince you that you're a bush, then perhaps a weed, and so forth."

"Why are we doing this if the Healer can't help me?"

Wanderspoon stroked his beard and sighed. "Ah, inane child, I suppose there's no alternative but for me to wallow in your psychonecrotic fantasies in the vain hope that I shall be able to find some common ground of communication. Therefore, though it will be like attempting to converse with a slug or a centipede, I shall begin asking questions to which you will mumble responses as your intellect allows. Is that understood?"

"Whatever." Amanda was just too tired to argue.

As the cart creaked along, Wanderspoon began grilling her. For hours he wheedled, browbeat, and badgered until, just for the sake of shutting him up, she had told him about the plane crash, meeting Bellwind, Tori falling into the frame, the tree in the sky, and the horse in the stadium. The only thing she left out was her experience in the tower. That was just too personal. Finally Wanderspoon sat back, grimaced, blew air out of his cheeks, and shook his head.

"Well, it's little wonder that your body is in a state of gross envegetation. You're nothing more than a collection of disjointed and incoherent hallucinatory stimuli. And since it is ineffably true that we are the sum total of all that we psychologically ingest, I can say with absolute authority that you are not really a person at all, but rather a foul-smelling stew on two legs, lacking a single unifying flavor. Worse than that (if such were possible), you have been utterly misled. First, you've been deceived by your own brain." He pulled a filthy handkerchief from his pocket, blew his nose, and then wiped sweat from his forehead, leaving a streak of mucus in the grime. "Take this Bellwind fantasy. In the form in which you have described her, she could not exist at all. Clearly she is a delusion based upon your repressed desire for a nurturing mother figure to replace the stupefyingly insane, narcissistic excuse for a human being who birthed you. It's like all the rest of your preposterous fabrications, such as imagining that you came from another planet called Chicago and then floated in the ocean with an old woman and a dog."

Amanda just couldn't take it anymore. As weak as she was, she exploded. "Don't you talk about my mother that way. You are such a *jackass*! Chicago is a city not a planet and I did float in the ocean and Bellwind is real and my mother is not crazy! You're just a filthy little man who lives in a filthy house, and there isn't a single book on any of your walls because you probably don't even know how to read. You might as well just *shut up* because I'm not going to listen to anymore of your babbling garbage." The baby started clapping.

"Is that so? That's what you think, is it?" Wanderspoon stared at her malevolently. "Well, we'll see about that. You're going to be very sorry you spoke to me with such disrespect, you nasty, ugly girl."

"Okay, that's it. Just stop and let us out right here." Amanda tried to slide toward the back of the wagon, but suddenly she was in so much pain that moving was almost impossible.

"Let you out? Oh, no indeed. I promised to take you to the Healer, and the word of Pilfius Bordre Wanderspoon is his bond. No, no, no, you belong to me, my child. You are my prize, a gift from the gods to assuage the misery of my condition. So sit back and enjoy every agonizing bump as we go in search of your *miraculous healing*." He cackled with laughter. From that moment on the vile little man drove over every rut and hole he could find to make the journey even more unbearable.

A short time later the cart passed an outcropping of rock, and they left the gorge. Before them lay a broad plain that stretched many miles to the base of a mountain so gigantic that its summit was invisible in the clouds. In the middle of the plain stood a strange collection of dark jagged towers. The road led straight toward them.

Amanda squinted, trying to see. "What's that out there, those things sticking up?"

"Oh, you'll find out soon enough. That's where we're going to spend the night." And he would say no more.

For the next eight hours the cart creaked through miles of dirt. Twice more her thirst became so unbearable that Amanda had to demand a drink. Each time, Wanderspoon cursed and threw the bottle at her. The baby would take nothing and seemed no worse for it. Other than that, no words were spoken, and the only sound was the grinding squeak of the axle.

Even in her suffering, Amanda couldn't help but stare at the shadowy towers slowly coming into view. It was a city, or at least it had been, and the buildings at its heart were very tall. But they appeared to be broken and blackened. Spanning out from them were thousands of smaller structures that decreased in size like ripples in a pool of soot.

It was evening when they reached the outskirts of the city, and Wanderspoon began acting even stranger than usual. He began twitching and grimacing, jerking and sighing until Amanda thought he was having a seizure. When they approached the first low mounds, he suddenly jumped up straight as a tent pole. On his face was plastered a fatuous grin that revealed the rottenness of his teeth. Then he began bobbling back and forth, waving and bowing as though acknowledging the adulation of a crowd. Between grunts and groans, he yelled, "Yes. Yes, yes, yes. Beautiful ... exquisite ... mmmhhhmmm, mmmhhhmmm, my my my my ... how they gather ... how they love me ... yes, they do. Thank you. Thank you all so much. Shall I let them kiss my shoes? A small condescension. They're desperate to do it, and how can I refuse such devotion? But only clean lips. Dirty lips I cannot abide ... mmmm, yes. And perhaps only the sole not the top ... Thank you! Thank you! Of course you can."

It was the most amazing exhibition of nuttiness that Amanda had ever witnessed, and it creeped her out almost as much as the eerie place they were entering. The cart was moving down a main street lined with mounds and heaps of what must have been small buildings. All that was left were a few jagged walls of masonry that jutted out from the dirt. On they went, with Wanderspoon continuing his bizarre performance, which now included sticking his shoe over the side of the wagon and laughing uproariously.

After several miles the mounds grew into the blackened hulks of larger buildings that looked as though they had been eviscerated by a horrific explosion. Only stacks of cavelike rooms remained with twisting tunnel hallways that looked like vertical rat warrens. A chill wind started to blow, swirling up billows of dirt. Suddenly a huge dust devil blasted toward the wagon, and Amanda pulled the baby close, covering his face. The filth burned her eyes and stung her skin, but it didn't seem to bother Wanderspoon at all. He sneezed twice, and dark trickles began running from his nose, but he kept right on waving, smiling, and bobbling.

The last rays of sunlight were fading as they entered the canyons of the city. Amanda shivered. All around her loomed gigantic twisted ruins. Some were broken and jagged; others leaned precariously as though the slightest breeze would bring them crashing down. Many had fallen untold ages ago, crushing everything beneath them, turning the street into a nightmare of debris. The cart staggered through it, bumping and grinding with bone-jarring lurches. And every moment Wanderspoon's excitement grew. Shrieking with joy, he looked up, down, and around, screaming, "My people, my people ... yes, it's really me. Lick my shoe if you wish. Yes, lick it!" And he almost danced a jig, trying to keep his foot outside the wagon.

A few minutes later they turned a corner, and ahead appeared a great, twisted pinnacle of broken glass. Crimson light from the rising moon reflected on a billion grimy shards. Floor upon floor hung in teetering chaos. The whole shattered mass was draped like layers of crystal skin on an iron skeleton that looked as though it had writhed in a dance of death. When Wanderspoon saw it, tears began running down his cheeks. Raising his arms, he cried out in rapture, "My people, I have come back to you. Did I not promise to return and be your salvation? Though vast forces were arrayed against me, I have kept my word. So worship me, for I am greater than the gods."

The wagon creaked to a stop in front of the tower. A dozen long stairs led from the street up to a wide plaza beyond which stood a set of splintered doors. But it was an object in the center of the plaza that drew Amanda's attention. Out of a huge empty fountain rose a gargantuan statue that looked like a shrieking giant. Its fists were raised, and its mouth gaped open as though screaming at the sky. Suddenly Wanderspoon turned and struck a ridiculous pose with his fists in the air and his mouth open.

"Notice a striking resemblance?"

"What do you mean?"

"The statue—it's *me*!"

"If you say so, but why would they make a statue of *you*?"

Instantly he went almost insane with rage. "*Why?* I'll tell you why. Because I am their prophet, their priest, their king—their savior." Leaping into the back of the cart, he pointed. "Look at all of them. Look how they scrape and grovel. Look at the flowers they have strewn in my path. Look how they hang from their windows, sobbing with exultation at my return. Listen to their cries of fervid adulation. You can see all this and ask why they would make a statue to me, their god?"

"You're delusional."

"What?"

"All I see are broken buildings and all I hear is you."

Wanderspoon stared at her aghast. "The crowds—are you blind to the vast multitude all around us?"

"In your dreams! There's nobody here but us."

"Insanity! Lying, evil monster girl!" Jumping to the ground, he rushed up the stairs. When he was beneath the statue he turned majestically. Raising his arms, he cried out, "Silence. Listen to me, my people. Withhold for a moment your ravishing displays of affection. I must speak to you of horror. There in my royal carriage sits a craven criminal riddled with disease. A burglar, a miscreant, a scoundrel, a stealer of infants, remorseless, pitiless, the lowest form of life. Beyond all hope. Far worse, beyond all *therapy*. And why have I transported such a monster? Out of nothing but kingly compassion. Though she had broken into my house, I have carried her this long distance to alleviate her suffering. But in what coin does she repay my kindness? With denigration and insults, besmirching the character of me, your one true king."

He paused as though listening to the roar of an enraged mob.

"Yes, yes, I understand your desire to tear her limb from limb, but I urge you to restrain yourselves. Let her own diseased brain wreak the vengeance she so justly deserves. However, in your restraint, do not fail to show your displeasure, to reveal to her darkened mind the glory of my majesty, the god-like magnificence of Pilfius Bordre Wanderspoon." With that, he made a deep bow, then turned on his heel and strode toward the building. Pushing through the glass doors, he didn't seem to notice as they fell crashing to the ground.

Amanda looked down at the baby. "He's totally insane. He could come back in the middle of the night and kill us. We've got to get away." Desperately she struggled to push herself up, but the pain was so great that she fell back. "I can't do it." Looking down at herself, she started to cry. Prickling growths were shooting out of her elbows and knees. And something was sticking from her cheek that was beginning to block her vision. Suddenly the tears turned to anger. "Why did Bellwind send me out this way? She knew I'd never make it. I'm gonna die. We're both gonna die and nobody cares. I want to go home. *I want my mom.*" Amanda closed her eyes, and through her tears she whispered, "Just get it over with. Let me die so I won't hurt anymore. *Let me die right now.*"

As she lay, hurting and crying, a soft wind began to blow. Then she felt a strange vibration, and a voice she had never heard before spoke softly. "Stand up, child."

Without thinking, she replied, "I can't."

"You can."

So odd. Suddenly she wasn't hurting anymore.

"Stand up."

And Amanda stood up. The movement was easy, but everything felt weird, dislocated.

"Look down behind you."

Turning, she looked. Lying in the cart with the baby in her arms was a girl whose body was slowly transforming into a small white tree. Branches tangled in her hair, and her skin was thick and rough like bark. It took a moment to realize that she was seeing herself from the outside. Then she became afraid.

"What's happening?

The voice answered, "Do you really want to die, Amanda?"

"Who's talking? Where are you?"

"Because, if that's your wish, I'll grant it."

She grew angry again. "I'm dying whether I want to or not. I just can't stand to hurt anymore."

With great gentleness the voice answered, "So death is what you want?"

She began sobbing. "No! But I don't want to live either. I hurt so much, and how am I supposed to get to the mountain if I can't move?"

The wind grew stronger, and with it came the sound of distant singing. Once more Amanda felt the overwhelming love that had swept through her in Bellwind's tower. The voice spoke again with deep emotion. "I have searched for one whose heart could be broken and would not turn cold, because the task is great and the road I travel is filled with sorrow."

Suddenly all her anger vanished, and she whispered through her tears, "Who are you?"

"Do you really want to die, Amanda? Think carefully before you answer. All of your pain can end right now."

"What would happen to the baby?"

Silence.

"I've carried him a long way; I have a right to know."

"What is it that you know already?"

"I know he can't be left with that evil little man. But look at me, I can't even move. How can I protect him?"

"He is safe in your arms."

Kneeling beside her body, she looked at the little boy who was sleeping peacefully. "It isn't fair. I love him so much. I can't leave him this way."

"But what if loving him costs you everything?"

"I just don't see how I can get him to the mountain. It's impossible."

"Loving and never giving up is all that matters. Your journey to the Mountain began the moment you were born. You will reach it because the One Who Lives in the Mists has called you. He will make the way."

As she looked at the baby, his eyes opened and he looked back at her. "He loves me too. I can feel it," she whispered.

"Do you want to live, Amanda? Think carefully before you answer."

"I want to live . . . if it will help him."

There was a long pause. When the voice spoke, it was filled with tears. "You have made your choice, and it will be honored forever. Now, see and learn the sorrows of the past, for in them are shadows of what is yet to come."

There was a thunderous crash, and suddenly she heard the roar of screaming voices. As she stood up, everything changed. It was daylight, and no longer were the buildings black and broken. They were tall and majestic and glittered in the sun. Thousands of people surged in the street. Thousands more were leaning out of the windows. All were shrieking with rage. But they didn't seem to realize that she was there. Then Amanda smelled a horrifying odor. Staring at the people closest to her, she almost screamed herself. Their skin was sickly yellow, and they were covered with huge running sores. Their eyes bulged and their hair was falling out. And as far as she could see, everyone was the same. The city was full of plague. The odor was the smell of dying.

But none of this was what terrified her the most. As Amanda stared at them, she realized that, because she was outside her own body, she could see inside theirs. She could see beneath their skin. And behind every face a second shadow-face was visible. It was like double vision, seeing the spirit under a mask of flesh and bone. Although their bodies were all different, old and young, men and women, plain and beautiful, the shadow-faces were exactly alike. Every feature that made one person unique from another had been rubbed away as though they had become leprous and grinded and grated and scraped themselves until every mark of individuality had been erased. Their noses and ears had vanished. Their eyes were empty circles of horror. What was left of their jaws hung open as though trying to scream, but all that came out was an eerie mewing whine that sounded like the drone of bees.

The droning whine and the shrieking—Amanda couldn't stand it. She was about to close her eyes and cover her ears when the city shook with drumbeats. Instantly the screaming stopped and the crowd waited breathlessly. Then came the rhythmic crash of a thousand marching boots.

A block away, the crowd parted. Into view advanced an army, and at the front was a golden carriage pulled by white horses. To Amanda's amazement, standing in it with his fists was a man who looked vaguely like Wanderspoon. But she almost didn't recognize him because he was young and handsome. The only similarity with the ugly creature she knew was a vague cast of the face and an insane intensity in his eyes. Like everyone else he was covered with disease.

When the carriage reached the tower, a command rang out. It stopped and the army stopped behind it. Picking up a large covered basket, the man who looked like Wanderspoon jumped to the street, then rushed toward the stairs. As he passed, Amanda realized that she couldn't see beneath his skin. With him the double vision didn't work. At the top of the staircase he stopped beneath the statue and turned toward the crowd. There was another command and the army faced him. Then he cried out, "I promised that I would save you. And I have kept my word." Pulling back the cover on the basket, he held it up for all to see. Amanda gasped. Inside was the little boy she had been carrying. "Healing is ours! Out of death, life will come for us all."

Instantly the crowd went insane with joy. Wanderspoon raised his hand for silence. "But I ask you, my friends, why should we share this great gift with others? What have the ancient cities of Boreth ever done for us?"

The multitude screamed, "Nothing."

"And Lammortan, what has he ever done but take our children and tell us lies? Why should we serve him any longer?"

There were screams of agreement.

"Then let us overthrow the gods and become gods ourselves. Together we will rule the world."

For what seemed an eternity they raved and cheered. But when the sound began to die away, another voice rang out. *"You are all fools!"*

Everyone turned to stare, as out of the crowd stepped a beautiful young woman. She was tall and her dark hair hung almost to her feet. Though she was ill like everyone else, in her eyes there was a strange power. And beneath her flesh Amanda could see a being filled with light.

When Wanderspoon saw her, he shrieked, "*You!* You dare to come here? If you have something to say ... speak before you die."

Like a queen going to her execution, the young woman walked up the stairs to face him. Then she cried out, "Do you think this terrible act will save you?" She turned to the crowd. "How many times have you been warned and you have not listened? I bring you the final message. You killed your souls with your evil. And now your bodies will follow. *Let the judgment come!*"

Wanderspoon screamed, "How long must we live with the babbling of these false prophets? It is time to silence them forever." Then he shoved her down the stairs.

Instantly the mob was on her. Throwing the young woman to the ground, they began beating and stomping. As they pounded and kicked her to death, her face remained utterly peaceful, and the light that was inside grew brighter with every blow. At the moment of dying she looked straight up at Amanda and whispered, "Until Mountaincry." Then there was a flash of blinding brilliance and the light disappeared.

The young woman's broken body was lifted and passed over the cheering mob, her blood drenching those beneath her. With shouts of joy everyone surged forward, desperate for the drops to fall on them. Then Wanderspoon held the basket high and shrieked, "To the sacrifice!" A great cheer went up as he rushed down the steps toward his carriage. There were yells of command and the drums began to beat.

But just as they were at a fever pitch, Amanda heard a call that made every other sound vanish into silence. It started in a low moan that made the buildings tremble, then it lifted into a bloodcurdling scream. The mob froze. A man pointed and everyone looked up.

Looming above the skyscrapers was a gigantic bird hanging motionless in the air. Instead of two wings, it had six, and its feathers looked like shards of broken glass dazzling in the sun. And it was staring down with huge flaming eyes. Its beak opened and out of it came another scream. The people turned and ran, shrieking, trampling, clawing each other to get away. But it was too late. The ground began to rise and fall like the waves of an ocean. The pavement cracked into huge fissures. The buildings danced and teetered, then split and crashed. Thousands disappeared beneath the crushing debris.

From high above there came a wrenching groan. The universe seemed to grow black with boiling mist. Then fire vomited downward. Burning rivers poured from the sky onto the buildings, rolling down the walls, exploding and surging through the streets in mighty waves. Though the agony and destruction were unspeakable, the last thing Amanda saw was the most terrifying of all. As the people died, their spirits twisted out of their bodies and hovered in the air. For a moment they looked around confused as though not knowing what had happened. Then the bird gave a haunting cry, and with agonizing wails, all of them began rising toward him. Quickly they gathered beneath him like a swarm of flies. Then, majestically, the creature turned, his wings began to beat, and he vanished into the smoke. Like a stream of shadows in the fiery sky, a million spirits followed. And in a heartbeat, all were gone.

Day.

Daylight.

Amanda couldn't move. Everything was a blur. Try as hard as she could, her eyes wouldn't focus. Her jaw was frozen shut, and she didn't even have the strength to groan. Suddenly she heard someone climb onto the cart. Then a vague shape that looked like a head bent close, and out of it came the voice of Wanderspoon.

"There, you see? Just as I predicted. You can't move and you can't talk anymore, either. Silent as the forest on a winter night, that's what you are. And so much the better for me. I won't have to listen to anymore of your vicious insults. Since you can't see yourself, let me describe your appearance. In short, you've become a deciduous denizen of the thicket. Your skin has turned to bark, and your hair is a mass of dirty little branches. Nasty roots are growing from your feet, and since they aren't attached to the ground, no moisture can get into your ugly trunk, which means you'll get drier and drier unless I plant you someplace. But why should I do that when you're getting exactly what you deserve? Well, from now on it will be a much pleasanter trip for me. Perhaps I shall sing a bit."

Humming happily to himself, the little man climbed into the seat, and Amanda felt the cart begin to move. Slowly it rolled and bounced over the broken pavement.

Light.

Shadows.

Darkness.

Light.

Shadows.

Darkness.

The squeaking axle.

Wanderspoon's awful, tuneless gargling.

Light.

Shadows.

Darkness.

Darkness.

Darkness.

Darkness.

And then slow awakening.

When she awoke, Amanda was at home.

24

THE PINK AND WHITE ROOM OF TERROR

Dreams and visions, what are they?

Dreams come when the body sleeps. Visions come whenever they please.

Dreams drift away like a morning haze. But a vision is something you never forget.

And it was a vision that came to Amanda.

In it, she was lying in her old bed in the old bedroom. The little-girl room. And it was dark, but not the darkness of night. A misty darkness soft in the air.

Without knowing how, she knew that everything was just the way it had been in the Time Before Time so long ago. The room with the pink walls and the fluffy white curtains. The room she had tried so hard to forget. A different Amanda had lived here, the Amanda who had loved stuffed animals and collected them by the dozens, the Amanda who had sat for hours pretending they were all alive.

The pretending room—gone forever. Vanished with Amanda the child. But not forever. It was back again. And the animals were back, waiting in a pile in the corner where they always waited until she awoke. Imaginary friends, but not the closest friends. None of the ones on the floor had earned the right to sleep in her bed. Only two could do that: the bear with the broken eyes and the scrunched-up dog with eyes that wouldn't open—both furless because she had hugged them so much. They had been the hardest to throw away. For a long time she had allowed them an agonizing reprieve. From her bed to the floor, from the floor to the secret place on the garage roof where the rain and snow had obliterated their identities and unnamed them. That's what she had done. Letting them die had taken their names away. When their faces had disappeared and their seams had broken, she had ripped their stuffing out and tossed it to the wind. So strange. They were back again, resurrected beside her pillow. Old imaginary friends. Instinctively Amanda pulled them into her arms and felt their softness against her cheek. Yes, everything was just as it had been.

But it wasn't.

Because it could never be.

Why was she in this place, the room she hated, so full of lying memories? Like soft fingers running through her hair, her mother's fingers. Her mother sitting on the bed, listening and loving while little Amanda babbled on about the vastly important nothings of childhood. And when sleep was about to come, looking up into her mother's face. How beautiful she had been in the Time Before Time. Hearing her whisper-sing a lullaby, while Amanda, the child long vanished, hugged the bear and the dog. *How she hated those memories!* She had told herself so often that they weren't real until finally none of them *were* real. If they had happened at all, it was to another child, a different Amanda.

So what *was* real? Sorrow was real. Night after night, tiptoeing to stand outside her mother's bedroom, hearing the sobs coming from behind the closed door. How could her mother sob that way and go on living? Fear. That was real too. Maybe she was dying in there, slipping away one horrible sob at a time. Terrified, Amanda had listened ... and listened ... until the sobbing faded into silence. And then, like a little shadow, she had cracked open the door and slipped into the room. Over to the bed. Standing breathlessly now. A careful examination in the darkness. Yes, breathing. The blanket was going up and down, which meant her mother was still *alive.*

Thank you, God. Thank You, thank You, thank You. I'll be good from now on. Just don't take her away.

Then, tiptoeing back to the room with the pink walls and the white curtains where her own sobbing would begin. That's when she had discovered that the bear and the dog were a hiding place for tears. So much sorrow — more than she should ever know.

As she lay in the vision room, once more Amanda was little Amanda, pouring out her heart to the furry creatures in her arms. Words on top of words. Mixed up. Jumbled. The heartaches of two worlds.

Alex, where are you?

Tori, I never got to say good-bye.

Daddy, why did you leave us?

Mommy, why did you stop running your fingers through my hair?

Alone, so alone. Walking through a wilderness carrying a baby. Such a burden across so many miles. Alone, so alone. Walking through her house after her father had gone. Hearing sobs behind closed doors. Yes, Alex had sobbed too, though he never would admit it. Burdens on top of burdens. Trying to carry the people she loved. Child mother to a child whose name she didn't know. Child mother to her mother and brother and sister, willing to give up her own childhood as a gift of love. Wanting to carry them, but unable to do it, because the weight of their sorrow was too much to bear.

Stumbling ... falling ... sobbing beneath the load.

And through it all, who had been there for little Amanda? No one but the furry animals. No one but the bear and the dog. Had no one ever cared about her sorrow? Had no one ever stood outside her door and listened to the sounds of her broken heart? Was she so worthless? Was that why her father had left her?

Tears. And the echo of tears.

But then a strange memory began to seep in around the edges of her weeping. Alone? Had she *really* been alone? Was there something that she had forgotten? A silvery shadow at the back of her mind? No one had ever taught Amanda to pray. No one had ever said there would be anyone listening. But she had done it anyway, night after night. And as the words tumbled out a strange warmth had quieted her sorrow. She had decided that the warmth was God. At first it had brought great comfort, so she had poured out everything in a jumble of mixed-up words and heartaches. But as the nights passed the jumble distilled into one begging, burning cry.

Please, please, please bring him back to us. Make him love us again. Make him love me.

But in the warmth there was only silence. And finally one night she had decided that warmth was not enough. She wanted her father back right now! Was that too much to ask? Just one little thing?

More silence.

And silence.

And silence.

In spite of all her prayers, her tears, and pleading promises, her father had not returned. Then one day the news had come that he had married someone else. That night there was no sobbing in Amanda's room. And there were no prayers either. Why keep mumbling words into empty darkness? It was like talking to stuffed animals. And that's what Amanda had decided she had been doing all along, praying to the bear and the dog. In her anger she had banished them to the floor, vowing never to pray again. From that night on, the warmth had turned to emptiness.

But now, in the vision—this odd, soft vision—she felt the warmth return. And there was something in it. No, not *something* ... *Someone.* And she heard a voice whisper, "Amanda ... little child ... look at me."

It was the same voice that had spoken to her in the city. She strained to see, but no one was visible. "Where are you?"

The words came again, "Amanda ... little child ... look at me."

"I'm looking, but I can't see you."

"I'm standing in the past, in a room of many sorrows. Do you know this room?"

"I know where I am right now and I hate it. Why am I here?"

"Because you have never left."

Instantly her mouth went dry and fear raced through her. "I don't know what you're talking about."

"In this room there are wounds that have never stopped bleeding."

Suddenly the darkness deepened and there was a damp, suffocating odor. *What is that smell?* Amanda began trembling.

Sweat.

It was the smell of sweat.

And it brought terror. She tried to jump up, to run away ... but she couldn't move. She began struggling, but the blankets seemed to tighten around her. *"Help! Let me out. Somebody help me!"*

Silence.

And silence.

And silence.

The silence before something. The silence of an abyss. The silence of the Time When There Was No Time. The silence between *Then* and *Now*. The silence of things Never To Be Remembered. The silence of a door after it is shut. More silence than a child should ever have to bear. And then, in the silence, sobbing, echoing through the years as though life itself were sobbing away. As Amanda sobbed, the warmth encircled her and the air shimmered with crimson mist. In it stood the outline of a man whose face she couldn't see, but the warmth of love was flowing from him.

"I'm standing in the past and you must stand with me."

"I don't want to."

"If you don't, you will die."

"But remembering hurts so bad."

"Little child, give me your hand."

"I'm ... afraid."

"Don't be afraid. I will never leave you."

Slowly she lifted her hand and felt a strong, warm hand take hold.

"Where are we going?"

"Through it all ... to Sorrow's End."

Gagging ...

Suffocating ...

Screaming ...

Crushing ...

Searing ...

Burning ...

Sobbing ...

Sobbing-sobbing ...

And all in total silence.

Shhhhh ... not a sound.

Not ever!

Killing words.

Secret words.

Drowning under waves of secrets and silence. Gone. Everything gone.

Dying ... shriveling ... vanishing ...

But then in the silent darkness Amanda felt the strong hand holding hers and heard the voice whisper, "Stand up, child."

"I can't." The words came from her mind not her lips. The weight on her was too heavy for her to breathe, and the smell of sweat was choking her.

"Stand up, child."

"I said, I can't!" Angry now! She was angry. Wanting to sleep. Wanting to forget forever.

"Stand up!" It wasn't a request. It was a command.

So odd. Suddenly Amanda stood up. The hand lifted her to her feet. "Now turn and see and don't be afraid."

Turning, she looked down at her bed. "What *is* that?"

Covering it from top to bottom was a thick pool of oily blackness that slowly oozed back and forth like a feeding amoeba. Out of the pool rose a reeking haze. As she watched, the pool receded until she could see her own head lying on the pillow. Her eyes were open, but they were frozen as though she had gone blind.

"What's happening? What's that all over me?"

And then the amoeba congealed into a man. He was lying on her bed and her body was under him. In that moment Amanda remembered all that she had tried so hard to forget. From out of the deepest part of her, it came up in a desperate wail. The terror. The horror. The pain. The shame. The self-loathing. The loss. The Fear. The Fear. *The Fear.* Night after night. Lying awake in the silence. Waiting in terror.

The door opens. The door closes. Softly, so softly.

She closes her eyes, trying to die, willing herself outside her body into a place without feeling. But she *does feel.* Crushing weight. Hurting. Burning. Drowning. On and on. And always, the soft, hideous voice whispering ... grinding lies into her ear.

Her fault.

Hers.

Not his.

Warning. Whining. Threatening. Pleading. Wheedling. *Killing. Murdering*!

Yes, *murdering*! Choking away the last little pieces of childhood that had been left to her. The end of little Amanda.

The door opens. And the door closes. Softly, so softly.

And she sobs herself to sleep hoping that tomorrow will never come.

But morning always does come. And with it shame. A breakfast of self-loathing at the kitchen table. From her mother, jittering talk. From her brother sullen silence. From her sister breathless babbling about plastic dolls with perfect female bodies. And *him*! *Him* looking at her. Her mother's brother who had come to stay with them six months after her father had left. Looking and looking and *looking*.

Don't look back or you will die.

All she can do is stare down at her untouched food, trying to make herself deaf to the jittering jumble of "Why-aren't-you-eating? You-never-eat. Don't-you-feel-well? You-need-to-eat. You-can't-go-to-school-without eating." Sticking a spoonful into her mouth. Wanting to vomit. Like eating garbage. Like *being* garbage. The food, so ugly on the plate. Pieces of her own face reflecting on the shiny surface around the eggy goo. So ugly. That's why her father had left. Who could love such an ugly girl broken all into pieces?

Only him!

That's what he had said to her.

That's exactly what he had said in the grinding whispers.

Night after night!

In the vision Amanda shrieked and leaped onto his back. She pounded, tearing, pulling his hair, trying to rip his eyeballs out—to choke him—to feel him die in agony and go to hell forever. But no matter what she did, he didn't seem to feel it. So she tried harder until all her strength was exhausted and she slid into a sobbing heap on the floor. How many times she had imagined tearing him into bloody pieces. But it meant nothing. Because she was weak and he was strong. She was alone with no one to protect her. Without a father who loved her enough to stay!

Long after the door had closed for the last time, the memory had scorched her heart. And it was more than she could bear. Only one answer. Lose herself within herself. Close off. Shut down. Lock tight. And never, ever open the Room of Darkness, the room of rage and pain and sorrow with pink walls and white fluffy curtains.

But now it *was* open.

And she was helpless in it. As Amanda lay choking and gasping, she felt someone kneel beside her and gently lift her in his arms. He was crying too. So strange. No one had ever cried like that. She could feel within him an eternity of sorrow as though all the tears that had ever been shed had been stored in a single broken heart. And he was crying with her; no one had ever cried with her before.

She was *not* alone. Amanda buried her face against his chest and for a long time they cried together.

Finally, when quiet came, he said. "Daughter, I want you to understand. Look with me once more."

Lifting her to her feet, she faced the bed. The man, her mother's brother, was rising. As he stood up, she looked into his face, and just as within the awful city, she found that she could see beneath his skin. With the double vision, she saw the hideous thing that lived inside him. Sleek. Soft. Putrefied. Rotting. Eyes that were empty circles bleeding drops of death. Torn lips. A jaw hanging open in a silent scream. Yes, all of this and something more. Weakness! The thing that lived within him was weak, disgusting, pitiful, no longer a man, a slave, trembling with fear.

But what was he afraid *of*?

The one who was standing beside her whispered, "Look down at yourself." She looked. A strange radiance was coming from the bed. It was glowing from inside little Amanda. Beneath her skin was a soft white light. The thing in the man saw it and was terrified.

"He's afraid of what's inside me."

Unable to stand the light any longer, he rushed from the room.

"He was *afraid* and he *hated* me."

"The power that controls him hates all children."

"Why?"

"Because a child knows things and never questions."

"Like what?"

"What did you know when you prayed?"

"I guess that there was someone listening."

"And why did you stop?"

Amanda didn't answer.

"Look down at yourself again."

The soft light was fading.

"What's happening? Why is it going away?" As she watched, a second face appeared beneath the face of little Amanda. No longer was it the face of a child. Its eyes were old and in them was anger and sorrow and pain. "Why do I look like that?"

"The disease that was in him has entered you. This is what the Dark One wants for every child. Death before they're born, and if not that, hate and bitterness in their souls. That's what you are seeing."

"Is that what I look like inside right now?"

"You're older."

"So you mean it's *worse*?"

Silence.

"No, that isn't me! That's not what I look like! I don't believe it! I'm leaving. You can't keep me in here." She rushed to the door. But when she tried the knob, it wouldn't open. "Let me out!"

"Amanda, this room is buried in your heart. Long ago you closed and locked it. But you locked yourself inside."

"That's not true! That's a lie! I want out right now!" Then she screamed and pounded until she collapsed against the door.

"I'm so tired. I just want to die and sleep forever."

"Even if your mind sleeps, your soul lies awake in this room. Amanda, do you really want to leave this terrible place?"

Burying her face in her hands, she sobbed, "Yes."

"Then you must trust me and do a very hard thing."

"What is it?"

"You must call him back."

"What?" She stared in horror.

"Call him back and give him to me."

"I can't do that! I can't bring him back in here."

"If you don't, he will keep returning. The hate and rage inside you draws the Evil One. It unlocks the door to your heart."

Amanda groaned and covered her eyes. Suddenly she had a burning headache. For a long time she didn't say anything, then she whispered, "If I call him back what are you going to do to him?"

"You must leave that to me."

"I want you to *hurt* him. I want him to *die* and I want to see it."

"Which do you want more, to hate or to get out of this room?"

"You saw what he did. I have a right to hate him. I have a right to want him dead."

"Yes, and no one can take that from you. You must give it up on your own."

"I can't. I'm going to hate him forever."

Then she heard a guttural sound and looked over at the bed. Slowly the head of little Amanda turned toward her, and she saw the face within her face. It was choking with rage, grinding and scraping itself against the inside of her skull. As she watched, its nose and ears began to rub away. Its mouth opened in a scream, but all that came out was an eerie, mewing whine, like the drone of a giant insect.

Amanda covered her ears and shrieked, "Stop it. Stop it. I'll do anything. Just make that go away."

"Then call him back ... and give him to me."

"I ... don't know ... if I can." She was gasping and tears were streaming down her cheeks.

"Try!"

"You'll ... be here? You won't leave me?"

"I'll be right beside you."

Instantly she was back on the bed, trapped beneath the covers. The blankets were so tight that she could hardly breathe, but finally she managed to gasp out, "Come ... come back ... now." At first she heard nothing. Then as she stared at the door, the knob began to turn. Softly, so softly it opened. And he entered.

Step by step he walked across the floor until he stood above her. Once more she saw the face within the face, and it was *smiling*. Slowly he bent down and the double face drew close to hers. Then came *the whispering ... the laughing*. She felt his terrible weight begin to crush her. But just before her mind drowned in darkness, she looked straight into his eyes and whispered, "I don't want to hate you anymore. I give you ... *to him*."

Instantly the weight was gone. The double eyes, the eyes within the eyes, stared at her. The smile within the smile faded. Slowly the creature rose and came face-to-face with the One in the Mists. It groaned, and from its mouth gushed oozing bile. With a gagging croak it began to sink into the pool of its own darkness. Screaming, it clawed at the bed, trying to reach Amanda, but its arms were shriveling and drying up. Finally only its head stared up at her. And then, with a gurgle of hate, it was gone.

At that moment something happened inside Amanda. It was like an icy shell melting, falling away, and with it, the terrible weight, the crushing heaviness of sorrow that had been on her heart for so long, completely disappeared. It was as though a child buried in a grave had been reborn.

Sobbing, but sobbing with happiness. Sobbing with unspeakable joy.

"Stand up, child."

Amanda jumped up. She wanted to run and sing, but she stood in front of the man whose face she couldn't see. His arms encircled her. She buried her face in his chest, and all she could say over and over was, "Forgive me, forgive me, forgive me ... for throwing you away with the bear and the dog."

Gently he whispered, "Daughter, now you are ready. *Awake and be strong.*"

Swirling streaks of crimson and gold. Swirling mists of fire. So soft. And in them, the pink and white room of terror and sorrow faded from her heart.

25

ESCAPE

"That's a *skull.* I don't like skulls." Tori was staring at the pile of bones and dirt on the chair.

"It can't hurt you." The moth was sitting on her shoulder.

"And look at *that.*" On the wall above the chair loomed a huge stained-glass window. Suspended in it was the image of the regal-looking woman with the terrifying face. *"That's the one who was sucking on the bottle."*

"During the day the Painter keeps the spirits of his slaves frozen in glass."

"You mean she's alive up there?"

"Well, a kind of living. There's no reason to be afraid. I'm taking care of you."

"Yeah, right."

"And just exactly what does that mean?"

"You're a *bug.* If she comes down what can you do, fly up her nose?"

"I assure you that if I chose to do so, her nostril would never be the same. However, she is blind and deaf until nightfall—unless you make a lot of noise. Any disturbance will cause the Painter, who sees through her eyes, to know that you are here, which would precipitate a distinctly undesirable conclusion."

"You're sure they never come down before night?"

"Almost never."

"Almost?"

"Lammortan is weak right now. His body is in a kind of prison. He doesn't want to waste his power. His slaves can't stand the daylight. It burns their strength away, and it's up to him to keep them alive. Since he has been in prison, only once in all the centuries has he sent them out when the sun was shining."

"Why did he do that?"

"A year ago two of them traveled to your world to look for the thing that had been hidden. But it cost him a great deal of energy."

"Did they find it?"

"Yes, but one of the Worwil stopped them, so now they're desperate. It's time to go. Do you see those doors at the back? Go through them."

Hurrying through the doors, Tori found herself in a sweltering corridor. The walls were covered with paintings that dripped with mold. The moth began fluttering ahead.

"Why is it so hot in here?"

"Have you ever had a fever?"

"One time when I had the flu."

"This building is full of disease. That's why it's so hot."

"Why are there so many pictures of kids?"

"Lammortan likes to remember his sacrifices."

Suddenly she began smelling something horrible. "Peeeeuuw, what's that?"

"The dining room."

"It smells like *poo*." The odor got worse until they were outside a pair of ornately carved doors. As they hurried past, she held her nose. "If that's the dining room, why does it smell so bad?"

"The Painter can read your mind. He takes all the ugliest, most disgusting thoughts inside your head and paints them into imaginary food. Then he feeds it to you and makes you think you're eating a delicious meal."

"But it's really eating poop?"

"If that's what's in your mind, then that's what'll be in your mouth."

"What do they drink, pee?"

"He calls it sweet wine."

"Ewww. Has my brother eaten in there?"

"You'll have to ask him about that."

"Where is he?"

"We'll be there soon."

"How'd he get in this nasty place?"

"He landed in the ocean in a raft. But he was alone. When he got to the shore he chose a road that brought him here."

"Why doesn't he leave?"

"He tried, but he can't. He's become one of the Painter's slaves."

"Like the things in the windows?"

"Almost."

"But we can save him, right?"

"If he lets us. He's very ill. We've got to take him to a place where he can get help." Mirick fluttered to a grimy door and landed on the knob. "Okay, this is it. He's in this room. But you've got to be ready for what you're going to see because your brother is *in between*."

"In between what?"

"The living and the dead. His body isn't dead, but it's dying, so part of him is trapped in a window and part on a bed. It's not pretty. When we go in, don't try to wake him. And one more thing. When he does wake up, I've got to stay hidden." The moth fluttered to her shoulder and his light went out.

"Why?"

"Because his mind belongs to Lammortan and he'll think I'm an enemy." He crawled into her hair.

Tori winced. "Not this again."

"Yes, this again. Here's what you have to do. Whatever I whisper in your ear, you tell him exactly that. Do you understand how it will work?"

"I think so. Just don't start tickling."

"Heaven forbid that I should do that. Now, go in quietly."

Easing the door open, Tori slipped into the room and stared in amazement. On a wall loomed a massive stained-glass window, and in it was the stupidest thing she had ever seen. It was supposed to be an image of her brother, but gone was the sloppy slouch and the half-snarling smirk. The stained-glass version of Alex stood with his shoulders thrown back and his chin jutted forward as though a steel rod had been shoved up his spine. Sunlight shone through dumbly fearless eyes, and on his mouth was plastered an idiotic grin as though he had been quick-frozen in a drug-induced stupor. And then there were his clothes. He was dressed in grime-slimy jeans and a T-shirt slick with greasy filth that had been rendered in excruciating detail. Adding to this grandeur, around his shoulders hung a cape made of rat skins, their flattened little bodies exquisitely created from tiny chips of gray glass. The entire image made Alex look like the brain-dead king of Sewer World. But then Tori looked down and almost screamed in horror. Beneath the window was a bed and on it lay a filthy shadow wrapped in skin. Alex's eyes were open, but there was no life in them. They were sunk in a face so gaunt that it looked like a skull. His greasy hair lay matted; his shirt was off, and rivulets of gray filth ran down his bony chest. Walking over to him, she began to cry.

"All right, I admit this is a bit more than repugnant," Mirick whispered. "But if you want to help him, stop making those snuffling sounds."

"He looks dead."

"Well, he isn't. Now find a place to sit. We've got hours to wait before the sun sets."

Tori looked around the room and froze. On a wall behind her she saw the picture frame. Its glass was gray and empty. "That's like the one ..."

"Don't worry. It can't hurt you."

"Are you sure?"

"The Painter can't see you until your brother awakens. But if it makes you feel better, go pull the curtain and hide it."

After cautiously doing this, she sat down on the floor and leaned against the bed. For a long time she stared at the curtain. Finally she fell asleep.

"Wake up."

Tori's eyes flew open. Sunlight was fading and the shadows were growing deep. Mirick was still in her hair.

"Stand up and watch the window."

Something was happening. As the sunlight faded, the colors began to drain from the glass and form a mist in the air. For a moment they hung in a watery blur, then suddenly there was a cracking sound, and a streak of brilliance flashed down into Alex's body. There was a sucking gurgle and his chest heaved.

"All right, get ready. The next part is going to be singularly unattractive."

With a muffled shriek Alex lurched and every muscle in his body went rigid. Then he began thrashing. A mass of drooling spittle erupted from his mouth and covered his chin.

"He's choking."

"He'll be fine. He's just getting put back together."

Shuddering to the edge of the bed, he flopped to the floor and landed on his face. Tori rushed over and bent down. Mirick whispered, "Don't do or say anything until he looks up at you."

Slowly Alex quieted, and with a grunt he opened his eyes. Seeing his sister's shoes, he twisted his head and squinted up at her through a blur of mucus. "What . . . ?"

She knelt and hugged him. "Alex . . ."

"What's this? Who're you?"

"I'm Tori."

"Tori . . . ?" He tried to rub the mucus away, but his vision wouldn't clear. "You're not Tori. Go'way and leave me alone."

"I *am* Tori."

"No, you're not. You're just a dream." He laid his head back on the floor.

Mirick whispered, "Get him up. There isn't much time."

She looked at the curtain. It was moving as though in a slight breeze.

"Alex, get up. We've got to get out of here." She pulled on him. Nothing. Then she pinched him hard.

"Ow, stop that."

"I'm going to keep doing it until you get up." She pinched him again.

"I said, stop it." He struggled to his knees. "Will you leave me alone?"

"We've got to get out of here before they all wake up." When he was on his feet, she began dragging him to the door.

"This is a dream. I know it."

"I don't care what you think it is, *just move.*"

Stumbling into the hall, he almost fell, but she caught him. Then she began pulling him down the corridor. After a few moments he stopped and stared at her. "Wait a minute. Who are you?"

"*I'm Tori, you jerk.* We've got to get out of this horrible place."

"If you're Tori, how'd you get in here?"

"I'll tell you later. Now would you come on?"

"There's no way out. I've tried."

"Somebody's gonna help us."

"Like who?"

Mirick whispered to her what to say.

"He's here, but you can't see him," said Tori.

"What?"

"He's sort of invisible, but not quite. You've got to trust him or you'll die."

"This is some kind of trick. I don't even think you're really my sister. I told Melesh *I don't want any more games*."

Tori kicked him in the shins as hard as she could.

"OW!"

"Does that feel like a trick?"

At that moment a strange, shrieking roar came from far down the hall behind them.

"They're awake." Mirick whispered urgently. "Tell him if they catch you they'll kill you."

"Alex, they're coming and they're going to kill us. Now let's go." The sound was growing louder.

"I told you, there's no way out. This is a stupid waste of time." But he let her grab his hand and together they began running. With Mirick whispering directions, they rushed down reeking corridors, through mold-choked rooms, then up and down a series of slippery staircases. After that, on and on, constantly running, climbing, descending in what felt like meaningless zigzags, with Alex complaining every step of the way, while the shrieking behind them grew louder. Finally they burst through a door and stopped cold. They were inside a small room; on the wall hung an ancient lantern, and from it came a dismal flicker just bright enough to show that they had come to a dead end.

"This is it? This is where your invisible friend has been taking us? Well, it looks like the game's over," Alex sneered. The roar was very loud in the corridor they had just left. "But there's nothing to worry about. Everybody in here thinks I'm some kind of god, and they'll do whatever I want. So if you're really Tori, when they get here it'd be a good idea if you were kneeling and worshiping me. Then everything will be fine."

"Tell the little 'god' to pick up the lantern," Mirick muttered.

"Pick up the lantern."

"What?"

"Pick ... up ... the lantern. Are you deaf?"

"Why should I?"

Jumping two inches from his face Tori shrieked, "Pick it up, you ass!"

"All right! But you're going to be sorry for calling me that." He grabbed the lantern from the hook. Instantly there was a deep grinding rumble. Then the floor started tilting and a crack appeared across the bottom of the opposite wall. As they struggled to keep their balance, the floor tilted more and the crack yawned wider. They began slipping toward it. Yelling, they slid through and began sliding with unbelievable speed down a stone ramp as smooth as oiled glass, down thousands of feet in huge circles it took them until it felt like they would slide forever. Finally they tumbled out onto the floor of a cave, and there they sat, dazed and breathless. And the lantern was still burning.

Alex groaned, "I bashed my shoulder. Where the heck are we?"

Mirick whispered in Tori's ear, "There's a big hole in the wall. Go through it and you'll find a tunnel. *Hurry!*"

Jumping up, she grabbed the lantern. "Come on."

"Where's your stupid invisible friend taking us now, to the dungeons?"

Beyond the hole was a corridor. They had gone a hundred yards when a strange object appeared up ahead.

"What's that?" Tori raised the light.

They approached cautiously. In the gloom soared the stern of a long narrow boat. Once it had been painted in bright colors, but long ago they had faded to a rusty brown. Alex stared at it. "It looks like a Viking ship."

"Climb in," Mirick whispered.

"He says, climb in."

"Why?"

"I don't know. Let's just do it." She struggled to get over the rail. "Help me, Alex."

Lifting her, he groaned and swore. "My shoulder's really screwed. You know, we haven't escaped anything, we're just deeper in the mountain."

"Get in."

Throwing a leg over the side, Alex dragged himself up and flopped to the floor next to her. The deck was empty except for a long box sitting in the middle.

"Okay, now what's *that*? It looks like a coffin." He went over to it and bent down. The lid was ornately carved with words in a strange language.

Mirick whispered, "Find the flower and lay your hand on it, then tell him to open the lid." Joining her brother, Tori began searching.

"What are you doing?"

"Looking for something." At one end of the box she found a carved flower, and in the center was the outline of a hand exactly like hers. Carefully she placed hers over it. "Now, open the lid."

Grasping the wood, Alex pulled and the lid creaked opened. Tori held up the light and both of them stared—lying in the box was the body of a man. He was wearing a simple white robe, and his hands were folded on his chest as though in prayer. Though he must have been dead a thousand years, his body was amazingly preserved. Long silver hair flowed down over a pillow of stone; the skin of his face was as dry and thin as paper, but in it they could still see the creases and lines of great suffering. But even sorrow and ancient death could not conceal his gentle strength.

They were looking into the face of a king.

"Who is it?" Tori whispered.

"How the heck should I know?"

"I wasn't asking you." But before Mirick could answer, they heard the sound of running water. Grabbing the lantern, Alex moved to the rail.

"The cave is flooding."

Tori joined him. As they watched, water rushed in faster and faster. Suddenly they felt the boat lift. Then they were moving. Trying to see, Alex ran to the prow, but the light wasn't strong enough. All he could tell was that they were traveling with increasing speed through an underground tunnel carried along on a river of rippling shadows.

26

BUG ISLAND

I'm sick of riding in this tub down a thousand miles of sewer pipe. Where are we going?" Alex had been complaining for an hour.

"Tell him to stop whining or I'll fly into his mouth and drill a hole all the way to the back of his head."

"You wouldn't do that." Tori was trying to deal with both of them at once.

"Wouldn't do *what*?"

"Not you, Alex. I'm talking to my friend."

"You're crazy, you know that? There's nobody here but us."

"Then why do you keep wanting me to ask him questions?"

"I must tell you that my patience with your brother is fading rapidly. And a moth doesn't have a copious supply to begin with," Mirick whispered loudly in her ear.

"Stop it! Both of you."

"Look at me, Tori. I am only one person so both of me can't do anything."

"Shut up!"

"What a superlative idea. If only he would do it."

"You too! Everybody just be quiet! You're driving me crazy." Tori marched to the stern of the boat and plopped down. Alex continued slouching near the prow.

"Fine! But maybe you could tell your stupid imaginary friend that I'm starving to death."

"I told you, I've got nuts and berries."

"I hate nuts and berries!"

"Then go eat poop."

"That was not poop. It was the best food I've ever had."

"Then just pretend you're eating more of it and leave me alone." Closing her eyes, she leaned her head against the carved wood. They had been speeding down the underground river for hours, and Alex had become more and more obnoxious. Mirick, who was still nestled in her hair, whispered, "I should warn you that in a few minutes he's going to get very, very nasty."

"How can it get worse than now?"

"Oh, believe me, this is nothing. It's almost dawn outside, and he's away from his window."

Suddenly there was a loud guttural rasp. Tori froze. "What was *that*?"

"It's begun. Now, no matter what he does or says, just stay away from him and remain calm."

A jittering gurgle came from the prow. Tori jumped up and looked at her brother. He lay slumped on the deck with spittle drooling from his mouth. She rushed up to him.

"Don't get too close."

Slowly Alex's empty gaze shifted down to his arm. The flesh on either side of the metal band was swollen and running with pus. Suddenly his mouth opened, and from it came a choking roar. Then he began tearing at the wound, raking it with his nails and teeth.

"Alex, stop that!"

"He doesn't hear you."

"He's biting himself."

"That's the least of his problems. He's like a dog on an invisible chain, and his master is jerking on it."

As Tori watched in horror, he began shrieking and beating his arm on the deck. Then he leaped up and rushed back and forth, screaming and flailing. After a few moments his eyes rolled into the back of his head, then he staggered and crashed to the deck where he lay unconscious. Tori ran over and bent down.

"He's dying!"

Mirick fluttered into the air beside her. "No, he isn't. His master won't let that happen. He's far too valuable."

"We've got to do something."

"Why? The silence is refreshing."

"His arm is all bloody."

"It's only a few drops. There will be help when we get where we're going."

Suddenly there was a swooshing gurgle and the boat slowed so abruptly that Tori was almost knocked off her feet. "What's happening? Are we sinking?"

"We are not sinking."

"It feels like we're sinking."

The moth groaned. "After riding with you and your brother, I have to admit that sinking is an attractive idea, but look around."

Rushing to the rail, Tori looked. Though it was still dark, she could tell that they weren't streaking down the tunnel anymore. The boat was bobbing aimlessly with water lapping against its sides. "Where are we?"

"On an underground lake called Leresh Mirickgard." The moth fluttered to the rail and landed next to her.

"Is it big?"

"About a thousand miles across."

"We're not going anywhere. Are we just gonna float like this?"

"Look ahead."

She turned and looked. "I don't see anything." But then she did see something. Far away appeared a pinpoint of green light. "What's *that*?"

"Some friends on their way to meet us."

Quickly it grew larger, weaving and glistening as it came.

"It looks like a *ghost*."

"It isn't a ghost."

"Then why does it look like that?"

A few more moments and it became clear. Streaking toward them was a massive swarm of sparkling lights, and from it came a loud hum.

"It's *bugs*!"

"Quite correct."

"There are millions of them."

"Close. But I can't give you an accurate count."

"And they're *huge*!" She wailed.

"Now, listen carefully. I expect you to be on your best behavior. These are very dear friends of mine who have come to help us. They have highly developed olfactory nerves and will be extremely upset if your first reaction to their presence is some form of regurgitation."

"Ooooooo . . ."

And then the swarm was all around them, a million twinkling insects, like gigantic fireflies, buzzing and swooping. Tori slid down under the rail, closed her eyes, and covered her head with her arms. "Keep 'em away from me."

"Will you *please* not do that? It's *quite* embarrassing."

"I can't help it."

A moment later she thought she heard Mirick buzz as though he were having an intense conversation. Then there was a roar of buzzes, and the sound vanished with a strange kind of plopping noise as though a million pebbles had dropped into the water. Slowly she opened her eyes. The insects were gone. "Where'd they go?"

"To do their job. Look over the side."

Pulling herself up, she stared into the water. Beneath the boat was a shimmering green light. The insects had submerged and were swarming under them.

"They're in the water. How can bugs fly in the water?"

Suddenly she felt the boat lift and turn, and it began moving with increasing speed. They were traveling through the air.

"They're carrying us. They're that strong?"

"They're warriors. It's a detachment from the 222nd Light Brigade that has come to escort us home."

"Can they fight?"

"When necessary they can be quite lethal. Of course, their desire is to be insects of peace."

"Where are they taking us, to some big beehive?"

"Since they aren't bees, they couldn't be going to a hive."

"Well, it's some kind of a yucky bug place, isn't it?"

"My home is not 'some kind of yucky bug place.' You will see it when we get there."

They were moving very rapidly, and it wasn't long before a strange shape appeared in the distance.

"What's *that*?"

"Isn't it beautiful? I haven't seen it in such a long time."

To Tori it didn't look beautiful at all, just exceedingly weird. Sticking up from the surface of the lake and growing larger by the moment was an island of tubes that appeared to be carved out of solid rock. A few were as huge as skyscrapers. Around those were clustered thousands of smaller ones. It was like a monstrous collection of smokestacks, and all of it was covered with a disturbingly iridescent glow.

"What are those things sticking up?"

"Pipes. Have you ever seen a pipe organ?"

"No."

"It's a big instrument that plays music."

"Do they play music?"

"They used to, but they've been silent for a long time."

As the boat flew nearer, Tori heard an astounding hum like the buzzing of a beehive as large as a mountain. "You said it wasn't bees, but it sounds like bees."

"There are no bees."

"So it's buzzing bugs."

"Yes, buzzing bugs. And you're going to see a lot of them, so prepare yourself."

Soon they were very close. The gigantic cluster of pipes towered hundreds of feet in the air and seemed to ripple as though covered with loose, glistening skin. The boat slowed and dropped back into the water. In front of them appeared a tall arch that led into a wide canal. The buzzing was so loud now that it was like an army of chain saws. But until they were very close, Tori couldn't see any bugs at all. However, as they passed through the arch she realized that every pipe was encrusted with them. It was their bodies that caused the green glow.

As they entered the canal, the buzzing changed into a strange kind of music, almost like a march being played by five million very large kazoos.

"Ah, the choir is greeting us with a new composition entitled 'Winged

Victory.' This is a very great honor, perhaps the greatest that has ever been afforded anyone in the history of Boreth. Now I want you to smile and wave."

"Do I have to?"

"You have to. They've heard about you for a very long time, and it's only polite."

Then, with a sickly grin, she began waving.

"Excellent."

"I think I'm going to throw up."

On either side of the canal, masses of insect-covered pipes towered above them, flickering and shifting as though covered with layers of green fire. The buzzing 'music' grew louder and more majestic. Mirick fluttered up and landed on the highest point of the prow. Instantly the buzzing rose to a crescendo.

"What's happening?"

"They're cheering our arrival. Just keep smiling and waving. Nod to the left and then to the right. Left ... right ... left ... right ... good. You're doing very well."

Suddenly a blast of buzzes reverberated around them.

"What was *that*?"

"They're beginning the funeral march for the Great King. They have waited untold ages for this moment."

The insect choir devolved into a grinding bellow.

"I hate that sound. It's awful."

"It's called 'The Lament of the Moths,' and it's a great masterpiece in the post lingual style. By the way, you can stop nodding and grimacing. We've begun a funeral. Just look serious and take your fingers out of your ears."

Slowly the glistening light under the boat guided them around a curve. Ahead stood a long pier, and above it hovered a swarming column of monstrous insects.

"Look at those! They're monster bugs!" She started to scream, but Mirick flew right in front of her face.

"This is a very solemn moment. You will not destroy it with prejudicial howling. Is that clear?"

"Okay. But they're as big as dogs."

"They are the Larggen. Their job is to escort royal coffins into the Chamber of Sorrows. Long ago, when the kings of Boreth died, this is where they were brought to sleep with their ancestors."

"To Bug Island?"

"To the Island of the Singer."

"Is he a bug too?"

"He is what he is."

"Am I going to have to see him?"

"When the time is right."

"Just tell me so I can close my eyes."

Gently the boat came to rest against the pier. The insects that had transported it rose from the water and flew away. As the endless bug-dirge ground on, the swarm of Larggen swirled above the boat. Tori had closed her eyes, so she didn't see them descend and slowly lift the coffin into the air. Then, with a great deal of majestic buzzing, they carried it over the pier toward a regal doorway that led into darkness. When the coffin was gone, another swarm descended on the unconscious Alex. None too gently he was lifted and hauled off in a different direction.

"You can open your eyes now. It's over." Mirick fluttered in front of her. "Come with me. A room has been made comfortable for you." He flew up onto the pier.

"What about Alex?" Tori looked toward where her brother had been, but he wasn't there anymore. "Where'd he go?"

"He's been taken to receive help."

"By the bugs?"

"Yes."

"What are they going to do to him?"

"Everything possible."

"But I need to be with him when he wakes up."

"No, you don't. It's daylight on the surface, and his spirit won't be able to find his window."

"He's going to be okay, isn't he?"

"We shall hope so. And you will see him soon. But now it's time to rest. You've had a very long day struggling to control your nausea. And heaven knows, my day hasn't been easy either." As Tori climbed up onto the pier,

Mirick fluttered to a small door tucked behind a mass of tiny pipes. Like everything else, it was covered with insects.

"Open please and allow our guest to enter."

The bugs on the knob turned it and the door swung open. Tori entered a quaint little room hollowed from clusters of baby-sized pipes. In the middle was a soft bed with a thick comforter. To her deep relief there were no insects anywhere except Mirick. "Good, no bugs."

"I have told them that great fatigue has made you quite irritable, and that exasperating unsociability in such a circumstance is one of the foibles of your bizarre race. They were disappointed, but being intelligent and sensitive creatures they understand. They were looking forward to hovering over your bed and singing you to sleep."

"Yick!" She shivered. "Okay, well, tell them I'm sorry, but I don't need anybody to sing to me right now." Suddenly she was so exhausted that she could barely keep her eyes open. "I think I'm gonna lie down and rest a minute." Without even removing her shoes, she dropped to the bed and went fast asleep. She didn't see the tiny winged creatures that began hovering over her, not singing, but guarding her life.

The window . . .
Where is the window?
Fighting to get out . . .
Screaming . . .
Struggling . . .
Arms reaching . . .
Almost out . . .
Then sucked back in . . .
Over and over . . .
Where is the window?

Alex's consciousness awoke to his own thrashing. He was caught inside a cage of stinking, rotting meat, a cage with dim glass holes that let in a sickening vision. Screaming, he mashed against the walls. What was that on the outside? He could see thousands of huge glowing things swarming everywhere. And he could hear them. The thrum of their wings was like the roar of some awful machine. And his cage was flying through the air along with them. He wailed and howled.

Why couldn't he escape this nightmare?

Why couldn't he get to his window? His soul was loose inside himself, mashing and thrashing back and forth. All that mattered was getting out, but something was holding him in, keeping him locked in this hideous place. Once more he leaped upward, struggling, clawing the air, only to be sucked back in again. Into the clotted, festering mass of skin and bone. If he didn't get out, he would die.

Suddenly the movement through the air stopped. The cage was lowered onto something flat and cold, and the swarming things vanished. But above him hovered a shape with gigantic glowing wings and a body of green fire. Even in the depths of his agony he knew that he had seen it before, in the feverish dream, lying sweat-drenched in the cathedral. It was the nightmare creature that had flown through the halls spreading suffocating heat and mold and destruction. And now it was hovering over him.

27

JOURNEY'S END

You-you evil-evil little-little fool-fool ... you-you evil-evil little-little fool-fool ... you-you evil-evil little-little fool-fool ...

Freezing words from a soft lilting voice.

A woman's voice.

Two voices together.

The same voice, but double.

Scattering words.

Then another voice, muttering, mumbling, whining, terrified.

Wanderspoon.

Fading ... gone ... silence ...

And then ...

Strange, pleasant feelings.

Fingers in her hair.

A woman's fingers softly caressing.

And Amanda heard a gentle voice whisper, "Wake up, my child. It's time to wake up."

Slowly her eyes opened. Everything was blurry like in the morning before the sleep is rubbed away. Amanda couldn't remember a single dream where there had been sleep in her eyes, which meant this could be *real*. If only the blurriness would leave her mind. Reaching up to wipe her eyes, Amanda realized something else. She *could* reach up. Her arms moved. And her body didn't hurt anymore. When her fingers touched her face, she felt soft skin.

So wonderful, just to wake up and not hurt. She rubbed her eyes; it was like rubbing away a layer of crusty glue.

Still blurry.

Where was she? Was that sky up there? And branches? She was lying on something very soft, and the air was heavy with a mulchy sweetness. And she heard bubbling, gurgling sounds. Running water close by.

Another rub and she could see more clearly. Boughs were gently bending over her and beyond them was an azure sky speckled with stars. *Daytime stars.* Finally the blur left her mind. Boreth. She was still on Boreth. Amanda sat up and looked around. And then began the enchantment.

She was in a small forest clearing that could have been the garden of a fairy princess. The bubbling sounds came from a little waterfall that spilled into a shimmering pool. Beneath her was a thick silky blanket of moss. And green. Everything was green. She had never imagined there could be so many different greens. Around her hung dark green ferns the size of pillowcases. And beneath those, tiny ferns with pale green leaves like fairy teardrops. There were tall spindly bushes of yellow green, fat little clumps of gray green.

There was brown green and black green and emerald green. And all of the greens glistened as though every leaf had been polished by a fanatical gardener with a huge bottle of wax. Splashed among the greens were masses of exotic flowers—little purple lippy things with red stamen tongues, clusters of pink blossoms that hung together like bunches of wrong-colored bananas, misty blue and yellow petal-swarms that looked like butterflies but weren't. And swathed across all of it was a rainbow of crimson and blue-green moss hanging delicately in the branches as though an angel had dropped her mantle on the way to Heaven.

Heaven!

There was an interesting idea. Amanda had never thought much about Heaven. But if there were such a place she imagined it would be like this: a lovely garden where all the ugliness would be swept away. And those crushed with sorrow and pain would wake up to find that everything was all right. In Heaven they would find healing. She looked down at herself. Her skin was smooth and soft. Nothing was growing out of her knees and elbows, no hard crusts of flesh anywhere. Crawling over to the pool, she looked at her reflection—no longer a twisted, ugly shape like a human tree, she was Amanda. Truly and really Amanda! But how had it happened?

She told herself that, dead or alive, it didn't matter. All that mattered was being this happy. But suddenly the happiness was sucked away in a blind panic.

The baby!

Where was the baby?

Jumping up, she stared around.

Nowhere! He was nowhere!

She was about to start crashing blindly through the bushes to search for him when a soft woman's voice whispered, "The little one is safe. Don't be afraid."

Amanda looked around but couldn't see anybody. "He's supposed to be with me all the time. If I'm not dead, I've got to take him to the Mountain."

A sweet laugh echoed from high above. "You're not dead and this *is* the Mountain."

"It is?"

"Yes, it is."

"The ... Big Mountain?"

"The biggest."

"You mean ... I'm ... here?"

"Here is exactly where you are. You brought the baby home."

For a moment Amanda stood in shock; then tears came. "You mean ... it's over? We made it?"

"Your journey has ended."

She felt dizzy and, in her dizziness, started babbling. "This-is-it. We-did-it. I-never-thought-we'd-get-here-but-we-did-and-just-look-at-it-it's-so-beautiful-I-can't-even-stand-it." She babbled until she almost fell into the pool.

The voice in the treetops laughed again. "Be careful or you're going to get wet."

"Okay-okay-I-will-it's-just-all-so-wonderful-and-I-*feel*-wonderful." Then she paused. "But ... could I still see him? I'm-so-used-to-having-him-with-me-we've-been-together-so-long-it-feels-weird-when-he's-not-here-could-I? Would-it-be-all-right?"

The laughing voice replied, "Slow down, my child. Of course, it's all right. Follow the path beside the stream. It will lead you to him."

Amanda turned and looked. Flowing away from the pool was a little stream, and next to it lay a path that led off into the forest. Rushing over, she began running through the trees, laughing and calling out. "We made it! We got here! We're on the Mountain! We did it!"

The soft voice came again. "Doesn't it feel good to walk and run without pain?"

She stopped, suddenly feeling very guilty. "Yes, it does. I don't know who you are, but if you're the one who healed me, I'm sorry for being so ungrateful." She fought back tears. "I didn't even say thank you. All I was thinking about was being happy and wanting to see the baby."

"Your joy is all the thanks I need."

"Are you the Healer?"

"I am. My name is Melania, and soon we will meet face-to-face. But go slowly and let my forest touch you. All that matters here is loving, and feeling, and being One with the beauty. Hurrying can take the joy away. Breathe deeply. Say to yourself, *Let peace and Oneness enter my heart for I am One with all things.* Will you do that?"

"Yes."

"Good. And I'll see you in a little while." Amanda heard a soft rushing sound in the trees, and she felt as though the person she had been talking to was gone. She looked around. Why was she hurrying through such a lovely place? Bellwind's island had been beautiful, but the beauty had been veiled in sorrow. There was none of that here. Melania was right; the terrible journey was over. Now was the time to rest. Lifting her head, she closed her eyes and began breathing deeply. Then she whispered, "Let the peace and Oneness of this lovely place enter my heart, for I am one with all things." Instantly she felt tension leaving her body, replaced with a joyful calm. The colors around her seemed to grow more vivid, and from far away came the echo of singing. It was all so peaceful that she thought about lying down and letting her mind drift in the dreaminess, but she just couldn't do that until she had seen the baby and shared the joy with him.

Breathing in the sweetness of the forest, she walked on. As the path wound through the trees, the gentle singing grew louder. It was like the voices of many women softly chanting words as old as the ages in a language she couldn't understand. But just hearing them filled her with joy, as though they were calling to her, telling her she wasn't alone, that sisters who loved her were waiting a little farther along just a few steps deeper into Heaven.

Closer.

The chant-song grew more complex, voices rising, falling, harmonies within harmonies weaving on the wind. Finally she entered what must have been the oldest part of the forest, and the singing was everywhere. All around her towered trees that looked as though they had been planted at the dawn of time, their trunks covered with ancient moss that hung like robes of dewy splendor. Though they were old beyond imagining, none was gnarled or misshapen. Each one stood straight and tall. Long ago their highest limbs and branches had woven together into an endless vaulted ceiling of pale green leaves through which fell shafts of hazy sunlight. To Amanda it was like being in a forest of tree grandmothers who had gathered to sing when the world was young and had enjoyed it so much that they had kept on singing for ten thousand years. Though all were stately and dignified, there was a softness about them too, like regal old women who love to take little children in their arms. As she walked among them, she realized that each tree had a voice all its own. Some were low and gentle. Others were like singing birds. Often she left the path and stood beneath a particularly beautiful tree so she could hear it apart from the rest.

As Amanda wandered and listened, she became aware of one magnificent voice. It took awhile to hear it clearly, but when she did, she realized it was like no other. It sang a haunting melody that would rise to the treetops, then vanish beneath the thousand harmonies below, only to soar again in heartbreaking loveliness. The more she heard it, the more it felt like the voice was singing the story of her whole life, heartache and joy, pain and happiness, every experience she had ever had, blended and interwoven. Often tears would come to her eyes, and she would find herself whispering, "Yes, that's the way I felt," and, "I remember that. How could I have forgotten?"

How long she walked, she had no idea, but constantly the one voice drew her on. Finally she rounded a bend and discovered that the path disappeared at the edge of a lustrous meadow, in the center of which stood a single tree. And it was *glorious*. Its long gentle branches were covered with silver leaves, and out of them grew clusters of shimmering black flowers. Glowing mist drifted from it, creating soft halos in the air. Though it wasn't tall, the tree seemed to be the center of everything with all the others gathered around it in worship. And the singing voice was coming from within it.

The singing stopped and the voice called to her, "Amanda, my daughter, I've waited so long. Come to me." With wide eyes she crossed the clearing. "Are you ... the Healer?"

"I am. Come closer."

Slowly she walked forward and felt the warm mist surround her.

"You're ... a tree?"

"Does that surprise you?"

"I guess nothing surprises me anymore."

"Trees are known for their music. Did you like my singing?"

"I loved it, but sometimes it made me cry."

"That's because the song was about you. Amanda, dear child of earth, your life is a song of faithfulness and courage."

"I don't know about that. All I did was get carried here in a wagon."

"Your great strength brought you here. But you have traveled far, and I know you are hungry."

Amanda realized that she was famished. "Well, I haven't eaten in a long time."

"Come beneath my branches."

As she stepped under the tree, she was bathed in a luscious fragrance. Among the flowers she saw fruit so ripe it looked like it would fall to the ground at any moment.

"Hunger you shall never know in my forest." The voice was coming from above. "I invite you to taste my children."

"Your children?" The girl was startled.

"Fruit are the children of trees."

"I never thought of it that way."

"In ages past all creatures knew such things. No one would take the children of a tree without asking permission of their mother. But that was in a time before time, and it doesn't matter now. All that matters is that you are with us at last and my forest is here for your pleasure. Take of my little ones. Their sweetness will continue your healing."

"Am I still sick?"

"Growing well is a journey of many steps, and you are far along. First came the healing of your body. But now must come Oneness to your soul. Eat as much as you desire."

Though she felt a bit odd about it, Amanda reached up and plucked a piece of fruit. When she bit into it, the taste made her forget everything else. A strange sweetness tingled in her mouth, and each bite made her ache for more. "It's so good." She mumbled as juice ran down her chin. After six pieces she had to stop. "I want to keep eating, but I'm so full." Then something began to happen. The tingling sensation grew and her eyes started to blur. She rubbed them and looked around. What she saw made her knees so weak that if she hadn't grabbed onto a branch she would have fallen.

She wasn't in a forest. It was a garden of spirits. The outer shells of everything looked like soft glimmering ghosts. Inside them were living creatures mingling, loving. That's why the singing had been so complex. She understood now. Every vine, every branch, even the roots under the dirt, all were *one.* Life entwined forever. She looked down. Beneath her was an emerald carpet of soft slender beings, bending and weaving in the wind.

Grass.

That's what she had always called it. But each blade was different. And every tiny shoot knew who she was and why she was there. And they were singing too, in little voices that had been drowned out by the trees. For a moment she could think their thoughts and feel what it was like to be a blade of grass in a sea of brothers and sisters. No life apart. *One with all.* What joy there was in Oneness.

Slowly Amanda walked back out into the clearing. Before her stood hundreds of lovely tree-spirit women, their arms reaching toward her. Suddenly she could understand their language. Their chant-song was about her, and how brave she was, and how she had come home to them from a long and terrible journey. Most of all it was about how they loved her and wanted to make her One with the life that was in them. Amanda was about to run to them when she heard a rustling sound behind her.

Turning, she saw that the beautiful tree had disappeared. Standing in its place was a tall slender woman. Her skin was soft brown and her eyes were violet. Her long hair was like silver leaves and woven in it were clusters of black flowers. She wore a gown of moss and her feet were bare. Around her shimmered halos of silver mist. Her loveliness was so delicate and ethereal that Amanda felt like she was in the presence of a goddess of dreams.

"You're … Melania?"

The woman nodded and smiled. "Now you understand the true power of healing. The eyes of the soul must be opened because all creatures join hands in the rebirth of a single heart. Only when that takes place can we become free from the shadow of dying."

"I feel so happy." Tears were in Amanda's eyes. "I feel like this has always been my home and I want to stay here forever."

"This is your home. But there is one more thing that you must do before your work is finished."

"What is it?"

"An act of joy that will fulfill the purpose of your life. But right now it's time to go and see the one you carried over so many weary miles."

"Oh, yes. Where is he?"

"Come, I'll show you." The woman turned and led her across the clearing. On the other side the path became visible again. As Amanda walked, she had never experienced such joy. The whole forest was alive with singing creatures that reached out from every tree and bush and flower, trying to touch Melania. It was like a mother walking among her children. The air itself seemed to ripple with ecstasy. A kind of dreaminess entered her mind. This was Heaven. She knew it.

"All of them love you so much," Amanda said.

"They were dead and I brought them back to life again. But my power is limited to this mountain. You have walked through my poor world, Amanda. What is it like away from here?"

"It's awful. So ugly."

"But it will live once more because a new Healer is among us."

"Really?"

"It's you, my child. You are the Chosen One. Within you lies the power to make this world into what it was meant to be. That's why you were called to bring the baby home."

"I don't know how to heal anything."

"The gift will be awakened. All you need is a little of the courage that brought you here."

"It was Wanderspoon who brought us here. We never would have made it otherwise."

"Speak carefully. That name is a curse. He brought you because he wanted a reward. He's a pitiful creature."

"I know, but sometimes I almost felt sorry for him."

"He wasn't always the way he is now. Once he had great gifts."

"We spent a night in this dead, empty city, but he thought it was full of people and he was their king. While we were there, I had a dream. In it, there was an earthquake and a fire and a lot of people died."

Melania stared at her. "You dreamed the truth. It must be part of your gift awakening. What you saw happened long ago, during the last Great War. What else did you dream?"

"The buildings fell down, and Wanderspoon was right in the middle of them. How did he get away?"

"He isn't human."

"What is he?"

"When the Worwil came to Boreth we brought spirits with us to help us do our work. He was one of mine. I gave him power to heal all creatures. But he turned against me, choosing to rule instead of serve. So I took his power away. Now his life is cursed. He hoped that if he brought you here the curse would be removed."

"What's going to happen to him?"

"He will wander on and on, trying to fill his hunger."

At any other time Amanda would have found the words very frightening. But in her dreaminess she simply walked on looking at the pretty flowers and trees. They had been climbing for an hour when Melania left the path and led her into a tiny clearing. There, in a patch of sunlight, lay the little boy fast asleep.

"Shhh," Melania whispered. "We don't want to wake him. I'm sure he hasn't slept like this in a long, long time."

Amanda whispered, "He's so beautiful, and I love him so much. I want to pick him up." The woman smiled and led her away. When they had gone a short distance, Amanda stopped. "There was a question I wanted to ask, but I can't make my mind remember it. Oh, I remember. What's his name?"

"My sister Bellwind didn't tell you?"

"No."

"Did she tell you anything?"

"Not much."

"Perhaps she thought you weren't ready. His name is Aloi, and he is the Living Presence of the Spirit that is in all things."

"He's a spirit?"

"Listen to a little song that we used to teach the children." She began chanting softly.

> *One. Yes, one. The universe is One.*
> *When Boreth was shaped from the dust of the stars*
> *In that Oneness was born Aloi.*
> *One. Everything is one.*
> *From the tiniest leaf to the tallest mountain.*
> *And we call that Oneness Aloi.*
> *One. Forever one.*
> *When he comes, he will sing the world to Oneness.*
> *And then, in him all things will be . . . Aloi.*

When she was finished, Amanda said, "That's so beautiful. But there's something I don't understand."

"What is it, my child?"

"If that's who he is, why does anybody want to hurt him? One night we saw evil things riding on horses. If they'd have found us, we'd both be dead."

Sadly Melania replied, "In the universe the great battle never ends, Light and Darkness, good and evil, love and fear, the circle turns on and on."

"I was really scared that night."

"Little daughter, let me take your fear away. In the world of Light and Darkness, which is good and which is evil?"

"What do you mean?"

"Which is better and which is worse?"

"I guess light is better. It lets you see."

"But too much light can burn your eyes with fire, and only in darkness is the crimson moon revealed. Deeper, child, go deeper, to thoughts that you have never known. Creating or destroying, which is good and which is evil?"

"Well, creating things is better than wrecking them."

"But how can new things come unless the old is swept away? If nothing died, could anything be born?"

"I guess there wouldn't be any room left, would there?" Amanda was struggling to make her mind work. "Okay, but there's one thing I know for sure. Hurting a baby is always bad. And there's nothing good about it."

"Ah, here is the secret within the secret, the greatest secret of all. Few there are who find it and fewer still who grasp its power. But to the Chosen it is revealed. And you are the Chosen, my child. Aloi is the light. The darkness tries to overcome him because it is the destiny of evil to fight against the good. But struggling against it makes him strong. Like a butterfly trapped in a cocoon fighting to reach the wind. Fighting, fighting, for if it does not fight, its wings will be weak and it will never fly. If there were no evil to fight against, there would be no light in Aloi. Chaos, darkness, and evil are only the names we give the cocoon out of which all light is born."

"I don't understand any of that. How can he fight against things on horses? He's just a baby. What if they had killed him?"

"No creature of the Light can ever die."

"They killed a huge stone horse and he was a creature of the Light. I saw them do it."

Melania paused and her eyes filled with tears. "So, my brother Sandalban is gone."

"I'm sorry. I forgot he was one of you."

"It's all right. You saw him die?"

"Yes, and it was horrible."

"But what happened when his body was destroyed?"

"His spirit rose in the air and he flew away."

"So, he didn't really die at all, did he?"

"Well, not exactly."

"Don't you see what happened, Amanda? The Servants of the Night released him. They set him free from a world of pain. Wasn't that for his good?"

"I . . . guess so. But it was terrible too."

"Yes, evil is always terrible. And what they did to him was very evil. But tell me, wasn't he happier to be free?"

"Well, he looked happier. He'd been chained to the ground for ages."

"So good came out of bad. Hasn't that happened to you? Aren't you a better person for all that you have suffered?"

Softly Amanda replied, "A lot better. I was so selfish and angry before. But I don't think it's that way for everybody. What about Wanderspoon?"

"Some creatures learn more quickly than others. But slowly, through the endless wheel of life and death and life again, every being, even Wanderspoon, grows toward the Oneness of all things." She stopped and knelt down. Near the path, there was a tiny flower. "Look, child. Do you see the lovely spirit inside?"

Amanda knelt and looked. Flowing up the stamen and over the petals was a misty little creature with the eyes of a baby. "Oh, it's so cute."

"Pull it out of the ground."

"But I don't want to do that. It'll kill it."

"Just do it and see."

Reluctantly Amanda picked the flower. A startled look came into the little spirit's eyes, but then it changed to excitement and joy. With a soft cry, it leaped into the air and vanished.

"Where did it go?"

"Where did my brother Sandalban go? To be reborn. The flower was glad to leave the dead shell that you hold in your hand, just like Sandalban was glad to leave his chained body. Don't you see? Good and evil need each other. They're like two sides of a single leaf."

"I'm so confused. If that's true, what *is* good and what *is* bad? What's the difference if it all comes out the same? Why does it matter which one you choose?"

"Because every creature must fulfill the purpose for its life. Look how Wanderspoon brought you here. He chose evil because that's his destiny. You chose good because that is yours. Both of you had to be what you are for it to work together."

"But if it's our destiny, we aren't choosing at all, are we? We're just doing whatever we're supposed to, and that isn't good or bad. It just *is*."

"My daughter, your wisdom is very great. Now you understand the secret. All that matters is being who you are in the Oneness of Life. And remember, above all else, there is love. Love guides all things. Good and evil, light and darkness, creation and destruction, even life and death, all work together in eternal love. My world is moving out of chaos into love and light. Evil was necessary for good to be reborn. Aloi is the power of healing, and you will be the healer. The ancient prophecies foretold that one would come who would be the Bearer of Life for all. And so you are. But our time is short. There is much to do when the baby awakens. We must prepare you for your great task." She clapped her hands. Out from the trees stepped dozens of lovely girl-spirits. "Come, children, prepare our little sister for the Great Awakening."

With cries of joy they came and took Amanda's hands. Then, laughing and singing, they led her off into the forest down a long path to a hidden glen. There she found a silvery pool. In the sparkling ripples, she thought she could see tiny beings made of foam dancing and vanishing. Then the preparation began. First she was bathed in the deliciously warm water, then anointed with sweet oils that made her skin tingle. She almost fell asleep as her hair was brushed and braided with flowers. Finally a simple white gown was brought, and on her head was placed a thin circlet of gold that looked like a crown. When they were finished, Amanda stared at her reflection. She was pretty, *really pretty*, in a way that she had never thought possible. The sun was setting when the laughing spirit-girls led her back to Melania.

"Amanda, my daughter, you are so beautiful." There were tears in the woman's eyes. Amanda wanted to cry herself. How often she had dreamed of hearing those words from her mother, dreamed of hearing them and knowing they were true. But they had never been true, not until this moment. And looking up at Melania, she could almost see her mother's eyes. To keep from bursting into tears, she looked away and whispered, "You've done so many wonderful things for me, and I don't deserve them. I love you."

Melania smiled. "Daughter, the joy is all mine. But I have one last gift to give." From out of the trees, a spirit-girl brought a stone chalice. Lifting it high, the woman's lips moved as though in prayer. Then she turned to Amanda.

"Dusk is the time when night and day join hands. At this sacred moment I give you the most precious thing I possess. It came with me from beyond the stars and is called the Tears of Heaven." She handed the chalice to Amanda. From it came a bittersweet fragrance. Inside was a mysterious liquid. The surface was calm, almost like oil. But beneath raged a tiny ocean. Miniature waves crashed and swirled in frothing luminescence.

"What is this?"

"Drink it, my child. It will show you all that you were meant to be."

"It looks kind of scary."

"You need fear nothing that comes from my hand."

Amanda hesitated. But such love was in Melania's face that her fear vanished. Putting the chalice to her lips, she drained it to the bottom.

28

THE MEANING OF ONENESS

At first, nothing.

Only a faint sweet flavor that Amanda had never tasted before. Then slowly came a distant roaring.

What was it? A voice? A thousand voices? Whispering, chanting, a single note, a single tone deeper than any ever heard before.

Louder, and louder still ...

Thundering Deepness ...

Ten Thousand Voices in One ...

An Ocean of Roaring Sweeping Down from the Sky ...

An Ocean Crashing over her ...

Gasping ... struggling to breathe ...

Drowning ... Dying ...

And then ...

Exaltation!

Fire ...

Her soul was turning into flame ... her mind exploding. Blazing! Consuming the shell of her flesh ... Rising higher and higher ... Above the forest, above the mountain, above the planet. Flaming beyond the universe. Entering the Greatness ... the Ecstasy ... the Rapture of One. Of One Alone! Complete in Splendor. Beyond All! In All! Light, Darkness, Good, Evil, Love, Hate, Life, Death ... meant nothing in the Endless Oneness of the One. All that mattered was drowning the Amanda-girl of long ago in the Vastness of the Presence. Becoming One ... One that was God ... Is God ... Beyond God ...

To be God ...

One!

Then from far away she heard Melania whisper, "Beyond good and evil, beyond all fading dreams, you are the Presence and the Holy."

And Amanda-god whispered, "I am One."

But then her mind began sliding backward through the stars. Down ... and down.

Suddenly below her was the planet. She saw oceans and mountains, deserts and forests, and heard Melania whisper, "All exists for the pleasure of the One. Now you must choose. Shall this dream live or shall it die? Nothing is real but the dreams of the One."

Amanda-god answered, "Today the dream will live because it pleases me."

"Then come back and bring it LIFE."

In an instant she felt her mind contracting, smashing through her skin back into her flesh. Gasping! Struggling to breathe! Once more she was looking out through her eyes. Too much. Too fast. She fainted. But Melania caught her.

Instantly Amanda's eyes opened. Then she spoke, but not with her lips, with her mind. "I don't want to be here. I want to be where I was."

Melania's mind replied, "Soon, my daughter, very soon. But first you must make your world live again."

"How?"

"By releasing the power of Aloi. Come."

Taking her by the hand, the woman led her through the forest. As they walked, Amanda felt strangely dislocated as though part of her had been split away and was floating high above. It was like seeing out of two sets of eyes, one in her body and the other in the treetops. Looking through the "treetop eyes" made the god-feeling return. And she found that she could shift her awareness back and forth from Amanda-god to Amanda-girl. It was jarring. For the first time in her life, she wasn't sure who she really was.

Finally they reached the place where the little boy had been sleeping. He was awake. Focusing through her "girl-eyes," Amanda reached down and picked him up. At first he stared at her, and then he clung to her. She kissed him. "I'm so glad to see you. I've missed you so much." But there was an odd echo in her voice, and she found it hard to keep her awareness in her body.

Softly Melania said, "It's time to go."

Moving through the trees, they came to a wide path that led up the Mountain. It was dark now and the crimson moon was rising. As they climbed, they soon left the forest, and the path began twisting steeply upward through barren rocks. Amanda heard singing, and looking back, she caught her breath. At first she thought every tree on the Mountain was on fire. But then she realized that it was the spirits living within the trees. The whole forest was blazing with tree-angels, thousands and thousands of them, singing for joy. Her awareness shifted above, and once more she felt ecstasy. The spirits were worshiping her, singing about her strength and beauty and courage. But then her "girl eyes" looked down at the baby. He was staring at her. For a moment she stopped feeling split in two and was only a girl again.

As she struggled to understand what was happening, Melania whispered into her mind. "Soon we will reach the place where all things are made new. Prepare yourself. Purify your soul."

"How do I do that?"

"Remove every doubt and look toward the stars where you were born. Hold the little one close. Feel his life. And speak the words of Oneness that I taught you."

Softly Amanda whispered, "Let peace and Oneness enter my heart for I am One with all things."

And Amanda-god returned.

As they climbed, mist began to appear. With her god-eyes she looked behind her. The fiery singing spirits of the trees were following, and, as they entered the mist, around each one appeared a glowing aura. It was like an ocean of crystal spheres with living flames inside, drifting up the Mountain. But soon the mist grew so thick that she had to look out of her "girl-eyes" or she would trip and fall. "Melania, where are you?"

"Right here, my child." She felt the woman take her arm. "Stay close. We're almost there."

Finally they stepped out onto a flat stone pavement. Here the fog was so heavy that she couldn't even see the baby in her arms. Melania said, "We are at the place where Aloi was born. And here his spirit must be released so that he can make all things new again."

"How will that happen?"

"I'll show you." A dozen more steps and they stopped. "Amanda, though you can't see it, you are standing above the Womb of the World. Say the words of Oneness."

She repeated. Instantly her god-mind was floating in ecstasy.

"This is where the Power of All Healing will come. Do you want that, my child?"

"Yes."

"Then lift Aloi and release him."

Instantly Amanda's awareness flashed back into her body. "What did you say?"

"Lift him and release him into the Womb."

"I ... I don't understand." With her "girl-eyes," she began struggling to see what was in front of her. But it was impossible. "What do you mean ... release him?"

"Hold him out and let him go."

"You mean ... drop him?" She was incredulous.

"Daughter, look down."

Amanda looked. Gradually the mist parted and a dim golden light appeared thousands of feet beneath her. She gasped. She was standing on the edge of a sheer precipice. As she watched, the light began to rise, and in it, arms were reaching upward. "What is that down there?"

"The Spirit of the Womb. The Mother Force of Boreth."

Suddenly she heard the anguished cry of a woman.

"She knows her child is here, and she is calling for him. Release him to her."

"But she's still ... a long way off."

"Don't be afraid. He won't be harmed. She will take Aloi to his true home, where he will be loved forever and his power will fill the world."

"But ... if I let go ... will he ... float?"

"He will fall to the Mother."

Amanda looked at the little boy. He was staring at her and clinging with all his might. She had never felt him hold on so tightly.

"Maybe ... we could wait until she gets a little closer. I think he's kind of scared."

"Aloi cannot feel fear. What you sense is your own dread of losing him, and you must overcome it. You saw what happened when the spirit of the flower was released. Much greater joy will come when he is loosed to make all things new again."

"But the flower died. Is ... his body going to die?"

"He can never die."

"But then how will his spirit be released?"

"Do you trust me, child?"

"Yes."

"Would I do anything to harm him?"

"No."

"Then believe my words and obey."

Amanda looked up at Melania. The woman's eyes were filled with overwhelming love. "Well ... if that's what I'm supposed to do ..." Breathing hard, she inched closer to the edge and held out the baby. But the little boy began struggling. Quickly she pulled him back. "He's scared. He really is. He's never been this way before. I want to do what I'm supposed to, but I just can't drop him."

Another heartbreaking cry echoed from the deep, and Melania spoke urgently, "Child, there are many things you don't understand. Soon the moment of power will be gone. The ancient prophecies must be fulfilled right now."

"Please ... just have her come up and take him. I know she wouldn't want him to be afraid."

A strange look came into Melania's eyes, "Child, she cannot. The eternal Laws are written. The power of Aloi must be released by the faith of the Life Bearer. It is from your arms that his spirit must fly. There is no other way. If you care for a dying world, *release him*."

Tears came to Amanda's eyes, "Melania, I want to, I really do, but ..."

"Look down at her, Amanda."

Far below, she saw a mother's face—and in it there was endless sorrow and yearning, and her arms were reaching upward.

"If you truly love him, give him back to his mother. Complete the task of faithfulness for which you were born."

The singing grew in majesty as though Heaven itself had been drained of splendor to give her strength.

"Release him, my child." Melania laid her hand on Amanda's head. Instantly waves of ecstasy swept through her and her mind floated upward.

Exaltation!

Oneness!

She watched from above as her body stepped to the edge of the precipice and held out the child. But just as she was about to drop him, she heard a different voice in her mind, and it spoke with power, *Amanda, wake up!* Instantly her awareness crashed back into her body. The feeling of being split in two vanished, and she awakened as though from a dream. She looked into the baby's eyes. In them, there was a searching presence that was staring into her soul.

With a gasp she pulled him back and cried out, *"No! I won't do it! I will not drop him down there!"* Then she turned away from the edge.

Instantly the singing stopped, and there was a silence so heavy it seemed to crush the air. Amada looked at Melania. The woman's face was changing. The beauty was fading away. Her skin was growing very white, and tiny lines were appearing around her eyes. Her mind whispered into Amanda's mind. *Child of the Wind ...*

But Amanda stopped her. "No, don't talk to me that way. Use your mouth." It wasn't a request. It was a command.

Another terrible silence. And then a soft eerie groan seemed to come from everywhere. The woman began growing taller. The skin of her face hardened. From her lips came a ghostly whisper, *"Lutakuan ... moleteva ... melesssss ..."* There was a scraping sound like something with huge claws crawling over glass.

But Amanda wasn't frightened. Instead, within her she felt a terrible, steely calm. In a soft voice she said, "You told me this was the Great Mountain. If it is, then I want to see the One Who Lives in the Mists. Bring me to him right now."

There was a sigh like the last breath from a dying body, and the woman whispered, "Amandamaaaa... you have followed liiies ..."

But before she could continue, Amanda cried out, "Yes, I followed lies. And they all came from you."

An eerie, creaking ripple trembled through the stone beneath her feet, and the scratching, crawling sound grew louder. But Amanda kept on. "You told me that Darkness is as strong as Light, that one can't live without the other. *A lie!* Darkness is so weak that the smallest candle can make it disappear!"

Taller. The woman was growing taller. Heavy wrinkles were appearing all over her body. The lovely moss of her gown was sinking into them and turning deathly white. But Amanda didn't stop, and her voice began echoing over the Mountain. "You told me that evil is as strong as good, that one can't live without the other. *A lie!* Good doesn't need evil to live. But evil can't exist unless there's something for it to destroy. It can't live a minute on its own because destroying is the only power it has. That's why evil is weak. *And you are evil!* You tried to destroy us. I let my mind go to sleep because I didn't believe that evil could be so beautiful. But I was wrong. Lies are always beautiful. You told me I was a god. I'm not a god, and I never will be. You wanted me to kill this child with my own hands, to drop him to his death to the thing down below. And I almost did it because I loved your lies. But whoever you are, *you've failed.* I do have the power to choose. And I have chosen. If you want this baby you'll have to kill me to get him."

A scream!

Out of the woman's body streaked a thousand twisted limbs that writhed, splitting and branching into the air. Higher and higher, she towered over the girl. But as Amanda stared at her, she was changing too. A blazing strength shone in her eyes. In that terrifying moment her childhood ended, and she became all that she was meant to be. Calmly she said, "This isn't the Mountain. My journey isn't finished. I still have to take the baby home."

From the tree came a shrieking voice: "I am Melania, Worwil of Life and Death, the Queen of Heaven. I give life and take it away. Now you will know who is stronger." The tree grew into a giant. But still the woman's face was visible, twisting and elongating high up within the trunk. Her limbs and branches cast a thousand shadows into the sky. Then the shadows and the Melania-tree became one. The air around her boiled and surged like a thunderhead. At that moment Amanda knew what she was seeing because she had seen it before. As the tree in the sky roared above her, she held the baby against her heart. A mighty rush of wind surged as the trunk tore out of the ground and rose. For a moment it hung motionless.

And then the lights appeared.

From inside the trunk flashed gigantic shafts of red and green and blue and purple. Up and down they swirled in a hurricane of brilliance, leaving trails of glistening mist. As they moved faster and faster, out of them dropped thousands of smaller lights that raced and spun in every direction like a dance of fiery stars. But this time Amanda felt no ecstasy and her mind didn't blur. She cried out. "You're no healer. I know who you are. You're the *thing* that gave me the disease!"

A wrenching groan reverberated from the abyss. Amanda looked down. The face and arms of the mother had vanished. Far below whirled a mass of shadows that congealed into a gigantic form with wings and a body of crystal. Within him flowed rivers of color. He was standing in a crimson canyon above a pit of blood.

A thunderous crash.

Amanda looked up. From high above, fingers of lightning were streaking toward her. She saw them coming and all she could do was hold the baby tight and bow her head. When the white fire touched her, she cried out in agony. Her body stiffened as her skin began to burn. Out of her grew branches and limbs. Her face faded beneath the crust of a tree. But as the transformation continued something unexpected happened. In the depth of her suffering ... as the last tears rolled down her vanishing cheeks ... from within her burned a silver light.

Brighter and brighter ...

Her soul was blazing ...

Suddenly around her swirled the mists, and within them flashed lightning the color of blood. The crystal being in the canyon disappeared. As the soul of a dying girl streaked upward, the burning hands of her spirit grasped the Tree in the Sky. There was a mighty shout as the sacrifice of Amanda's life called down the Fire of Heaven and with a roar the flames consumed every limb and branch. From Melania came one last shriek, and the mighty Worwil, the Fallen Healer, vanished, never to live again.

Daybreak.

A lovely white tree stood on the pinnacle of a mountain. It was all that was left of a girl named Amanda who had come so far from a place called

Earth. Though she was dead, wrapped in her silky branches lay a contented baby fast asleep. Gone was the beautiful forest of lying dreams. But in death the girl was not alone. All around her, covering the Mountain, stood the true forest that had been there all the time, white trees by the thousands, large and small, their arms reaching upward as though in prayer toward a far Greater Mountain with mists that shrouded a Crimson Throne.

29

THE PIT

A DEMON!

That's what it was. That's what it had to be.

Alex lay where the awful flying things had taken him. Inside the rotting prison of his own flesh, his spirit shrieked and cringed, trying to hide. Then out of the demon's mouth came a whisper, "Son of Darkness, be still."

Instantly he choked into silence.

"I must do things that will cause you great pain. Prepare yourself."

The monster rose into the air. From the end of its body appeared a needle-like stinger as long as a sword. The tip moved downward until it was above his stomach. Then it plunged.

His vision filled with jagged streaks. He lurched and spasmed. Every muscle went rigid. And then began a horror that he had never experienced. A tiny twitching in his guts, something moving from side to side. A twitching ... then a twisting and a writhing.

Something inside him. He was not alone. Not alone within the cage. Something else was living there too, and the poison of the sting had awakened it. Like a serpent, it was uncoiling. He could feel it expand. Then it started crawling upward, climbing through the tunnels of his body, through his intestines ... into his stomach. Nausea. Expanding. Expanding. And not just up his body, but into his soul. Alex screamed, trying to escape its slithering touch, but he couldn't; they were locked in the cage together. Through him passed waves of unspeakable knowing.

Food! He was its food!

As it crawled upward, he could feel it eating him, sucking his life, taking him into itself... chewing, swallowing, gorging, digesting, excreting. Passing over his heart ... into his throat. He heard the demon in the air whisper, "In the name of the One Who Lives in the Mists, reveal your presence."

A roar! A mighty roar came from Alex's mouth! Alex roared because it roared. Using his tongue and teeth and soul, in a shrieking rasp it screeched, "You dare to summon me as though I were a slave without a name?"

With icy calm, the hovering monster replied, "The ancient king lies in the Chamber of Sorrows. The time of the end is upon you."

The Alex-Thing screamed, "Yes, the end is near, but not the one you expect, my brother."

The demon hovered closer until its face was inches away. "You have failed. Melania is dead. The final sacrifice was not made. Without it, your power will be broken. You know the Law."

There was a long mocking laugh. And then, from out of Alex's mouth, croaked a song.

The Law, the Law,
Yes, I know the bloody Law
From the Mountain comes the singing,
The Crimson Light is bringing,
Death forever stinging in the Music of the Law.
The Law, the Law,
The horror of the Law,
From the witless depths of weakness,
Come the lies of love and meekness,
The end of lust and sleekness is in the Music of the Law.
The Law, the Law,
The screeching of the Law,
Childhood's blood is just a token
Of the Song forever broken,
And the curses I have spoken, against the shrieking of the Law.

The Thing laughed again. The tiny awareness that was still Alex heard the awful sound of children sobbing. Millions and millions of echoing voices, sobbing from far away. And up from an abyss within him spewed the memories of hell. Wave after wave of heartbroken screams and visions of horror. Children offered on altars of selfishness and fear, little ones torn from their mothers' wombs, children crushed, burning like straw on a fiery wind, drowning in darkness, their innocence vanishing in a flood of hate and tears. And the Thing within Alex tasted each memory, loving it all, leeching joy from their dying, bathing in their blood, cherishing their murders, treasuring their shrieks, storing each death within itself, so it could gorge on an endless banquet of horror. All of this Alex knew. But more than simply knew. Because he was one with the slithering Thing, he was forced to join in its memories, to taste the blood, to writhe in the agony.

Loathing!

How he loathed himself. How he hated his own soul. How he hungered to die. If only he could go back and die like the children, innocent and clean. And the Thing that sucked his life took joy in his wretched loathing and showed him more and more, making him smell and taste and see.

But then the creature in the air cried out, "Enough! While you are in my chamber you will look at me alone!"

The hellish visions vanished. From Alex's lips came a groaning sigh, and the Thing hissed, "Oh, mighty Worwil, weak, pitiful creature, remember the fate of the ones who have stood against me. Sandalban—broken; Faylin—burned; Rindzac—frozen to the ground, a statue in a City of the Dead. And who is left for me to destroy? Bellwind, the old witch. She is nothing. Her life I shall consume in a single swallow. But you! You! For you there will be a special kind of dying, for it is you who plays the Music of the Law."

Suddenly strange sounds began to fill the room, deep, rumbling creaks and moans. The Alex-Thing began shrieking, "Stop it! Stop it!" But the sounds grew louder and wilder. High, shrill peeps and chirps and rasps in a hideous cacophony. The Thing in Alex's throat screamed and gurgled as though it were going mad. Then, as quickly as they had come, the sounds ended and the hovering demon whispered, "The Song of All Singing, once you thought it was the most beautiful music in the universe. Now it sings your doom."

Spitting words came through Alex's gritted teeth. "How I long for you to die. How I long to taste your agony. Fool, what was your purpose in bringing me here, to torture me? Do you think that my arms have grown so weak that I cannot reach you?"

"You know the Law. Unless Aloi is sacrificed by the hands of one from another world, you will remain bound, living only through the creatures that you possess until the final test is over."

"Is that what you summoned me here to say? Then your task is finished. Now, return to me that which is mine. You stole my food! My brand is on its arm. It is cattle from my herd. Its spirit was sealed forever when it gave itself to me."

"On his arm are the marks of the Seeker."

"Listen to the screeching of your Law, oh, mighty Worwil. The soul that chooses evil, into evil it must go. The beast is mine. Return its rotting flesh. Play the music of its life. I call for the Judgment of the Song."

"His song will be played at the time ordained. Until then he will remain here. Now, by the name of He Who Lives in the Mists, return to the place where you are bound."

With shrieking curses Alex felt the Thing within him contract inch by inch down his throat, through his chest and into his belly. There it receded into a pinpoint of fire. But it didn't go away.

Once more the winged creature spoke, "I did this so that you would know what you have done and what lives within you. Remove him." Instantly the monster disappeared and the gigantic glowing insects returned. Alex screamed and thrashed as they lifted him into the air. He kept on screaming and thrashing as they carried him down fiery-walled tunnels to a black hole in the floor. Then they lowered him into a deep stinking pit and flew away leaving him in total darkness.

More shrieking.

He shrieked until he was hoarse. Over and over he tried to jam and shove himself out of his body. All that mattered was getting to his window, but he couldn't break free. Not an inch of his soul could crack through the muscle and bone. Finally, exhausted, he lay twitching and grunting. It was then that a seeping discomfort began to plague his fuzzy awareness; slowly his eyes became eyes again and not just mucus coated windows. Underneath him he felt a slithery slop. The floor was coated with a thick layer of slime.

It had soaked through his clothes and was oozing over his skin, and it smelled like sewage. Yelling curses, he struggled to stand up. But he was too dizzy. He teetered into a squat, but that was worse. Finally, with a croaking burst of foulness, he tipped over and flopped back into the muck, slipping and sliding around until he was even more covered than before. This provoked a new string of obscenities that went on until his energy was spent and all he could do was huddle in miserable silence.

During his tantrum his eyes had adjusted to the dark, and very slowly he began to see things. Slime wasn't his only problem. Something putrid was on the walls. Hanging like vertical pools in the blackness were vague glowing clusters, so dim they were barely visible. He squinted hard.

They were *moving.*

Some kind of stringy things were slithering around, leaving blurry trails of iridescence. They looked like clumps of centipedes twisting and writhing on top of each other. Alex shivered. He could almost feel them crawling up his pants and wrapping around his legs, but as the minutes passed they stayed where they were, and he began breathing again.

Slowly Alex became fully aware of his surroundings. He was huddled at one end of a narrow tunnel-like cavern with a high ceiling. The opposite end was too dark to see. He was in a dungeon. Something hard and prickly brushed against his ankle. He yelled and jumped. There were scratching and swishing sounds everywhere. Terrified, he shrieked, "Keep away from me. Get away," and began kicking and flailing. This only brought more scratching and swishing.

"Help! Somebody help! Get me out of here!"

But no one came and the sounds faded. Whatever had caused them didn't touch him again, but he couldn't stop shivering. The terror had driven the last patches of fog from his brain, and now, in the darkness, his mind exploded with disjointed pieces of memory. He seemed to remember sliding down a tunnel with Tori, then being in some kind of boat with a body in it. After that, everything dissolved into a terrifying nightmare about bugs.

As Alex tried to make sense of it all, he decided that none of it was real. He had been hallucinating again, which meant that he hadn't *escaped* to anywhere at all. He was somewhere in the cathedral. But who had put him in this awful pit? And why? They had said he was a hero, a god. You don't throw a god into a stinking pit. A god belongs in a nice cool window. If that dirty little witch Melesh was responsible for this, he would tear her to pieces.

In his despair Alex buried his face in his arms. But when his head touched the wound he *screamed* and fire shot through him. The pain was so intense that he almost fainted. Slowly the fire turned into a bone-throbbing ache, and sweat poured down his face.

He was burning up all over. And he couldn't breathe.

What was wrong with him? The illness was coming back. That's what was wrong. He was burning up with fever. The wound was infected and the fever had made him delirious. It must be coming in waves, which meant that soon he would go crazy again. The way he felt, he must be close to dying.

The hot turned to freezing cold. Now he was shaking uncontrollably and his eyes hurt. He groaned and rubbed them. When he opened them again, something had changed. A subtle shifting. A deepening of the darkness. He realized that the ooze on the walls had disappeared. And what was that? A new thing, a kind of wheel glistening in the distance, sparkling like a cluster of stars. More hallucinations. He shook his head, trying to make the sparkles vanish, but they wouldn't; instead, the wheel was rolling toward him, growing larger and larger. And it wasn't stars. The sparkles came from broken glass, giant shards, and little splinters twisting and turning as though a crystal galaxy had exploded. Then they were all around him in an endless stream.

In the pieces he began to see things. The shadow of a skateboard, the glimmer of a comic book. Clearer now: a bed, a poster, a baseball cap, a desk, a chair. More and more. And he recognized them; they were things that had belonged to him and, in each one there was a memory. Wind in his hair. Sleeping late on a Sunday morning. Hero faces on the wall. *Things.* Things he had taken for granted. Things that had just been there and he had thought would never go away. How he longed for them now. If only he could ride the skateboard again. Sit at the desk even at school. Lie in his bed and read comics. *Longing.* Longing for a life that was gone.

But as he watched, the images changed. In the glass he began to see splintered faces. And he recognized them too. His family. His friends. *People* he had taken for granted. *People* who had cared for him and he had thought would never go away. And with each one came a torrent of memories. Talking.

Laughing. Hanging out. Doing nothing. Just being together. How he longed for those moments now. How he longed for those *people.* If only he could go back and be with them. As he saw each one, he called their names. Slowly their eyes turned toward him. And in all of them there was hurt.

Why were they looking at him that way?

Without knowing how, he knew. The hurt was because of him. Things he had done, things he had said, a thousand cruelties large and small flickering sorrows on broken glass. Streaming by. Streaming away forever.

Then out of the darkness came fragments of an image crushed more than all the others. The pieces were horrifying, the edges streaked with crimson. At first he couldn't tell who it was, but soon he realized that it was his mother; in her broken face were a thousand glistening splinters, and all of them were tears. Her eyes were tired, so tired and filled with sorrow, yet still they looked at him with love as though she would give her life to take away his pain. He had never really *seen* his mother's eyes before. Never seen the hurt they carried. So many things he could have done to take that hurt away—a word, a smile, a hug. But instead, he had hurt her even more.

Suddenly Alex was filled with a longing so great that he couldn't bear it. If only he could see her one last time; if only he could tell her that he loved her. He hadn't said those words in years. Why not? Why hadn't he? It was such a small thing. And how much she had wanted to hear them. Yet he had remained silent. Why? Because silence was the hammer that he had used to smash her, the silence of contempt, of derision, of disdain. And with each raging silence her broken life had been shattered even more. Now the jagged pieces ripped through him.

Alex began to sob, sobs so deep it felt as though they would crush him, but he was already crushed, and he had done it with his own hands as he had smashed his mother and all the people who had ever loved him. Smash and run. Smash and run. Smash with hate and vicious words, then run from the guilt when he saw them suffer. Run from their anger. Run from their pain. Run from every whisper that told him he was wrong. Because he *couldn't be* wrong. Not ever.

If he were wrong just once, he might be wrong about *everything.*

So when guilt whispered, smash it and run. If someone said you hurt them, hurt them more and blame them for it. Smash and run. Better that others should be broken and not you. Always, always, smash and run.

But as Alex stared into the darkness at the glistening fragments of his mother's life, he couldn't smash and he couldn't run. The shame and guilt overwhelmed him. What would happen when you couldn't? All that was left was to cry. But as he wept, a soft, cold voice began whispering that there was something else he could do, something that would take away the pain forever.

Clench his mind.

Twist it into hardness.

Freeze the sorrow.

Strangle the shame.

Swallow it whole.

Turn his soul into a glacier of solid ice.

The voice whispered that if he did it long enough and hard enough, the guilt would go away and never return. Nothing could ever hurt him again.

And Alex obeyed.

Closing his eyes, he clenched his teeth until it felt like his jaw would snap. Then he twisted, froze, strangled, and swallowed. When he opened his eyes, the vision of his mother had disappeared. He was back in the darkness of the cave, staring at the glowing ooze. And he felt much better. Sorrow? Gone. Shame and guilt? Gone along with it.

He took a deep breath. What had made him see such awful things and feel so bad? Clearly it was illness, fever, delusions. But he wasn't shivering anymore. He was still sick; yes, still very sick. The fever would come again, he knew it. And the hallucinations would get worse, so he had to prepare for them. He would be brave, and being brave meant telling himself the truth while his mind still worked. And what was the truth? The visions were all lies. He was not a bad person! Oh, maybe he had done a few unkind things, but he had never intended to hurt anyone. Especially not his mother. Even though she had hurt him terribly. Was he so much worse than anyone else? Of course not! So why was he stuck in this hideous place? He knew a lot of really horrible people, and none of them were sick and rotting in a filthy cave. No matter what he had done, he didn't deserve this.

It wasn't fair.

But nothing had ever been fair in his life. Nobody had ever really cared about him. Not a single person. He hadn't hurt people; they had hurt him. Over and over he had tried to make them understand how really hurt he was. That's why he had done things—he was just trying to make them see. But they didn't want to see because all they cared about was themselves. Well, he didn't care about any of them either. And his mother? What was the truth about her? She had been glad to get rid of him so she could live her life in peace. That's why she had sent him to England.

More truth?

In spite of all the cruel people in his life, he had always done the best he could. Always! And he had tried so hard to please everybody. He had given so much and what had he gotten in return? Rejection! And now sickness and pain and death. Well, he hated them all, every last one of them, all the people in the broken glass. And he would hate them forever. But there was one creature that he hated beyond all others:

That dog!

And all he had done was try to save a girl from a terrifying monster, risked his life to help someone. And for that the dog had torn him to pieces, ripped his flesh, filled him with this disease. How he despised it, how he wished he could kill it all over again, throw it into the chasm, see it *smash* and *crash* against the rocks, shredding into bloody chunks of meat.

Alex continued to weep, cursing everything and everyone he knew. As he cursed, he began to hear something—soft at first, far away, but coming closer. He listened. It was *singing.* A soft sweet voice singing. A girl's voice. Lovely, so lovely, but filled with *sorrow.* Alex strained to hear. Where was it coming from? And the words, he couldn't quite make them out, but they were familiar. Where had he heard them? And then out of the darkness came . . .

Burning, burning,
Forever turning,
Icy ashes fall away.
Melting, reeling, the end of feeling,
Silver strings will never play.
Altars broken,
Death words spoken,
Childhood's blood from yesterday . . .

With that, the most awful vision of all appeared; it was as though the dungeon vanished and he was standing in the moonlight looking up into a delicate tapestry woven of mist, sprinkled with stars. Up, up it went into a crimson glow, and with the singing voice he heard ten thousand notes filled with wistful sadness.

Then she came, down the endless strands, the most beautiful creature that Alex had ever seen. A spider? It wasn't a spider. Her crystal body was only a shadow, a shell that held the loveliness of her soul. Walking toward him, with her fingers sweeping over the strands, was a girl, her beauty softer than the mist around her, and as Alex looked into her eyes, he felt the greatest love he had ever known. She came toward him, playing the instrument of her own creation, her wonderful eyes entering his soul. In one moment she understood his sorrows, saw every dark thing that he had ever done, and still she loved him.

And he loved her too with a passion that made him want to cry out, to fall at her feet, to be her slave, to swear his love forever. But then he saw a hand lift a torch and cast it into the Mist of Eternity.

And the hand belonged to him.

He screamed, but it was too late. The mist caught fire. The strands of the great harp broke and the loveliness turned to horror. As her creation burned, the girl began to burn with it. Her agony was unspeakable. But not once did she cry out. Her eyes just kept looking at him with unbearable love. Then, at the last moment, her face turned upward and she whispered ...

Webs of crystal that you gave me,
Words to weave, and harps to sing,
Through the universe I served you,
Now to your heart, my soul I bring ...

Then the last of the strands gave way. For a moment the lovely face hung over a chasm. And with a sigh she was gone. Screaming, Alex wanted to leap after her.

Instantly he was back in the darkness overcome with the terrible thing he had seen. In that vision all of the lies crumbled around him. The lie of his comic-book dreams. The lie of the girl with the long black hair. The lie of the Cathedral. The lie that he was a hero.

The truth?

His whole life was filled with murders. Not the murder of bodies, the murder of hearts and souls. And before every murder he had been warned. His conscience had warned him. But he had murdered it too. Finally it had led to this. The murder of the most beautiful girl he had ever seen. And the dog had tried to stop him. The dog who had been his friend, who had saved him in the dead city, who had shown him where to get food, who had tried to lead him down a different path away from the nightmare on the mountain. And he had destroyed it like all the others.

Into his heart came the pieces, the shards, the splinters of every selfish choice that he had ever made, every choice to hate and rage and hurt another person, every choice to care only about himself, to smash and run, to hide in a world of twisted heroes, of murderous images smeared on the walls of his soul. All the lies, all the smashing and running, had prepared him to believe the greatest lie of all, the lie that would destroy him forever, the lie that he was his own god. The dog had been his last hope, had brought the last warning. Not with a whisper, but a roar.

Lost!

Lost!

And no one to blame but himself. Alex sobbed, but this time it was from a truly broken heart. And through his tears he whispered, "Oh, God, help me."

Silence.

Deathly silence.

The silence of eternity.

Then out of the silence came a voice. And when Alex Lancaster heard it, he froze.

Softly it said, "Alex, Alex, Son, you've got to stop doing this. You're driving yourself crazy." It was the voice of his father.

30

THE PEARL

Tori awakened.

Not that she wanted to. Her dreams had been soft. Something about kittens. But there was a wonderful smell in the air, a smell that reminded her of home. She stretched and yawned. And then her eyes popped open.

Chicken strips!

It was the smell of hot, fresh chicken strips!

To her amazement, someone was sitting on the end of her bed, and he was holding a plate full of them — and steaming French fries too. It was an old man in a robe with a craggy, wrinkly face, and he was smiling at her.

"Good day, granddaughter. Might I inquire about the state of your appetite? Could it be ready for a bit of a nibble?" His eyes were twinkling.

Tori stared. Something was *very* familiar about him. She had seen him someplace, and not very long ago. Then she remembered and pulled up a pillow to hide behind. "I know you."

"Do you, indeed?"

"You're the one who was on the boat ... in that box."

"What an intelligent and observant girl. You are quite correct. The last time you saw me I was well crated and professionally shipped, if you will."

"You were dead."

"Strictly speaking I still am. Or I should say my body is."

"That means you're a ghost!"

"Well, let's consider this carefully. Do ghosts normally deliver huge platters of fowl, thickly encrusted and carefully shaped into unrecognizable portions that people of your world find ravishingly delectable?"

"What?"

"Do ghosts deliver chicken strips? That was a rhetorical question, and the obvious answer is that, indeed, they do not. Do you have any idea what a 'ghost' even looks like?"

"Sure. They're kind of foggy and you can see through them."

"An apt description. They are the essence of fog. In fact, I have known one or two who were in such a state of fog that they couldn't pull themselves together enough to look like anything more than a layer of pestilential gas. Pitiful creatures. Hmmm, I don't think I feel like one of those. But you decide. Here, touch my hand." He extended it toward her. Slowly Tori reached with one finger and gave his skin a quick poke.

"Well, you don't feel foggy."

"What a relief." His eyes twinkled even more.

She dropped the pillow down an inch. "But you could still be a ghost."

The old man laughed. "Well, whether I am one or not, the only thing that matters are these heavily encrusted clumps of fowl. Now, to me they look rather like the squeezings from a mineshaft rolled in river sand. However, it is my understanding that you fancy them to the exclusion of all other foods." Lifting the plate, he examined them closely. "I would suggest, granddaughter, that haste is required in consuming them. I imagine that they are less than flavorful cold."

"Why do you keep calling me granddaughter? You're not my grandpa."

"Not your most recent one, that's for certain. But I am your grandfather with about forty-two 'greats' in front of it."

"I don't know what that means."

"Not important, but you'd best get started ingesting these before it becomes impossible to pass them over your tongue." He held out the plate. She took it.

"I don't suppose you have honey-mustard."

Without batting an eye he pulled out several tiny plastic tubs.

Tori took them. "Thank you." Opening one, she stuck a strip into it. A single taste and she groaned with pleasure. "*I love chicken strips.* They're so much better than rat food."

"I shall inform the chef, but I shall not tell the rats."

She continued stuffing her mouth. Then she picked up a fry. Instantly the old man produced a red plastic bottle. "It is my understanding that next you will require a squirt of liquefied vegetable matter."

"It's called ketchup. Yes, thank you." Taking it, she squeezed a big dollop onto the plate and swooshed the fry through it. Then she tucked it into her already overcrowded mouth. "You didn't happen to bring a Coke."

"Ah, I knew there was something missing: dirt-colored water. We'll have to go to the kitchen for that. Come along." Rising, he headed toward the door. But Tori stayed where she was. He turned and looked back. "Well?"

"I don't want to go out there."

"Why not?"

"Way too many bugs."

"There are no bugs in the kitchen."

"There are a billion right out that door. I saw them when I came in."

"If you want a drink, I'm afraid we have no choice. I'll be waiting outside." With a smile, he opened the door and left the room. Tori stared after him. She was very thirsty. But thirsty enough to face 448 hexatrillion insects? Finally she crawled out of bed, and cracking the door open an inch, she peeked out. What she saw was so startling, that she pulled it open all the way.

On the other side of the door was an outside world, and in the silver moonlight stood a big tree with a swing. The old man was swinging on it, pumping higher and higher, with his robe flapping around his bony knees. Laughing joyfully, he called, "Did you ever wonder whether you could swing so high you'd go all the way around in a circle?"

Tori almost started crying. It was her backyard on Earth. There was her house just the way she remembered it. Slowly she walked out into the grass. It was covered with dew.

"This is my backyard. My home, where I grew up."

Smiling, he dragged his feet and came to a stop. "I imagine that you've spent a lot of time on this swing."

She stared at him. "This is a dream, isn't it? I'm not really home at all."

"My child, you are wise for one so young. Let's call it half a dream. You really are home, but only for a visit."

Wistfully she looked around. "I've missed it so much. Will I ever come back to stay?"

"That is a question I cannot answer. The path of your life is not visible to me."

"Is my mom inside?"

"She is."

"There aren't any lights on."

"It's the middle of the night. Let's go see her, and on the way we'll get some of that special dirt water that you love so much." Taking her hand, he led her to the back door. Quietly they made their way into the laundry room and then the kitchen. Tori went to the refrigerator and pulled out a can of Coke. Popping it open, she took a long drink, then looked around. "It isn't the same in here. Something's wrong." A kind of shadowy haze hung over everything. "What's that in the air?"

"It's sorrow."

"What do you mean?"

"When there is great sorrow the world around it begins crying. Most of the time the mist of tears can't be seen. But you're walking in the twilight realm, and here it's visible. Come, let's find your mother."

As they went through the dining room into the hall, the haze grew thicker. Finally they came to a bedroom door. As he opened it, the old man whispered, "We must speak quietly or we will enter her dreams."

Tori peeked in. Misty softness hung everywhere, but over the bed it was so heavy that she could barely see through. Walking over, she looked down. A figure was lying under a blanket. A dim shaft of moonlight struck a sleeping face. It was her mother and there were tears on her cheeks.

"She's crying in her sleep. Why is she doing that?"

"Her dreams are of you and your brother and sister. She knows of the plane crash and thinks that you have died."

Tori looked up at him. "Did we die?"

"No. But that is hidden from her. The future she cannot see and the present she cannot bear. So it is in the past that she lives where memories break her heart. Would you like to see what she is seeing?"

"Yes."

Instantly the room was filled with flickering images of Alex, Amanda, and Tori. In all of them their mother was reaching out, trying to touch them, to take them in her arms, but they were never quite close enough. Then came echoes of pain. Every angry, hurtful word that she had ever spoken filled the room. And tears ran down her cheeks.

"Her mind wanders endlessly through all the things that she has done and said to each of you. She longs to go back and be the mother that you needed, but you have vanished from her life."

Tears filled Tori's eyes. "She's a good mom. She loved us and took care of us. I don't want her to be sad. Can I wake her up?"

"No, but there is something that you can do."

"What?"

"Whisper into her dreams. Tell her you love her."

"Will she really hear me?"

"Her heart will hear."

Sitting on the edge of the bed, Tori bent down and whispered, "Mommy, don't be sad. I love you so much. You were so good to us. You took care of us every day. You made me a birthday cake with yellow flowers."

The sorrow in her mother's face seemed to deepen and more tears came. And then suddenly Tori could see inside her. Beneath the face of her mother was another face, the face of a little girl. She and Tori looked so much alike that they could be sisters. And the little girl was crying.

"Is that my mother the way she really is?"

"Is and was. She has been crying for a very long time."

"Why?"

"Long ago things happened that broke her heart. Broken hearts can get angry and they are easily frightened."

"What happened to her?"

"Her father left and never came back."

"She told us he died when she was little."

"In a way, he did. But leaving and never coming back is worse than dying. It tears a ragged hole in a child's heart. In your mother that hole remains. When she was little she tried to fill it with dolls."

"So that's why she loved them. When our daddy left the hole must have gotten bigger."

"Much bigger, for she saw her own pain echoing in your eyes and blamed herself."

"But it wasn't her fault."

"The little girl inside can't understand that. She blamed herself back then too."

"I want to kiss her. Couldn't I do it? Wouldn't she feel it?"

"It will be like the kiss of a butterfly."

"I want to do it anyway." Tori bent down and kissed the tears. Then she ran her fingers through her mother's hair. The lines of sorrow softened. "I want to give her something to make her feel happy again."

"What would you like to give?"

"This." Reaching up, she removed her necklace. The light within it shone like a tiny star. "When I was so scared it made me feel happy again."

"Granddaughter, that was given to protect you."

"Could it protect her instead?"

There was a moment of silence. When Tori looked up, the old man's eyes were filled with tears. "It will be a thousand times stronger, because it comes with your love, and it is all that you have to give."

Carefully she laid the necklace into her mother's open hand. "It'll be here when she wakes up, won't it? It won't be just a dream."

"It will be real. And she will wear it always."

"Will she know it's from me?"

"Her heart will know. Now it's time to say farewell. We must return."

Gently Tori kissed her mother and whispered, "I love you. Don't be sad." Once more she ran her fingers through her hair. Then she rose and the old man led her toward the door—but just before they reached it, he stopped and they looked back. The light from the necklace was glowing in her mother's hand, and the mist of sorrow was gone. Looking at Tori, he smiled and said, "Though you have given away the pearl that casts out terror, its strength will be with you always. Now go, and never, ever be afraid again." With that, he opened the door and ushered her through. Instantly her mind was lost in the soft darkness of sleep.

31

FATHER OF THE PIT

Alex could hardly breathe for trembling.

Slowly he turned and stared into the darkness. At the opposite end of the cave a dark form sat huddled against a wall. It spoke again. "Did you hear me, Son? Did you hear what I said? You've got to stop this."

Covering his ears, Alex screamed, "No! No, no, no ..." Jumping to his feet, he shrieked, "Go away! You're not real!"

Silence.

Alex gasped for breath. Suddenly he was so dizzy he couldn't keep standing. Sinking to the floor, he buried his face in his hands. "I'm going insane."

Another soft whisper. "Son, I've come to help you."

Alex covered his ears again. "I'm not listening, I'm not listening ..." Over and over he screamed it.

Finally when his breath was gone, the voice said, "Alex, you're dying. I don't want you to die alone."

"Not-real-not-real-not-real-not-real ..."

"Please, just listen for one minute. After that, if you want me to leave, I'll go."

"Not-real-not-real-not-real-not-real ..."

"I came to be with you. There are things we need to talk about."

"Not-real-not-real-not-real-not-real ..." Alex began sobbing, "Go away, go away."

"But we haven't talked in such a long, long time."

"And whose fault is that? Not-real-not-real-not-real-not-real ..."

"It's my fault, Son. When you needed me, I wasn't there. But I'm here now. Won't you give me a chance, Alex? It's the last time we'll ever be together. I don't want you to die hating me. Please, don't do that."

"Oh, God, I'm so sick. I feel so bad."

The voice was filled with deep sadness. "I know that. But soon it will be over. If you don't want me here, I'll go. Just tell me to leave *one more time*."

Alex said nothing.

The figure leaned toward him. "I want to tell you something, Son, and I mean this with all my heart. No matter what has happened, you're still a hero to me."

Alex sobbed as though his heart would break. "No, I'm not. I know the truth now."

"Listen to me. I know you better than anybody. Even when you were a little boy, you were brave."

"Stop saying that! It's a lie!"

"Do you remember the slide at the water park? The one that was five stories tall? I was afraid to go down it. But you didn't even blink. How old were you, seven? We went down that thing together, and it scared the heck outta me. But we must have done it ten times because you didn't want to stop. And baseball! You were the home run slugger. You faced pitchers twice your size and blasted them out of the park. I thought then, when my son grows up, he's going to be a hero. And you are. I'm so proud of you, Alex. And I've missed you so much."

"You are ... such ... a liar!" Alex whispered through his tears.

"What did you say?"

"I said, you ... are ... a liar."

After a long silence the voice replied. "You're right. I have been a liar. I've lied about a lot of things. I haven't been the kind of father you needed."

"What kind is that? The kind that's actually there? Why am I doing this? Why am I talking to myself?"

"Alex, you're doing this because in your heart you know it's time to make things right. When death is about to come strange things happen. Sometimes people who are far apart can talk to each other mind-to-mind. Maybe that's what's happening right now. A kind of miracle. Maybe I've entered your dream or you've entered mine to give us one last chance together."

"Our last chance came a long time ago, and it's gone!"

"No, it's not. While there's life, there's hope. Death makes things clear. Maybe now we can understand each other. Don't you want to give it a try?"

"Oh, I understand you. I understand you really well."

"Do you? People have told you lies about me, and you've believed them. I can hear it in your voice."

"Nobody has told me anything. I know what I've seen. I know what you did to us."

"You think I just walked away, don't you, that I didn't care about you and your sisters? Well, it isn't true. I didn't want to leave you, Alex. I tried to take all of you with me to England, but the court wouldn't give me custody. I spent sixty thousand dollars on attorneys, but it didn't do any good."

"You left us a long time before you moved to England."

"You're right. I moved out. But that wasn't just for me. I left because your mother and I were fighting all the time. I thought, at least if I wasn't there you could have some peace and quiet."

"And why were you fighting all the time? Why was she screaming at you? You want to tell me that?"

"I'm not going to say anything bad about her. No matter what she's done, she's still your mother."

"How noble of you. But go ahead. I'm never gonna see her again. Go for it. Say anything you want."

A broken whisper came from the darkness. "You don't know what it's like marrying someone and seeing her change. Step by step, day by day, watching the one you love turn into a different person. When I married your mother, she was so beautiful, and I loved her so much. I tried, Alex, I really tried."

"So why did she change?"

"I don't know. She began … imagining things that weren't true."

"Like what?"

"Crazy things. She would shriek at me for nothing. I was afraid to sleep at night. Nobody can live that way."

"So she went nuts. Is that what you're saying? She went nuts and you moved out. You left us with a crazy person."

"She was never crazy with you kids. Never. She was a good mother. You know that."

"Either she was crazy or she wasn't. You can't turn off craziness like a faucet."

"For some reason my presence just pushed her over the edge."

"And why was that?"

"I don't know."

"So you moved into an apartment twenty minutes away, but it was too far to ever come and see us."

"I was working long hours, trying to support two households and pay for a bunch of attorneys. I was exhausted all the time."

"So to get a little rest, you moved to England."

"I had no choice about that. It was move or lose my job."

"You moved because you got a big promotion."

"If I hadn't taken it, all of us would have been out on the street. If you were me, what would you have done, Alex?"

"I would have stayed with my kids even if I had to be a garbage collector and live in my car."

The voice spoke with deep emotion. "I did the best I could. We don't have long together, Son. Won't you at least try to understand me?"

With burning eyes Alex stared into the darkness. "You don't think I know about your life, do you? You don't think I really know."

"What do you mean?"

"I mean the truth, the real, total truth about who you are."

"What are you talking about?"

Tears ran down Alex's cheeks. "I always thought you were a hero. I wanted to be just like you. When I started reading comics, all the superheroes had your face. You were never around, so I'd tell myself stories about you. You'd be fighting the bad guys and I'd tag along. That's who you were to me. That's who you were."

"I'm not a superhero, Alex, but maybe I'm not as bad as you think."

Alex started laughing. It was a cold, bitter sound. "This is amazing. I've got your lies so deep in my brain I can actually hear you saying them. I can have a whole imaginary conversation as though you're right here with me. How sick is that?"

"Look, I know your mother said terrible things about me. And you never got the chance to hear my side. But I'm here now to make things right. I just want you to know that, no matter what you've heard, I never consciously did anything to hurt our family. I deeply loved your mother. In many ways I still do. We just couldn't live together anymore."

"Tori cried for a year after you left."

"I'm sorry."

"And Amanda. I don't know what happened to Amanda. She just changed and was never the same again."

"I love them both very much."

"Liar!"

"That is not a lie!"

"Hey, can I tell you something? You want to know about the worst day in my whole life?" Alex fought to control his voice. "There were a lot of bad days, but this one was the worst of all. You want to hear about it?"

"If you want to tell me."

"Yeah, I think I do. One Saturday when I was twelve, I had a baseball game. You were supposed to be there, but like usual you had to go into the city and work."

"I missed too many of your games. I'm sorry."

"I was so upset that you weren't gonna be there that I didn't even want to play. So I skipped out. And you know what I did instead? I followed you into Chicago on the train. Pretty slick for a kid, huh? I was tall and got away with it. You never saw me. Well, guess what? You didn't go to the office. Instead, you changed trains and went up to the north side. I followed you to her house, Dad. You weren't at the game because you wanted to be with her. Mother found out, didn't she? And it broke her heart. She found out what kind of a man you really are."

After a long silence the voice spoke. "What do you want me to say, Alex?"

"Nothing! I want you to shut up and go to hell forever!"

"That's the easy way out. You don't want to know the truth about me, do you?"

"I know the truth!"

"No, you don't! I was hurt and lonely, Alex. Can you imagine a man being hurt and lonely?"

"What you did killed your children. Didn't you ever think about that?"

"A man has to take care of himself before he can help anyone else. That's a rule of life, Son. I did what I had to do to survive."

"And you survived by murdering all of us. You might as well have slit our throats. What I knew about you killed me. It killed me inside just like if you'd stuck a knife in my guts and watched me bleed to death. And I never told anybody because I was so ashamed of you. Since you weren't around, I took everything out on Mom. I made her life hell." Alex's voice broke. "You were supposed to be a hero, Dad. Heroes are brave. They defend people who are weak. They give their lives to save others. But the only one you cared about was yourself. I hate you so much that I can't stand it. And I'm going to hate you forever."

Silence.

Deathly silence.

The silence of eternity.

Then out of the silence came a voice. "Alex, Alex, Son, you've got to stop doing this to yourself. You're driving yourself *crazy*." Then it laughed. And it wasn't the voice of his father.

Alex stared at the dark figure huddled against the wall. He knew that voice. Suddenly a slithering movement rippled in his belly. He gasped. It slithered again. Something was down there. Something that wasn't part of him. And then he remembered.

The Thing.

The raging Thing.

The Thing that had crawled up into his throat.

The Thing that had screamed through his mouth.

Quietly the voice continued. "You're absolutely right. Your father wasn't a hero. All he cared about was getting what he wanted, a beautiful woman with long . . . black . . . hair. You forgot what she looked like, didn't you, Alex? She was lovely. Much more beautiful than your mother. But you know that because you saw her. You saw them together. Hate him, Alex. Hate him. He deserves it. Dream about killing him. Think of all the ways to do it. Shriek and rage and hate. And do you know what will make your hate so much more delicious? Here is something that will drive you insane. What your father did to you, his father had done to him. Yes, your grandfather left his family just the same way, for a beautiful woman. Oh, but there was a major difference. She had long *blonde* hair. Now, consider this—what kind of a man would go through agony as a child, then inflict that same agony on his own son, daughters, and wife, a wife whose father had abandoned her? Yes, that's the dark poetry of it. That's who he married, someone just as hurt and angry as he was. People like that are drawn to each other like moths to a flame. It's horrible, Alex. Horrible. However, lest you think too harshly of him, remember that he had a congenital weakness. He couldn't control his lust. But you can understand that because you have the same weakness. Here's the secret, my friend. It isn't your fault. It's just something that gets passed from father to son. The males of every species are meant to lust and leave. Men are just animals hopelessly tied to the evolutionary chain. Didn't you learn anything in school? If you had lived long enough to mate with a suitable partner, you would have left her and your children just like your father and grandfather did."

"That's a lie!" Alex shrieked. "I would never do that!"

"Oh, that's what they all say. Every son swears he won't be like his father. The truth is you're exactly like him, only worse. He may have been a weak, selfish fool, but at least he didn't actually kill anybody to get what he wanted. At least, he didn't do that."

Alex was staggered.

"Now, don't misunderstand me. You did the right thing. A man has needs. And I am always there to help him meet those needs. You needed her, Son, the girl with the long black hair. And you were willing to kill to get to her. You needed her to prove to yourself that you were as good a man as your father. And you did it. You proved it. Just like your father proved it with the woman we dangled in front of him."

A long satisfied sigh came from the dark form. "So sweet! So delicious! So enjoyable! We're going to spend eternity creating scenes just like this from your past. Think of all the infinite variations of sorrow, regret, hate, and rage that we can play out in excruciating detail. I'll be anyone you want, your father, your mother, your father's mistress, your father's new wife, your father's new children, individually, collectively, in complex configurations. A million times we'll do it. Ten million! We'll never grow tired. And at the end of each I will suck the hate and agony from your soul. You see, you're like my cow. I feed you and milk you, and we both get what we need." Very slowly the figure rose and began moving across the floor toward him. It didn't walk. It seemed to glide. And as it moved, he felt the Thing crawling within him.

Shaking, Alex backed away. "Get away from me! Oh God, help me ..."

"There you go again. You tried that before and look who came. Now, Son, listen to me ..."

"I'm not your son."

"Oh, but you are. And I am more than just your father. I'm the voice in your head that tells you what's right and wrong. When you pray, I'm the one who answers. Be honest. What else could you want in a god? Ah, but you need a hero, don't you? Someone to save you from this terrible situation. But there are no heroes in the universe, Alex, only hunters and prey. Look at all the children who have died, sacrificed on altars of selfishness, fear, and greed. Their blood cried out for a hero. But no one ever came, and they died like little animals. Now if you insist on praying, perhaps I can be of help. For untold centuries I've heard the finest in futile prayers. How about words like these, 'Oh, God, get me out of here. Do what I want and I promise I'll be good. I won't ever lust after girls with long black hair. And I won't murder any more dogs and beautiful angels. And most of all, I'll never, ever be like my father.' Well, go ahead, say it, pray it, scream it, sob it, and let's see what happens. Alex, try to understand this. Your life as you have known it is over. Stop trying to run from me and remember the pleasures that I can bring."

From out of the figure came the soft, sensual voice of Melesh. "You saved my life. Do you remember what I told you when I brought you to your room?"

Alex heard his own voice answer, "Tell me again."

"I said I was your slave."

"Is that right? So I can tell you to do anything and you have to do it?"

"Why don't you find out?"

Alex screamed, "Shut up!"

But his voice continued, "If you're my slave, kiss my shoes ... now my hand. Your room, let's go."

"Shut up! Shut up!"

The black form grew larger. "It is time to go, Alex. We've been in this awful place long enough. I'm going to be your hero. I'm going to help you escape."

As he backed away, suddenly Alex pressed against the wall. He felt something sticking into him.

"Behind you is a door. Do you feel the knob?"

Desperately he grabbed it and turned it. The door opened. Beyond was darkness.

"It's the way out. Escape, Alex! Run! Run for your life!" Then the voice started laughing.

Alex stumbled through the door into a narrow tunnel. Ahead he saw a dim green light. As he groped and staggered toward it, suddenly everything began to shake. A high-pitched whine shrieked, the light shimmered, and a great organ began to play. From the stone around him rose a terrible crescendo.

And Alex Lancaster began to hear the Song of his Soul.

32

THE MUSIC OF THE LAW

Gasping, Alex rushed out of the tunnel and fell into shimmering light. There he lay, unable to move. The music was shaking him apart. The deepness of it, the roaring. It was as though his body had turned to iron and he was being struck with a gigantic hammer. It reverberated in his bones; it crashed in his brain. And then …

Silence.

Every sound passed away.

Now there was nothing but light … and the rasp of his own breathing. He cracked open his eyes.

Pain — a splitting, throbbing headache. He was almost blind. He had been in the darkness too long. The brilliance was excruciating. He covered his eyes, but the light seeped between his fingers and through his lids. No way to stop it. Where was he? Where was this awful, blinding place with sounds that tore you apart?

He heard footsteps. Groaning, Alex struggled to his hands and knees. The movement made his head pound.

"Who's there? Is someone there?"

"I am." The voice creaked with age. It was a man's voice.

"I can't see. The light hurts."

Instantly it grew dim. Alex tried to open his eyes, but even the dimness was too bright. He squinted upward through narrow cracks between his fingers. Towering above him was the vague outline of a man in a long robe.

"Please … I need help."

"What is it that you want me to do?"

"I'm sick and hurt." He held up his arm.

"The injury will not kill you."

"How do you know that? Are you a doctor?"

"I know all about dying." The words were so strange that Alex tried to look up at him again. But now the figure was bending down, holding something. "Are you thirsty?"

"Yes." His tongue felt like scorched sand.

A cup, the man was holding a cup. With trembling fingers, Alex took it and put it to his lips. Water. Sweet. Delicious. He drank and drank. It ran down his face and onto his filthy shirt. And the cup didn't empty until his thirst was quenched. Finally he handed it back and whispered, "Thank you. I haven't had a drink in a long time."

The man rose. Alex squinted at him again. A little clearer now. He was old, with a white beard. But his face—he still couldn't see it.

"Can you stand up?"

"I don't know. I'm awfully dizzy." But the drink had made him feel better. His head wasn't aching anymore.

"I'll help you." Reaching down, he took Alex's hand and helped him to his feet. "Hold onto my arm." For a moment they stood without moving.

"Where am I?"

"In the Chamber of the Witnesses."

"What's that?"

"Look around."

Alex forced his eyes to open, but it was still difficult to see. It appeared that he was at one end of a gigantic room, a kind of stadium carved out of solid rock. On every side rose tier upon tier of wide stone shelves, and on them in long, straight rows lay boxes that looked like coffins. Thousands of them stretched upward into the dimness. The ones nearby were covered with ornate carvings.

"What are all those boxes?"

"This is the burial place of the kings."

"A cemetery?"

"A place of waiting. Let's try to walk."

With great care the old man led him toward the center of the chamber.

Alex squinted. Something was up ahead. It looked like a single coffin surrounded with seven pillars that rippled with fire. As they drew closer, he saw that the pillars were made of tiny glowing insects. Thick masses of them slowly swarmed in perfect circles. And it was a coffin. The lid was open. When they reached it, he stared. It was the one that had been in the boat. And inside lay the ancient body. "So it wasn't a dream," he whispered. Then he turned to the old man and for the first time saw his face. It was the same face that was lying dead in front of him. He pulled away. "That's ... you."

"Yes, that is my body."

"How can you be dead and standing next to me? This is another dream."

"It isn't a dream. And death isn't what you think."

"Who are you?"

"The one who will guide you through the test."

Alex felt a thrill of fear. "What kind of a test?"

"Tell me, how did you escape from the dungeon?"

"There was a door. I opened it."

"The end, the end, when he comes all things will end. The Lord of Death has told him, no prison bars will hold him. The darkness will enfold him, Son from a distant world. They are the words of an ancient prophet. There was no door in the dungeon."

Alex stared at him. "Of course there was a door. You think I'm lying?"

"No, you are speaking the truth. But there was no door."

"So how did I get out?"

"By the will of the One Who Lives in the Mists. And by His will your test shall begin."

Suddenly the chamber was filled with blazing light. But this time Alex wasn't blinded. He looked up and what he saw staggered him. In the air, a hundred feet above, stretching across the entire ceiling was a shining horror with wings of flame. Fire roared from its eyes. And Alex remembered those eyes. It was the demon that had stung him and awakened the Thing in his belly. But now it was gigantic. He stood transfixed, waiting for it to descend and engulf him. But it didn't move. It just hung there. And as he continued staring, it transformed. The fire deepened and parted. Within it he saw a creature of searing radiance.

The old man cried out, "You stand beneath the Worwil of the Throne. Prepare your heart to worship!" Then he fell on his face with his arms outstretched.

Alex didn't move. He couldn't. For a moment more the winged being hung in silence. Then it opened its mouth, and from out of it came a piercing call. Like the sound of a trumpet it filled the air, growing louder until the chamber trembled and shook. And then the call became a Song. From the Worwil's lips poured a thousand voices sweeping downward.

Rushing ...

Crashing ...

Rising ...

Falling ...

Crescendos of overwhelming loveliness in a language that Alex could not understand. But just hearing it brought unbearable ecstasy. Tears streamed from his eyes. Splendor broke his heart. Without knowing a single word, he knew that this was the Song Above All Others, the Poetry of Fire sung when stars were born, rhyming light from the darkness, form from the chaos, the poem that had hovered over the endless deep. It was the Song of atoms and galaxies, of oceans and teardrops, of eternity echoing in the cry of a bird. It was the Song that had called them, the Song that had formed them. In it was all of Life that would ever be. And as Alex listened, in the glory he saw a glimmer, a single cell of starlight within a mother's womb. So tiny in the vastness, yet within it was the Rhyme of Heaven, weaving flesh as it had woven light on a billion worlds. Cell upon cell, whispering softness, lullaby in a woman's body, knitting a child with a poem of love. Bone and flesh, soul and spirit, weaving and breathing from the Song of Songs. Never had he understood before. Never had he imagined the grandeur, the hope, the promise, of a single child awakening in the morning of a womb.

And he was that child.

From the heart of singing his heart had come. And his life was meant to rise and join the greatness. Bone and flesh, soul and spirit, all of him was meant to be a song. As Alex sobbed, unable to bear the beauty, suddenly the vision faded into darkness ... and he saw the place where the Song was born.

Gigantic in the starlight!

A vision of Eternal Majesty!

Vast!

Endless!

Crowned with crimson.

Crying out with wildness and joy!

The Great Mountain bathed in blood-mist, rising above the Heavens.

"Worship! Worship!" The voice of the Worwil called, "Fall down and worship, for this is the Throne of the Endless One."

Desperate to worship. Thirsting for it. And Alex knew what worship was now, knew how to do it, knew how to grovel in the presence of Crushing Power. But he couldn't. His knees wouldn't bend. It was as though rods of steel had been shot through him. His spine was rigid and his head cocked back. He tried to force himself to kneel, to fall on his face, but he couldn't move. Couldn't kneel. Couldn't worship. Because something inside wouldn't let him. All he could do was shriek in an anguish of desire. And then the vision disappeared.

Gone.

Silence.

Once more, above him hung the creature with the mighty wings. But the singing had ended and the fire had dimmed. Alex gasped, shaking, gulping. Then he felt a hand on his shoulder. Quietly the old man spoke, "You have come to the place of judgment, the hall of the Living Song." Then he turned and looked outward. "Brothers, awake!" Instantly above every coffin appeared the form of a king. Some were wearing regal robes, others were clothed in armor as though they had just come from battle. Thousands and thousands of them stood stretching upward into the light.

With great sadness the old man looked at Alex. "You saw the moment when you were formed within your mother. You heard the Song that gave you breath and wove your soul. You witnessed the glory that your life was meant to be. Because you came from singing, your life has formed a song. With every thought and choice and deed you have written the words and music. And you must sing it for us now. It is the test that comes when life is over."

"What? What do you mean, when life is over? Am I dying?"

"The life that you have known has ended. Beyond this room is a place of glory. Not a single note of evil can enter there. So every life is measured by the Music of the Law."

"What kind of music is that?"

"It is the singing of the Endless One, the music in His heart. In Him, there is no evil. To be in His Presence is ecstasy forever. But to enter His Glory, your life must be without a flaw. No discord can mar the splendor. If you have lived one false note the test will show it."

Alex stared at him in horror. "But that's impossible. Nobody could be that perfect."

"Nevertheless, it is the trial of every living soul."

"So what happens when I don't make it? What happens then?"

"You will go to the place that you have chosen."

Alex's terror deepened. "But that isn't fair. I didn't know. Nobody ever told me."

"From the moment you were born, the Singing of the Mountain has echoed within you. It was always there. To listen or not was the choice of every day and every hour. And from all your choices will come the music of who you are."

Suddenly Alex felt a dreadful writhing in his belly and a soft voice whispered, "Ah, now you understand the little game of Heaven. What does fairness matter when a soul is about to die?" Then it began a mocking rhyme.

At the end of life, all songs are measured
By the Music of the Law.
And if you hope to live forever,
You must sing without a flaw.
But think hard before you do it,
Know what perfection really means.
Not a clanking creak of vileness,
No raging, ugly scenes.
Don't let a note fall flat,
Nor a word go out of rhyme,
For a flicker of lust and madness,
Is considered an eternal crime.
One mistake however minor,

And the light you will never see,
A glitch in the joy and gladness
And your soul belongs to me.
So sing with perfect freedom,
Sing of all that you have known,
And when your singing's finished
Then I will sing you home.

Alex screamed, "Shut up, shut up!" But the voice in his head droned on.

Since I helped you write the music, let me suggest some subtle themes.
Sing of the kindness you showed your sisters,
Sing of the love that warmed your mother's heart.
Sing of your father and forgiveness.
Now that's a place to start.
Sing the little secrets,
The slime within your soul.
Sing of the supple phantoms,
When pleasure was your goal.
Sing of guilt and grief and murder,
Sing the truth of who you are,
Sing of rage and hate and sorrow,
Heaven isn't far.
Sing with pride and lust and passion,
Sing it all without regret,
Sing it the way you wrote it,
And prepare to pay the debt.
So sing with perfect freedom,
Sing of all that you have known,
And when your singing's finished,
Then I will sing you home.

Alex held his ears and shrieked, "Stop it! Leave me alone! I'm not gonna do it!"

"My son, you must." The old man had tears in his eyes.

"I won't! I can't! Please, don't make me!" But then, from the stone beneath his feet, he felt a soft vibration. Slowly it rose in waves of ever-increasing power. Shaking, rumbling, like the tones of a mighty organ.

Louder!

Into his body!

Into his chest!

Crashing into his skull!

He felt himself splitting, separating, dividing—bone and flesh, soul and spirit.

And in every part of him there was a song.

Alex fought desperately, trying to keep silent. He gritted his teeth. He bit his tongue until it ran with blood. But the deepness of the organ was calling and he couldn't stop it. His lungs filled with air, his mouth opened, and out of him came . . .

Horror!

Voices upon voices!

Rising—

Screaming—

Shrieking memories out of every crevice and corner of his soul. Vomiting curses and secrets. Revealing every lie, every thought, every deed of vileness. No rhyme. No music. Just jabber-screeching. Spewing out rage and lust and hate. Filling the chamber. On and on, squeezing, draining, sucking, bleeding, until his heart was empty and he was naked for all the universe to see.

And then—

It was over.

His mouth snapped shut and he dropped to the floor as though dead. In the chamber there was silence. Finally the old man spoke. "Rise, my son."

Weak and dizzy, Alex struggled to his feet. Turning toward the vast crowd, the ancient voice trembled with emotion. "Brothers, tell me what you heard."

And all the kings whispered, "The song of Lammortan."

With great sorrow the old man looked at Alex. "The prophets wrote of one who would come from another world. They said his soul would be filled with evil and the end of all life would be in his hand. They told us that we would know him by his song. You are that one."

Alex stared in horror. But before he could say a word, he felt an awful surge within his belly, a crawling rush writhing upward into his chest and throat. He knew what it was and now there was nothing to stop it. He screamed as it wrapped around his soul.

Lost!

Lost forever!

They were the last words that were his own. His mind was alive, but no longer could he control it. From his mouth came a guttural laugh. And out of him roared the voice of his god. "Blood for blood! The creature that does evil belongs to me. The Judgment has been rendered. Your work is finished. Slaves of the Mountain, go back to your tombs."

Instantly all the kings who had stood on the coffins disappeared and the old man with them. The Thing that was now Alex turned toward the great angel in the air. But the ceiling was empty. The Worwil was gone. Out of Alex's throat came another laugh. "So you run, my brother? Where is the courage of Heaven? Don't you know that I will find you wherever you are?" Then he cried out, "Come!"

The call was answered with thunder, ten thousand iron hooves crashing over stone. In a swirl of black mist the phantoms entered the chamber, horses and riders streaking through the air. And leading them was a giant stallion with no one on it. It stopped in front of Alex. Smoke swirled from its body, enveloping him in a shroud.

Leaping onto the creature's back, Alex lifted his fist and cried out, "Die until death is all that remains!" There was a great cheer.

Then, with Alex in the lead, the horses and riders streamed into the air. With a pounding roar, they surged forward. And when they reached the wall of the chamber ... they disappeared.

33

WELL OF THE LOST ONES

"Tori! Tori of Lancaster, *wake up! Open your eyes!* Tori, we've got to get out of here."

Tori's eyes popped open. Mirick was fluttering two inches from her face, and the air sang with whining screeches like a million chainsaws slashing through a steel forest.

"What's wrong? What's happening?"

"War! That's what's happening. We are at war. The island is under attack! You must do *exactly* what I say."

She sat up. There was a deep rumble and the door burst open. Into the room flew four insects the size of German shepherds. Their bulbous eyes stared at her, and from their heads hung jaws with jagged teeth that looked like ripsaw blades. As they hovered at the end of the bed, the wind from their wings almost blew her covers off. Tori was terrified.

"Lie on your stomach and stick out your arms and legs!"

"What?"

"Do it! They have to carry you, and there's no time for squeamishness. These are the greatest warriors of the Larggen, and they're here to save your life. *Lie down and turn over!"*

Shivering with fear, Tori obeyed. Instantly wind plastered her clothes as powerful talons slipped around her arms and legs. Then she rose into the air.

"Ooo, I don't like this."

As they hovered toward the open door, Mirick fluttered into her hair.

"Terrible things are happening outside. Close your eyes." Then he yelled, "Go!"

The Larggen took off. Out of the room they flew and beyond the pier. Then came a blistering right turn, and they streaked down the canal a foot above the water. Suddenly a huge mass of Larggen swooped around them like an escort of fighter jets. Though the wind blasted her face, Tori didn't close her eyes. She had to see what was happening, what was causing the terrible, buzzing screeches. She looked up.

The air above Mirick's island roared with green fire. In mighty waves it surged through the canyons between the giant pipes. And from the fire came the awful sounds. All the trillions of insects that had covered the island were swarming, raging, attacking something that she couldn't see. Then for a moment the waves parted and she did see.

High up, horses and riders flying through the air, half ghosts of flesh and darkness, streaming smoke, racing back and forth, roaring, thundering. And the insects were attacking them. By the billions they poured down from the sky, blanketing, stinging, blinding, burning. As they struck the horsemen, their tiny bodies flared, then dropped in avalanches of fiery death. Into the water, onto the pipes, glistening, dazzling, then gone.

"Do you see?" Mirick's voice was filled with emotion. "My people are giving their lives. Look at them! Such bravery! The battle is hopeless, but they do not stop. On and on they die, the glorious legions. Their greatness will be remembered forever." Then his voice broke. "And my place is with them ..."

Suddenly, from high above, two of the horsemen plunged straight toward Tori. Instantly twenty of the Larggen veered to intercept. With a roar their bodies clashed. The horses and riders screamed. Then twisting and thrashing and covered with huge burning insects, they plunged into the canal, disappearing in an explosion of green flame.

Chaos!

The whole island was ablaze. Tori could hardly breathe. On and on she hurdled down the twisting canal. The breakneck speed and hairpin turns made her so dizzy that finally she did close her eyes.

Because of this she didn't see what happened. But suddenly the sounds of war vanished.

Tori opened her eyes. They were flying down a black tunnel and the escort was gone. Only a single Larggen remained in front, lighting the way with the glow from his body.

"Where are we?"

"In a secret passage."

"Where'd the other bugs go?"

"It's safer now if our group is small. They went back to fight and die."

"What were those flying horse-things?"

"The Army of Shadows. The hour of evil is upon us."

Suddenly Tori yelled, "Wait a minute, what about Alex? Where's my brother?"

With sadness Mirick replied, "He is among our enemies."

"What? Stop, stop! We've gotta go back and help him!"

"I'm afraid that isn't possible."

"Why not?"

"He has chosen darkness and with darkness he must remain."

"What do you mean?"

"Your brother is one of them now."

"Those horse-things?"

"Yes."

"We've got to save him."

"That power is not in our hands."

"But you told me I'd see him again."

"And I fear you will."

"We can't leave him like this." She was sobbing now.

"We must. There's nothing we can do."

"You told me the bugs were going to help him."

"I said we would do everything we could, and we did."

"I'm never going to see him again."

"You don't know that. Your brother's life is in the hands of One Who Is Greater Than All ..."

"You promised me, you promised ..."

"I'm sorry."

For a long time Tori cried. Finally she quieted. "Where are we going?"

"There's only one safe place for you now: the Great Mountain."

"Is it far?"

"A long way. First we must get to the surface, and after that there are still many miles to travel. It's night outside, which makes the journey much more dangerous. The riders are creatures of the dark, and they'll be searching for you."

"Why?"

"You escaped from Lammortan and he wants you back."

They flew on in silence. Finally Tori said, "You want to know something? I'm not afraid of bugs anymore."

"I'm glad to hear that."

"Could you tell your friends 'thank you' for saving me?"

"They heard and it fills them with pride. To them you're a queen."

"I am? You mean, like a bug queen?"

"No, just a queen."

More silence. Then she whispered, "You know what I'm doing right now?"

"No."

"I'm praying for my brother."

"That's the very best thing you could do for him."

They had been flying for almost an hour when Mirick said, "There's something that I must teach you, something very important. You must learn to talk without using your mouth."

"What?"

"Soon we will enter a strange and frightening place, and the sound of your voice could make it dangerous."

"What kind of place?"

"I'll tell you more about it in a minute, but right now we have to learn a new way to speak. Start by thinking of me. Then think the words in your mind that you want to tell me, and I'll hear them."

"How can you do that?"

"It's a unique attribute found in highly advanced moths. We call it attenuated cranial fibrillation, and it's used only in times of great danger. Let's try it. First, think of me, then talk to me without using your lips."

"Okay, here goes." She squinted into the darkness and concentrated hard.

Calling Mirick, calling Mirick, hello Mirick, come in Mirick ... "All right, what did I say?"

"You said, 'Calling Mirick, calling Mirick, come in Mirick."

"And I said, 'hello, Mirick.' Did you hear that?"

"Yes, I heard it."

"This is fun. Is it like reading my mind?"

"No, I can't hear you unless you think of me first."

"Let's try it again."

"All right."

"Here goes."

"You don't need to say, 'Here goes.' Just start."

"Okay ..." *BZZZZZZZZZZZZZZZZZZZZZ.*

"Would you stop that?"

"You said to say anything."

"Anything but buzzing."

"I thought you'd like to hear some buzzing."

"Would you like it if I started babbling stupid, meaningless words straight into your brain?"

"I don't know, maybe."

"Well, I don't. To insects, buzzing is a very sophisticated language filled with an endless array of subtle nuances. When people buzz it sounds like very loud drooling."

BZZZZZZZZZZZZZ ... Tori laughed uproariously. "Okay, okay, I won't do it anymore. I just couldn't help it."

"You are an amazing creature. In the direst of circumstances you maintain the ability to be monumentally irritating."

Suddenly the Larggen slowed.

"What's happening?" She tried to peer ahead.

"We're almost there. It's time to take a rest."

The insects settled to the floor. After releasing Tori, they hovered a distance away, forming a protective circle. Mirick fluttered out of her hair. "Are you all right?"

"Just a little sore where they were holding me. But I'm fine." She rubbed her arms and legs. As the whirring of the Larggen's wings quieted, she began to hear something odd. From far away came an echo. And though it was very faint, it sounded like screaming and crying. "What is that? I hear something."

The moth spoke gravely. "I told you that we would be entering a strange and frightening place. The island on the lake is miles underground. The normal passage that my people use to reach the surface is long and blocked with enemy riders. But there's a shorter way. Do you know what a volcano is?"

"Sure, a mountain full of lava."

"Well, there's one up ahead, but it isn't full of lava anymore. The fire went out a long time ago. Now it's a giant shaft that goes down into the heart of the planet. To reach the surface we're going to fly straight up through it. No matter what you see there, do not be afraid. Nothing can hurt you."

"Nothing can hurt me?" Tori was struggling hard not to be afraid.

"That's right. Now it's time to go. Lie down." Mirick nestled in her hair.

Stretching out on the floor, she extended her arms and legs and the insects lifted her.

"Remember, when we reach the shaft, talk to me only with your mind." Once more they began flying through the tunnel, and as the minutes passed, the screaming grew louder. Suddenly the walls disappeared and they were in dizzying emptiness. Heavy mist billowed around the Larggen's wings as they started flying straight up. The shaft was feverishly hot as though they had entered a boiling wound in the flesh of the planet. And the heat reeked with a cloying stench.

It's so hot and it smells in here. The words almost came out of Tori's mouth, but at the last moment she remembered to say them with her mind.

"Yes, it's quite unpleasant. I suggest that you think nice thoughts, maybe something about sunshine and flowers. That sort of thing."

I can't think about sunshine and flowers when it smells like I'm in a toilet.

"We'll be out soon."

The Larggen were flying hard, but the moisture dragged at their wings. And as the mist saturated Tori's clothes, she grew heavier, which slowed them even more. They were pounding upward, but it didn't feel like they were moving at all, just hovering in the stink.

The longer they flew, the more Tori became aware of the awful sound echoing far beneath them. It was like the thunder of a mighty ocean, millions of screams and wails and curses, rising, falling, surging with grief and rage. And it never stopped, never lessened. Every few seconds, a single shriek would climb into a pinnacle of despair and then vanish in the roaring. What are those horrible noises? Nothing that you want to know about. Try not to listen. But she couldn't stop listening. And as she listened, a strange terror gripped her. It felt like the ocean was sweeping upward, like she was about to drown in a sea of tears.

Suddenly she knew something. Knew it with an awful certainty. Her family was dead! Her mother. Her father. Amanda. Alex. Everyone! Dead and gone forever. She was alone! In her mind, she gasped to Mirick, *We're never gonna make it. I'm gonna die here. I'm never going to see my family again.*

"No! Stop thinking that way! It's the air. It's polluted with desolation."

How much longer are we gonna be in here?

"Just a few more minutes. Make your mind think about other things. Fun things. Happy things. Think about those vile chicken streaks."

Strips! Chicken strips! It makes me very sad that you can't ever get that right. It's such a small thing, and it would make me so happy.

"Okay, okay! Chicken strips! I'll never say chicken streaks again, I promise. Just don't cry!"

Tori looked up. She sniffled, but she didn't cry. Instead, she began thinking about the huge insects, how brave and good they were, how they were trying so hard to save her. Suddenly she felt thankful. And the more thankful she felt, the more the sad thoughts began to drift away. Soon the screaming dimmed, and the air wasn't quite as heavy, which allowed the Larggen to fly faster.

I'm feeling better now.

"Good, we'll be out of here soon. Can you see the moonlight?"

She craned her neck. High above was a sliver of crimson. *I think so.*

"That's the top of the shaft."

Suddenly, from far away, there came a low mournful sound. It started like a moan, then grew louder and louder, until the darkness echoed with a bloodcurdling scream. Then it fell back into silence. Instantly the voices below grew silent too.

What was that?

"This volcano is called the Well of the Lost Ones, and it's like a prison.

Deep down, no one knows how far, are kept the spirits of people who did terrible things a long time ago."

Do you mean ghosts?

"You can think of them that way."

What did they do?

"Do you remember the dead children in the cavern when you awoke?"

Yes.

"These are the spirits of the people who sacrificed them to Lammortan. They're kept in darkness until the day when their lives will be judged. But each night, one of the Worwil calls them out of their prison to make them remember what they have done. He sends them to the cathedral of Lammortan to worship the god they have chosen. I hoped we'd get out before the Call, but we didn't, so we'll just have to make the best of it. They're very frightening to see, but they can't do any harm. In fact, they won't even know we're here because they're blind. But they have excellent hearing. And if they hear a child's voice, it will drive them mad. That's why I taught you how to speak without using your lips."

The shriek came again, this time even louder. It was answered from below with a wave of fearful groans. Tori shivered. *Are they coming?*

"They're getting ready to gush out. Now, I want you to close your eyes and don't open them until I tell you. Is that clear?"

Yes.

"Do it now."

She closed them.

"Remember no matter what you hear or feel they can't hurt you."

I'm going to feel something?

"Maybe a little bit of cold when they pass by."

You didn't say I was gonna feel anything.

From below came an eerie flapping, as though a million bats had awakened. The Caller screamed again and the flapping grew louder.

"Okay, they're coming. Get ready."

A moment later the shaft was swollen with a reeking presence, and flapping air pounded in Tori's ears. Then something cold brushed across her face, icy strands slithering, creeping. She gulped and almost gagged; close by, a woman sobbed as though her heart would break. Desperately Tori tried to keep her eyes shut, but she just couldn't. She had to see who was crying that way.

She opened them.

The dim glow of the Larggen's bodies illuminated a river of shadows. Around her swirled thousands of ghostly shapes streaking upward. Heads, faces, arms, hair, things that had once been people, but now were phantoms. And it was impossible to tell whether they were men or women, old or young. Behind them and around them trailed streams of dusty filth like flapping shrouds. Suddenly one of the faces lurched within an inch of her own. Its eyes were blind and dead and its mouth hung open. Out of it came a stinking hiss. Tori couldn't help it. It was too terrifying.

She screamed!

And not with her mind, with her mouth.

The response was instantaneous. The phantoms began shrieking and swarming around her. Their breath filled her nose. Their fingers brushed her skin. Over and over they screeched, "A child, a child, where is the child?"

Tori screamed again and the phantoms grew thicker.

Mirick yelled in her mind, *Tori, stop it! Stop screaming! You're making it worse. Close your eyes!*

They were already closed, but it didn't help. Out of her came choking sobs. And the phantoms kept swarming, their freezing fingers reaching, stroking, caressing.

Mirick yelled, "They can't hurt you! Nothing can hurt you! We'll be out of here in a minute. Hang on!"

It was unbearable! Now the voices were calling names, children's names. Desperate parents overcome with despair, crying out for their lost ones. Another moment and Tori knew she would go insane. Then the scream of the Caller drowned out every other sound, and they were out of the shaft.

For a moment more the shrieking continued. Then it faded as the ghosts streaked off into the sky.

"They're gone." The moth breathed a sigh of relief.

Still sobbing, Tori opened her eyes. High above hung the crimson moon. Below yawned the blackness of the shaft. Extending away from it in every direction was a rolling crater, a vast wasteland of dirt and rocks that went on for miles, and the walls of the gigantic caldera were scarred with jagged cliffs.

"Go north! We've got to get out of here," Mirick yelled to the Larggen.

"I'm sorry, I'm so sorry. I just couldn't help it." Tori struggled to control her tears.

"It's all right. It was a terrifying place, and you were very brave. What's done is done. Let's just pray that their shrieking wasn't heard."

With a roar of wings the insects flew toward the crater wall. They were almost to the top when Mirick said, "Too late."

"What?" Then Tori stared in horror.

Shadows were rising on the cliffs. Drifting shapes that suddenly took form. Above them appeared thousands of black horses and riders in a line that stretched for miles along the rim. The insects slowed and hovered, and Mirick spoke quietly to them. "Brothers, we can't escape. You know what to do. Brave friends, be faithful." Then he whispered to Tori, "They're going to capture us. But I will stay with you no matter what. Just remember to talk to me only with your mind."

The Larggen flew upward until they reached the summit of a cliff and flew forward. Instantly they were surrounded by the horsemen. With great gentleness the insects lowered Tori to the ground and released her. As she struggled to her feet, she saw how the Larggen chose to die—each picked a rider, then with all their strength, they attacked. With five terrible flashes, the insects dropped to the ground, their bodies and wings on fire. For a moment they writhed ... and then they were gone.

In tears, Mirick whispered, "My brave warriors, I salute you. I swear that your lives were not given in vain. May you find peace in the heart of the Great Mountain."

But there was no more time for words. The horses and riders parted, and in front of Tori appeared a stallion. Smoke swirled around his body, and on his back sat a figure wrapped in darkness—only his face was visible.

Towering over her in the moonlight ... was Alex.

34

NIGHTFALL

"Alex!"

Tori stared up into her brother's face. Icy waves of hate almost knocked her down. A darkness like a universe without stars filled his eyes, and out of them drifted wisps of black mist. She had seen that mist before. It was the mist that had oozed from the frame on Bellwind's wall, the mist that had crawled across the room and drawn her away to die. Now it covered her brother's body like a shroud.

"Alex?" This time she spoke his name in a whisper.

Then she heard Mirick's voice in her mind. *He's there, but he can't hear you. Lammortan is squatting in his brain like a toad in a teacup.*

A strange look came to her face. Walking over, she stared up at the Thing that was Alex and said, "You're like a toad in a teacup. My brother doesn't belong to you. Get out of him!"

With a roar, it kicked her in the mouth. She fell to the ground, bleeding. Then it shrieked, gagging out screeches about toads and teacups until spittle ran down. Finally it screamed, "Take the little witch so I can kill her slowly!"

One of the riders jerked Tori up by her hair, grabbed her around the waist, and pulled her onto the horse in front of him. As he gripped her, his arm felt like steel.

"Are you all right?" Mirick whispered.

My lip's cut, but I'm okay. She wiped blood from her mouth.

The Thing that was Alex cried out, "Follow!" and the giant stallion leaped into the air. In a moment all of them were high above the crater, racing over mountains and valleys, forests, and deserts. And as they flew, in their wake roared clouds and slashing wind. Tori began sobbing, *I'm so stupid. I'm just so STUPID.*

"No, you are very brave," Mirick replied gently.

I'm not brave. We got caught because I started screaming. If I had kept my eyes closed like you told me to, this wouldn't have happened and your friends would be alive.

"We don't know that."

Well, I do.

"No, you don't! Child of Earth, we walk the path that has been set for us. Our lives are in the hands of the One Who Is Above All. The Larggen didn't die only for you. They died for Him."

But it's still my fault, and I'm so sorry.

"You are forgiven. Now stop crying. What's important is to think clearly, and you can't do that with salt water and mucus bubbling out of your head."

Okay, you're right. I'll stop. Tori wiped her eyes. Suddenly, in the distance, she saw something. She squinted. It looked like a shimmering cloud of dust streaming through the air. *What's that ahead of us?*

"The spirits of the Lost Ones."

We're following them?

"Before this night is over you're going to see terrible things."

I'll close my eyes.

"This time it won't do any good."

The shimmering cloud began to descend, and the riders followed. A gleam of moonlight was on water. They were heading toward a line of cliffs that ran along a shore. Rising from them were dark shapes that stretched inland for miles. As the phantoms descended, suddenly there was an echoing moan and they disappeared.

They're gone. Where'd they go?

"Into the ruins of an ancient city, the oldest in the world. It was called Arringale, the Garden by the Sea. The people who lived there were the first to sacrifice their children. They strangled them on beds of flowers."

That's awful!

"It's where the horror began."

The riders started circling. Tori stared down. *I don't see a city.*

"The buildings are covered with vines."

They circled lower. *Okay, I think I see them now. It looks kind of like a jungle with streets.*

And then she heard it. Rising above the wind came a scream.

Is the Caller down there?

"He is."

Lower and lower the riders flew. When they were just above the buildings, Tori saw a grotesque form. Standing in the moonlight was the statue of a giant bird with its wings outstretched.

Is that him?

"He is imprisoned inside."

Where are the ghosts?

"Look across the city."

Down a vine-choked street a dark river was flowing. Thousands and thousands of phantoms were marching toward the stone figure.

I see them. What are they going to do?

"What they have done every night since the Caller was imprisoned in a battle long ago. But this night will be the last."

Suddenly the Thing on the stallion screamed, "Ended! No more will you march!" The ghosts shuddered and froze. Then the voice from Alex cried out, "Rindzac ... come forth, you old monster!"

Within the statue appeared a fiery shape. It had the body of a man but the wings and head of an eagle. Its burning eyes looked up at the rider and it screamed, "Blood for blood, Lammortan! Hear the last oracle of the Crimson Throne."

In Heaven you were formed,
With crowns you were adorned,
For your horror I have mourned,
Oh, Painter of the Sky.
For the curses you have sworn,
For the children you have torn,
For the blood you have scorned,
Mighty Worwil, you will die!

The Thing that was Alex shrieked, "*You curse me?* Never will you scream again!" With a roar the stallion flashed down and vanished into the burning figure. A pillar of fire engulfed the statue. The Caller lifted his head and one last scream filled the air. *"The Curse of the Blood … let it fall!"* With a rumbling crash the statue was no more. The fire blazed upward and the Worwil was gone. From out of the smoke rose the stallion with Alex on his back.

In a strange room on a distant island an old woman stood before seven golden frames. In one, the glass was shattered. Taking a deep breath, she bowed her head and started circling the room making peculiar reaching motions. On the fourth circle she began to sing. A thick vapor rose from the floor. Slowly it drifted higher, and the room became filled with radiance.

Seven times.

Seven circles.

And at the end of the last one the vapor congealed into streaks of crimson. Four of the frames were running with blood. The old woman whispered, "Angel fall! Only two of us left to stand against him. Indeed and forever, the night has come." Moving to the frame with the broken glass, she raised her hand and cried out, "Spoken, spoken, foretold and spoken! On this night all truth will be revealed. In the Name, the Very Name, I command you … paint your presence before my eyes!"

The darkness swirled and, line-by-line, in the broken glass of the seventh frame appeared the work of a great master. It was the face of Alex, and from his eyes flowed crimson tears. When the portrait was finished, the face smiled and whispered, "My sister, I come." Then it faded and was gone.

Coldly the old woman replied, "Long, yes, long, have I waited. So come and do not delay!" She turned and walked to the wall. Passing straight through the bricks, she went outside.

Moonlight and mist.

A world of blue-green shadows.

As Bellwind stood on her porch, all the creatures of her island gathered before her, strange and lovely beings, large and small. "Dear ones, yes, my very dear ones," she began. "For untold ages, this night we knew would come. Through wars and endless dying, safe we were upon our island because to the shore of darkness we were not allowed to go. Died, our brothers and sisters, in untold millions. And now, this night, our night it is upon us. Be brave, my children. I love you still and will love you always." Raising her hand, she cried out, "Look to the Mountain! At the end of sorrow will come the Dawn!" Then she turned and walked back inside her house.

Quickly Bellwind began to climb the stairs of the tower. And with each step the marks of age fell from her. Higher and higher, through floor after floor, from wrinkled and old to beautiful and young. When she reached the top, the soft light of her loveliness filled the tower. Calmly she turned and looked toward the land; far away, she saw it, a streaming cloud blotting out the stars. But her heart held no fear, for beyond the cloud she saw the Mountain. With joy she whispered, "Tonight, yes, this night ... I will be home."

Where are we going now? Who's he gonna kill next? Tori couldn't stop trembling with rage.

"He's destroying the last of his enemies," Mirick replied.

How many more are there?

"Only two."

They were flying above the ocean. Far below, waves crashed and foamed. In the roaring hurricane behind the riders streamed the phantoms of the Lost Ones, moaning and shrieking. Suddenly, in the distance, appeared a soft green light that glowed on the water like a floating star. The riders veered toward it.

What's that up ahead?

"It's the island of the Watcher."

Who's that?

"One of the mightiest of the Worwil. Her name is Bellwind."

That's the old lady who was with us in the raft. She's one of them?

"She is."

Then he's going to kill her too. She started crying. *Somebody's got to warn her. She's got to get away.*

"She knows he's coming. She's been waiting for this night for ten thousand years."

As the light drew nearer, the riders descended until Tori could see the crimson cap of each moonlit wave. And then the source of the lovely light became visible. It was streaming from a tower that rose high above a mantle of glistening mist. She stared—something was *in* the tower. No, *someone.* Closer still. The light was coming from the shining form of a lovely young woman. It was flowing from her body.

I see a girl in a tower. And she's so beautiful.

"That's Bellwind."

But she's young. Bellwind is old.

"Her spirit is young forever."

She's just standing there. It's like she doesn't even see us.

"Oh, she sees us."

Then why doesn't she do something?

"Watch!"

The attack began. Like a typhoon of smoking filth, the riders swept down. With the Lost Ones screaming behind, they began circling the island. Around and around they went, and each time they passed the tower, Tori saw Bellwind's face. It was so strange. She wasn't looking at them. She was looking up as though at something far away, and her eyes were filled with blazing joy.

With each revolution the circles grew tighter. And then a bell began to toll. Deep and clear it rang. With each mighty peal, waves of light began rippling outward. Tori had never seen light that looked this way. It was thick and soft, and as it flowed from the tower, it pulsed like blood from a wound. When the first wave slammed into the horses, they went insane, screaming and shrieking, as though they had been covered with burning oil. Hundreds plummeted into the ocean. The rest scattered. The horse carrying Tori bucked and thrashed. It was all the rider could do to keep them on its back as it raced away.

Over and over the bell tolled, and the waves of light rolled on. From out of Alex the deep voice raged, "Stop running! Come back and form around me! Obey!"

But the horsemen couldn't control their mounts. The ones that didn't fall into the ocean vanished into the darkness. All that was left were the ghosts of the Lost Ones, circling and moaning in the hurricane. Finally, with a raging shriek, the great stallion turned and raced alone toward the tower.

Within the room of the frames there was a thunderous crash. Out of the seventh frame flew a spear of darkness. As it streaked across the floor to the stairs, it became the stallion with Alex on his back. They climbed, and with each step, the horse's hooves struck lightning. The tower began to burn.

Outside, Bellwind gasped and whispered, "Oh, Father ... I am dying." As she stood in the roaring night, no longer could she see the Mountain. The crimson mists were lost in horror. As flames rose within her body, the agony deepened in her eyes. Yet the bell continued ringing.

Up the staircase the stallion pounded. As the rider passed each landing, the stairs behind him vanished in howling flames. Through floor after floor he raced until he was at the top. Above him was the crashing bell, roaring sound, and pulsing light. He shrieked, insane with rage. Leaping up, he grasped the iron and screamed, *"Ring no more forever!"*

The bell stopped, but the reverberations grew, ringing light and fire. Suddenly there was a mighty explosion. As the tower fell, Bellwind lifted her hands and cried out, "Lord of the Mists, I come!" With a streak of burning light she vanished in a cloud of crimson.

From out of the firestorm leaped the stallion. Rising into the air, the rider gave a cry, and once more his army gathered. They drew their swords. Tori closed her eyes and tried to cover her ears, but still she heard the horror. Over and over the horse that carried her swooped down, slashing and screaming, killing Bellwind's lovely creatures. The dying seemed to take forever, and all she could do was sob. Finally the Thing on the stallion gave a call and the shadow-riders leaped into the air. Below, the lovely island of emerald mist vanished into the waves.

When she felt the wind on her face, Tori opened her eyes. Still sobbing, she asked, *They're all dead, aren't they? They killed all the beautiful things on the island.*

"Yes."

I hate him! Isn't there anybody who can stop him?

"He will be stopped. And when it happens it will be forever."

When is that? After everybody's dead?

Mirick didn't answer. As they flew on, the ocean vanished behind them. Below, in the moonlight, flowed a landscape of forested hills and, beyond that, a broad, empty plain. Tori cried for a long time, but she was so exhausted that her eyes finally began to close. In spite of the awful clouds and beating wind, she fell asleep.

Then suddenly she awoke.

The horse had slowed. They were descending. *Where are we? Where's he taking us now?*

"To a terrible place." Mirick spoke with great sadness. "What's about to happen will be the most awful of all."

What do you mean? A cold knot formed in her stomach.

"Prepare your heart and pray for strength."

She looked down. They were passing over a desolate mountain, and on its slopes stood a forest of dead trees. Stark and leafless, their twisted limbs reached up into the crimson moonlight.

"Below is the Mountain of the Faithful Ones. Long ago many brave people died here, murdered because they wouldn't sacrifice their children." Then Mirick's voice changed. Somehow it became hard and soft all at the same time. "Tori of Earth, your heart is about to be broken. What you are going to see will test all of your faith and love."

What am I going see? Her mouth was dry.

"One of the greatest heroes who ever walked through this dark world, the bravest of the brave."

The riders began to circle. Beneath them was a barren peak. At the very top, all alone, stood a small white tree. The leader on the stallion raised his hand, and ten horsemen followed him downward. One of them was the rider carrying Tori. They landed on the mountaintop. Then the Thing that was Alex dismounted. "Put her on the ground!"

The rider dropped Tori off the horse. She landed in a heap. As she struggled to get up, she suddenly saw something very odd—in the branches of the small dead tree there was a strange bundle. She took a step closer. What was it? It looked like a *baby*. She walked over. It *was* a baby; the bundle in the tree was a real baby held as though in a mother's arms. And he was alive. His eyes were open. He was looking at her. Tori couldn't believe it.

It's the baby who was in the raft. What's he doing here?

"Take the *thing* out of the tree!" The roaring command came from Alex's mouth.

She turned and glared at him. "Why should I? You're not the boss of me."

"Obey!"

"Do it, Tori. Take the child."

Giving a vile look to the Thing that was Alex, she began pulling back the dead branches, but as she did so, her eyes fixed on the trunk. She stared—what was that? There was a shape in the bark almost like a face. She bent closer. It *was* a face, a dead face, though its eyes were open.

Tori staggered back. She knew that face.

It was *Amanda.*

35

ALOI

Steady, child. Be strong," Mirick whispered.

But Tori was screaming, "Is that my sister? That's her, isn't it? That's her and she's dead."

Out of the Thing that was Alex came a horrible laugh. Shrieking, she rushed at him.

"You killed her! You killed my sister!" With all her strength she started hitting and pounding on him. He shoved her away, but she came back. He struck her.

"Tori, stop it!" Mirick yelled, but she didn't stop. Finally the Thing that was Alex kicked her in the stomach. Gasping, she doubled over and dropped to the ground.

Mirick pleaded, "Tori, listen to me. Your sister was the bravest of the brave. She died trying to protect the baby. He needs you. Will you help him?"

Choking, sobbing, wanting to die, she lay with her face on the cold stone.

The command came again. "Take it out of the tree!"

"Look at him. Look at the baby," Mirick whispered.

Though she didn't want to, Tori raised her head and looked.

"What happens to him now depends on you. Amanda did all she could."

Suddenly she thought she heard another voice calling softly to her from far away.

Tori, come to me. It was her sister's voice.

Sobbing, Tori struggled to her feet. Then, as though in a dream, she stumbled to the tree. From a broken heart she whispered, "Amanda, I love you, I love you." And a sweet voice seemed to whisper back, *I love you too. Take him and don't be afraid.*

With tears streaming Tori began untangling the branches that had been her sister's arms. The little boy was finally free. He was so light. He didn't weigh anything. As he clung to her, she looked down into his eyes. She had never seen anything like them. Deep, not like a baby's eyes. And as he looked up at her, she heard soft voices like mist, rising, falling, lilting in her soul, singing away the rage and horror, singing peace and strength beyond anything that she had ever known. And in the singing Tori changed forever. Within her heart a brave young woman was born. Holding the baby close, she whispered through her tears, "It's all right. I've got you now."

The Thing that was Alex climbed back on the stallion. "Take her!"

The rider who had carried her before reached down and jerked her up. But this time he didn't lock her in with his arm. Instead, with one hand, he gripped a knot of clothes on her back and with the other her hair.

"Stop that! It hurts!" she yelled. But he kept on.

"Bring the filthy weed to burn on my altars," the leader roared.

Two of the riders pulled the little tree from the ground. It was easy because it was small and the roots weren't deep. After tying it on a horse, they mounted. Then all of them rose in a raging cloud and, with the army of shadows following, streamed away.

The rider behind Tori was still holding her by her clothes and hair.

"I told you to stop that! You're hurting me!"

But the grip only tightened.

Why is he doing this? He didn't do it before.

He's afraid to touch the baby. To them he's like poison.

Oh, really? A nasty look came into her eyes. Jerking around, she pushed the little boy toward the rider and yelled, "Why don't you grab *him* for awhile?"

The baby reached out a tiny hand that vanished into the mist around the creature's body. Screaming as though it had been stabbed, the thing fell from the horse and disappeared into the hurricane. Instantly other riders moved in, but none touched her. Tori hugged the little boy. "I wish you could kill them all."

As they flew on, she started crying. *I want to know about Amanda. What happened to her?*

"She died trying to take the baby home."

Where is that?

"The Great Mountain that stands above the world. You can't see it because of the clouds, but it's there. It's the place I was taking you."

And she was doing it all by herself?

"There was no one who could go with her."

What about Bellwind?

"Not permitted. Her task has been to watch and remember for the record of the ages. If she or any creature from her island had stepped onto the shore, they would have died. It is the Law."

So Amanda went alone. She was brave.

"Yes."

Tori looked over at the little tree tied on the horse. *How did my sister die?*

"Her enemies gave her a disease that changed her body."

It must have been awful.

"She died in great pain, but she never gave up."

I'm so proud of her. She fought back tears. *Who is this baby? Why do they want him so bad?*

"His name is Aloi, and he is the Angel of the Children."

You mean, like an angel from Heaven?

"You can think of him that way. Long ago, when the sacrifices began, when the first drop of child blood fell from the dying, the heart of the Great Father was broken. As He watched from the mists, He heard every cry, from the tiniest whisper of one torn from a womb to the screams that rose from the altars. Ten thousand ways they killed them. And the death of each child was the agony of Heaven. From that agony Aloi was born. He is the angel of the innocent ones, the face of all their faces, the Spirit of Childhood that was meant to be, the promise of life for all the lives that were destroyed."

Like the dead children in the cave?

"Those and countless more."

Where has he been? He was with us on the raft when we first got here.

"He was hidden on your world, kept from the eyes of Lammortan until the prophecies could be fulfilled. Then the Darkness was allowed to find him. Now they want him to be the last sacrifice. If his blood is shed this world will belong to Lammortan and the children will sleep forever."

That's not going to happen, is it?

"Soon we will know. I have not understood many things until this moment. But now all is clear. Your sister lived and died to bring Aloi to the place where you could take him from her arms. 'Hidden in weakness is the last. But to the last the first is given.' That's an ancient prophecy and it's about you. You're the last child of your mother and father, and Aloi was meant to be the first child of a new world. You are the one who has been chosen."

Chosen for what?

"To stand against Lammortan face-to-face."

I can't do that.

"Yes, you can. You weren't ready before, but you are now. And you won't be alone. They thought they had killed the Carrier. But you are the Carrier."

What's going to happen?

"There is an ancient Law that even Lammortan must obey. It says that if Aloi is to be sacrificed, the offering must be made from the hands of a child from another world. That's why you and your sister were brought here, at the end of time, to fulfill the final test."

He wants me to kill the baby? I'll never do it! Never!

"If you refuse, he will kill you."

I don't care.

"You see, you are ready."

What about Alex? Could he do it?

"I don't know. He isn't a child, but he isn't a man either. If Lammortan tried to use him, it would be a great risk. It might not work. And even to try, he would have to give up control of his mind and body. The sacrifice must be made in freedom."

So he could still win even if I die?

It took a moment for the moth to answer. Finally he whispered, "Those who serve the Great Mountain must walk without seeing what lies ahead. But remember this—the One who loved the children loves them still. And it is He who guides our path."

After a stomach-wrenching lurch, the riders began falling from the sky.

Tori screamed as the horse plunged beneath her. Twisting, spiraling down she flew in a blur of smoke and shrieking wind, past moonlit cliffs into darkness. Her fall ended with a bone-jarring jerk deep inside a canyon. The horses began racing through an eerie gorge, between massive walls strewn with boulders. Tori gasped, trying to make her stomach leave her throat. *Why ... did they ... do that? Where are we going now?*

"To the throne of evil."

The gorge widened. The riders rounded a bend and Tori saw it. Straight ahead, high above, sprawled a vast building. Tortured walls and twisted pinnacles snaked for miles across a sheer cliff, and in the center stood a monstrous heap that looked like a tomb.

What is ... that? She could hardly form the words in her mind.

"The Cathedral of Lammortan."

As she stared at it, a terrible coldness entered her heart. Something inside whispered that when she entered those walls she would die, but her eyes hardened and her mind answered, *Shut up. I don't care.*

Carved into the cliff leading up to the cathedral were a thousand stairs, and it was to these that the horses flew. On a wide landing halfway up they came to rest. The riders dismounted and the voice from Alex snarled at her, "Get down!"

Carefully she lowered herself and the baby onto the stone.

"Follow!" Then he began to climb.

Tori looked up. The stairs were so high and there was no railing. Worse, they were crumbled and covered with debris.

"Don't be afraid," Mirick whispered.

I'm ... I'm okay. I'm gonna count. My mom taught me to do that when I was little so I wouldn't be scared. Carefully she started climbing and counting each step.

"One ... two.... three ... four ... five ..."

When she reached a hundred, she turned and looked back. Behind her was a vision that would have terrified the bravest man. Crawling up from the chasm were thousands of silhouettes shrouded in mist, the phantoms of the Lost Ones.

"You're trembling," Mirick whispered.

I ... just feel a little weird.

"Well, I can understand that."

I should be scared, but I'm not. And it makes me feel kind of freaky.

"Wait a minute. You're trembling because you're not scared?"

Yeah.

"Such a strange child."

Tori began climbing and counting again. "One hundred one, one hundred two, one hundred three, one hundred four ..."

Two hundred ...

Three hundred ...

Four hundred ...

Suddenly she heard singing, a host of deep voices rising in a roaring chant. She looked up. Above her soared the vast cathedral, and its gigantic walls were encrusted with carvings. Broken bodies. Raging faces. Screaming gods and shrieking children. But the horror of it only made her eyes grow harder still.

Finally ten more steps ...

Then two ...

Then one ...

And she was at the top. Before her, giant doors stood open, and from out of them poured waves of dripping steam. A rotten stench filled the air, and the ground shook with triumphant singing as the Thing that was her brother vanished inside.

"Remember, you are a queen," Mirick whispered.

"But not a bug queen." Her voice was steady.

When the moth spoke again, his was trembling. "No, not a bug queen, but a queen that the mightiest Larggen would follow forever. So hold your head high, Tori of Earth, for you are the Queen of the Children."

Lifting her chin and hugging the baby, Tori walked through the doors ... into the steaming glow.

High above, on a Throne of starlight, there was One who saw. And in the seeing, knew that the night had come. Stepping down, He began the long descent, from the Crimson Mists toward the Cathedral of Sorrows, from glory into a humble form, from the Great Mountain ...

Into the Night of Blood.

36

VEILS VANISHING

Veils of mist, veils within veils …
Golden, glistening, shimmering …

What is this?

As Tori entered the cathedral, she experienced exactly the opposite of what she had expected. Gone was the stench and horror; the air was filled with gentle perfume. No longer did the singing crash and groan. It was like soft voices whispering from Heaven. And the mist—the lovely mist—where it touched her skin, it tingled with soft, gentle coolness. As she breathed it in, all she wanted to do was dream—dream in the mist that swirled and danced around her. Slowly she took a few steps forward … and the mist began to fade.

Amazing!

Was it real?

Before her lay a chamber so vast and high that the ceiling was lost in twilight. The pillars that held it up were the trunks of huge old trees, and the floor was covered with moss. Among the tree-pillars stood golden statues that seemed to hover like singing angels.

But the light …

All she cared about was the dazzling light. It swept through the room in a dance of rainbows with such loveliness that she wanted to cry. Forgetting everything else, Tori began walking toward the light. No, not walking—drifting, dreaming. And then she saw it, far away, at the front, a place of such glory that it had to be the Heart of Heaven.

A golden staircase.

And above it a gigantic painter's canvas that seemed to be coming down from the stars. Over it, out of it, roared a waterfall of fiery colors that crashed and splashed, transforming into the rainbow light that filled the room.

Walking ... walking toward it, and the soft singing was all around her.

Walking toward the waterfall of light.

There was something under it. Something at the bottom. Something reaching out from the waves. A lovely hand. It was the crystal hand of a woman. And though it was very large, never had she seen anything so gentle and delicate. It was like the hand of a mother beckoning to her child. From the fingers ran streams of crimson starlight. Then came a sound that almost made her stop breathing. Out of the singing mist, a voice called her name.

"Tori ... Tori ..."

Shock! Had she really heard it? It came again, louder.

"Tori ... where are you?"

Amanda!

It was Amanda's voice.

She couldn't believe it. "Amanda, I'm over here," she yelled. And then she started crying.

"Tori, look up. Daddy's home!"

The canvas—no longer was it flowing with fire and light. It was like glass. Like a window. And through it she could see into a home. Her home! Yes, her real home back on Earth—her living room, with her couch, her chairs, her pictures. And there was her family—all of them—Amanda, Alex, her mom ... and her dad. He was right there, smiling at her. They were all smiling and laughing and waving from behind the window. Her sister yelled, "Come on, slow poke, what are you waiting for?"

There was a trembling vibration. She felt her body freeze. Then a tingling strangeness. Separating—she felt herself being pulled apart. Suddenly she was floating in the air, and the baby wasn't with her anymore. Looking back, she saw herself, standing very still, with the little boy in her arms. But she didn't care. Nothing mattered anymore but getting to the window. She turned toward it, closer and closer, drifting until she was just outside the glass. She tried to touch it, but her hand passed right through. Alex grabbed it and pulled. Instantly she was standing in her living room, staring at all of them as though she had just awakened from a long nap.

Her brother yelled, "You're home. We didn't think you were ever gonna get here. You walk like a slug."

They were all laughing and happy, so happy they looked almost like different people. Gone from Alex was the sneering coldness, and Amanda … in her eyes, there was no more hurt and pain. And most all, her mom. The terrible sorrow wasn't there anymore. Gently her mother kissed her. "Oh, honey, I'm so glad you're home. I've been so worried about you. Look who's here."

"Hello, princess."

And then Tori was in her father's arms, hugging and crying and whispering, "Daddy, you're here, you're really here."

"Yes, I'm really here."

Then he twirled her just like he used to do when she was little. Twirled her round and round …

Dizzy, laughing, hugging, crying …

Yes, crying for joy.

"All right, you two, it's time for dinner. The pizza's done." Her mother's eyes were so beautiful when there was no sorrow in them. "Amanda, set the table. Alex, get the drinks."

They crowded into the kitchen. The smell of hot pizza, oh, it was so delicious. And she was so hungry. Her mother took it out of the oven, dripping with cheese and stuffed with pepperoni and Italian sausage (but no vegetables, not a single crunchy thing). Then they all sat down, and her father cut a big slice and laid it on her plate. That first bite … she thought she had died and gone to pizza heaven. Tori started eating. And eating. Everybody laughed because she ate so much. When she couldn't hold another bite, her dad yelled, "Table games! It's Tori and me against all of you." Of course, Alex and Amanda groaned. They always did that because they knew they were going to lose.

While the table was being cleared, her dad went to the closet and pulled out all of her favorite games, Clue and Sorry, Chutes and Ladders, Uno — boxes that she hadn't seen in years. While they played, her mom made huge banana splits with vanilla ice cream and hot gooey fudge (but no nuts, only maraschino cherries). The first heaping spoonful dripped chocolate down Tori's chin. She laughed so hard that more fudge ran from her mouth, which made everybody laugh until they thought they would throw up. Then she and her dad proceeded to win every game. And Tori was not a good winner. With each victory she gloated and giggled and snickered until it drove her brother and sister nuts.

Finally her mother said, "All right, everybody, it's time for bed. You've all got school tomorrow."

Of course, there was the usual whining. Tori begged, "Can't I stay up just a little longer to be with Daddy?"

"It's late and you've had a busy day. He can tuck you in."

"Hey, I have a surprise for you." His eyes twinkled.

"What is it?"

"It's in your room. Hop on." Jumping onto his back, he jiggled and joggled her into her bedroom and plopped her onto the bed.

"Butterfly kisses!" Bending down, he laid his face next to hers and tickled her cheek with his eyelashes. But instead of laughing, she started to cry.

"Hey, butterfly kisses aren't supposed to make you cry." He ran his fingers through her hair.

"I just can't believe it," she whispered. "You're really here. I've missed you so much, Daddy."

"And I've missed you, Sweetheart. I'm never going away again."

"You mean that?"

"I promise."

"But what about your family in England?"

"My only family is right here. I love each of you so much. And most of all, I love your mom."

"I thought you hated her."

"Oh, Tori, that isn't true. I love her more than words can say. This is the only family that means anything to me."

"But you left us."

"Yes, I went away for a while and I made you cry. Will you forgive me for that? Will you forgive me for hurting you?"

She nodded, hugging him and sobbing even harder. "Every night I cried because you were gone."

"And I'm going to make it up to you," he whispered. "I promise you're never going to cry again."

"Will it always be like tonight? This is just like it was when I was little and we were so happy."

"It'll be just like this forever."

But as she hugged him, a strange feeling came over her. *"Forever?"*

"Yes, always and forever."

Then she saw something. On the wall was a frame that hadn't been there before. And in it was a picture. "What's that?"

Smiling, he replied, "Oh, that's the surprise, the little gift I told you about."

The strange feeling grew. Climbing down from the bed, Tori walked over and stared at it. In the frame was a picture of her. She was surrounded with black clouds and looked very frightened. In her arms was the baby. Bending down, her father said, "Do you remember that awful place?"

"Yes."

"Well, you never have to go back there again. You can stay here forever with your brother and sister and Mom and me."

Tori looked at him. "I know what this is," she said softly. "This is my dream, the one I had every night, that you would come back and love us again."

"And now it can be real. But there's something you have to do first."

She felt a creeping coldness. "What is it?"

Gently he answered, "It's about the baby. You have to leave him over there in the place where he belongs."

Tears began running down her cheeks. Her father saw them and hugged her. There were tears in his eyes too. "Honey, I'm sorry. I know you love him. You've been carrying him close to your heart for so long. But you need to do what's best for both of you. I know you understand that."

"What do I have to do?"

"It's very easy. You won't even have to leave this room. Just look at the picture. Go ahead and look, Sweetheart."

Tori turned toward the frame. Suddenly, looking through it was like being in two places at once—in her bedroom, yet standing in the cathedral with Aloi in her arms. She could feel him nestled against her. Through the frame, she saw the canvas flowing with mist and rainbows. And beneath it . . . the crystal hand.

"Now, think of yourself walking toward the stairs."

It was so odd. Standing and not moving, yet at the same time walking and feeling the moss beneath her feet. When she reached the bottom of the staircase, she stopped.

"All right, now go up the stairs and lay him in the beautiful hand. You've brought him home, Tori. He'll be happy here forever."

With tears brimming she looked up at her father. "So many times I dreamed this dream—that you would come home and be with us. And every time when I woke up I cried."

"And now your dream has come true."

"No, it hasn't. Because to get it I have to kill the baby."

"No, no, no, Sweetheart. What are you talking about? It isn't killing him. It's doing what's best for him. It's placing him in the Hand of God."

Suddenly Tori's eyes didn't look like the eyes of a child anymore. In them was a great sadness. Quietly she said, "I know something now that I didn't know before. Do you want to know what it is?"

"What is it?"

"You can't make a dream come true by hurting someone else. That's what you tried to do, Daddy. That's why you went away. You hurt us to get what you wanted. And you're not coming home. Not really. Not ever." As she said the words, she felt her heart breaking and the beautiful dream begin to die.

Her father rose and towered over her. "Don't you want me to stay, Tori? Don't you want our family to be together?"

"Yes," she whispered.

"Then you've got to prove it. You've got to show me that you really love me—that you love all of us—by doing this one small thing."

Into the room walked her mother and Amanda and Alex. Her mother was distraught. All the sorrow was returning. "Sweetheart, why won't you do it? We need for you to do it."

Desperately Amanda grabbed her hands. "Please do it, Tori. Do it so we can be together. If you don't, it'll be like it was before, and I can't stand that. I'll kill myself."

"Save your breath. She doesn't care about us. She's just a spoiled little brat." The rage and bitterness were back in Alex.

Her father bent down and stared deeply at her. "If you don't do it, Tori, I'll have to leave. And this time I'll be gone forever."

Tori looked at each of them. Then through her tears she said, "When I dreamed this dream, all it ever did was hurt me. And I don't want it to hurt anymore. The dream isn't real. But the baby is real. And I'll never do anything to hurt him ... even if I have to die."

With a grinding crash, instantly she was back in her body. She felt Mirick nestled in her hair. *"Well done!"* he whispered. *"Now, prepare for his rage."*

37

THE SINGER

Shrieking wind roared around Tori. It was all she could do to keep from falling down. Gone was the loveliness of the cathedral, gone was the Heart of Heaven. The soft singing turned into a wrenching wail and the perfume into stench. Before her lay a chamber so vast and high its ceiling was lost in gloom. Veils of steaming mist and churning mold swirled between gigantic pillars. And in the billowing veils swarmed shadows and shapes — a sea of dead faces, rising and falling in the glistening dark.

The phantoms.

The Lost Ones.

The cathedral was infested with their terror. Stumbling backward, Tori bumped into something and almost fell. Looking down, she started to cry. On the floor beside her lay the little white tree with the face of Amanda. But before the tears could come she heard a whisper:

"Turn and see!"

She turned. In front of her were the golden stairs, and soaring above them was the canvas. No longer did it dance with rainbows. Down it poured waves of thick green oil that oozed onto the staircase and then simmered into the steam that filled the room. The delicate crystal hand had vanished. In its place, reaching through the waves, was the golden hand of a giant with gnarled fingers the size of tree trunks.

Suddenly at the top of the stairs appeared a silhouette shrouded in wreaths of smoke. Slowly the smoke parted. Standing above her was Alex. She was about to call his name when his mouth opened and from out of it came a roar.

"Praise to that which is fallen! Praise to the Lord of the Night!"

And all the shadows answered, "Sing the Song of the Lost Ones. Glory to the God who Burns Away Light!"

Then silence.

The chanting stopped and the wind died, and in the silence there was soft surging. Something was slithering in the oil on the canvas. A shape was beginning to form. Stroke by stroke, line by line, there appeared a face of such majesty and splendor that every creature in the cathedral froze in breathless awe. Eyes of shimmering starlight, soft skin painted in a thousand hues, male-female-angel-god. Towering in the mist, as though descending out of heaven was a Face of Glory.

Worship!

Worship!

The creatures in the cathedral fell prostrate in worship—all except for Tori and the little boy she held. Upon her came a crushing weight—she gasped, struggling to breathe. From out of the lips on the canvas came a sighing whisper, *"Life ... I would have given it. All of your hopes and dreams fulfilled. But you turned away. Now death is all that remains."*

Threads of smoke. From the giant hand appeared wisps that formed into ghostly fingers. Drifting ... rising ... reaching toward her. The moment had come, she knew it. Hugging the little boy, Tori closed her eyes and prayed. All she wanted was to be as strong as Amanda, as strong as her sister until death came.

Waiting, waiting to die.

But then ... *a shriek*!

What was happening? Confused, Tori opened her eyes.

"Alex!"

The fingers were wrapped around her brother, and he was writhing. Screaming, he crashed down the stairs and fell at her feet, jerking and spasming.

"Stop it! Stop doing that to him!"

But it didn't stop. It grew worse.

"Leave him alone! Get away from him!" Sobbing, Tori knelt and touched his hair. His face was drenched with sweat, his teeth were clenched, and his eyes rolled back.

"Will he live or will he die?" the Voice cried out.

"I hate you!" Tori screamed.

"But do you love your brother?"

"Yes, I love him!"

"Then look into his soul."

As she stared, Alex's skin became like smoke. Suddenly she could see inside his body, down, down, through flesh and bone, into the depths of who he was, into a terrible pit of darkness.

And something was living there.

Cowering and moaning was a tiny luminous shadow with her brother's eyes. And wrapped around it hung a glowing serpent that was eating his life, sucking it away. Tori screamed and the vision disappeared. Over and over she sobbed, "Alex, I love you, I love you."

"But do you love him enough to save him? Give me the child and I will set him free."

Staring up at the face, Tori screamed, "No!"

"Then you do not love him."

"I do love him!"

Waves of hate and rage, she could see them flowing from the fingers like black tendrils, strangling her brother's life.

"Give ... me ... the child."

Dying, Alex was dying. His life was slipping away. She couldn't stand it. Suddenly her heart was drowning in darkness. She was killing her brother. Shaking, sobbing, she cried out, "Oh God, help me." Then she looked into the baby's eyes.

Such love!

He was crying too, as though he could feel her anguish. And in that moment the darkness broke, and her soul was flooded with light. Her sobbing stopped. Rising to her feet, she cried out, "I won't do it. I won't kill this baby ... not even to save someone I love." As she hugged the little boy, her face was shining. "If you want him, you've got to kill me first. So come and do it! You've murdered all the other children, kill me too!"

Instantly the monstrous face roared and the cathedral shook. The fingers left Alex and wrapped around Tori.

Agony!

She felt her life being crushed away.

But what she didn't feel was a tiny movement in her hair.

A rush—a shriek of wind—and then, *raging fire*!

Suddenly she was surrounded by a wall of emerald flame. The fingers vanished and she could breathe again. Tori looked up. Soaring above her was a Creature of dazzling Brightness. The phantoms were rushing away, as from the Creature came a voice like singing thunder. "Enough! The test is over and you have failed."

The eyes in the oil were staring and out of them flowed hate. *"So, my brother, you have come."*

"How blind you are, Lammortan. I have been here all along, hidden in the hair of a child."

Mirick, what's happening? Tori cried out in her mind.

From above, strange flaming eyes looked down at her. "Little Queen of the Children, the time for hiding has passed."

She felt her hair. The moth was gone. "Mirick . . . ?"

"Yes, Mighty Mirick," mocked the Voice from the oil. *"Mirick, Singer of Curses . . . Mirick, Worwil of the Throne."*

Tori stared up. It *was* Mirick. But he was huge, and his wings glistened with green and yellow fire. Around him burned a shimmering halo, and his eyes were flaming multifaceted globes. He was so different, so strange and frightening, and yet the same. As he looked down at her, she could feel his love.

Then he turned toward the face in the canvas. Once more the singing thunder echoed in the room, "I will not let you destroy the last innocent child on Boreth. You know the Law. The Choice of the Carrier has been made, and it cannot be changed."

"Yes, her choice is made," the Face hissed, *"but do not think that I am defeated. There is one last child from another world . . . and he will obey."*

Mirick looked down. Alex lay unconscious on the floor. "The Law, Painter, the Law. To perform the test you must release him. His choice must be free."

"Do not speak to me of law, my brother. Speak only of blood. For this is the night of all nights . . . when the last of the Worwil die." The golden hand began to glow. Slowly the huge fingers reached upward.

Mirick looked down at Tori. His eyes were soft, as one last time she heard his voice in her mind. *Daughter of Earth, I love you. Be faithful, and we will stand together before the Crimson Throne.*

Before an eye could blink, the Creature that was Mirick became a living flame. As the giant hand streaked toward him, Mirick's wings engulfed it and thunder shook the chamber.

Shrieking! The Face on the canvas was shrieking, and the cathedral was filled with the stench of searing death. Though Mirick was in agony, from him came singing in a language that Tori had never heard. And then, above, she saw a vision. The ceiling of the cathedral disappeared, and down in an avalanche of splendor rushed millions of tiny flaming stars. As they encircled Mirick, she saw what they were.

Fireflies!

The fireflies of Heaven had come to escort him home.

The monstrous hand and the body of the Angel burned together, as the Face in the canvas shrieked. Then Tori heard something so wonderful that she never forgot it for the rest of her life; words weaving sorrow, full of anguish and love, higher and higher they flew. It was Mirick's Death Song. As the fireflies swirled around him, his flame grew bright and he began to change. He was singing his soul out of his body—shedding his dying form like a burning chrysalis. Then his spirit broke free, and the most beautiful creature that Tori had ever seen hung in the air. His wings were living flames in a thousand colors, and his eyes were filled with the Fire of Heaven. Lifting his head, he cried out with joy, "Larggen of the Throne … lead me home!"

Blazing light and singing, such brilliance that Tori couldn't stand it! She closed her eyes. Then silence and dark.

When she opened them again, all that was left of the gigantic hand was a blackened stump sticking out of the wall. And Mirick, the Singer, the tiny moth and Mighty Angel … was gone.

"Mirick, Mirick …," she sobbed. But there was no answer.

The Voice, full of agony, screamed, "Take her!"

Instantly she was surrounded with glassy beings. Leaded fingers gripped her body and she was lifted into the air.

Then the voice cried out, "Awaken!"

38

THE MASK

The Voice . . .

The Terrible Voice . . .

Within the soul pit Alex's consciousness groaned. Writhing, he tried to burrow deeper into the darkness where the last shred of who he was had crawled to escape the sucking horror.

"Awaken!"

The Voice . . .

The Terrible Voice . . .

No escape! The Voice was dragging him out, forcing him to fuse with the prison of blood and bone. Slowly he began to feel the heaviness of the flesh, to hear the beating of a heart, and he hated it; he wanted to be dead. Then splinters of remembering, splinters of the last things. The old man and the singing monster. The shrieking. The surging up from his belly.

"Awaken!"

The Voice . . .

The Terrible Voice . . .

But what was this?

It was coming from *outside* . . . through the ear holes. Alex began to realize that he was alone—alone inside himself. The crawling nightmare was gone. But it brought no relief, no joy, because what he wanted most of all was to be dead, dead and gone forever. His soul had been sucked down to nothing, the consciousness that had called itself "Alex," the thing that had lived in his body from the moment he was born, that had strutted and lusted and raged and hated, what was it now? A speck without a name, a pinprick quivering in the darkness where the horror had squatted and sucked until there was nothing left but the invisible "skin" of "self" that had contained the knowledge of who he was.

"Awaken!"

Gasping ... wheezing ... grunting ... Alex opened his eyes. He was lying on his back and above him drifted a blurry vastness.

"Stand up!"

Flopping over onto his belly, he struggled to push himself to his hands and knees.

"Stand up!"

Finally on his feet, teetering back and forth like a bag of blood propped on a two-legged stool. As he rubbed his eyes, vague images appeared; in front of him were stained-glass demons and they were holding something, no, some*one*. A girl. And the girl was holding a baby. Who was the girl? Somebody ... somebody ... trying to remember. And then she screamed, "Alex!"

His name.

Yes, that was his name.

And hers ... it was ... Tori.

Why did he know that? Now she was crying, calling out his name over and over. He whispered hers. She saw him do it and it made her cry even more.

"Turn around!"

The Voice ...

Turning, he saw the Nightmare above him.

Run ...

Hide ...

Crawl back into the pit.

But he couldn't move. All he could do was stare and twitch and tremble.

"Take the child! Take him from her!"

What was he supposed to do? The girl named Tori was screaming at him, "Don't ... Alex! Don't! Please, don't kill the baby!"

"Take the child! Take him from her!"

Stumbling forward, he tried to obey. But the Tori-girl fought and kicked.

Finally the glass monsters forced her to let go, and the baby fell into his hands. He stared into its eyes.

He knew who he was.

He was Alex Lancaster. And the girl named Tori was his little sister. As he stared into the eyes of the child, all of it came flooding back. He was someone! He was a person and he was alive!

"Look at me!"

Alex looked up ... and his heart shriveled. Above him was another set of eyes, and from them flowed waves of loathing that obliterated all but the vilest memories. Staring up into the Darkness of those eyes he knew who he really was and who he would be forever. *No one!* A vile, empty, worthless slave! The eyes told him all of that, and in the depths of his being, he knew it was true. Suddenly he was burning with thirst, but not for water, a thirst for dying, a thirst to drown the filth of his nothingness in an ocean of eternal sleep.

"Walk up the stairs. Walk!"

He stumbled to obey. Such excruciating pain! The flesh was so heavy. Like an old man, one step at a time, Alex lurched and staggered up into the steaming mist. Roar-singing voices drowned out his sister's screams. He heard scraping, the grinding rumble of stone on stone. When he reached the top, the floor was broken in front of him. The oil was oozing into a chasm of velvet darkness. As he stared into the hole, a voice whispered, "Think only of yourself. Think only of sleep without dreams, without guilt, without sorrow. All you have to do is hold the child, close your eyes, and fall. Death will bring eternal sleep."

So tired.

So desperate for sleep.

And the darkness looked so soft and inviting. He leaned forward.

Almost ready to do it. Almost ...

But something held him back. He felt a strange warmth in his arms. Looking down, he caught his breath. The baby ... the warmth was coming from Him and His eyes were so beautiful. As he stared into them, he heard a soft voice whisper in his heart.

"Alex, I love you."

A new voice. Not the voice of a child. A voice that was gentle and strong.

In the voice and in the eyes there was such sorrow. Sorrow and love … for him.

"Alex … I love you."

A sliver of light.

"ALEX, I LOVE YOU …"

Juddering shock.

"ALEX, I LOVE YOU!"

The soft voice was drowned out by a mocking, rasping taunt: *ALEX, I LOVE YOU!* That voice! He knew that voice! It was the voice he hated. It was the voice of his father.

"Listen, Son, I'm sorry I can't be with you, but I've got a big report due in the morning. I just wanted to call and say good-bye. I know you're thinking about killing yourself. Let me say that, in my opinion, it really is a good idea. You're such a screw-up that you'll never amount to anything anyway, and this is your chance to do something right for a change. Of course, you're so spineless you probably don't have the guts to pull it off. So when I come home and find you alive, it'll be just another reason for me to be ashamed of you. But hey, maybe someday I'll have a son who'll make me proud."

The words made no sense, but that didn't matter. Instantly the sliver of light vanished, and the gentle voice was drowned in a wave of rage and hate. Weeping, suddenly Alex couldn't stop weeping. Needed to die! Desperate to die! To forget his father! To forget the "truth" that broke his heart! In his mind, a voice that he thought was his screamed that "truth" over and over in words that Alex had heard a thousand times.

My father doesn't love me. He's ashamed of me. He went away to have a son that he could love.

The voice didn't belong to him. But he had listened to it all of his life, and it had so filled his brain that he thought every vile word it whispered was his own. And so the Evil Spirit had gorged on him, veiling its presence behind the words he called himself, "I," "Me," "My," "Mine," every foul sentence in his head carefully formed to sound as though he were saying it, when it wasn't his voice at all. Nestled deep within him, it had vomited an incessant spew of hate and lies, always twisting the agony, screwing it into his soul, making him dance like a puppet to the jittering syncopation of self-pity, guilt, and rage. And while he danced, lashing the people who loved him. But now the dance was almost over.

"Look down," whispered the Voice.

Dark mystery! What was this that he was holding? A beautiful child? No, its face had changed. Stroke by stroke, line by line, in colors drawn from Alex's heart, the Master of Lies had painted a small, soft phantom. The face ... it was the face he had seen in pictures. The child he was holding was his father's new son, the son who had replaced him! That it couldn't be real didn't matter. It was real! Then came the death whisper.

"One chance! One shot at paying him back! Take away his freaking precious son. Kill the little piece of garbage that he loves. Make him lose both of us together. Just do it. Jump and fall!"

Staring into the tiny, phantom mask, for one moment Alex hesitated. Then he leaned forward ... and dropped into the hole.

39

THE CLOT OF DYING

Falling into emptiness ...

Falling and falling ...

Hurtling down with the child in his arms.

But something was wrong. He wasn't asleep. He was awake. Death was supposed to be sleep without dreams. But suddenly Alex was more awake than he had ever been in his whole life. What had he done? He had jumped to kill himself and his father's child. But that was insane. The baby wasn't his father's. It couldn't be.

In a single second all the lies that had clouded Alex's mind turned to ice and shattered. Down, down he fell into an ocean of total darkness. Darkness that smothered! Darkness that bled all life from the soul! And in that Darkness he knew what Death really was. Death was not *sleep*, because Death was not *dead*. It was a hungering Presence all around him, thick and black like clotted blood.

Fool! Stupid fool!

He had thrown his life away.

Murderer! Horrible murderer!

Not enough just to murder himself, he had murdered a baby. Sacrificed Him! Destroyed Him out of nothing but jealousy, hate, and rage. How could he have been so blind?

Down ...

Down ...

They were dying together.

And in the dying, Alex loathed himself, loathed every minute that he had ever lived, loathed with a perfect revulsion, because in the clarity of Absolute Darkness he saw who he really was. He was *evil*. Evil had lived in him from the moment he was born. Tiny and soft at first, it had been like a seed. Every day he had chosen to water it with a flow of little selfish sins. And as he had grown older, the flow had turned into a steady stream of sewage, the purest feces of self-pity, hate, and pride. Fertilized with filth, the plant had grown into a mass of reeking roots and bloody vines buried so deep in his flesh they were part of him. Why had he murdered? Because for years the hate of murder had been rotting in his soul, waiting for a chance to spill out.

And in the clotted Darkness he knew what Hope was. Hope was the Glistening Shadow of God's Presence that had haunted every moment that he had lived. Hope was the Echo of Beauty, the Song of Songs. It was the voice that had whispered, "I love you." Yes, even at the end, in the swarming hate, it had whispered, trying to make him see that he was loved in spite of who he was. And in that Love there was Hope enough to last forever.

But now there was no forgiveness—in the Dark it was blindingly clear. Hope was the *chance* to be forgiven, the *chance* to say, "I'm sorry." The Glistening Shadow that had haunted him with hope had whispered that even *he* could be forgiven. All he had to do was ask. But asking meant giving up his favorite poison, the endless drink of sweet slime that he had sucked into his soul. To get forgiveness you had to give it, you had to forgive the ones you hated and stop sucking their blood in your mind. He had gagged at the thought of forgiving. Never could he have done it. And now the choice was sealed.

For the first time, "never" really meant forever.

As Alex fell, he began weeping with a sorrow that he had never known. Yes, now he knew what Death was. It was the place of the broken heart, the place where Love and Forgiveness were only memories because the glistening shadow had been thrown away.

Weeping, weeping . . .

He would never stop weeping.

But then he heard a sound that froze the tears. From far away came a whispering moan, and then another and another! Nothing human could make those sounds. The moans were everywhere; all around him he could feel the heat of circling creatures like sharks in a bloody ocean. And they were moaning with hunger! Hugging the baby, he screamed, "Go away! Leave us alone!"

Suddenly, a rush! Iron claws gripped him.

He tried to fight, but it did no good. Shrieking, they dragged him down. And Alex learned another awful truth. The Clotted Darkness was only a doorway. Waiting below was the Deepest Death of all.

Slowly it began. A tremble. Then another. As Tori lay sobbing on the floor of the cathedral, she felt the whole building began to shake, and after the shaking came pounding. The hideous chant of the phantoms stopped, and every face turned toward the great doors. Something was pounding on them. Pounding! Pounding!

For a heartbeat there was silence, followed by an *explosion*! The doors were blown to dust, and Tori saw Him.

Instantly all the dark creatures of the cathedral screamed as though they had entered hell. For a moment the One from the Great Mountain stood like a statue and His eyes swept the room. With the softness of a whisper, the waves and veils of steaming mold froze in the air, and all the thousands of creatures froze with them, hanging from floor to ceiling in tapestries of icy filth.

Then He began walking.

Slowly, with the crimson moonlight around Him, He walked through the vast room. Old! He was old beyond imagining and covered with scars as though He had spent all of time locked in a vicious war. Old, yet His eyes were young as the morning and the crimson fire that burned in them was from beyond the stars.

He walked slowly through the darkness and the evil. When He reached the front, He stopped and looked into Tori's eyes. One brief moment.

Then He turned ... walked up the stairs ... and leaped into the chasm.

40

SONG OF THE BLOOD

Shrieking, his mind frozen, Alex was dragged down through waves of Darkness. And every moment the Thickness of Death grew heavier. Suddenly he saw something, far away, a tiny pinpoint of light! Rapidly it expanded into an eerie glow.

Was that hell?

Were they taking him to hell?

A moment more and he could see what it was: a gash that looked like a burning wound. And he heard a new sound—weeping! Soft weeping. The weeping of children. Millions of them!

Billows of stench churned around him, burning his eyes and throat. Then he was in the gash, streaking down thousands of feet between smoldering walls. He screamed as the bottom raced toward him, but before he could smash into it, he wrenched to a stop, almost dropping the baby. Alex found that he stood at the bottom of a gigantic gorge. On either side towered walls coated with crimson mold. It grew like steaming fur from every slope and crevice, and under the mold the chasm was caked with clotted blood that drooped in pendulous waves. It was a gorge that had been carved by a mighty river of blood. And the soft crying of children was everywhere.

Alex spun around. In the billowing steam behind him loomed a hundred twisted forms decayed almost beyond recognition. They were the Mighty Ones of the cathedral windows, the Lords of Glassy Darkness. What was left of their flesh was embedded with shards of softly tinted crystal, and through the splinters Alex could see their starving, raging souls. Among them was a face veiled in long black hair. Once more he tasted the spittle on her lips. As he stared into her eyes, the disease of the cathedral that had never left him began to burn.

They shoved him forward. Slipping, he fell to his knees, sloshing in a sluggish rivulet of half congealed gore, all that remained of the torrent that had flowed here. Jerking him up, they shoved him again.

They wanted him to walk.

Trying to obey, he began dragging one foot at a time out of the bloody muck. But with each step, the oozing thickness sucked at his shoes. Hugging the baby and struggling not to vomit, Alex stumbled up the twisting gorge, splashing through half-scabbed pools, splattering through turgid bogs, on and on between walls so narrow that he had to push through layers of mold that left him slick with bloody spores. And with every step the weeping of the children grew.

Finally he rounded a bend and saw it. In front of him loomed an arena carved from bleeding stone with walls so high they disappeared into the blackness. And in the center was a hole shaped like an open grave. From out of it boiled clouds of burning light. And it was toward this that they drove him, through blood so deep that it gurgled around his knees. When he reached the edge of the pit, the creatures lifted him. With a crimson cord they bound him with the baby in his arms. Then together they were lowered into the hole. As Alex lay on the bottom, he felt his back settle into a pool of warm bloody ooze. He was burning with fever; sweating, shivering, teeth chattering.

Carved on the walls were the faces of children, their eyes deep-cut with agony and their mouths torn in silent screams. It was their blood that had formed the river. He knew it. And it was their spirits who were crying. Soon he would share in their endless death. But never could he share their innocence. And the most innocent of them all would be murdered in his arms. Tears streamed down his cheeks, and he whispered, *"I'm sorry."* But the words meant nothing.

From far away Alex heard a roar and froze; it came again, a guttural shriek like a lion awakening to its prey. High above in the blackness appeared a shimmering streak—something was falling, rushing down in a rainbow of flashing glory. Instantly Alex knew what it was and began to sob. As the falling rainbow grew, a suffocating heaviness mashed the air from his lungs. He wanted to scream, but no sound came.

So hideous—so beautiful!

The starry streak was taking form. Falling toward him was a Mighty Angel covered in a mist of rainbows with wings that flashed like shattered diamonds in the sun. As he descended into the arena, all his creatures fell prostrate, screaming, "Praise to the God who has fallen. Glory to the One who burns away light."

Like a monstrous crystal sculpture, Lammortan hovered, then came to rest in the swamp of blood. Slowly he bent down and peered into the hole. Alex tried desperately to drown in the muck. But he couldn't move, couldn't even close his eyes. Above him, within the glassy flesh, flowed rivers of blood in ten million colors. With infinite hunger the eyes gazed at him, and Alex felt his mind begin to crumble. But from the Angel's lips came a caressing sigh, *"Not yet. The taste of the blood means nothing if there is no soul within the flesh to feel it pour."* The Angel began a juddering chant.

Childhood's End, Childhood's End,
Blood of Childhood's Angel quench my thirst for Childhood's End,
Spilled and poured to Heaven's madness,
My joy forever His rage and sadness,
And I will wear the Crown of Steaming Gore,
And as my soul is soaring,
You will feel his life-drink pouring,
Over your skin, over your skin,
And with the scream of his last breathing,
Your soul will leave its fleshy sheathing,
Never to rise again, never again,
For of all the children lies have bought me,
It was only you who brought me,
Childhood's End, Childhood's End.

From one of his wings the Angel drew out a long crystal splinter caked with blood. Bending down, he lifted the baby's head and bared his throat. Alex screamed as the dagger rose. But suddenly, a vibration; the dagger hand began to shake. The Angel was trying to stab with all his might; he was pushing down, but his arm wouldn't move. Then came a sound so low that Alex wasn't sure it was real.

The air shuddered with a soft murmur: *"My children ... my children ..."*

The crystal eyes froze.

The murmur came again, louder, *"My children ... where ... are my children?"*

High above, the darkness stretched and rippled like the fetid scum on a pool of sewage, and then it burst! Down from the darkness roared a sheering wind, and in it a Voice cried out in agony, *"Crimson River, bloody sea, the screams of my children cry out to me. Where are my children?"*

Shaking, gagging, the Angel slavered out, "It's ... mine. The Law ... followed it. Given to me. All mine ..."

Lightning words streaked the air,

Established forever and cannot be broken,
My Law was a promise, but only a token,
Of a Law that is deeper, a Law that is strong,
It cries out in love, it whispers a Song,
With it I painted children in wombs,
And now they lie in endless tombs,
My greatest art I gave away,
Birthed in fools you led astray,
And now you claim them by right of blood,
Their souls to drink in one black flood,
But there is a law for One who has painted,
Who loves his work though by excrement tainted,
When works of art are to be destroyed,
Ravaged and slashed, burned in the void,
The artist who loves them may buy them again,
Paying the price so their rape will end.

In the terrifying silence that followed, Alex saw a great shadow high above. Finally the Angel croaked out, "Buy? Buy? With what? The price must match the purchase."

With iron sadness the Voice replied,

One Price only for flesh and bone,
For children scorched on arms of stone,
The life of the Artist is worth more than all,
The works of His hands both large and small,
My life I offer for each slaughtered child,
Bathed in blood in worship defiled,
My life for every girl and boy,
And my life for the slave who offered Aloi.

Alex was so stunned that he couldn't breathe. What had he heard? "My life for the slave ...?" Suddenly into his heart came a desperate hope. He stared at the glittering face. The Angel was looking up. The Shadow of the Crimson Throne was growing brighter. But the throne was empty. Into Lammortan's eyes came raging joy, and in his crystal flesh appeared a jagged reflection. Alex couldn't make out what it was. As it grew, a strange, rough voice echoed in the bloody walls. Never had Alex heard anything like it. The ground shook with each agonizing word, *"Blood for blood ... mine ... for all the blood. The Death Thirst ... to quench it. Yes, mine. I have come."*

Alex couldn't see who had spoken. All he could see was the Angel's face filled with a terrible ecstasy. "Is it really you? The Great Seeker has left His Crimson Throne? And would you leave it forever? Yes, blood for blood. By the Law it must be accepted. Your blood instead of theirs. I will grow drunk on the finest Wine of Heaven. If this is your choice, lie down."

And then it happened. Into the hole leaped a Being who glistened with mist and crimson moonlight. And the baby laughed for joy. Alex thought he was dreaming. It couldn't be! But standing over him, looking down into his eyes, was the One he had cursed and thought that he had murdered. Standing *over* him, standing *above* him, standing *between* him and the horror beyond was the One he had thrown into the chasm. And in that moment he understood a great mystery of Heaven, that Eternal Power and Glory can be hidden in the humblest form.

Seeker, that's what He had been called and that is what He was, the Seeker who had searched for him and found him and had tried to keep him from harm. But much more than that. In His eyes Alex saw the One who had painted the starry hosts, had woven the oceans and mountains on every world. With the Breath of His Spirit, had formed the galaxies, flinging them out like grains of sand. And then, in a moment of time on a tiny world, had called his life from nothing, had painted a child named Alex into the warm darkness of his mother's womb. In the eyes above him, Alex saw the One who knew him as no one else ever could, knew all the horror, hate and evil that had brought him here. Knew it all, and yet, to save him had leaped into the bloody pit of his soul, leaped in with a Love so great that he could feel it burning.

As Alex stared up into His eyes, he knew that in them was Forgiveness enough to last forever, forgiveness for every evil thing that he had done, forgiveness for the asking. As he lay in the reeking hole, he found the only hope that mattered. In tears he whispered, "Forgive me ..."

But then a flash of jagged crystal, and the dagger fell. With a shriek the Angel plunged it, crying out, "Now I will rule upon the Crimson Throne."

Screaming ... screaming ... Alex screamed as over and over, the knife slashed into the One who stood above him, slashed his back, slashed his neck, slashed his head. And around the pit, all the glassy creatures joined in. On and on it went. The eyes of the Seeker filled with agony, but never did they falter or grow afraid. And in them, Alex's dreams came true. He saw the eyes of the Father who would never leave him, the eyes of the Hero who would give his life to save a lost and dying child. In them, Alex saw the Heart of God.

Blood rained down, blood thick and warm, drenching through Alex's clothes, soaking his skin. It was a feast of murder. And the murderers were laughing, shrieking, dancing. A hundred hideous faces clustered around the most awful face of all. A hundred fists gripped daggers, groping down to gash and gouge.

Finally the One who stood over him could stand no longer. With the daggers falling, he lay down by Alex's side. Sobbing, Alex whispered, "Let me die with you." The Great Eyes looked at him with overwhelming peace, and then the Life of the Seeker faded away. But the slashing frenzy went on. Alex screamed, "Stop it! Can't you see he's dead?" They didn't hear him. They just kept shrieking and stabbing, licking themselves, drinking the blood.

But then ... *so strange*; Alex began to hear distant singing. In their ranting orgy the creatures were deaf to it. Slowly it grew, a lovely voice singing a Song.

Where was it coming from? At first he couldn't tell. Then he realized that it was coming from all around him. *It was coming from the blood*, growing louder because every moment there was more of it. So much blood pouring from the body. Alex began to hear words. Where had he heard them before? It was the Song of the Burning Angel of the Chamber, the Song that had crushed him and broken his heart, full of splendor and majesty, it soared. The words ... now he understood them. He knew the Song and what it meant.

It was the Song Above All Others, the Poetry of Fire whispered when the stars were born. But wonderful mystery, *the Song was about him*. All the loveliness and splendor was a promise sung before time began, a promise to reach down into the depths of his horror, to save him, to change him, to fill him with Life that would never die. And singing in it, he heard the secret of who he was.

So tiny in the vastness,
Like a single cell of starlight in the heart of God,
Bone and flesh, soul and spirit,
His life was woven into the Song.
Never had he understood before.
Never had he imagined the grandeur,
The hope, the promise that he could be reborn,
From the Heart of Singing,
A new heart for him would come,
And his life was meant to rise and join the greatness,
Bone and flesh, soul and spirit,
All of him was meant to be a song,
And now, he could sing it,
Now, he would sing it,
For the River of Blood was rising,
Singing him out of the pit,
Lifting him out of the horror,
Drowning the evil that had drowned his soul.

The Beauty, the Glory, Alex couldn't bear it. Weeping ... weeping ... and as he wept, the vision faded. His eyes began to close. And he found the peace that he had always longed for ... in the Song of the Blood.

To the slaves of Lammortan the song was the Curse of Heaven. Too late the Angel and his creatures heard it. Too late they knew that the Song was in the Blood. Covered with it, bathed in it, it was the Song of Death. From out of the pit it roared up in a burning fountain.

Shrieking, covered with blood, the crystal flesh of the Angel cracked and melted. Out of his broken jaws gushed the soul sewage of a dying world. He shrieked and thrashed, crushing the burning creatures beneath him. Higher and higher the fountain roared ... into a pool ... a lake ... and then a mighty river. Crashing down the canyon! Dragging the dying angels with it!

Screaming ...

Gagging with blood in their throats ...

Like drops in the ocean of eternity, Lammortan and all his slaves vanished into the chasm of Angel Fall.

*I*n the cathedral Tori stared up in wonder. The ghosts and the phantoms had disappeared; no longer was the great canvas flowing with oil. Slowly, down poured a crimson wave, and the vast room was filled with singing, the loveliest voice that she had ever heard. As she watched, the blood flowed from the canvas down the stairs. On it came until it reached the little white tree lying on the floor. There, gently, it pooled beneath the broken branches.

Melting ...

Melting ...

The little tree began melting into the form of a girl.

Sobbing, Tori knelt beside her sister's body. Amanda's face was so peaceful. Whispering her name, Tori lay down and wrapped her sister in her arms. Such a weight of sorrow! Such a heavy weight to be carried by a girl! Hovering above her, the gentle voice sang on ... sang rest ... sang sleep ... into the broken heart of a child.

41

THE KING OF THE CRIMSON THRONE

Song of the Blood.

Song of Forgiveness.

Song that sings the Darkness away.

At the moment of awakening, even before he opened his eyes, Alex knew that everything had changed. The black pit where his soul had crawled, the jagged hole where his heart had drowned was gone. In its place was lightness, a wonderful soaring lightness. Never before had Alex felt anything like it because never before had he felt joy. All he had ever known were ragged shreds of pleasure. Always the shreds had been eaten up by sorrow, hate, and rage. But now the deepest part of him was soaring with Lightness. Blazing Lightness! In it he could hear the Song. To feel like this forever, that's all he wanted. And he was so afraid that if he opened his eyes the Lightness would go away.

So don't open them.

Don't move.

Don't even breathe.

Just lie here and stay like this always.

But he couldn't stay like this. Because staying like this meant keeping it in. And the Lightness wouldn't stay in. Suddenly he was so overwhelmed with joy that he had to yell it out or he would explode.

Sitting up, Alex yelled—yelled with all the joy that burned within him. And when he yelled ... he opened his eyes.

What?

What was this? Stunned! Where was he? He knew this place, but didn't know it. The Cathedral! He was in the Cathedral. He was sitting on the floor at the foot of the stairs, and the vast room was empty. He was alone! What had happened? How had he gotten here? The last thing he remembered was rising out of the horrible pit, rising on a river of Singing Blood, then falling asleep.

It wasn't just empty—the Cathedral had totally changed. Gone was all the horror and darkness, gone were the ghosts, gone was the stifling heat and reeking mold. Around him towered an ancient ruin that looked as though it had been deserted for a thousand years. The walls were covered with moss and the pillars were draped with vines. Empty? Was it really empty? A freezing thought. The face.

Jerking around, Alex stared in terror. Not there! No face! No canvas! Nothing! Then he looked down at his arm. The terrible ache, he couldn't feel it; the wound was healed! And the golden band—the mark of his slavery—it was gone.

Free!

He really was free!

He knew it now!

Tears came to his eyes as the Singing Lightness swept back over him. So beautiful! The Cathedral was so beautiful! Everything was so beautiful when the fear was gone. Even the air seemed to dance and glisten. And the light . . . streams of crimson sunlight were weaving soft patterns across the stone. Maybe he would sit here and watch it forever . . . watch the sunlight dance with joy.

Crimson sunlight? How could that be? Where was it coming from? Alex looked up . . . and gasped. The roof of the Cathedral was gone. He could see straight into the sky. And there it was! Towering in its vastness, rising into the stars like the Throne of a Mighty King stood the Mountain. Wild, burning, swept with winds of fire! And the Summit glistened as though wreathed in a Crown of Blood.

Worship!

Worship!

Soar and sing!

And now he knew what worship was. It was a soul soaring and singing for joy because it has been set free. Soaring, singing with thankfulness forever.

As Alex looked up at the Mountain, suddenly he was filled with such ecstasy that he couldn't bear it. On fire! His soul was burning with joy! In tears he struggled to his knees. Just to look up at it! To kneel beneath the Mountain! To kneel and soar and sing!

But then he felt a Shimmering Presence.

Slowly he turned. Mists of Glory! Alive! He was Alive! At the top of the stairs was the One who had stood above him, the One who had stood over him, the One who had shed the Singing Blood. And then the form began to change from the humblest of creatures into a Man of Mighty Splendor filled with Light greater than all the suns, and He was wearing a crimson robe. Blinded, Alex fell on his face. As the Glory streamed around him, he lay sobbing. Suddenly he felt a hand on his shoulder. Through his tears he looked up. The Man was kneeling beside him. Gone was the blazing Light. He could look into His face. Old He was, old beyond imagining. And covered with scars as though He had spent all of time locked in a vicious war, a war that He had won. Yes, old . . . but young.

So young!

In His eyes was the Light of Heaven's Morning. He was young like a King who has just arisen to put on His Crown. And Alex knew Him — not because of the Splendor, but because of His eyes. In them was the Love that had whispered into the depths of his misery. In them was the Love that had pursued him even in the blackest caverns of his soul. Kneeling at his side was the Great King, the Lord of the Mountain, yet He was still the Seeker, the One who had chosen to die for him in a pit of blood.

Gently He lifted Alex to his feet. For a moment they stood in silence. And then the Great King took him in His arms. Never had his father hugged him. Not once in all the years. But now Alex felt a Father's arms around him, and he couldn't stop crying. The King was crying too. Tears of joy because the past was gone forever. Tears of joy because a lost child had finally come home. For a long time they stood. Then the Seeker King led Alex away. Out of the Cathedral of Sorrows. Out of the place of his shame. Into the light of Morning.

Into the Crimson Dawn.

A tiny buzzing sound penetrated into Tori's mind and fitted perfectly with a very delightful dream that she was having. In it she had become a bug. Well, not just a bug, the Bug Queen, and she was flittering around in an endless sea of daisies. There were lots of other bugs with her, millions of them. And Mirick was there too. They were all flittering together. The only problem was the daisies smelled like pizza. Italian sausage and pepperoni daisies. Which seemed odd but made her want to gobble every one. Then the buzzing got louder and it started calling her name.

"Torizzz ... Toriizzz ... Toriiiizzz ..."

Instantly the dream vanished and her eyes popped open.

Dazed and confused, she sat up. "Mirick?" It had been his voice, she was sure of it. But now it was gone. Where was she?

She was in the huge cavern, the terrible place where she had first awakened. And just like before, it glimmered with eerie light—the light from thousands of blue candles standing above endless rows of dead children lying on stone tables.

"Mirick, where are you?" Tori was about to cry when she felt tiny hands patting her arm. Looking down, she couldn't believe it. Beside her on the table sat Aloi. He was staring at her with his deep, wonderful eyes ... and he was giggling.

"You're alive! I thought you were dead, but you're alive!" Picking him up, she hugged him so hard that he grunted. "What happened to you? How did you get here? How did we both get here?"

Then a tiny voice buzzed her name, "Torizzzzzzz ..." High above, she saw a tiny sparkling light. As it danced back and forth, Mirick's voice buzzed, "Szzzzooo, laaaazzzzzzyyyy girl, you finally woke up."

"Mirick, is it really you?" She started crying again.

"Yes, little Queen of the Children, it is I."

"Come down here so I can see you."

"Not yet. Work time, not play time."

"What do you mean? Why am I back here? What happened to the baby? And where's my brother?"

"No time for questions. Questions will be answered when the work is done."

"I don't have to crawl out through that crack again, do I? I just can't do that with the baby. I'd squish him."

"No more crawling through cracks."

"So what kind of work is it?"

"You have to wake up the children."

"What?" Tori stared up at the fluttering light.

"Are your ears full of beeswax? I said you have to wake the children. Some of them have been napping for thousands of years."

"Nobody in here is taking a nap. They're all *dead*."

"Dead to you, napping to me."

"How am I supposed to wake them up?"

"Pick up the baby and stand on your table."

"Why?"

"Just do it!"

So Tori did it. "Okay, now what?"

"Well, go ahead, wake them up!" The tiny light danced closer.

"How?"

"You are still a most difficult girl."

"I'm difficult because I don't know how to wake up dead people?"

"How did you wake up your sister on a Sunday morning after you'd tried and tried and all she'd do was pull the covers over her head?"

"I'd start screaming."

"What did you scream?"

"Wake up, slug! Wake up you big pile of hair! I'm going to scream until you wake up! Stuff like that."

"Did it work?"

"Most of the time, but she wasn't happy about it."

"Well, do the same thing now. You could leave off the slug and the pile of hair, but yell at them. Tell them it's *morning*."

That's exactly what Tori did. Holding the little boy in her arms, she turned around in a circle yelling, *"Wake up, children! Wake up! It's morning! It's time to get up! It's time to get out of bed!"* While she yelled, the baby clapped and laughed.

Softly ... so softly ... it began.

At first, just a whisper.

In the blue twilit chamber of death Tori began to hear singing, a voice singing the Beautiful Song. And as it sang, high in the air appeared waves of

Crimson. Slowly they spread out across the room. And then, as the voice rose higher, they fell on each small body like drops of rain.

Tears began running down Tori's cheeks, as she understood the gift that she had been given. To see the moment of awakening. The stirring! The yawning! The stretching! The cooing! The gurgling! The giggling! The whispering! As all around her the thousands and thousands of children began to brush off the dusty sleep of ages and awaken into the Singing Light. A little girl on a table looked up at Tori and asked, "Is it time to play?"

As though Heaven were answering, at the end of the cavern the dark wall vanished and golden light flooded the room. Mirick's voice called to Tori, "Tell them to bring the babies and come outside. The Great Sleep is over. Tell them ... *it's time to play*!"

When Tori yelled it, there was a cheer. All the bigger children jumped off their tables. The older ones grabbed the little ones. Some of them had two babies in their arms. Then, laughing and yelling, they rushed toward the Light. Holding the little boy, Tori jumped down and ran with them. In a moment she was out of the cavern.

What she saw was so beautiful that she stopped and stared and trembled. Sweeping down and away from the Cavern of Death was a valley of Living Rainbows. Rainbows and more Rainbows. So many she couldn't count them. In arcs and streaks and circles, they rose from the ground into the sky ... spiraling ... weaving ... darting ... dancing. The whole valley was filled with music as though an invisible choir of harps had joined in the Dance of Light. Deep and soft, high and sweet, endless melodies and harmonies soared around her. At first Tori couldn't tell where the music was coming from. Then a little rainbow swept close and she knew. *The colors.* Each one was like a string. The rainbows were harps of mist, and all of them were playing the Song of Songs.

As the children raced down the gentle slope, it was as though the rainbows had been waiting for them. In a rush of joy they swirled, caressing each child with Singing Light. Laughing, spinning, swooshing the colors into streaming waves, the children ran on. Tori wanted to run with them, to jump and twirl, but something held her back. Something inside whispered that this was for them, that for her there would be a different joy. So, holding the baby close, she stood and watched and waited.

The last group of children was pouring out of the cave as the first reached the heart of the valley. Rippling through it was a stream that flashed as though the water were made of soft lightning. Clustered on the banks were trees with leaves so bright they sparkled. Each was a different color, and all were heavy with fruit. When the children reached them, they picked the fruit, and as they ate, they jumped in the stream, yelling and splashing each other with glistening drops.

Suddenly Mirick's voice whispered, *"Little Queen of the Children, look up."*

Tori looked ... and all the loveliness below paled into dim shadows. What she saw made her so weak that all she could do was kneel before the Splendor.

For the first time she saw the Mountain. Towering in the Heavens it stood, so vast and radiant that the stars vanished in its Presence. Sheer cliffs rose above sheer cliffs in endless processions of jagged glory. And each one flashed like a precious stone. Peaks of emeralds! Pinnacles of rubies! Spires of amethyst, jasper, and jade! Crests of silver. Crowns of gold! And between the peaks spilled a thousand waterfalls of diamonds drifting in the air like veils woven in the heart of the sun. Across it all swept Winds of Singing Fire flowing down from a Crimson Wreath of Mist that hung at the Summit like a Diadem of Blood.

As Tori stared, transfixed, it seemed to rise higher and higher until all the galaxies of the universe became like dust before it. On a mighty slope, there was a streak of brilliance. And the streak was moving. A Shining Wave was pouring down. A Fiery Avalanche was rushing toward the valley. What was it? She squinted, trying to see. Then she did see.

The wave was a host of Shining Beings, so many and so dazzling they were like a burning flood. Down and down they descended to the foot of the Mountain. With a great cry of joy they swept through the children, rushing among them, picking them up, twirling them in dances of light. For every child there was a Shining Being. Every baby was held and hugged and loved. Not one was left alone. All the children who had been given away, betrayed, and murdered by those who should have cherished them, all the children who had slept so long in darkness, each one was caught up in arms of love. It was so beautiful that Tori couldn't stop crying. The voice of Mirick whispered, "Do you know who they are, the Shining Ones?"

She shook her head.

"They're the Guardians, the Gift of Heaven to every child who was ever born. Their work was to watch over and love them. But since the race of men chose Darkness, the power of Lammortan held them back. Through all of time, they watched in agony as their children were given away to die. For age upon age they have longed for the Awakening. And now it has come."

"Do I have a Guardian?" Tori was staring in wistful awe.

"Indeed, you do."

Suddenly she saw a beautiful being running up from the valley toward her.

"*Is that her? Is that mine?*"

"Indeed, it isn't."

Then she heard a voice calling her name, "Tori! Tori!"

The being was Amanda! It was her sister, and she was shining. Her whole body was full of light. Never had she looked so lovely. Then they were together, hugging and crying. Through her tears Tori whispered, "You're alive. You were dead, but now you're alive. Are you an angel?"

Amanda laughed and wiped her eyes, "Of course not. People don't become angels. Those are the angels down there."

"But why do you look like this? Why are you shining?"

Amanda smiled, "Oh, Tori, there's so much to tell you. But right now, it's time to take the baby home. Come on, we get to do it together."

Together they began walking down into the valley. When they drew near, all the Shining Ones stopped dancing and turned toward them, opening a path. For the first time Tori really did feel like a queen. As they made their way, the Guardians and the children followed. But Tori didn't see them. She was looking up. As she stared, she gulped. The Mountain was so high that it seemed to go on forever.

"Do we ... have to *climb it*?"

"No, all of our climbing is finished."

The moment they touched the foot of the vast slope, a soft mist enveloped them and they heard a new kind of singing. Not one voice. Not ten thousand voices. It was as though every star in the universe had a voice. The high, the soft, the sweet, the piercing, the rumbling ... it was like a *mighty wind of music*, and the girls felt it blowing straight through every cell of their bodies filling them with a wonderful, terrifying *Lightness.* Holding the baby between them, they began to rise. Tori yelled, *"Amanda, we're flying!"*

Higher ... faster ... the Wind of the Singing Voices drew them upward. The girls looked down and Tori whispered, *"Oh, it's so beautiful ..."*

All the Shining Ones and all the children were rising too, flowing like a river of starlight up the side of the Mountain. And below lay a world ... forests and rivers, peaks and plains, oceans sparkling in the sun. Higher and higher they went, until the rim of the world was a glowing arc in the starry blackness. And still the Singing Wind carried them on. But now it was singing like a hurricane. Another moment and everything below paled into a distant memory. Swirling down toward them were waves of Blood-red Splendor, the Mist of the Mountain's Crown. Then they were in it! Blinded in a Cloud of Piercing Joy! The Voices rose in a great crescendo. The mist parted and their feet came to rest at the top.

Staggering ...

Shattering ...

Glory!

Before them lay a crystal ocean bluer than the bluest sky, an ocean without a wave or ripple. Beneath the surface blazed a Living Fire whiter than the purest snow. Around the ocean stood a Host of Beings that stretched into the endless reaches of eternity. Many looked like people. Others were like creatures out of a dream. Some were small, some were gigantic, but all burned with *Splendor* as though their hearts were made of Singing Flames. It was their voices that had called them upward. As wonderful as they were, the girls barely saw them ... for above the ocean, above the Singing Host, soared a Crimson Throne.

And on it sat a Man robed in Lightning,
Whose Face was brighter than ten million suns.
Around His head flowed a Diadem of Rainbows,
And in His Hand was the fire from which the stars were born.
Terrifying Majesty!
Irresistible Joy!
All the glory of the universe was like a flickering candle lost
in His Splendor.

The galaxies were like fireflies swarming at His Feet.
The girls fell on their faces ... and time ceased to be.

Worshiping and weeping!

Weeping in the Endless Joy!

How long they lay like that, they didn't know. But suddenly a gentle hand caressed Amanda's hair. She looked up. Kneeling beside her was a tall, lovely woman with eyes so blue they seemed to burn. Amanda cried out, "Bellwind!" And Bellwind took her in her arms. Tears and more tears. The Great Worwil could hardly speak for crying, "Little Brave One ... welcome home!"

Then Tori felt a tickling beside her ear and yelled, "Mirick!" There was a rush of power, and next to her stood her friend in all his glorious strangeness. "Yes, little Queen of the Children, didn't I tell you that, if you were faithful, we would stand together before the Crimson Throne?" Sobbing, Tori hugged him and his wings swept around her. "My Courageous Little Queen, how proud I am of you," he whispered.

Finally Bellwind said, "Now, my girls ... now, yes, now ... bring the baby and come."

Holding the little boy between them, Amanda and Tori were led out over the crystal ocean, over the pure white flames.

And as they walked, everything vanished but the Shining One. On and on they walked toward Him, until finally they could walk no more. The Glory was too great. They fell to their knees. Then the Splendor parted and they saw His Face. Never had they seen such a Face. So much anguish and so much love. Quietly He spoke words that Amanda and Tori remembered forever.

"My little children, my strong and faithful ones ... *well done.*"

All the kingdoms on all the worlds, all their riches and all their grandeur could not compare to this. His words descended upon them like shining crowns and no sovereign on any world had ever known such glory. Then He stepped down. Yes, stepped down from His Throne ... and bent down. Gently He lifted Amanda and Tori to their feet and took them in His Arms. And all their weakness vanished.

Love beyond imagining!

Soaring . . .

Singing . . .

Blazing Love . . .

His Heart . . . they felt it!

His Heart . . . they entered it!

And in His Heart they were One.

In the Oneness their lives were spread before them, every second that they had ever lived. And in them all was the Burning Shadow of His Presence.

For Amanda, He was the Man in the Robe who had held her with such gentleness in her greatest sorrow, giving her strength to face the terror locked within her soul. He was the One who had flown above her like an eagle easing her pain with drops of His Blood. When she had been offered life that would last forever, He was the One who had given her strength to choose death instead. And when her body had burned with fever, in the last moments when life was slipping away, He was the One who had stilled her anguish and rocked her to sleep in His Arms like a Father holding the little daughter that He loved.

Yes, He was the One.

For Tori He was the One who had never left her, even when she had drifted in the Darkness of a Night Without Stars. He was the One who had sent Mirick to guide her and had shown His Love through the baby's eyes. He was the One who had given her strength to climb the steps of the dreadful mountain and walk with her head held high through the terrifying doors. When she had entered the softly painted vision, the laughing, happy nightmare of her most cherished dream, He was the One who had shown her the truth and given her the courage to destroy the lie. And when she had faced the rage of the Painter, He was the One who had turned her heart into a Blazing Flame so great it could look at Death and not be afraid.

Yes, He was the One . . .

And He was the King!

But not a King like the kings of earth, the rock stars and film stars and sports stars, who live pampered and perfumed and draped with baubles. No, not a king like that. In the Face of this King was a strange and terrible Glory, and that Glory was in His scars. So many! So deep! Scars upon scars! Scars within scars! The girls knew why they were there because now they knew

His heart. Every wound given to the smallest and least of His children had been a burning wound within His body. Amanda's wounds, Tori's wounds, Alex's wounds, all the wounds of every child on every world, the knives that had slashed them, the fires that had scorched them, every touch, every word that had broken their souls, all had scarred Him forever. And the worst of the wounds were still bleeding, for they were the wounds from the Pit of Blood.

Laughing, He opened His hands. Instantly the girls knew what to do. Together they gave the little boy to Him, the baby they had loved and carried so far. And from the Host of Heaven there rose a mighty shout of victory! But then the King raised His Hand and there was silence.

"You have brought a precious gift, a gift that cost you everything. And now I have a gift for you."

He turned and from beneath the Throne stepped their brother. Oh, the tears of that moment! All they could do was hug and cry. Bending over them, the King whispered, *"Little daughters of Earth, you are mighty warriors, and your brother will be a mighty warrior too. But now, dry your eyes. It's not a time for weeping."* With the baby in His arms He rose and cried out a single word in a language that only He could understand.

A Word that shook the Heavens!

A Word that streamed with Fire!

A Word that became a Living Song!

In tears Bellwind whispered, "Mountaincry ... oh, finally, yes, finally it has come."

42

MOUNTAINCRY

The brilliance parted.

Alex, Amanda, and Tori found themselves standing on the edge of a gigantic precipice. Below lay the slowly moving circle of a sleeping world. Down ... down ... the Singing Cry swept toward it, like a shaft flung out of Heaven. And from deep within the planet came a pounding, rumbling Roar.

Louder and louder, the Thunder-beat of a heart awakening, the music of a mighty organ built to answer the Singing Voice of God, loosening the crust of continents, shaking the shroud of oceans, preparing the flesh of a world to be reborn.

And then the Cry struck it ...

Driving deep ...

Exploding outward in a wave of Singing Flame.

And the face of the world defiled by the Painter began to scorch and peel away.

On and on roared the Fire, over the clawed-out craters of ages, the fields, the ditches, the bone-troughs of war; on and on ... over the scabs of long-dead cities, over the blood-drenched temples with their altar-mouths that had sucked the slain.

On and on ... over the howling deserts, the shadow valleys, the dried-up rivers that had flowed with tears.

On and on, swirling, scorching, searing, swept the Singing Cry of God.

Suddenly it came upon a forest, endless miles of dead white trees. In a rush of joy it whispered through them, caressing every branch and limb and twig. And beneath the Singing Touch, the mask of death began to fade. No longer gnarled and twisted, pale and withered, across the mountains and the plains stood a forest of living people, and the King knew them all by name. They were the Faithful Ones who had refused to sacrifice their children, so with their children they had died, murdered by the plague of Melania, the fallen Healer, the Tree of Horror in the Sky. Now they stood with arms uplifted and began to sing the Song of Songs. Many were old and many were young, but all were children, for childhood is the ageless life of the heart that has learned the Song of the Blood.

But the Cry didn't stop in the forests. On and on it burned, through desolate tracts and deserts until it came upon a sea of graves. There it hovered with a Fiery Passion. Then into the ground it flew, down to bones asleep in corruption, down to the dust of memories that were deeply loved. For these were the graves of the fathers and mothers who *had* sacrificed their children, but then, with cries of anguish and broken hearts, had realized what they had done. In endless tears and prayers and sorrow, they had repented. These Lammortan had slaughtered, but now the Cry of the King found each one and drew them out to join their lost children in the singing of the Song.

When every child, both old and young, had been awakened and all were gathered from around the world, out of a Chamber deep within the planet rose the righteous rulers of Boreth, dancing, laughing, singing, for Mountaincry had finally come. Then the Host below streamed upward to meet the singing Host above, and never had there been such a hurricane of dancing, shouting, laughing, not since the world was born.

As it spun and swirled around Him, the King cried out, "SANDALBAN ... GREAT THUNDERER ... IT IS TIME!"

There was the crash of mighty hooves. Suddenly, beside Alex, Amanda, and Tori, appeared a creature that looked like a gigantic stallion, but his body rippled with lightning. In a rumbling voice he boomed, "Well, children, are you ready for a ride? If so, climb on."

As terrifying as he looked, they weren't afraid. Bellwind and Mirick helped them onto his back. Then he rose in the air and leaped over the cliff. A hundred thousand feet straight down he streaked, then swooped outward in a blinding flash.

Soaring!

And the air around them burned with the Singing Cry.

Below, newborn mountains heaved and rippled. And down toward them they flew. Into valley rifts with roaring rivers, through misty forests laced with streams, above wild gardens with rainbows painted in their leaves, over a waterfall that crashed into a chasm. On and on ... sweeping out over a broad, flat plain.

Suddenly beneath them was a surging sea of animals. Herds and gaggles, packs and flocks, prides and droves, rushing, leaping, racing together unafraid. Never had there been such a choir of squeals and grunts and roars and bellows, and every voice was filled with joy. Above them swirled a typhoon of wings and feathers, calling, crying, blending with the Song of Songs, for the Curse of men and angels had been broken and all the fear was gone.

On flew the Worwil, leaving the land, streaking low above crystal waves, splashing the children with tingling spray. And from the depths they heard a mighty chanting. The great creatures of the ocean, with their retinues of fins and scales, rose to meet them, singing, rolling, crashing, for even into the heart of the oceans the Song of the King had come.

How long they flew, they didn't know and never could remember. Time lost all meaning as they watched a world reborn. But finally Sandalban began descending into a forest of moss-covered trees and gently came to rest at the edge of a clearing. In it stood a circle of seven ancient thrones. On four of them sat the remaining Worwil of Boreth — Bellwind the Watcher, Rindzac the Caller, Faylin the Weaver, and Mirick the Singer of the Song. When the children had climbed down, Sandalban the Thunderer took his place among them. On the center throne sat a little boy of five years old. He looked familiar. Laughing, he waved. Bellwind and Mirick stepped down and joined them.

Tori stared, "Is that ... ?"

Mirick nodded, "Yes, that's Aloi."

"But how did he grow so fast? He was just a baby." Amanda couldn't believe it.

Bellwind replied, "His world ... yes, our world ... is alive again. It's growing and growing, and it will never stop. And He will grow with it, for the throne of the Dark One, whose name I am forgetting, is now the Throne of Aloi."

Filled with wonder, Amanda and Tori walked over to Him. Jumping down, He hugged them.

But Alex wasn't looking at the child. He was staring up at the most beautiful young woman that he had ever seen. Around her, like a woven halo, drifted a glistening web. Slowly he walked over and stood before her. He tried to speak, but tears drowned out the words. Stepping down from her throne, Faylin took his hands. Then, bending down, she kissed them. And no words were ever needed.

Softly Bellwind spoke, "So indeed, yes and so, young Lancasters, this is where your journey through our world will end."

They turned and stared at her. "What do you mean? What happens now?" Suddenly Alex was afraid.

"Well, and what always happens when a journey is finished? The travelers, do they not go back home?"

Tori's eyes grew wide. "You mean ... home ... like ... back-to-Earth home?"

"The last time I checked, that was the place where you were born, my dear."

"But ... we want to stay on this world. We love it here with you."

Alex was desperate. "Please don't make us go back. It's awful on Earth."

Mirick turned his burning eyes toward him. "Yes, awful it is. But not forever. There is a Mountaincry for every world, and soon it will come to yours. But before that time there will be great hardship. And in that time there will be a war."

"A war? I don't want to be in a war." Tori stared at him in horror.

"Little queen, it is the end of the war that you were fighting here. The evil in the universe is like a hive of wasps and every one of them must be destroyed."

Bellwind nodded. "The ugliness, the bubbling, stinking nastiness won't be gone until your world is washed clean like ours."

"But why do we need to be there?" Alex was feeling ill.

Mirick replied, "There are many on your world who are chained to Evil.

You know the ways of the Dark Ones. For some, you will be their only hope."

Tori began to cry. "I don't want to go back. I'll miss you too much."

Gently Mirick knelt and hugged her. Once more she was surrounded by the soft warmth of his wings. "I have brought a gift. Would you like to see it?"

Wiping away the tears, she nodded. Instantly she felt something around her neck. On a delicate chain hung a little golden moth. "Oh, it's so beautiful. I'll wear it always and every time I look at it, I'll think of you."

"It's a gift to bring you comfort in times of need. And remember this, no matter what happens, the mark of the King is upon you, and no child of His will ever be alone."

"What about Alex and Amanda? Are there gifts for them?"

"Your brother will wear his gift as long as he lives."

"What is it?"

Slowly he lifted his arm. "It's my scar."

Bellwind smiled. "The scars, yes, the scars from wounds of the King, are the greatest gifts of all. And yours runs deep and strong."

"What about Amanda? What's her gift?" But before Tori's question could be answered, they heard a honking wheeze. They turned and stared. Clunking and bumping out of the forest was an ancient, rust-red limousine. Creaking to a stop, the door opened and out stepped a gangling old man in a ragged uniform. Tori yelled, "Mr. Hydrogen!" Then she ran and hugged him.

"Well, well, well, I see I got to the right place again. If it was wrong I sure wouldn't get such a great big hug, now would I? Looks to me like you young folks are about finished with your vacation."

"Our what?" Alex choked.

"And now that all the fun's over, it's time to get home again, is that it?"

"Are we going to ride in old Malleus?" For Tori the thought softened the sorrow of leaving.

"You sure are."

As Alex looked at the ancient chauffeur, all he could think about was their first meeting. In shame he turned his eyes to the ground.

Smiling, the old man walked over and put his arm around him. "Ain't nothin' to worry about, Son. You turned out just fine, just like I told your mom you would. All right, all aboard who's goin' aboard. We gotta get. There's a nice wind startin' to blow an' we're gonna jump on its tail." Moving to the limousine, he opened the passenger door.

Tori hugged Mirick one last time, then she and Alex started for the car. They were climbing inside when Tori realized that Amanda hadn't moved. "Come on. If we've gotta go back, we might as well get it over with. And I really do want to see Mom."

But there were tears in Amanda's eyes. Quietly she said, "I'm not going with you."

Alex stared at her. "What are you talking about? If we've gotta go back, so do you. Come on!" But as he said the words, he felt a touch of fear.

"I can't."

Tori rushed over to her. "Of course you can. We're not leaving without you."

"Look at me, Tori. Do I look the same as I did before?" She was so beautiful and light was still streaming from within her. "Up on that mountain my body really did die. The one I have now is made for this world. It can't live on Earth until Earth is changed."

"No, that isn't true." Tears were in Alex's eyes and there was no holding them in. "You're coming with us. We're not going anywhere without you."

Tori was sobbing. "If you don't go back, what do we tell Mom and Dad?"

"Tell them I love them. Tell them about the Great King. Tell them I want to see them when Mountaincry comes to Earth and all the worlds are one."

What followed were a lot of tears, a lot of hugging, and a lot of forgiving. But finally the old chauffeur put his arms around Alex and Tori and drew them away. Before they got into the car, they saw an amazing sight: Bellwind led Amanda to the last empty throne. Quietly she said, "My daughter, though you are not a Worwil, it is the desire of the King that this throne that once belonged to Melania be yours forever. And with it her gift of healing. She believed the lie of Lammortan, that when he ruled the world, she would be crowned the Queen of Heaven. Under the power of his Darkness, she became drunk with blood. You will not be tempted to such evil. Sit down, Daughter of the Mountain, and take your place in a new world." Slowly Amanda sat down and around her swirled streams of Crimson Glory.

As the limousine rose in the air, the last thing Tori and Alex saw through the window was Amanda waving and blowing kisses. Then suddenly the circle of thrones was filled with Shining Brilliance, and in the center stood the King. Smiling, He lifted His hands toward them.

Then the Brilliance faded and they entered a darkness filled with stars.

EPILOGUE

TWO CHILDREN FROM DOWNED PLANE
FOUND IN RAFT
AFTER 36 DAYS IN OCEAN

(Reuters) — Two children from downed American Airlines flight 466 were found alive floating in a raft in the North Sea, 500 miles from where their plane had crashed 36 days ago. The raft, sighted by a helicopter crew on their way back from the Aileron Petroleum Platform, was drifting 7 miles off the coast of England's Lindisfarne Island. After being extracted by a search-and-rescue team from the British Navy, the children, who had traveled alone and whose names are being withheld, were transported to a British naval hospital where they were examined and found to be in excellent condition. From there they were flown to London, where they were reunited with their parents.

That was the story that electrified the world, the miracle that splashed across every front page and babbled its way through all the talk shows from Sacramento to Jakarta. Of course, the members of the rescue team were interviewed endlessly; it was the best that could be done because the Lancaster family refused to be interviewed at all. Along with the interviews, everyone saw dramatic footage of the boy and girl being plucked from the heaving waves. But the video and the interviews didn't tell the whole story. Because the whole story just couldn't be told.

Something had happened during the rescue that the team members refused to talk about even among themselves, because what had happened was impossible. Even worse, it hadn't appeared on the video. Though they had seen it with their own eyes, somehow the camera had refused to record it. So to talk about it would have made them all look crazy.

The girl was inside the helicopter and the extraction of the boy was almost complete—he was dangling in the arms of a diver ten feet under the craft. The pilots and the crew were looking down, making sure that everything was going correctly, when suddenly on the ocean they saw something that hadn't been there before. Next to the raft was floating a rusted Cadillac limousine up to its wheel wells in sloshing water. That was bad enough, but standing on the hood, smiling and waving in the blinding spray was a crazy old man in a chauffeur's uniform. All of them saw him. The children saw him too because they smiled and waved back. Then the whole awful vision—limousine and crazy person—simply vanished into thin air. And that was the story that could never be told.

It was Sunday when Alex and Tori Lancaster were pulled from the ocean. It was Sunday and only thirty-six days had passed. Thirty-six days and a lifetime. It was Sunday when they came back to their world.

And the Wind from Heaven was still blowing ... toward the last Angel Fall.